Praise for

"This moving story of a fictional soldier in a real Mississippi regiment in the real Civil War was inspired by the experiences of the author's great grandfather. The novel's descriptions of combat are realistic and powerful; the portrayal of wounds, death, and destruction are stark enough to turn the reader into a confirmed pacifist. Although I have read many books on the Civil War, I learned more about the psychological impact of the war on the men who fought it than from anything else I ever read."

— James M. McPherson,
author of *Battle Cry of Freedom* and *The Civil War Era*

"Civil War enthusiasts will enjoy Van Temple's novel of America's bloodiest war, *Whisperwood*, told from the perspective of an ordinary Confederate soldier and based on the real adventures of the author's great-grandfather. Readers follow young Anderson Temple as he enlists in the 20th Voluntary Mississippi Infantry Regiment, undergoes training at a camp in Iuka, Mississippi, and eventually sees ferocious combat and eventual defeat across the South. Throughout, the novel is peppered with letters to and from the narrator's relatives. Although billed as a work of fiction, *Whisperwood* ends with a description of the narrator, Anderson Temple, on his deathbed in 1929, so the reader is left wondering how much of the book is history and how much literature. It's a bracing chronicle of the Civil War told in a fashion many readers will not have encountered before."

— Robert J. Hutchinson,
author of *What Really Happened: The Lincoln Assassination*

"*Whisperwood* is a truly enjoyable read that brings to life not only Anderson Flowers' Civil War experience, but also the struggles of all those Mississippi volunteers who risked so much, so long ago."

— David A. Welker,
author of *The Cornfield: Antietam's Bloody Turning Point*

WHISPERWOOD

A Confederate Soldier's Story of
War and Conscience

Van Temple

Distribution by
KDP- Amazon and Ingram Spark
P.O.D.

Printed in the United States of America
Title: Whisperwood
Names: Temple, Van - author
Illustrator: Anna Zakelj

Description: An Intimate Portrait of the Civil War Through A Soldier's Eyes

ISBNs: 9781087921761 (soft cover); 9781735332703 (eBook)

Published with Talk+Tell
www.talkplustell.com

LIFE STORY OF ANDERSON FLOWERS TEMPLE*

Anderson Flowers Temple was born in Copiah County Mississippi on the 13th day of January, 1841. On or about the first of March following his birth, his father, James Herbert, moved his family to Attala County, and settled across Big Black River from Durant.

The new place was a double log house with plank floors, a gallery on each side and a hall between. The kitchen was situated about forty feet away from the main building; this being the custom in those days as a way of preventing fire from spreading to the main building. The chimneys were made of sticks and dirt and the window shutters were made of wood.

The farm was the principle source of food and many necessities. From the farm the people had their corn, cotton, wheat, potatoes, sugarcane, peanuts, garden vegetables, fruit and honey. Cows provided milk and meat. Sheep provided wool and meat. In the nearby swamps there was a bountiful supply of squirrels and other wild animals, and fish from the river. Hogs were loosed in the fall to fatten on the bountiful mast in the swamps.

A.F. Temple, a volunteer, joined a company made up at Kosciusko in July 1861. This company joined the 20th Mississippi Regiment at Iuka, Mississippi.

"I shot more than one hundred shots at Yankees in one day. I shot at a man every time I fired. This was picket fighting and we were out between the lines. I saw men fall when shot but could not know that I killed a man, and am glad that I do not know that I ever killed a man, though I took as deadly aim as I could every time I shot."

On November 30, 1864, at Franklin, Tennessee, the army lost six thousand men. General Hood ordered his army to charge the breastworks and the Federal guns cut them down. Another charge was ordered, and again they were cut down. And so the battle raged and very little damage came to the Federals, their fortifications being impregnable. The area was covered with the dead, the dying, and the wounded. Men were lying three deep in places. For a hundred yards one could have walked on dead men. Night came on and the firing ceased, but now instead of the noise of cannons and muskets there came the cries and the noises of groaning and dying men from every direction.

Excerpts from Van Benson Temple's 1963 booklet about the life and times of his father, Anderson Flowers Temple (author Van Temple's great-grandfather).

MISSISSIPPI

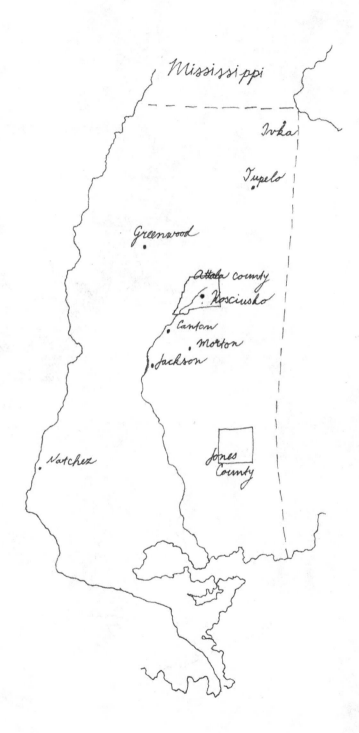

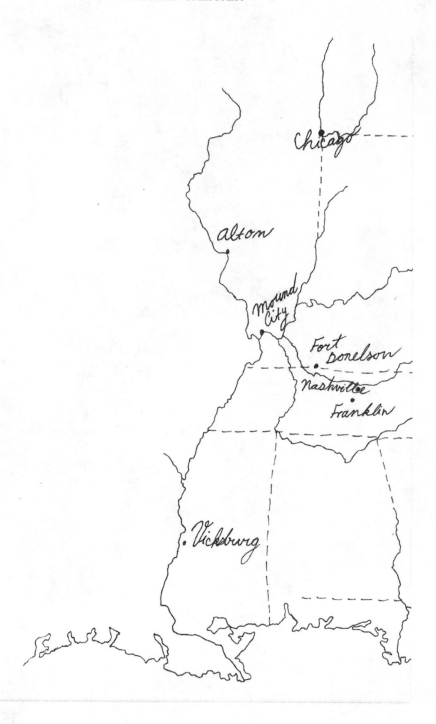

Fayette
County

Lynchburg

Knoxville

Greensboro

Kinston

Atlanta

PREFACE

Have you ever wondered if memories of your ancestors inhabit your soul?

On a cold, rainy day in February 1964, I was a restless twelve-year-old longing to play outside. My mother sent me to the garage to crack a grocery sack full of pecans. An hour later I finished but was still at loose ends, so Mom handed me a bronze-colored booklet, smiled and said, "I think you'll like this."

I opened my bedroom curtains wide to keep an eye on the rain, crawled in bed, and two hours later finished reading the booklet. The rain persisted, but I was no longer anxious, and no longer locked in my own little world. I met a special person for the first time. The booklet was about the life and times of Anderson Flowers Temple, my paternal great-grandfather — born 1841, died 1929. He had spoken directly to me across the years and I was spellbound.

His story helped me begin to see life as a long tapestry of lives — the lives of my forebearers: farmers, soldiers, teachers, mothers and fathers. People who struggled, who sought to find a true path, who succeeded or failed to different degrees. A few years later, as a draft-eligible young man during the Vietnam war, I re-read the booklet and was again captivated by his spirit. The life lessons in Anderson's story seeped into my soul and guided me at that pivotal point in my life.

Whisperwood is a work of fiction, built upon the bones of my great-grandfather's lived experiences. Twenty years ago, I began researching the history of the 20th Mississippi Regiment, the Civil War, and the language and customs of 1860s rural America. I found firsthand accounts, letters to and from home, and an abundance of historical information. Three years ago I began writing the story I've long wanted to bring to life.

Whisperwood is my way of saying thank you to my grandfather Van Benson Temple, for writing a narrative of his father's life and sharing it with the family, and to my great-grandfather Anderson, for his hard-earned wisdom about war and honor.

Herewith is an account of my experiences as a soldier in the Confederate army, written some years after but true to the best of my recollection. I experienced the depravity and addiction of war and lost my best friend and brother. Battles still ring in my ears and memories haunt.

Anderson Flowers

Chapter 1

SKIRMISH IN THE WOODS
November 1861, Fayette County, Virginia

Dallas and I followed Lieutenant Oldham through a thick morning fog across a field of knee-high switchgrass. The double-file of fifty Mississippi riflemen moved wordlessly, crossed a split-rail fence and headed west down a densely wooded hill. My heart beat fast and I breathed in the cold air deeply. I was determined to do my duty and be brave no matter what came. A quarter mile into the woods a small creek wound its way through a hardwood flat. The ground was covered with brown leaves, wet from recent rain. Our lieutenant positioned us fifteen paces back from the creek on a rise crowded with trees and boulders. We spread out in an arched line, a few paces between men and hid behind whatever we could find. Dallas was to my left; Will, my right. Our orders included no talking and no smoking, and we were not to shoot unless Oldham pointed his sword toward the heavens.

Our skirmish line stretched eighty yards along the edge of the creek flat and our commander hid behind a clump of swamp grass near the middle where we could see him. Amos, our shortest man, stood by a crooked ironwood tree twenty paces in front with orders to squat if he saw the enemy.

Like all soldiers in Company K, I wore the same clothes as the day I left home. We were supposed to get uniforms at training camp and coats for winter, but army promises were hollow. Oldham was easy to spot in his gray lieutenant's double-breasted frockcoat.

I settled behind twin elms in a swirl of pressed-down grass with a good view of the bottomland and rested my rifle. Two split-heart prints, fresh deer tracks, marked the mud near my boots. One boot was held together with a piece of rope, the sole and upper having separated. The woods were quiet and cold, and a light wind pushed in from the north, brushing the broken clouds along. We blended into the landscape without a trace and soon the woods came alive again. Birds flittered about and a squirrel on the other side of the creek barked nervously. Just-fallen leaves drifted downstream and a stand of Virginia pines hugged the hillside behind me. Pines in my native Mississippi grew much taller and had longer needles. Doc Perry, our regimental surgeon, had lived in Virginia when he was a boy and he taught me the names of trees that didn't grow back home.

With one bullet in my rifle and thirty-nine in my cartridge case I waited. Except for being hungry I felt quite peaceful. My mind drifted back to deer hunting on Apookta creek with Dallas the winter before when we were both nineteen. It had been five months since we enlisted, and I figured we'd surely be home for Christmas. I thought of the folks at church and longed for Mary Ann, remembering our last time together in the woods. Now that time seemed far away.

Suddenly, loud *caw, caw, caw*, sounds surprised me from behind. A hawk flew just above the treetops chased by two angry crows. In seconds they passed out of sight, then out of hearing, taking their fight westward. I saw Amos come to a squat and hair stood up on the back of my neck. In the woods across the creek, bayonets flashed in the sunlight that knifed through the bare trees. An enemy patrol moved quickly through the creek flat, sticks snapping under their boots. The light settled on their dark blue uniforms, and they stood out against the green swamp grass. I raised my rifle and tried to steady a racing heart as four dozen enemy soldiers moved closer. I was afraid my beating heart might give away our position. Our lieutenant's sword was still at his side.

Suddenly a rifle fired to my right! *Crack!* A billow of white smoke rolled toward the creek, dispersed a bit and drifted back. Shots broke out along our line though no order to fire had been given. *Splat!* A bullet slapped a tree near my head. Blood splattered on my jacket, but I felt no pain. *Crack, crack, crack,* firing quickened on both sides, sounding like hard sleet on a tin roof. Red fire spouted from enemy guns and the drifting smoke brought the acrid smell of black powder to my nose. Never before had I seen the deadly end of a rifle fired at me. Fierce energy swelled within my chest and I felt unleashed. One enemy soldier appeared in sharp detail, so I sighted him and squeezed the trigger. The kick pushed me back, a spark burned my eye, and everything became a blur.

The woods were alive with the crack of rifles fired at close range. Bullets pulped tree trunks and ricocheted off boulders. My eyes watered and I fumbled the next cartridge, dropped my ramrod and stopped to clean off the mud. I fired through the haze of gun smoke in the direction of the enemy and reloaded. Oldham signaled our left flank to regroup near the center where the enemy was concentrated. He looked older and tired, like my father in his sweat-soaked hat at the end of a long day in our cotton field. The right side of my head felt wet and warm. I wiped blood off my neck and fired again.

In five minutes, the shooting lessened and the Yanks retreated across the creek, up the rise and disappeared. I scanned the woods for a target, but found none, and then the firing stopped completely. Oldham ordered us to be perfectly quiet and wait at the ready. My right ear was clogged with blood and my heart pounded like I'd just finished a footrace, though I'd not taken a single step. My mouth was dry, and stomach knotted. *Have they had enough?*

We surprised the Yanks, though not as completely as Oldham had planned. Daniel had taken a bullet in his thigh and Doc Perry tended to him. Our regiment, eight hundred strong, was only half an hour away. Oldham was well schooled in tactics and would send for reinforcements if needed. *Surely those Yanks won't come through here again!* My ear throbbed and I squeezed it tight with my handkerchief.

Oldham sent Amos and two others out front to search. They moved slowly through the valley, pausing at intervals. No birds flew. The woods were completely still except for our searchers. Upon return, Amos was excited and grinning.

"Three dead Yankees, Lieutenant! Left 'em where they fell, jis like ya said."

"Good work."

"I found this." Amos handed over a revolver.

Oldham sent Ray back to Captain Patterson with a written report:

Engaged enemy infantry, strength estimated at fifty, three killed, enemy withdrew west. Patrol suffered one wounded. No reinforcements needed. Will hold position and observe remainder of day. Lt. J. R. Oldham

The affair was our first close-up battle and seemed to prove we could whip the Yankees when our commanders let us get at them.

I took the handkerchief off my ear and looked over at Will.

"What's it look like?" I whispered.

"Like a bullet took the tiptop off." He grinned. "Still bleedin'."

We sat in the unnatural quiet, each soldier alone with his thoughts. Dallas was only a few yards away, but Oldham had ordered all of us not to say a word. My lifelong friend winked at me and pulled his hat low. He'd always been able to fall asleep in an instant. Six bullets were gone from my cartridge case.

An hour passed with no sign of the enemy then Oldham let one man at a time take a look at the dead. When it was my turn I went to the creek. The gurgling water ran clear and a blue cap lay on the bank. Wood thrushes flitted around feeding on the ground. Upstream I came upon the body of a blue-coated man in the water, his face submerged. Wet leaves clung to his coat and one shoe was missing. A floating stick drifted up his trouser leg. *Who is this man?* His left hand bobbed up and down in the current. His brown hair was curly and thick. Might have been in his early twenties, same as me. A cold sadness flooded my soul and I sensed someone was watching me. *Has his spirit departed?*

I couldn't take my eyes off the lifeless body. *Did a bullet from my rifle kill him? Is he the one who nipped my ear?* I looked at my hands, bloody and scratched, but still alive and useful. I pondered these things in my heart, watched the flowing water and listened to the wind passing through the valley of leafless trees.

A blue jay landed by the dead soldier's cap. *Jeer, jeer, jeer.* I tossed a stick, the jay took off, and I watched it swoop through the valley in the direction of the Yankee retreat and disappear in the gray forest. The trees looked familiar. *Have I dreamed about this?*

After filling my canteen, I returned to my position in the skirmish line and ate the last of my peanuts and a hunk of bread. We'd been on half rations for a week. Bare branches swayed in a gust of wind and I heard a voice whisper, *Thou shalt not kill.* I glanced to my left, but Dallas wasn't there. I looked across the bottomland and saw him step haltingly along the creek. Several hours passed in silence then Lieutenant Oldham gathered the patrol around. He struck a match and took five or six quick pulls on a new cigar. The smoke lingered among the men and my belly growled.

"Ya fought well today, men," Oldham said. "But we could've done better. Anybody know what went wrong?"

"We started firing 'fore ya signaled," Daniel said.

"That's right. You gotta learn to keep your britches on! This ain't no huntin' trip!"

4

Oldham glared at Jack but didn't call out his name. Everyone knew Jack was the most anxious to fight.

"A top notch fightin' squad obeys orders down to the last detail!"

Oldham took a deep draw on his cigar, held it a couple of seconds, and blew the smoke toward his boots. The strong burning grass smell tingled my nose.

"If we'd held our fire, we mighta captured the whole bunch!"

He turned in a circle and looked squarely at each man.

"As it stands now, we'll likely face those boys again! And next time … they might surprise us!"

He shuffled his feet and looked up. The clouds had cleared and the sky was deep blue. Shadows grew longer and a chill settled upon us.

"I know you're all new to soldiering, but I expect ya to toe the mark. Mistakes have consequences. Just ask Daniel! Understood?"

"Yes, sir," the men responded together.

He paused and looked sternly at us once again.

"Okay." He smiled. "Let's go!"

Back at camp everybody wanted to talk with Daniel.

"How did it feel?" Dallas asked.

"Like a sharp pinch. Didn't know I 'as hit. When I looked down, my trousers were bloody and there 'as a hole in my leg. That's when it started hurtin'!"

"Does it hurt now?"

"Yeah it hurts like hell! What'd ya think? Doc pulled the bullet out with long-nose pliers."

Everyone laughed except Daniel.

"You gonna mend?" Will asked.

"Yeah. Doc says it didn't hit bone. Wanna see the bullet?"

We passed it around and then gave it back. Daniel slipped the bullet in his pocket.

In our tent that night, Dallas and I talked about what we'd do if seriously wounded, and then we played a game of chess by candlelight. Although I had captured his queen, he managed to put me in checkmate.

5

Chapter 2

LEAVING HOME

Five months earlier — July 1861, Attala County, Mississippi

When I awoke my Bible was beside me. From the Book of II Corinthians, I read the passage I'd marked the night before — "While we look not at the things which are seen: for the things which are seen are temporal: but the things which are not seen are eternal." Then I asked God to give me courage for the day ahead.

I smeared my bare feet with grease, especially the places blisters like to form, and put on my thickest socks. I laced my boots to the top, ending in a tight bowknot. I checked to make sure Father's watch was clipped in my pocket, and then went out back of the cabin to the kitchen shack. Sister was already up, simmering a big breakfast for Dallas and me. Bacon, grits, and gravy steamed on the stove. I hugged her from behind as she turned the bacon, and she gave me an elbow to the ribs. I laughed, but she didn't. She didn't smile or even raise her eyes from the stovetop.

Sister didn't want me to join the army, and she'd made that very clear. I'd lived with her, husband Eugene and daughter Henrietta since Mama died a couple of years before. I helped them with the hogs, vegetables and cotton … everything on the farm. Eugene joined up a month prior and we hadn't heard a word from him since. When I left, there'd be no man at home to help out.

Behind us, there was a noise at the cabin. Dallas was watching us from the doorway. He motioned for me to come over.

"Leave her alone," he whispered. "She's missin' Eugene. Better ya jis leave her alone."

He was right, but I hated to leave home this way. My oldest brother, Jesse, was married and lived one county to the west, and he'd joined the army a few months earlier. We didn't see him very often, but always at Christmas and Easter. My brother John, two years older than me, had decided not to join. His wife Ellen was pregnant for the first time. He would help Sister while we were away but had his own farm to manage too.

Sister served two plates of steaming food then went to her room and slammed the door shut. Dallas and I ate in silence and looked out the windows of the double log cabin as the summer sun warmed the countryside. We'd shared many good mealtimes at the table and plenty of laughs, but there was no celebration that day. Sister's absence at the table left me sad and worried.

"She'll be alright," Dallas whispered so she wouldn't hear us through the wall.

"It jis doesn't seem right."

"We won't be gone long. I hear the Yanks have no heart for fightin."

"I hope you're right about that."

A blue jay landed on the front porch rail. *Jeer, jeer. Jeer, jeer.* Another jay out back answered loudly, *Jeer, jeer. Jeer, jeer.* We ate to the chatter of the dueling birds and I wondered what lay ahead. *Will I be brave in battle? Or will I turn and run?* Dallas kept his thoughts to himself, too. When we finished, I slipped my Bible in my pack and tapped on Sister's door. My heart bounced when the door opened, and she threw both arms around me.

"Please don't go!" she sobbed. "Please!"

We held each other in a long embrace and in a minute she quieted.

"We'll fight off the invaders and be back 'fore Christmas," I said.

"For sure," Dallas added, grinning at Sister.

We all laughed, but it was part of pretending to be brave. I had no idea what I was getting into. Like all the other times we'd talked since the outbreak of the war, it was of no use. My mind was made up and wasn't going to change. She wiped away her tears, pushed me aside and spoke.

"Wait here."

In a minute she returned from the kitchen and gave both of us packages.

"Food for your long walk. Might be your last good meal for a while." There was a hint of a smile at the corner of her mouth. "Promise you'll write. And let me know when you're comin' home."

"I will … for sure I will," I said.

"I'll cook ya up somethin' special."

"I'd be happy to come for dinner too," Dallas kidded and we all laughed.

"When y'all find Eugene," she said, "tell 'em he'd better write, or I'll make him do his own cookin' for a month!"

Fighting back tears, I tucked Sister's food parcel in my pack and gave her a final hug.

"Keep the big hog happy," I said. "We'll roast her up good for Christmas." I tried to sound confident.

Sister sat on the wooden trunk and patted it with her hand as tears streamed down her face. We both knew the meaning full well. Father's violin was tucked inside with the winter blankets. He had taught me to play the year before he died, and she often sang when I played. I'd decided that the war was not a good place for our family treasure, and she'd promised to take good care of it till my return.

"Give Henrietta a hug for me," I said.

Henrietta, who was seven at the time, had spent the night with cousin Jane because we knew the leaving would be hard. As Dallas and I walked away, Sister stood on the porch, hands at her side. I felt more than I could show.

"I left a little surprise for Henrietta," I yelled back. "On her bed."

My wide brimmed hat shaded the sun as we traveled the dusty road east toward Kosciusko past the corn patch head-high with ears almost ready to pick. My heart was filled with love for my sister and the anguish of leaving. In my twenty years, I'd never been further away from home than Yazoo City, a fifty-mile journey. We took our cotton there each summer to sell and buy flour, salt, and supplies for the year. It was comforting knowing John was staying home.

"We'll all be back takin' harvest next year," I said.

"You talkin' to me?" Dallas asked.

"Nope. It's nothin'."

The sun bore down upon us as we walked along. It was my patriotic duty to defend our soil from the invaders. It was simple, it seemed. Mississippi joined the Union voluntarily, so seceding was our right. The fever to join up spread through our county like a brush fire on a windy summer day. You were supposed to be at least seventeen to join, but some younger boys lied to get in. It was the sort of crowd fever that the preacher tried to whip up at revivals. Being a soldier would honor my family name and I'd prove myself a man. I wanted to talk with Dallas, but my throat was too swollen with emotion and pride. He strode along steadily

9

with a look of determination on his face. He'd made up his mind too. *There might not even be any fighting.*

In the slowly drifting summer clouds I pictured my Father walking behind the plough and mule furrowing rows for seedbeds. A barefoot boy chewing a straw of yellow tallgrass walked behind Father, stepping on either side of the upturned dirt.

The cloud bank drifted off to the northeast and I came back to the present. Sweat beads tickled my back as the relentless sun bore down from the blue sky.

Chapter 3

ENLISTMENT
July 1861, Kosciusko, Mississippi

Shortly, we came to Sultan's ferry at the Big Black River.

Dallas yelled out, "Good mornin'! How 'bout a ride?"

Sultan's house was situated on a bluff overlooking the river with a thick stand of sweetgum trees out front. After hearing no reply Dallas hollered again. I moved up the hill a bit and saw old man Sultan sitting quite still in his chair. Dallas rang the bells at the ferry posts and Sultan finally got up. He wobbled down the bank looking like he might have been hitting the joy juice. Deep creases crossed his leathery face almost shrouding his sunken eyes.

The ferry was a rectangular flatboat with a rough plank deck just big enough to hold one horse-drawn wagon.

"How much?" I asked, even though I knew the fare.

"Two bits," Sultan mumbled. "You pull."

Sultan released the tie and Dallas and I pulled the towrope hand over hand. The ferry moved slowly across the swirling brown river toward the landing posts on the other side. Large white sand bars jutted out from the banks.

Sultan pulled a pipe from his pocket, lit it, and leaned both elbows back on the rail, gazing at the sky. He never was the friendly sort, nor was he ever in a hurry, as far as I know. I'm not sure Sultan was his actual given name, but that's what everybody called him, including his wife. In that part of Mississippi, his ferry was the only way to get across without swimming, and he acted like he was some sort of Lord or something, holding power over folks.

We paid our fare and continued east along the Durant-Kosciusko Road for a good while till we found ourselves a spreading live oak to sit under and take lunch. I checked my pocket watch — twelve-fifteen. As soon as we unpacked Sister's fried chicken, biscuits and blueberry pie, two dozen black flies appeared out of nowhere. We made short work of the food and then fell asleep. I dreamed I was cane-pole fishing with Father. He had just hooked a good catfish and started to pull it in, when a stark *caw, caw, caw* woke me. A crow was perched high in the tree above us and I jostled Dallas awake. We picked up our canvas knapsacks, put on our hats, and stepped back into the searing sunshine.

A few miles down the dusty road a familiar voice shouted from the other side of a rail fence.

"Hey, hey boys!"

We stopped to talk with Uncle Willie, working his field near Sallis. He offered us a drink from his jug, but we both declined. I didn't want to smell like whiskey at enlistment. Willie wasn't my uncle and he wasn't Dallas' uncle either, that was just what everybody called him. The story was he was living in Texas and came to Mississippi when he lost his family. He wouldn't talk about it, but the rumor was his house caught on fire one night while he was away at market and it killed his wife and two young daughters. He abandoned his farm, his cow ... everything, and moved to start over. At cotton harvest times, we went to help Uncle Willie with his crop, and he came over to help us.

"Where y'all goin'?" he asked, though he already knew.

"Fixin to whip the Yanks!" Dallas replied. "Gonna show 'em Mississippi can do jis fine without 'em."

"Ya darn right!" Uncle Willie boasted. "Don't need any comin' here tellin' us what to do!"

"Cussed fools! They should jis leave us alone."

"Kosciusko?" Willie asked.

"Yep. They're formin' a company."

Uncle Willie grinned and sent us on our way. From behind I heard him holler.

"Show 'em Mississippi boys can't be pushed around, ya hear?"

Dallas turned and shouted, "Duty calls and we have answered!"

On we went, our spirits bolstered.

As we walked along drenched in sweat, dragonflies lit on our hats and shoulders and we swatted them off each other. Soon our water was gone, and we weren't anywhere near a creek. We passed through a shady section of tall pines and I heard a distinct whisper voice say, *Thou shalt not kill*. I stopped and looked around, but Dallas kept on walking.

"Did you say somethin'?" I shouted at Dallas.

"Nope. Come on, I'm thirsty."

As we walked through the shade of the pines, the voice came again, and I pondered it in my heart. My mind was full of questions and fears. Home was only a half-day behind, but I already felt lost. The place that defined our lives, provided our food and drink … our shelter, music and play — *how long before we return*? A verse from Ecclesiastes that Momma taught me came to mind. "All go unto one place: all are of the dust, and all turn to dust again."

In midafternoon, we reached Kosciusko, tired and parched. Thirty or so men and boys were gathered in the center of town. First, we got ourselves a good, long drink at a well. A man in a gray, double-breasted frockcoat sat at a narrow table with two stacks of papers held down by palm-sized stones.

"Who's that man?" I asked a fellow standing nearby.

"Lieutenant Oldham," he winked. "Enlistment officer."

Dallas and I got in line and waited our turn. At the front Lieutenant Oldham asked for my name.

"Anderson Flowers from over near Durant," I said. "My friend Dallas and I walked twenty-five miles today to get here."

"How old are ya, Mr. Flowers?"

"Twenty."

"Ya married?"

Dallas poked me in the ribs. He liked to kid me about Mary Ann.

"No, sir, I'm not."

He filled in the blanks on a single sheet of paper and I signed.

"Welcome to the army. You're Private Flowers now," Oldham said.

After Dallas was signed up, he asked, "What do we do next, sir?"

Oldham told us the plan was to wait a few more days while they recruited a full company of a hundred men, or as close to it as they could get. Then we'd walk to

Iuka to join the Army of Mississippi. He directed us to the camp east of town where we could meet the other men, get food, and rest for the night.

We joined others who'd been camping for days in a picked-over, trampled-down cotton field. Every man looked hot and bored. I was anxious to get to the fighting and afraid that a few days delay might cause us to miss it. We met several enlistees including Jim Bunyan, Bob Waddell, Monroe Wallace, Amos Watson, Daniel Woods, and a tall redheaded fellow named Jack Stanley. They were from all over Attala County and ready to whip the Yanks.

After we'd all met, Jack challenged the group.

"How many Yanks ya gonna' kill?" He waved his arms up and down.

"As many as it takes!" Jim shouted back.

Other men started gathering around.

"Don't think there'll be much of a fight," Bob said. "Yanks don't know which end of a rifle matters!"

Jack howled and jumped up and down. He ran to the edge of the field, pulled a long, straight stick out of a brush pile and held it in his arms like a rifle. He aimed it level toward the woods and pretended to squeeze the trigger. *Bam!* he yelled and then stumbled as if the recoil had pushed him backwards. Bob caught him, joining in the game. The men roared and egged him on. Jack pretended to ram a bullet down the rifle muzzle. He cocked the hammer, aimed and fired the pretend rifle again. The men all yelled out together, *Bam!*

Jack's face got as red as a beet from cavorting around and a bigger crowd of men gathered to watch.

"Ready to kill some Yanks?" he hollered.

The men yelled back, some wanting action so much they were ready to start fighting with sticks. After a few minutes of hollering in the summer heat, the excitement was over and the group dispersed. We got Jack a drink of water, poured some over his head and made him sit in the shade. The only thing the army had for us to do was wait, so we bided our time as best we could. Monroe, a plain-looking man except for having enormous protruding ears, told stories of the gallant deeds he expected he'd do once we got a shot at the Yankees.

About the time the mosquitoes got to biting, we were ordered to the kitchen wagon for supper. There we met the cook, Walker, an older fellow with a bushy, gray beard. He'd cooked up a mess of black-eyed peas, salted beef, cornbread and coffee. When we finished up, a tall gentleman in a gray uniform jacket and a wide brim hat rode up on a fine-looking brown steed. He had a scabbard and sword at his side. The men who had been in camp a while told us he was Captain Patterson, our commander, from Yazoo City. He dismounted, turned his horse over to a negro servant and stood easy as the recruits gathered around.

"Good evenin' gentlemen. Good evenin'," Patterson addressed the group in a booming voice.

"Understand all y'all want to be soldiers. Is 'at right?"

"Sure do," Jack spoke, never at a shortage of words. "Sure do, sir," he corrected himself.

Several fellows chuckled.

"I'm Captain Duncan Patterson and I want to welcome you to the infantry. You are now part of Company K of the 20th Voluntary Mississippi Infantry Regiment," he said, evidently quite proud. He moved among the men shaking hands and talking us up.

"Did Walker feed ya well?" Patterson asked.

"Yes, sir, he did," Amos said. "But nothin' like home."

"You'd better get used to that, son," Patterson said with a deep laugh. "This ain't gonna be downhome cookin'."

"When do we get uniforms, sir?" Dallas asked.

"And rifles?" Bob added.

"Not sure 'bout that. Should be equipped at Iuka."

I was anxious to find my brother-in-law Eugene and see Doc Perry, our beloved doctor from home. Doc took care of our whole county, almost. I saw him at Old Lebanon Church on Sundays when he wasn't off taking care of someone. He did his best to help my father when he was ill.

"Is Doc Perry here?" Dallas asked Patterson.

"At the hospital tent," he pointed with his sword.

"Hospital? Has the fightin' already started?"

Patterson chuckled.

"Easy to tell ya jis got here. So many men gettin' sick, Doc can't hardly keep up!"

Dallas and I headed toward the south edge of the camp. There was about a half-hour left before sunset and the orange ball touched the tops of the trees at the edge of the field. A bevy of doves swooped over our heads heading west toward the Yockanookany River.

"Doc Perry here?" Dallas asked the orderly at the tents.

"He's awfully busy, but I'll see if he can talk to ya."

He ducked inside a large white tent. A dozen men lay on bedding on the ground, right next to one another, coughing and moaning. In a minute Doc emerged.

"Well who do we have here?" he smiled. "Dallas Townsend and Andy Flowers. Good to see you boys."

We shook hands and talked for a while. Doc was a round bodied man with a full beard and a monocle he used to see up close. He was quite a talker and quick with a funny line.

"Why so many sick?" Dallas asked.

Doc wiped his brow with a handkerchief.

"Some have malaria and I've got quinine to treat 'em. But we've got cases of measles, typhoid fever, and tuberculosis too. Never seen anythin' like it."

The orderly tapped Doc on the shoulder.

"You're needed, sir. Frank wants more opium pills."

"Sorry to have to cut this short, men," Doc said. "Duty calls."

He tipped his fingers to his forehead in a casual salute.

"Do me a favor boys," he said with a grin. "Don't get sick! My hospital's already full!" He disappeared behind the canvas flap.

Back at the main camp, I wandered off a ways to be away from the others. I came to an old barn by a burned-down house and sat in the last shadows of my first day as a soldier. *Coo ... coo ... coo*, the mellow call of a mourning dove came from the pines.

The adventure of soldiering was beginning to swallow me up, but my mind came around to Mary Ann. She was almost sixteen and I'd had my eye on her for three years. She was one-of-a-kind, at least of the girls I'd known, determined and independent, and not hesitant to speak her mind. We'd gone on walks in the woods and been swimming in the river alone. I walked her home some days after church and she let me hold her hand. I missed the sound of her voice and the way her wavy brown hair fell on her neck. The last time we were together was the day before Dallas and I left home to enlist. After church she led me off so we could be by ourselves and gave me a handful of pink crepe myrtle flowers.

"What's this for?" I asked.

"To remind ya of beauty."

She smiled, stood on her tiptoes, and kissed me lightly. Then she tucked a tiny green pinecone in my shirt pocket.

"And what's that for?" I asked.

She poked my chest hard and said, "I want ya to give it back to me when ya come home for good."

I pulled her up close so there was no space between us and felt my heart beating fast against her bosom. *The two shall be one flesh.*

The soothing sound of the wind slipping through the pines nudged me and the mourning dove called again, *Coo ... coo ... coo*. I checked and the little pinecone was still in my pocket.

Chapter 4

TRAINING CAMP
July 1861, Iuka, Mississippi

We stayed in camp at Kosciusko for a week doing nothing, till finally the day came to begin our journey north to join the Army of Mississippi. After breakfast, we helped Walker pack the kitchen wagons and hitch up the mules. Company K, seventy-eight strong, set out on foot behind Captain Patterson on his horse and there was great excitement among the men. Walker, a strong baritone singer, led us in round after round of the camp song, "Tenting Tonight."

We're tenting tonight on the old campground,
Give us a song to cheer our weary hearts,
A song of home, and the friends we love so dear.

Under full sun we walked mile after mile north toward Iuka. Early chatter gave way to long periods of silence then Bob got overheated and fell out. Walker and Daniel stayed behind to revive him. By noon our whole group was exhausted, so Patterson let us take shade, water and eat cornbread and peanuts.

"How far we goin', sir?" Jack asked Patterson while we rested.

"Aimin' for twenty-five today."

"How far to Iuka?"

"'Bout a hundred and sixty. Northeast corner of Mississippi."

"Is fightin' goin' on there?" Jack asked.

"No, son. That's where the army's assembling. We're joinin' up with other companies from all over our state."

Tending the farm and taking cotton to market took a lot of steps, but it was rare to walk twenty-five miles in a day. By afternoon bad blisters made me long for a riverbank to cool my feet. The July heat was stifling and not a cloud crossed the sky. By the third day of walking, sweating and sleeping in the same clothes, I stank to high heaven and so did everybody else. My feet were in bad shape and the heel of one boot was loose. We walked for seven days straight with no break in the heat nor a drop of rain.

When we arrived at Iuka, men were gathered around dozens of campfires cooking supper. The mass of new soldiers stretched as far as I could see. Captain Patterson had us wait and he rode off to headquarters, a white wood house in the middle of the fields. He returned in a half hour and boasted, "Company K is now officially part of the Army of Mississippi!"

"How many soldiers are here?" Bob asked.

"Several thousand and more'll arrive this week. Tomorrow you'll be issued guns and equipment."

"Yeah!" Jack hollered, and other men joined in. "Let's kill some Yanks!"

Dallas and I gathered firewood while Walker and others got our supper going.

"Ya gonna write Sister tonight?" Dallas asked me.

"Think I'll wait till tomorrow after we start training. She'll be interested in knowin' about camp life."

After supper Dallas and I sat around the fire and watched the flames. I pulled out my pocket watch and handed it to him. It was a silver Railway Timekeeper made in Liverpool with a tiny second hand where the Roman numeral six would have been. He turned it over in his hands, opened the face and held it up by the chain. It turned in circles and light from the flames glinted off the silver and glass and danced around the tree trunks. It had belonged to my father, and Momma gave it to me when he passed away. It was all I had left of him. Missing our fathers made our friendship stronger.

We added more wood to the fire and watched the flames. *Hoot hoot, whooo, whooo* came the sound of a great horned owl. Dallas fell asleep on the ground and I watched the fire burn till only a few flames flickered. From deep down in the coals I heard my father's voice calling me, *I am here, I am here*, and shivers went down my spine. He passed when I was nine and this was the third time I'd heard his voice from beyond. Once was from inside the orange sun when it broke through dark clouds after a thunderstorm. The first time I heard his voice it came from the Big Black, just upstream from Sultan's Ferry. I told Momma about it and she believed me. Father's words were always the same, *I am here, I am here*. It gave me courage to know he was looking in on me from time to time.

After drills the next day, the mail came, but there was nothing for me. Captain Patterson got a <u>Daily Richmond Examiner</u> with accounts of fighting in Virginia. Several of us gathered around and he read out loud.

General Irvin McDowell led a Union force of twenty-eight thousand from Washington to attack Confederates under General P.G.T. Beauregard protecting the Manassas Junction rail station. General Joseph E. Johnston's army of nine thousand men arrived to reinforce Beauregard on July 21st.

We listened with great interest as Patterson read. This was the first big battle of the war we had heard of.

Confederate General Thomas Jackson ordered his men to charge the Union artillery, but to wait till they were within fifty yards before firing. He told his men to yell like furies when they charged. Jackson's brigade charged with fixed bayonets, overran the Yankees, captured prisoners and guns, and changed the outcome of the battle. The Union lost two thousand eight hundred men and our side lost two thousand. The newspaper said the battle was a great Confederate victory.

Patterson put the newspaper down when he finished, and the men stood in silence. The blood ran out of my head. *Two thousand of our soldiers lost in one day's battle! Our whole regiment is less than a thousand!*

I had a hard time getting comfortable that night and kept turning over trying to find a softer position. Eventually I fell asleep but slept poorly. In the morning Dallas was gone and I discovered dozens of gumballs under my bedroll. I decided

21

not to say anything to Dallas, but to play high jinks on him later when he wouldn't be expecting it.

That day, each man was issued a camp kettle, skillet, two pans, a knife, fork and spoon, canteen and bedroll. We were also given old smoothbore guns with a bayonet, cartridge box, and cap pouch. The company was supplied with a set of picks, spades, saws and axes.

"A smoothbore?" Jack asked the quartermaster.

"Move along," he motioned.

"When do we get uniforms?" Jack asked.

"Soon, maybe," the quartermaster replied.

"And when do we get ammunition?" Dallas asked.

"Don't know! Move on!"

"What good's a rifle without ammunition?" Jack asked.

We pulled Jack out of line before he got in trouble and went back to our camp.

"This the best they can do?" Jack complained. "Smoothbores? I hear the Yanks all got new Springfields. You know, they shoot a lot farther."

"Guess we'll have to sneak up on 'em," Dallas replied.

"Or hit 'em over the head with picks and spades," Woods added.

The men laughed.

I found Patterson.

"Captain. Can ya help me find my brother-in-law?"

"Well sure. What's his name?"

"Eugene McAdams. I'm purty sure he's in the 20th."

"I'll see what I can find out, son."

July 23, 1861

Dear Sister,

After a long, hot day of drilling, I sit to write. I'm happy to report that I'm healthy in all regards, not counting the blisters on my poor feet. You may find it odd that my health is the first thing I mention, but there is good reason. Doc Perry is our regimental doctor and he's easily the busiest man in the army. Martin Baines took a fever a week ago and can't keep food down. Luckily Dallas and I have been spared from all the fevers and ailments so far. The gathering of armies is killing us, I fear, before we even see the enemy.

Our days start at five o'clock when a bugle sounds reveille and we assemble for roll call and then breakfast. After breakfast a bugle sounds sick call. Eight in our company were sick today. There's a different bugle call for mail and one when we're supposed to go to sleep.

Our lieutenants led our company to a parade field next to camp, divided us into three squads, and taught us the commands and formations of marching and attacking. I was assigned to Lieutenant Oldham's group. He has a negro servant named Able he brought to war with him. Some officers in other companies have servants too, but Able and Captain Patterson's are the only two in ours. After practicing in squads, the whole company formed up and drilled together. You should of seen all the dust we stirred up stomping around. By noon we'd just about baked to a crisp, so they gave us a rest for water and food and then we got right back at it. The whole regiment drilled together this afternoon. There's almost nine hundred of us. I hope my feet get toughened up, so I don't get blisters so easily.

We have no tents and sleep on the ground. Each man has an oilcloth just big enough for two men to lay side-by-side. So far, the weather has been hot and dry, and then some days are even hotter and drier.

In our spare time, we play cards, write letters, play horseshoes and read. I'm sure glad I brought my Bible for it's a comfort to me every day. The most popular thing in camp is gambling. Gambling for knives, soap, books, food, pistols … you name it. If we ever get paid, I'm sure money will be flying around like bats at twilight.

Some companies have special names. Company D calls themselves the Noxubee Riflemen. Company F, from Scott County, are the Forest Guards. Another company raised from Scott County goes by the name Morton Pine Knots. We're just plain old Company K.

Have you heard from Jesse? I miss you dearly.

Your loving brother, Anderson

P.S. Please send more socks. Mine are all worn through.

For two weeks, more men arrived and were issued the tools of war, and we practiced loading and firing our rifles. One evening Captain Patterson assembled the company. One of the drummer boys arrived carrying a fancy purple and white flag with brown tassels at the top of the standard, and he held it up high.

"The flag of the 20th Mississippi!" Patterson shouted.

The men cheered and the boy waved the flag back and forth for all to see.

"We'll carry it wherever we go. If it falls in battle, I expect the man closest by to carry it forward."

The men cheered and waved their hats. Our Captain continued.

"Men of Attala County. Proud, brave men. Our flag will lead us to victory and back home again!"

All the men cheered and threw their hats in the air. Bob put the boy on his shoulders and marched in circles around the company waving the flag.

Confidence grew as we learned to be soldiers. After drills, groups of men gathered and jawed about fighting and defending our homes. Many expected a decisive and victorious engagement that would last a few weeks or months at the most. I was beginning to wonder if we would have an army left to fight when the time came. More men were sick with measles and stomach pains and just about everybody had quick-step. Doc gave us gum sap to help with that. By the fourth week in Iuka, a third of our company was too sick to drill.

That week I got a letter from Sister.

July 20, 1861

Dear Brother,

I finally got a letter from Eugene. He's in Company G and he says he has done nothing but learn how to load and fire cannons and what dozens of bugle calls mean. Martha also heard from Jesse. He's in the 5th Infantry, posted in Virginia and has seen no action.

Henrietta loves the arrowhead and note you left for her. She borrowed a history book from school and is suddenly interested in learning more about Choctaw Indians. Where'd you find the arrowhead? I'm sure Henrietta would love to hear more about your adventures. You know she's kind of a tomboy. She's missing you a great deal and so am I.

It's been very hot here since you left, and the garden is about dried up from lack of rain. I'm planning to use the rest of the beans and peas for next year's seed. It's so dry even the mosquitoes look parched.

The cotton crop looks good, but the problem there is getting it picked. There's talk about putting together a crew and rotating from farm to farm, so all the neighbors with missing men can get picked. It's an interesting idea, but no matter how you organize it, there are a lot fewer working hands. The war is causing a great deal of excitement here at home. I'd say it's sort of turned everything upside down.

We've heard very little about the war. Please do tell me what you and your comrades are up to.

Love, Sister

The first Sunday of August, rumors spread that we would be leaving camp soon to join the fighting. Extra rations arrived by wagon train that afternoon and we were told to cook up food for several days. Little groups of men sang and danced. We were in great need of a change of scenery and a decent bath after weeks of drilling and sweating. After supper, Will and Bob invited Dallas and me over to talk. They seemed unusually excited. Turned out they had gotten a hold of two bottles of joy juice.

"Where'd ya get it?" Dallas asked.

"Let's just say — higher up," Bob winked.

My folks were teetotalers, but I had occasion to drink a few times on the sly. The four of us started out sipping and before you know it, we were in a loose state and asleep on the ground. At daylight, I heard a horse snorting and awoke with a start. My head felt like it had been stomped on and my mouth tasted of blood. I rolled over and looked up. Captain Patterson stood beside his horse, dressed in his best coat and hat. He tapped an empty whiskey bottle with the tip of his sword and the high-pitched sound stung my ears.

"You look like ten miles of bad road, Private."

I stood up slowly and saluted.

"You get in a fight?" he said.

"I think I'll be alright, Captain."

My comrades were still asleep on the ground and I remembered getting in a row with a man I didn't know.

"Good then," he said. "Get your buddies up and eat breakfast. We're breakin' camp in two hours."

Chapter 5

TRAVELING EAST
August 1861, Mississippi to Virginia

On August 10th, we marched to the railyard at Iuka. A locomotive sat on the tracks puffing slowly, its polished black and red paint gleamed in the midmorning sunlight. The engine pulled a tinder car brimming with cut wood, followed by several boxcars. Soldiers, rifles, gear, and rations — the whole of the 20th Mississippi was packed almost as tight as cotton bales for the journey. Rumor had it we were headed to Lynchburg, Virginia to join Floyd's Brigade as part of General Lee's Army. Doc told Dallas and me to take care of Martin who was still peaked and hot with fever. We made a place for him to lie down between us in the boxcar and put a blanket on him. With a jolt our train began rolling east on the Illinois Central Railroad, my first time on a train.

I remembered a hot summer day from childhood helping Father pick cotton. I was off by myself at the far end of the field when I heard a sharp, high-pitched *WOOooOOOH, WOOooOOOH, WOOooOOOH* coming through the woods. The crickets and birds went quiet all of a sudden. I untied my bag and ran toward Father. The loud, shrill sounds pierced the silence three more times. Father pointed to the woods and motioned, giving me the okay to go, so I slipped into the shade of the pine trees.

I heard more sounds through the thick trees and underbrush. Hammers, men talking, and a slow *chug, chug, chug*. Then the great black form of a locomotive rose up high. *The railroad! The railroad's finally coming to our county.* I moved to the edge of the clearing and watched the men and mules working. They packed dirt and stones for the railway base and lay large wooden crossties. Crews of men lifted long, steel rails in front of the engine. When the rails were laid in place and measured, other men hammered in metal spikes. The locomotive pulled cars packed with gravel, rails and ties. The railroad was being extended up from Durant to Goodman. Father had told me it was coming.

Our train rolled along and Dallas and Martin lay asleep near my feet as the boxcars rocked from side to side. Leafy trees and pines slid by the open door, and locomotive smoke stung my nostrils. I pictured the engineers wearing long, leather gloves and thick round glasses, throwing split wood into the firebox. Before we loaded up at the station, I watched the men tending the engine and wondered how burning wood made the big steel wheels turn.

The new world I traveled through made me excited and afraid. Until the war started, I knew what my whole life would be like, I thought. I'd get married, build a cabin and barn, and work hard clearing land for my farm. If lucky, I would be blessed with children and surrounded by family the rest of my days. As the train took us farther away from home, I felt uneasy and alone. Martin's face was red and sweaty, and he moaned when the train bounced hard. I thought I heard Mary Ann's voice, but there were no women in our midst. She was often on my mind.

As our train rolled on overnight and through a second day, we ate all we had in our haversacks. Around midnight we stopped and were issued more rations. We built fires beside the tracks and cooked up everything because the train would not be making any more stops.

My mind was considerably worked up about the adventure that lay ahead. I imagined our great army of valiant, armed soldiers, standing shoulder-to-shoulder like trees in a thicket. Our enemy would turn and run at the sight. When the war was over, I'd be welcomed home as a victorious hero. Underneath my swaggering thoughts, I was scared to death and suspect most of my comrades felt the same.

We gave Martin bits of food and sips of water, but he couldn't keep anything down and he burned with fever. I stood by the door to get fresh air while Dallas tended to Martin. About three in the morning Dallas tugged my trousers. He looked frightened.

"Martin's not breathin'," he said.

I knelt and listened for his heartbeat, but it was not there.

"I'll stay with him till we stop," I said.

"No. I'll do it." Dallas pulled the blanket over Martin's head and draped his arm over his body.

The trees stood as shadows against the black sky studded with stars. I fixed my eyes on a single bright star and pretended it was Martin. His mother would be devastated. Her husband had been killed in a fire the year before and Martin was her only son. The day after Martin left to enlist, his mother broke down at church and the women comforted her. As self-evident as it was, I had not considered the prospect of death and my comrades never talked about it. Light clouds drifted across the night sky, blocking out Martin's star. *What if I never see Mary Ann or Sister again?* Hour after hour, home and all that was familiar grew farther away. Martin was our first to die.

After three days and nights on the train, we arrived in Lynchburg, Virginia late in the afternoon. I smelled smoke as soon as we got out of the boxcar and knew an army camp must be nearby. Alongside the tracks, near the middle of town, stood rows and rows of cannons and loaded wagons. The sky was overcast, and the air hinted of rain.

Lieutenant Conway asked for volunteers to help bury Martin. Dallas, Pyrrhus, and I carried his body and followed a local man to a cemetery by a church where an open grave was waiting. The old fellow wore a pine straw hat and chewed on an unlit cob pipe. His clothes were soaked through with sweat.

"How'd ya know?" Pyrrhus asked the old man.

"Been diggin' graves for two weeks," he said, his voice weary. "Ever since the army trains been comin' through."

We buried Martin and the minister of the church read from the Bible. He talked about how all men are dependent upon God's almighty strength. After the burial, we rejoined the rest of our company and formed columns by the tracks.

As we marched out of town, a light drizzle began to fall, the first rain we had seen in weeks. I carried Martin's rifle and Pyrrhus carried his other things. The rain felt good on my head and it hid my tears. We walked on as the light faded, following the men in front. I wished the rain would wash away my sadness, and I prayed to God for Martin's soul. About four miles north we reached the camp near East Fork Mulberry Creek and slept on the ground in the drissly.

Chapter 6

CAMP DAVIS
August — September 1861, Virginia

Thousands of men were assembled at Camp Davis, a city of fields awash with wagons, cannons, and horses. Men gathered in groups and milled about. A few companies sported gray uniforms, but most wore the clothes they brought from home. Pride swelled up within me and I was confident that the war would go our way. Company K joined in the daily routine: an hour of gun drill followed by maneuvers and then baseball in the afternoon. I also wrote letters and read my Bible.

Our third afternoon in camp was August 16th, Mary Ann's sixteenth birthday, and also the anniversary of her father's death four years earlier from tuberculosis.

A hard, half-hour rain fell and then the sun came out. Lieutenant Conway sent Dallas and me to scavenge for food. We walked back along the road toward Lynchburg, turned east, and followed the lane for a quarter mile till we came to a cabin with a barn. Dallas knocked on the door and a woman appeared. She wore a yellow apron, had brown hair tied up in a knot, and carried a baby on her hip.

"Ma'am," Dallas asked. "Ya have some food ya can sell us?"

"Don't they feed ya in the army?"

"Not too well, to be truthful, Ma'am."

She disappeared back inside. I hated asking for food, especially from poor farmers like myself. Directly she reappeared and a girl stood inside holding the baby. The mother led us to the barn where she pulled the big doors open, revealing a wagon and farming tools. She handed me a basket to hold, put in some turnips, carrots, and a few dried apples.

"How many men?" she asked.

"They're seventy-seven in our company," Dallas said. "But we're just hopin' for enough to feed our sickest."

She went to the back of the barn and came back lugging a whole barrel of dried apples.

"Put this in the wagon," she ordered.

"Oh, no, Ma'am," Dallas said. "We can't take the whole barrel."

"You said there's seventy-seven of ya, right? Come help me!"

She filled a basket with potatoes and radishes. "Load this."

She started loading another basket and Dallas shook his head: no.

"Ya gonna watch while I do all the work, myself?" she said.

It was clear that she would have her way. Shortly, the wagon was loaded with eight baskets of food and we pulled it out in the sunlight. In a minute, she returned with a gray mule, hitched it to the wagon, and I paid her.

"Bring my rig back by sundown or I'll come lookin' for y'all! Now get on afor I sour on it."

"Thank ya kindly, Ma'am," Dallas said, and she went back inside with her children.

Lieutenant Conway was surprised to see us with a whole wagonload. The men unloaded the food and I took the mule and wagon back.

"Thank ya most kindly, Ma'am," I handed her a newspaper we got the day before.

"What's your name?" she asked and I told her.

"And yours, Ma'am?"

"Loretta Dixon."

"We're much obliged to ya, Miss Dixon. Much obliged. Hope someone out there is bein' as kind to your man as you've been to us."

The next evening during supper there was a loud explosion south of camp. Captain Patterson asked for volunteers and Pyrrhus, Jack and I took off right away. A dense mass of black smoke rose from the center of town. Two railyard buildings were on fire and men rushed to keep it from spreading. The flames roared as we carried buckets of water to the railroad workers. When the fire was under control I spoke to the officer in charge.

"Yanks sabotage the train?"

"No Yanks 'round here!" he said. "Unloadin' powder kegs when somethin' set 'em off. Help us get the powder outta here 'fore more blows up!"

For the next half-hour we rolled barrels of gunpowder to another warehouse and covered them with wet blankets.

"Help with the bodies!" the officer pointed. "Take 'em to the depot over there. Wheelbarrow's behind that building."

We stepped gingerly through the blast area, still smoldering. A charred arm wearing a long, canvas glove lay on the ground. My throat clogged, but I was able to keep it down. I picked up the arm and placed it carefully in the wheelbarrow. We retrieved body parts piece by piece and tried to keep the ones together that might have belonged to the same man.

I came to a headless torso. The shirt was buttoned up and a white handkerchief stuck out of the breast pocket. *Who was this man?* I held my breath and laid the dead man's torso in the wheelbarrow. Burned clothing, skin and blood stuck to my clothes and hands. The putrid, sweet smell of burned hair and flesh was too much and I puked. *Almighty God watch over me!*

I counted seven bodies in all. I hoped death had come quickly and they had not felt pain, but I knew better. We returned to camp, reported to Patterson, and then I went to the creek to clean up and settle my nerves. The occurrence was so gruesome I couldn't talk about it. Several days passed before I stopped smelling burned hair.

August 20, 1861
Dear Brother,

I'm so glad to hear from you and grateful to learn that you are well. Your letter was the first report about Martin's death. I couldn't bear to tell his mother myself, so I told Preacher Small in case the army letter had not already reached her. That's the preacher's job.

Some good news — Mr. Simon agreed to advance us flour, coffee, and sugar since we didn't have enough money this year. He's such a good man. He even gave me a bolt of cloth. Remember when we were little and he used to sneak us candy sticks behind his back? With the war, his store is even more the place for gathering and gossiping and he can't keep enough newspapers.

The news from the battles in Virginia is terrible. We're all in shock at the loss of life and everyone is afraid their men may be next to die. I sure hope Eugene, Jesse and you are never in that kind of fighting. Everybody wants to know about the battles, but then they don't want to know, if you see what I mean.

Tomorrow Uncle Willie and Elga should be back from Kosciusko so they can take Mary Ann's cotton to the gin. They are both willing, but awful slow. I shouldn't complain because you're far from home and living out from under a proper roof, but we're feeling the effects of the war too.

Mary Ann visited us last Sunday and asked about you and the others. She's most concerned about you, of course — she's looking forward to hearing you play the fiddle when you get home.

I'm having trouble sleeping these days. Henrietta is rambunctious and more than I can keep up with by myself at times. She thinks she can do anything a man or woman can do and she may be on the money. She said to tell you she's keeping the axe good and sharp and can split some of the smaller logs by herself now.

Do be safe and stay out of the way when you get in the shooting.
Love, Sister

After three weeks in camp, Ted and Jim started talking about deserting. This kind of talk was kept away from the officers, of course. One day a salesman from Port Gibson made the rounds selling tobacco, coffee and sugar out of his wagon. It took nothing to get him jawing.

"Did you boys hear 'bout the deserter they caught last week?" the salesman asked.

"No," Ted said. "What happened?"

"Fellow named Henry Alexander, I b'lieve that's right — from Hattiesburg — in the 13th. Well, Henry stole a captain's horse one night and got a good head start 'fore roll call. Colonel sent three men on horses to track him down and they caught up with him in a little town named Coldwater, 'bout twenty-five miles southwest a here," he pointed with his horsewhip.

A crowd of men gathered around to listen, and the salesman continued.

"Henry stopped to take a bath and spend the night in a proper bed, but he made the mistake a leavin' the horse out front of the hotel, so it was right easy to find him."

"Did they bring him back?" Ted asked.

"Yep. They brought him back and the colonel assembled the whole regiment and called out the names of five men to bring their rifles. Two sergeants took the guns and went off a ways, loaded 'em and brought 'em back. The colonel had Henry's arms tied across his chest and sat him on a coffin."

"Did they shoot him?" Ted asked.

The salesman puffed his cigar. "Don't rush me, now. I'm tellin' the story." He blew a smoke ring and watched it drift up and away.

"The sergeants gave the rifles to the soldiers and lined 'em up about ten feet from Henry. The colonel told 'em to aim at Henry's chest and fire at his command. The shooters were aghast at bein' ordered to shoot Henry 'cause he was a likable fellow and didn't mean any harm. He was jis one of them."

The crowd of listeners grew quiet as the salesman took another drag on his cigar.

"The colonel had the sergeants point their pistols at the firing squad and said he'd have them shot too if they didn't obey. By then every witness was sweatin' at the gravity of the situation. Then the colonel said ready, aim, fire, and all five guns went off at the same time. Henry slumped over dead right there on top of his own coffin and his shirt turned dark from blood."

The salesman took a deep draw on his cigar and blew the smoke into the silent crowd.

"You made that up, right?" Ted asked.

"Nope. It's the godawful truth, I swear."

He put his hand over his heart, dropped his cigar butt in the dirt and mushed it with his boot.

"Then the colonel told the soldiers that only one of the rifles was loaded with lead."

The story was a lesson for all who heard it and it put an end to Ted and Jim's talk about going home.

September 2, 1861

Dear Mary Ann,

I'm in good health and tolerating army life. Occasionally we get newspapers with the mail which is great because the men are eager to learn of progress in the war. There've been some ferocious battles, but so far, we've not seen any Yanks ourselves.

The weather is hot and ticks and chiggers are murdering my skin. I think the mosquitoes are only staying alive by feasting on the army. We've been on half rations for three weeks now. How often I think of the ample stores of food we have at home.

This past Sunday, the chaplain held a church service. He preached from Galatians 5, about the fruit of the Spirit being love, joy, peace, long-suffering, gentleness, goodness and faith. I read it later with my own eyes. In his closing prayer he said we should have no reason to doubt that God will help us. After the service, I was thinking about being in battle soon. It's difficult to see how love, joy and peace are going to figure in.

I hope you and your mother are well. For all the drilling and waiting around we're doing, we would be better off, it seems to me, to be back home. They could just call us back when there is actual fighting to be done.

Sister said you want to send me a present. Living outdoors and drilling day after day in the heat and rain is taking a toll on my clothes. The army has still not issued uniforms to our company and we have no good way to clean our clothes — so anything in the way of clothing that you would like to make would sure come in handy, especially shirts.

I'm not practiced at tender words in letters, or in person for that matter, but since this is the only way I can be with you now, I'll do my best. I miss our walks and talks. Being with you makes me feel alive and peaceful, and when you hold my hand my heart flutters like a thrush flying from bush to bush. I yearn for the day when I'm home and we can walk in the woods and swim in the river again.

Fondly, Anderson

A week after the explosion and fire at the railyard, Doc took Sunday afternoon off from the field hospital and came to visit our company. It was a cloudy afternoon with a light breeze, and we enjoyed the break from the intense sunlight. Before the war, at church picnics when I was a youngster, Doc told stories, so I knew we were in for a treat when he arrived that day. He took a seat and a good group of us gathered around to listen. He entertained us for a couple of hours with tales from Mississippi's past. His stories might not have been true, but that didn't matter because they were true enough.

Sometimes when he was telling a long, rambling tale, I got to thinking maybe he had lost track of where he was going, but eventually he came back around, and the story was all tied together. That afternoon with Doc breathed new life into the men of Company K.

When he had to leave, I walked back with him to the hospital. I thanked him for taking care of Father in his last days and told him about the explosion and my nightmares about burned bodies.

"Every man has to die," Doc said. "It could be a bullet through the neck or somethin' piddlin like measles, but it'll be somethin'."

He paused for a minute, then continued.

"I don't know for sure, but I believe what's most important is a man live a principled life and do the best he can with what comes his way. We'll see God in heaven eventually and we'll have no more of this foolishness."

I shook his hand, thanked him again, and watched him step into a white tent. As I turned to leave, his big, cheerful voice came from inside.

"My you're looking better, Davis. Maybe I should go away more often."

It's good we have men like Doc.

Chapter 7

BOXCAR JOURNEY
September 1861, Virginia

September 13, 1861
Dear Sister and Mary Ann,

Eugene and I talked again yesterday. I'm so glad he's here at Camp Davis. He misses you, I can tell that for sure, and he's ready to come home, just like everyone here.

Another week of drilling, eating and sleeping, but that's supposed to end soon! We'll be boarding boxcars, so I want to get this letter posted before we leave. Captain Patterson told us that there'll be no mail while we're on the move. There's

39

an air of excitement among the soldiers. We're to travel west to Lewisburg. It'll certainly be good to be moving again after a long encampment.

The weather's been fairly hot, but our food supply has improved to a tolerable level and some of the sick are getting better. Remember the short, dark-skinned boy from over at Wells Corner, name of Grimes? The one that plays the fiddle real well. He got so sick they sent him home yesterday. Right before he went home, he gave me his fiddle and told me to keep it for him and play for the fellows while he was away. I didn't want to take it, but he wouldn't take no for an answer. The nurse said he'd been telling her about it, so I took it just to make him happy.

I hid the fiddle in my bedroll so only Dallas knew about it. I was reluctant to play for the men because I don't know many tunes. Then Jack found out and nagged me to play, so tonight I slipped out of our camp and followed my ears till I found a fiddler playing up a storm, a fellow named Zack from Jackson in Company B. He had me join in and I learned some new tunes. Tomorrow night, I'm going to play for our company although I can't play nearly as fast as Zack. One new one I learned is called Stepping on My Toes and it's a real good toe-tapper. I'll play it for you when I get home. Henrietta will love it.

You should be proud of me because I've learned how to make biscuits in a skillet. They aren't nearly as tasty as yours, but for soldiering life they aren't too bad. We heard a rash of rifle fire while making breakfast the other morning. It turned out our pickets encountered two Yankee cavalrymen and captured them both. Apparently, they were lost and rode in the wrong direction. One was shot in the arm, but he patched up all right. We got horses, two tents and a little supply of coffee from their capture. The Yanks seem to have plenty of food. Our men were certainly excited to see Yankees for the first time and the bragging talk has picked back up.

Last week, two men from Water Valley disappeared from our camp. They were missing when we woke up and nobody knew they were leaving. Their guns, bedrolls — everything except canteens were left. We think they've deserted and are on their way back home.

Please do get help with firewood before winter sets in. Ask Dennis. He's strong and dependable. It would be all right with me if you let him use my shotgun. He loves hunting but doesn't have his own gun. Tell him he can use mine if he gives you a quarter of his kill. That should keep you in meat this winter in case we aren't home soon. Be sure to tell Dennis to take good care of my gun and to clean it after each hunt and oil the works.

There was a rumor a few days ago that we're going to get leave for visits home, real furloughs, but so far no one has been issued papers as far as I know. We get a lot more rumors than truth. That seems to be the army way.

Any word from Jesse? Keep your wonderful letters coming! I miss y'all.

Anderson

P.S. I didn't get the letter posted in time, so I'll add on. The generals decided we would travel tonight, so we loaded up quick, didn't even get to eat supper.

As we roll along, I'm watching the trees and countryside go by and remembering days back home, especially hunting in the river bottom near Abrams. I like to picture the shade trees around our house and remember afternoon naps on hot days. Compared to what we've done so far, plowing and planting seems much more favorable. Right now, even the idea of picking cotton seems a little exciting.

The winds of fall are stirring the leaves here. I imagine the fields at home have started to turn brown already. Sometimes I wonder what I've gotten myself into and would give up a month of soldiering pay for a single day back home. When I do get home, I'll play you the new fiddle tunes I've learned.

Anderson

After finishing the letter, I moved away from the doorway and squeezed between other men in stinky clothing. The train moved along at a good clip. Lee, a short, sandy-haired boy from Valden, started singing "The Yellow Rose of Texas" and some of the men joined in. I was surprised at the way our singing renewed my spirit and took my mind off the hunger in my belly. It felt a little like singing a favorite hymn in church.

Several hours later I awoke in the dark and my eyes and cheeks were wet. I was stiff and cramped from head to toe. A light drizzle fell as the morning light grew above the clouds. I pictured Momma and Father sitting together on the porch on a rainy autumn day.

Suddenly two men in the center of the car started arguing. Then it turned into a fight, waking the others.

"Give it back," the big one said.

"I didn't take your money," the other screamed.

The men tried to restrain the bigger, wilder one, but he broke free. Newton, the bigger man, grabbed Wesley, the short one, and ran him into the wall, hitting his head powerfully hard.

Bob, a big man himself, yelled, "Let him go," and he brought up his fists to fight Newton.

By this time everyone in the car was up and had moved away from the fighters. Newton grabbled Wesley by the collar and pushed him hard. Wesley stumbled and fell clean out of the open doorway. I leaned out and saw him lying face down in the gravel as the train moved on.

Jack, who had become quite agitated himself, attacked Newton, but Dallas pulled him back. Jack was a restless soul, skinny as a beanpole, and always primed to explode. Other soldiers restrained Newton and tied him up. The sudden violence shook up the whole bunch and I wondered what would happen to Wesley. After a while the company settled back down as our train rolled on. Men took turns at the doorways to relieve themselves and we stopped for a couple of hours in Lewisburg to cook. Jack told Captain Patterson about Wesley and the men turned Newton over to Lieutenant Hemphill.

September 15, 1861

Dear Henrietta,

There's a short, funny man in our company named Amos. You'd like him, I know. He wakes up raring to go every day and is good for our spirits. He also gets into situations a lot. About a week ago he was out looking for food with a buddy named Jack. Jack is the tallest man in our company, so standing side-by-side they look sort of funny. They were gone for the whole afternoon before Amos came back carrying a beehive in a potato sack. Everybody was excited to have honey to put on our johnnycakes. After the hub-bub died down a bit somebody asked Amos where

Jack was, and he said he didn't know. The men pestered Amos with questions till he told the whole story.

Turns out Amos and Jack were together when they found the beehive. It was about fifteen feet up in the crook of an oak tree that was hollowed out some, he said. Amos convinced Jack to climb the tree. The idea was plum crazy, but he did it anyway. When Jack got up to the hive, the bees attacked him, of course, but he managed to pull the hive out of the hollow and drop it to the ground.

The problem was that Jack was stuck up in the tree and the bees stung him all over and he couldn't climb down on account of fighting off the critters. Amos, to hear him tell it, bagged up the hive, ran back to camp and left Jack in the tree to fend for himself.

As Amos was telling us the story, a tall man walked out of the woods and up to our little gathering. His head, neck and arms were red all over and his face was so swollen up it was hard to recognize him — but it was Jack. When he spotted Amos, he went to chasing after him yelling at the top of his lungs. Amos skedaddled out into the woods with Jack a few steps behind.

About a half-hour later they both came back and it looked like they'd had a bruising fight and Jack had gotten his anger out. Walker made johnnycakes while the two men were off settling their differences and he offered Jack some cakes with honey, but he was too sick to eat. Three days passed before Jack was back up and walking around.

I knew you'd get a kick out of the story since you had that little incident yourself last summer.

I hope you're being Momma's helper this fall. I'll be home as soon as I can.

Love, Uncle Andy

Chapter 8

FACING THE ENEMY
September — October 1861, Sewell Mountain, Virginia

Three days after we lost Wesly, our train stopped at a place called Kanawha. A row of empty wagons stood beside the tracks next to a rocky, fast-running river. Clear water ran over and between green, moss-covered boulders. Except for the narrow space running along the tracks, there was no other flat ground. We were situated between two mountains covered with towering green trees. High, grayish-white clouds blocked the sun for seconds at a time.

"No farmin' here," Will said with a smile.

"But still plenty of work," Captain Patterson said from atop his horse. "Get the wagons loaded, men!" He sounded gruff and impatient.

We loaded supplies and our procession started up a narrow cut of trees on the side of Sewell Mountain. The ascent was steep and tiresome. A wagon ahead of us hit a fresh-cut stump and one of its wheels broke. Boxes of ammunition slid downhill among us.

"What're ya standin' there for, slackers?" Patterson shouted.

"Any spare wheels?" Will asked.

"No!" Patterson yelled and pointed.

We loaded the boxes into other wagons and trudged up the hill for a quarter of a mile more. Then Patterson redirected us.

"Top of this ridge," he yelled.

We followed Patterson and struck out through the woods, stepping over fallen trees. I fell and bloodied my lip. My heart pounded hard and some men stopped to catch their breath.

Our column leader found a narrow trace through the thick forest. After another half hour we finally arrived at the top of a great bluff overlooking a valley running southwest to northeast. A strip of trees about five paces wide had been cleared along the ridge. We collapsed in the wet leaves, rested and took water. The place was deathly quiet, and the smell of rain was in the air.

We learned from a lieutenant on horseback that our army was facing a Union force stationed on a similar ridge two miles distant. Lieutenant Oldham let us use his field glasses and we took turns looking toward the enemy's position on Miles Knob. The mountain on the other side of Meadow River was dense with trees, same as ours. I had never been on such a high piece of ground before. Billowy clouds coming from the east made giant shadows as they crossed the valley.

"Maybe we'll get our first fight," Will said.

"Hope my rifle still works," Dallas flashed a smile like our days growing up together.

A pair of blue jays swooped through the treetops. We were all excited and anxious to do our duty, so the closer we got to the enemy, the higher our spirits soared. The months of drilling and camping in the heat; the long, cramped train rides, and eating old food were finally at an end it seemed. I was glad Dallas and I would be fighting side-by-side. He had a good head on his shoulders and was quick afoot. He was also a good marksman and funny.

Captain Patterson brought the company together.

"The ridge we're on is Buster Knob. We're taking a defensive position in support of a Virginia artillery corps. Other regiments will be joinin' us over the next few days. Set up camp here and place a perimeter picket line along there." He indicated along the ridge. "Those not on duty may rest the remainder of the day. Rations will be arriving soon. Lieutenant Oldham will set the picket lines and choose shifts. Be alert men! Yanks may be movin' through the valley and across the river to attack us."

Our captain paused, spit a stream of tobacco juice on the leafy forest floor, and looked over the company.

"Remember what you've been taught," he said. "Do your jobs and serve with honor. You are good, loyal men and I'm proud to be your captain."

There was excited chatter among the men as we gathered firewood and unloaded supplies. In midafternoon, wagons filled with beef, vegetables, flour and more ammunition arrived. A dozen men unloaded our share and Walker got to work preparing a meal. Oldham named Will and Amos first pickets. Dallas and I tied our tent between two oak trees and peeled potatoes and cut onions. It had been three weeks since we tasted fresh beef or decent vegetables.

The aroma of wood smoke and tobacco floated in the cool autumn air. The dense growth made it hard for us to move around, but an attacking force, moving uphill, would have been hard pressed to overcome us.

The next morning, an hour before sunrise, Captain Patterson sent me on scout.

"A solitary scout must be alert at all times," he said. "The enemy can be behind any tree or boulder and a sharpshooter can put a bullet through your chest from eight hundred yards away. Your best protection are your eyes and ears. Use your senses to the utmost and never, never let your attention wander!"

"Yes, sir. I promise."

"I know ya love the excitement and danger, that's why I picked ya!"

"Thank ya, Captain."

"Take this pistol. Rifles and tree-climbing don't mix well. And one more thing." He handed me a headquarters' pass. "Show this to the pickets when ya return. I don't want my scout gettin' shot up."

The woods were quiet and still; the early birds flitted about. An hour after the sun rose, a north wind picked up and blew the fog away, first from the mountain tops, then gradually from the valley below. The easy wind stirred the day alive and I got a good look at the territory.

The tall mountain on the other side loomed up a thousand feet above the river. The scene was quite peaceful, but Patterson's warning kept me sharp. I scanned the woods for open approaches.

After the fog lifted, I found a pair of trees set close together, climbed up high to a good perch, and trimmed a few small limbs to open a better view. After a couple of hours, seeing nothing and hearing no gunfire, I grew sleepy.

Suddenly, out of the corner of my eye, I saw something dark moving up the hill. It was too late to climb down, so I sat still and watched while my heart raced. *Will I be shot out of the tree like a coon?* The dark form moved again, then all was still and the hair on the back of my neck stood up. *Is this what it feels like before a bullet strikes?*

47

Hrrrrrrwrrrwrrr. A low-pitched howl came from below. At the base of my lookout tree a black bear looked up. It sniffed the air and breathed heavily. I readied the pistol and tried not to breathe. The bear sniffed a while more then resumed its way uphill toward our camp. I did not tell Patterson or my buddies about the bear. They would have ribbed me unmercifully for the rest of the war, no doubt.

My second morning on scout, a herd of white-tailed deer crossed through the woods about fifty yards away. Beyond the deer I caught glimpses of men in dark blue uniforms carrying rifles moving across the mountain. My heart raced and blood pumped in my ears. *Should I run back and tell Captain right away?* 'Get an accurate count of enemy strength and composition,' Patterson had said in training.

Over the next few minutes, I saw squads of Yankees along the trace disappearing under the foliage. I estimated about a hundred men in all, then hurried back up the mountain to our encampment and reported to Patterson.

"Good work," he said. "Go back to your lookout, stay there and keep makin' observations. Under no circumstances do you fire. I'll send along a runner in an hour to get your next report."

I returned, climbed the lookout tree and observed as a threatening thunderstorm passed over the Union ridge, shooting lightning bolts into the treetops. Later I spotted my runner stepping slowly down the mountain, so I climbed down to meet him. It was Brantly, from Kosciusko, fourteen years old. He was high strung and tried to start a conversation.

"Son, my job is to look and listen," I said. "Your job's to report back. Tell Captain I've not seen any more signs of the enemy. And don't make any racket on your way back."

Another hour passed with no sightings and my forearms were sore like I'd been swinging an ax for hours. Off to the north came the *crack, crack, crack* of rifle fire deep down in the valley. Cannons boomed in the west, a good distance away. *Great armies testing each other.* The sky darkened and the wind stiffened.

That night about suppertime, a storm broke and rain filtered through the trees. Thunder and lightning lasted about an hour, but the rain turned steady and continued all night. By morning, my clothes and bedding were soaked.

For the next three days Captain Patterson put me on early morning scout. Occasionally the rain stopped, but the leaves kept dripping and then the rain started back up again. We began rationing our food supply. About every other day, food packed on mules came up the mountain from the east and sometimes they brought mail and newspapers. Owen Teames, a professor in civilian life, read articles out loud for the men who couldn't read well.

On our first Sunday on the mountain, Teames read a report about the battle for Wilson's Creek on the western front near Springfield, Missouri. The Confederates attacked the Union three times in succession but were unable to break them. After the third attack, the Yankees were exhausted and about out of ammunition, so they retreated. At the battle's end, at least two thousand men on both sides combined were dead or wounded. Wilson's Creek was the second big Southern victory of the war, after the Battle of Manassas.

After three days of continuous rainfall, we finally got a break in the weather and Dallas was able to kindle a fire. We strung up rope and dried our clothes. The ground was soaked like a sponge. Dallas and I were both so tired that we slept well even though a breeze swept water off the leaves onto us all night long.

When I got back to our tent, a letter from Sister and a package were sitting on my bedroll.

September 4, 1861

Dear Anderson,

I hope this letter reaches you promptly and that you are well. I'm anxious to tell you bitter news. Two nights ago, I was awakened by the smell of smoke coming from the back of the house. I got up to investigate and the kitchen was in flames. I threw buckets of water on the back of our cabin to keep it from catching. The fire and smoke were awful, and the kitchen was too far gone to save. There was nothing I could do except watch as it burned to the ground.

It rained all the next day and the coals were put out, but I was too upset to go through the charcoal to see what could be saved. The next day Mary Ann came to visit and brought a nice dinner. Marty from the lumber mill is coming over tomorrow to measure for materials. I don't know how we'll pay for it, but he says he'll work something out. Fortunately, most of our food stocks and canned goods were in the cellar and Mary Ann has loaned me some pans and utensils. I'm cooking in the fireplace in the meantime.

I've received no letters from you or Eugene in two weeks, so I hope you are on the move somewhere and not in any difficulty. Mary Ann keeps reassuring me, but that only goes so far. I don't want you to worry about Henrietta and me. Lord knows you have plenty to watch out for yourself.

Your loving sister, Sister

I opened the package and unfolded a new yellow and black checked shirt. Inside the shirt was a letter from Mary Ann.

September 6, 1861

Dear Anderson,

I hope you like the shirt. It ought to fit just right because Sister helped me with sizing. Making it made me feel closer to you even though we're many miles apart. I bet you'll look nice in it when you go to services on Sundays.

The cookhouse fire was awful, but Sister is strong, and folks have agreed to pitch in to build a new one. Luckily, Henrietta was staying at cousin Jane's the night of the fire, so she didn't see it burn.

The worst of the hot weather seems to be over now and we've gotten more rain this month. Beets, green beans, turnips, and radishes made a good showing, and the pumpkins are getting plump.

If you get home for Christmas, I'll make you a pumpkin pie. I'm missing you and looking forward to our next time together.

Fondly, Mary Ann

At noon on September 25th, we heard rifle fire coming from the river valley north of our position. The shooting was furious for a while, but by two o'clock it had stopped. A messenger on horseback arrived a while later and told us that three companies from our army had crossed over to the Union side of Meadow River. Our forces were surprised to find a large group of Yanks in the woods nearby and a firefight broke out. Outmanned, Confederate forces withdrew. Our side lost twenty men killed and wounded, and another fifty or so missing.

It rained hard the night of October 14th so I went to sleep early. Captain Patterson woke me in the night with a mission to go all the way down to the stream and look for signs of enemy movements. I packed food and water and headed off in the dark. It took two solid hours moving tree to tree and around large boulders to get all the way down the steep hill. At the stream, the sky had cleared a bit and the sun touched the mountaintops. I crossed over to the enemy side and found footprints of soldiers and horses, heading north.

There was no movement in the valley where Federal troops were seen a few days earlier, except turkey buzzards picking at a swollen carcass in a deep patch of grass. At midday, my canteen was empty so I leaned my rifle against a shagbark hickory, went to the stream, and drank my fill of cold water. When I sat up, a soldier in a blue uniform knelt on a gray-green boulder about twenty yards downstream and his rifle lay on another boulder nearby. I was afraid for my life, but caught in place, and we stared at each other. He looked to be about my age and clean-shaven. Unruly brown hair hung out from under his cap. Neither of us said a word.

In a few minutes, I refilled my canteen, keeping my eyes on the Yankee. He filled his too. When he finished he stepped back to the edge of the stream and I did the same. I retrieved my rifle and held it in one hand by my side, pointed toward the ground. The Yankee did the same and tipped his free hand to his cap. I returned his salute and stepped quickly back into the woods. He turned his back toward me and disappeared behind the trees. *Finally, a Yankee up close*! He reminded me of myself and I had no desire to harm him.

After retreating about a hundred yards upstream, I stopped to listen, then retraced my steps to the place of our encounter and crossed over. I followed his path into the woods, saw no more signs of the enemy and then headed back toward our camp. Near the stream, the clouds parted briefly and sunlight glinted off something. I moved closer and spotted a silver compass lying in the sand next to the water. I arrived back at camp about suppertime and told Patterson about seeing the lone Yankee scout and showed him the compass.

Chapter 9

FIGHT OVER NEW RIVER
October — November 1861, Virginia

October 16, 1861

Dear Mary Ann,

    The shirt is quite handsome! Thank you so much. Dallas is jealous through and through.

    We've been camped on top of a mountain for a good while and the forest here is most beautiful. I wish you could see the view! If I was good at drawing, I'd make a sketch for you. I saw enemy soldiers one day while scouting, but our company has yet to have a direct encounter or fire our guns. The food supply has been off and on since we arrived and some of our sick are getting better.

I'm busy several hours each day, chopping wood and helping Walker, our cook. And some days I'm out before sunup on scout. The weather has been nothing but rain and cold nights. Since we got to Virginia, being in the army is not bad. I enjoy being in the woods a great deal but worry that these peaceful days will soon end.

I'm going to close for now. I so look forward to being back home with you again. Fondly, Anderson

We spent several weeks overlooking Kanawha Valley from the ridge and saw the sun only a few times. Waves of fog drifted constantly through the shadowy, moss-covered trees. Towards the end of the month our scouts discovered that the enemy had withdrawn entirely. The big showdown never came. As we descended from our soggy mountain home, our company was in good spirits, singing and joking. The mountain was so beautiful I was sad to leave.

"One day closer to home," Dallas said.

"I hope you're right," I replied. "But I'm beginnin' to doubt it."

Late that afternoon, we arrived at a field, unplanted that season, and made camp for the night. My boots were wearing thin at the toes and any march over half a day resulted in renewed blisters on both feet. A new pair of sturdy, well-fitting boots would have made a big difference and a uniform would have been splendid. As we faced the edge of winter, I feared if we didn't get shoes and coats soon, we'd be the frozen and limping infantry of Mississippi, hardly fit for fighting mosquitoes.

Darkness crept over our army as Dallas and I ate supper. A messenger arrived and Captain Patterson left immediately for a meeting of company commanders. Gone was the talk about how many Yanks we would kill. I sensed that our days of limited enemy contact were drawing to a close.

At that moment, the rapid whispering *wheo-wheo, wheo-wheo, wheo-wheo, wheo-wheo* sound of wings came overhead. Two mallards flew low, winging their way to roost. I crawled in our tent and tried to sleep. Imaginary scenes of gunfire, smoke, and confusion filled my head and my heart beat more rapidly than it should.

At early light, my jaw was very sore — clenched teeth during the night. Lieutenant Oldham instructed us quietly.

"No fires, men. Pack everything up and be ready to go in half an hour."

As he alerted the others, Dallas attached his bayonet and returned it to its scabbard over and over. In the fog, men folded tents, rolled bedding, and tied their belongings up for the march. I put on an extra pair of socks and checked my rifle which had not been fired since training at Iuka. The mules snorted and complained as they were harnessed to wagons. When the troop column got moving, Dallas needled Oldham about the orders for the day.

"We headin' for battle, Lieutenant?"

Oldham said nothing.

"How many miles we goin' today, sir?" Dallas tried again.

He knew Oldham wouldn't tell us anything. It was part of a game we played — making up stories about the action ahead when we knew nothing. Sometimes Oldham laughed and that was all the encouragement we needed to keep up the banter.

About noon, we paused to rest under a stand of pines and the sharp, sweet smell relaxed me. Word spread that we were crossing Fayette County, a distance of twenty-two miles, to camp at a place called Cotton Hill. Dallas and I refilled our canteens in a stream. Father's pocket watch indicated twelve-fifteen.

"How long's it been since he died?" Dallas asked.

"Eleven years."

An orderly ran back along our procession.

"Yankee force movin' west of our location!" he said breathlessly. "We're goin' in to meet 'em!"

Energy surged through me as we marched into the windy afternoon. *Will I be brave and resolute? Or will I break and run?* We had read newspaper accounts of battles, but no one in our company had ever fired a shot at the enemy. I remembered feeling stunned and light-headed when we learned about the casualties at Manassas. Fear flooded my chest at the thought of nothingness and my ears turned hot. Jack began yelling and whipping others into a frenzy.

In late afternoon, the muddy road descended a long hill and we came to a narrow bridge built on wooden piles driven into the river bottom. Oldham told us it was the Gauley Bridge over the New River. The bridge looked sturdy enough for foot traffic, but I wondered if it would hold up under the weight of our long procession of heavy wagons and cannons.

The whole army, about four thousand men, plus mules, horses and wagons, was stretched out over two miles, all trampling the same mud. We crossed, ascended a wooded hill on the other side and camped on top.

October 29, 1861

Dear Sister,

Your letter dated September 25 got to me today. We're on the move again. We left the mountain five days ago and marched to Cotton Hill, Virginia. Our camp overlooks a valley where two rivers come together. They had us working day and night to build breastworks. Cannons are being brought in and we're building earth placements to protect them. This is the first break I've had from the dirt work since we arrived.

Our scouts have seen Yankees moving wagons across a river bridge. The rumor is we are to attack tomorrow to keep them from bringing in more reinforcements. The trees here are already turning and the nights are a good bit colder than they are at home this time of year. It's hard to know what's going on for we receive precious little news of plans. Our officers make it clear that our job is to do what we're told and not ask questions. When newspapers come with the mail, that's our most dependable source for truth.

Patterson sent a squad out yesterday to forage for food, my least favorite job. We have money to pay the farmers, but it takes more than a few farms to feed an army. If fighting was taking place at home, hungry soldiers would be coming to our house wanting everything you've got. I hate it and would rather eat acorns and mushrooms than take food from others.

The next evening, I finished the letter.

October 30

Today was a good day because Oldham sent me scouting. It calms my nerves and it's not nearly as hard as building breastworks. Of course, there's always a chance I'll get shot at, but I'd rather take my chances in the woods alone. I left before dawn with a pack of food and made the slow climb down. It took about half an hour to reach the river.

The land here is not at all like home. There are big hills and large boulders everywhere. I miss the flat, open fields, but I love the trees here. Doc taught me the names of some trees that we don't have at home. I now know what aspen, spruce, and Virginia pine look like. Oh, I almost forgot to tell you, Doc was promoted to Captain at the end of the mountain mission.

At the bottom of the hill this morning, I found a sheltered spot behind two large, moss-covered boulders. The sun was beautiful coming up over the misty treetops. Sitting in the quiet woods helps me know that God is watching over me even when I'm far from home. Surely God is watching over you too. "The Lord watch between me and thee, when we are absent from one another."

Both armies are massing and building emplacements, so I think there's going to be a real affair this time. I think of you often these days and wish I was there to share the work and read with Henrietta. I'll write again soon.

Your loving brother, Anderson

The next night, several companies, including ours, were moved down near the river, filling the woods with regular infantry and sharpshooters. As daylight broke, I saw enemy soldiers and wagons moving across the bridge. We sat still in the woods, no smoking allowed, and at nine o'clock we were ordered to commence firing. I aimed through the trees at a group of soldiers walking in front of a mule-wagon and squeezed the trigger, *crack!* My first hostile shot of the war set both ears to ringing. The kickback threw me off balance and a feeling of power swelled within. The pungent smoke brought tears.

The curved line of trees on our side of the river was popping with rifle fire. Clouds of gun smoke rolled forward and down the hill. Our firepower decimated the wagon train and a ferryboat. Enemy troops jammed the roads and bridge. Cannon shells screamed across the valley in both directions hundreds of feet above our heads. It was total chaos and in a few minutes the valley was choked with smoke. I fired in the direction of the enemy and added to the dreadful rumble of battle but had no idea of the effect.

A shell exploded in a tree above us and shrapnel hammered the ground. A shower of splinters and pine needles fell around me. The sweet scent of pine was interwoven with the stink of gunpowder. I looked over at Sergeant Dodd.

"Enemy cannons," he pointed to the ridge. "They musta lowered their barrels on us."

Dallas held his arm.

"You hit?" I yelled.

He grimaced. "Just a scratch."

The roar of exploding cannon shells was so deafening it made rifle fire sound like popping corn. My heart raced unnaturally, and my stomach ached. We kept blasting away at the smoke across the river and the rifle barrel burned my hands. After two hours, I crawled behind a wide beech tree, exhausted, and let my gun cool off. I drank from my canteen, ate a few peanuts, and promptly puked it all up. On the ground just uphill lay the remains of a blown-out squirrel nest.

The sounds of battle thundered, and the trees were shattered into kindling by exploding shells and splatting bullets. It was as though God had sent a fiery storm upon the whole forest. I expected an order to cease fire or to be replaced, but none came. Instead, runners slid down the hill to resupply us. My eyes burned from smoke and powder sparks and my ears rang ceaselessly. I fired again then felt a sharp prick. A splinter about six inches long stuck in the back of my hand. I pulled it out and wrapped the wound tightly with a handkerchief to stop the bleeding.

At seven o'clock, having fought ten hours straight, we finally received orders to cease fire and return to camp. When we got back some of our hilltop gunners lay asleep beside their cannons. Every soldier was exhausted. A handful of campfires burned, and a few men moved about in the dark with torches.

Thanks to captured supplies, we had a good, hot supper of salted pork with potatoes, cornmeal cakes, and coffee. The coffee was a real treat. We had been making do with boiled acorns and sassafras roots for weeks. The men who captured the supplies were our heroes that day. After supper, Dallas and I crawled in our tent. A charred cannon ball lay on his bedroll.

"Good thing we were fightin' down by the river!" he grinned.

In the morning, my stomach ached terribly. Captain Patterson told us four of the artillerymen supporting us from the ridge had been hit; three injured and one killed. Two men from our company, Elisha Sanders and Charles Bryan were wounded.

Doc joined us for breakfast. His clothes were stained with blood and it looked like he had not slept a minute. He chewed slowly and didn't join in the conversation. I asked him about my pains and racing heart.

He looked up from his plate and said, "Indigestion and soldier's heart."

"What can I do to make it stop?"

"Go back to farmin'!"

All the men laughed except Doc. He stood up, handed his plate to me and headed back to the hospital tents.

Early the next morning, we were ordered back to the river's edge. The enemy was again moving to reinforce. We resumed firing from the dense tree line about fifty feet above the river on the steep hillside. A bullet cut off a limb that then fell on my head. Another bullet struck my boot and lay on the leaves a few inches away. It was still warm, and I put it in my pocket. I didn't think it possible that I could die. The firing slowed, then a heavy downpour silenced both armies.

"Let's go!" I yelled at Dallas.

"What?" he screamed over the sound of the storm.

I pointed uphill. We headed straight up the incline toward camp. Streams of water from the flash rain made the going treacherous. Dallas slipped and fell, lost his gun and came rolling down past me with a wild look in his eyes. He crashed into the base of a large cottonwood and came to a stop. I went back to help, and we laughed. Taking another look across the valley, I saw a squad of Yankees struggling to get a wagon back on the muddy road. Our common enemy, the rain, won the day. Or maybe the rain was our guardian angel.

Back at camp, the rain came in torrents. Unable to build a fire to dry off or cook, we spent a miserable afternoon and night in our tent, which was barely long enough to pull our feet inside. War is a miserable business. Staying alive is not only a matter of avoiding bullets and capture, it's about keeping warm, finding food, and praying you don't get sick.

On the third day of battle, the Yankee cannons took a toll on our cannoneers. Company K helped them reposition, but they did not resume firing. We learned later from Captain Patterson that the Yankees had brought up rifled artillery, called Parrott guns. They could shoot five miles with remarkable accuracy and our smoothbore cannons were no match.

In the afternoon, our company was again sent to the firing line near the river to relieve others. Across the river, bodies of dead and wounded enemy soldiers were loaded on wagons and taken away. One of our soldiers lay dead by the river's edge, sixty feet below us, but we left him where he fell. The river glittered in the sunlight that occasionally cut through the moving clouds. It would have been hell-fired foolish to retrieve his body, but I wished that at least we knew his name. His family would be heartsick and might never know he gave his life to protect them.

At camp, we learned that our army had captured two dozen Yanks who had crossed over to our side of the river farther downstream. The prisoners were put in the center of our encampment surrounded by guards. I found it unnerving to have the enemy in our midst.

"They coulda been the ones who shot Charles and Elisha," Dallas said.

"Wish we could kill 'em now!" Jack's face was red with anger.

After one more day of fighting for possession of the bridge, our regiment packed up and headed off. The battle was not won or lost by either side and fighting had not been glorious like I imagined. It turned out I was no braver than any other man, nor less afraid. We did what we were told to do and hoped luck was with us. We marched four hours that day and camped at Laurel Creek. After supper when we were alone, Dallas spoke.

"When we enlisted, did ya think there'd be a shootin' war?"

"Not really. I figured when both sides were ready to fight, somehow the whole thing would be called off."

"Me too," he said. "Wonder where we got that nutty idea?"

A cannon fired in the distance.

"Feel like a soldier now?" Dallas said.

"I guess I do."

"Glad we're stickin' together."

"Me too, buddy."

Two days later, Company K was awakened well before dawn and assembled without eating. Lieutenant Oldham introduced a man to us.

"This is Mr. Ambrose. He'll lead our patrol this mornin'. He knows the countryside well."

Ambrose stood in the torchlight, in civilian clothes like us, wearing a tan hat of fine quality. His face was thin with a thick brown mustache that covered his upper lip. We followed him in single file and stayed close to the next man in front. Ambrose led us through a dense, pitch-dark woods, not following a trace as far as I could tell. Branches whipped my face and briars tore at my britches and coat. *Where's he takin' us?* This was the first time anyone other than Patterson or one of our lieutenants had led us. Just as the sun lit the edge of the sky, we came out of the woods into a little clearing and gathered around our guide.

"McCoy's Mill," Ambrose said in a hushed voice as he nodded toward a building in the center of the clearing. "We're about four miles northwest of General Floyd's army."

60

Oldham directed us into defensive positions in and around the mill. Amos climbed to the top of the mill tower as quick as a steel trap. While we waited, Ambrose talked to those of us hiding inside the mill. He was dressed like a gentleman and had no gun or anything else a soldier would carry. He told us Yankees under the command of General Benham held most of the territory to the west and were sending patrols from the main Federal body to probe Confederate positions. There'd been a few skirmishes, but no big battles. He was full of information and glad to share it, unlike our officers. I wondered who he was and how he knew so much but didn't ask.

The mill was a grinding house for corn. I wondered if corn might not have been picked that season due to so many men being in the army. War business disrupts everything that's important.

Oldham shushed our talk and I passed the rest of the morning swatting horseflies while others slept. We hadn't eaten since supper the night before and it was hard not to think about food. In mid-afternoon, the silence was broken by thousands of red-winged blackbirds that invaded the trees east of us. *Conk-la-reee, conk-la-reee, conk-la-reee.* Their busy, cheerful calls filled the air, and they swarmed about the trees surrounding the mill, stirring memories of home. By far the best part of army life was the natural world, the trees and meadows, the creeks, hills, and animals. Wildlife disappeared before battles and returned when the firing stopped. Somehow, they managed to keep life as it should be.

About four o'clock, all at once the blackbirds shushed and flew away, bringing me alert. Amos dropped a stick to the ground and signaled to the east. He held up four fingers and then a fist, indicating that forty Yankees without cannons were approaching. Oldham positioned our company to the east in a double line with short flanks slightly forward on the north and south ends, making a strong firing formation. Amos climbed down from the tower, got his rifle and joined the line between Dallas and me, all guns loaded.

A squad of enemy riflemen came along at a trot. When they were forty paces away, Oldham gave the signal. Our front row stood up, fired and stepped back to reload. The back row stepped forward and fired; two powerful volleys in five seconds. White smoke curled through the field and the sharp smell of burned black powder stung my nose. The enemy was taken by surprise and several fell. Their commander, on horseback, signaled retreat. We fired at the fleeing soldiers and they disappeared quickly over the hill and out of sight. The whole affair lasted no more than a minute.

Lieutenant Conway wanted to pursue, but Oldham disagreed.

"We don't know how many troops are behind 'em."

Seeing no further movement, a half-dozen men were sent to examine the fallen Yankees. I sat crouched with my rifle ready. Ambrose stood well behind us with his arms crossed, leaning on the side of the mill. He chewed a blade of tallgrass as calmly as a fellow fishing on a riverbank. *He must be a spy.*

Our men returned with a few things taken from the enemy including a pair of field glasses, canteens, food, and a leather pouch. Oldham looked at the papers inside.

"Gather up men," he said. "We're returnin' to camp."

As we departed a drizzle began. Shortly, the rain turned heavy and we were soaked through and cold before we got back to camp.

Chapter 10

ON THE MOVE AGAIN
December 1861, Virginia to Kentucky to Tennessee

On December 17th, our regiment boarded a train for Kentucky. A cold rain came in the night and water blew inside our boxcar. Only a few men had heavy coats. Most, including me, were underdressed for winter. When we arrived the next morning, the men were anxious to get out and build fires. Unfortunately, there was confusion at the station, so Captain Patterson had us stay in the boxcars. After a half-hour peering through the cracks and shivering, we were finally let out with instructions to stretch and be back on the train in an hour. The generals had changed plans again.

"Think they know what they're doin'?" Dallas asked.

I shook my head and helped start a fire.

Back on the train I tried to stay warm and sleep, then suddenly a man screamed. I woke and saw that his clothes were on fire. Men nearby splashed water from their canteens and put the fire out, but not before his legs were badly burned. He thrashed about and screamed as his comrades tried to comfort him. Dallas told me the burned man was named Chesley.

Doc wasn't in our car and we had no way to signal the train to stop, so we took care of him the best we could. Chesley got worse, quit drinking water and passed out. We were worried he might not make it, so Jack leaned out of the car and fired his rifle in the direction of the locomotive. The train slowed, came to a stop, and we carried Chesley to a car near the rear where Doc was riding with the sick men.

I wasn't able to sleep a wink after the incident. Since witnessing the aftermath of the powder explosion at the railyard, I'd been frightened to death of being burned. Cinders from the locomotive were a constant problem, as were sparks from the wheels. Each man carried a cartridge pack filled with ammunition and some boxcars were packed with barrels of gunpowder. Our train was a dangerous place to be.

December 19, 1861

Dear Mary Ann,

Riding the train in winter is dreadfully uncomfortable. I'm cold, stiff and hungry day and night. Two men got into a fight today over a newspaper and tore it all up in the process. We don't know for sure where we're going and have no idea how much longer we'll be riding in this cold box, squeezed up tight together like kernels on an ear of corn.

Not sure how much longer I can tolerate this life. We have none of the pleasures of home, of course, and we don't have enough food and much of what we get is rubbish. Even though we're poor, at least we have good food and plenty of it at home. My lips are so cracked I hate to open my mouth for fear of splitting them even more. We're all very much in need of winter clothing. The army has still not given us uniforms or coats. All in all, they are not taking care of us. I'd be much obliged if you would ask Sister to send my warmest shirts and trousers.

I've done nothing but complain so far, so will try to move on to more cheerful subjects. Back at Laurel Creek, Dallas and I cut several thin limbs from a birch tree and others from a hickory and then cut them in short pieces with a crosscut saw we borrowed from the quartermaster. We're carving them into a dandy set of chess pieces. That gives us a project to work on during the journey and keeps my hands from getting so cold.

We've had little news of the war recently, so can only hope the invaders are faring poorly or have stopped fighting for the winter at least. Please relay my news to Sister. I'm glad the two of you share letters. I'll write again when I can. Lucky to have you both to care about me.

Fondly, Anderson

After two more freezing days on the train, we disembarked and camped in a railyard. Wagons arrived bringing supplies, including fresh beef, tobacco and coffee. Walker cooked up a feast and we stuffed ourselves silly. The hot coffee was best of all. About the time we were getting settled in after supper, orders came to cook all the food for the remainder of the journey. I helped Walker finish up and slept reasonably well that night.

Early the next morning, we were back in our cars rolling toward Tennessee. We ate and slept … did everything a man must do, in our boxcar. With about a hundred fifty soldiers in each, there was just enough room to sit down with my knees pulled up close. Sometimes I looked through cracks to get a glimpse of the countryside. The train stopped several times during the day, but we were not allowed to get out and were given no explanations for the stops. A little sunlight sneaked through the cracks, but for the most part we rode in darkness.

That evening the train stopped in Knoxville and we disembarked. I was so cramped up I fell, bruised my forehead on a rock, and had to be helped back up on my feet. Who would ever have imagined that army life would include so much inactivity? The break in travel was short lived. We were issued several day's rations and within two hours were rolling northward again.

Walker sat next to me. "Light this."

I took a stick from my match brick and lit the candle. He pulled a folded Knoxville Journal from his coat. "War news," he grinned.

We settled down with our backs against the rough plank wall and read the newspaper in the flickering candlelight.

In November, the USS *San Jacinto* stopped a British mail ship, the RMS *Trent*, and captured two Southern political men, heading for France and England. They were on a mission to see if either country would aid us in our fight against the Yanks. The British disapproved of the violation of neutral rights and demanded that our diplomats be released. President Lincoln decided to let the men go free.

"Think we'll win?" I asked.

"Of course," Walker said. "We're fightin' for our homes and they're far from theirs."

"Sister says she can't sell our cotton and there's no coffee to buy. And we're sure not gettin' enough to eat."

"Don't ya worry. General Floyd and Lee ... they'll out-smart 'em. After the Yanks lose a few more battles they'll head back home."

My next letters to Sister and Mary Ann said we would definitely not be home for Christmas.

Chapter 11

GOING TO THE FIGHT
January 1862, Tennessee

At dusk on January 15th, after twelve consecutive days of travel, the 20th Mississippi rejoined General Johnston's army. The air was cold and the sky clear. After all that time in the boxcar, I left my rifle, haversack, and bedroll by the tracks and ran off a ways and back. The sudden movement left me swimmy-headed.

Officers from all units were notified to meet immediately in the station house. The men talked quietly among themselves until Jack jumped up on the raised platform and strutted about waving his hat wildly and calling out.

"Gimmy two Yankees to kill, not jis' one … gimmy three Yankees to kill, not jis' two …"

He got louder and drew up a rowdy crowd by the platform.

"Gimmy four Yankees to kill, not jis' three …" he kept at it, yelling as loud as he could.

More soldiers joined the chant and it rolled through the crowd. When Colonel Patterson stepped from the station house the chanting stopped immediately and Jack jumped back in the crowd. Patterson looked over the assembled men.

"Get all your gear and form up your units!"

A couple of ducks flew low over the railyard.

"We're marchin' tonight, men!" he said. "Goin' to the fight!"

Cheers erupted. Dallas and I quickly rejoined Company K and our lieutenants Oldham, Duncan and Hemphill.

"Is it true?" Dallas asked Hemphill.

"Yep. We're gonna join Floyd's Army. The Yanks are tryin' to take the upper Mississippi and we're gonna stop 'em. Flowers, Townsend, and Capshaw, to the loadin' dock. Bring back rations. Y'all be quick now. Not much time 'fore we set off."

We pushed three full wheelbarrows through the noisy, crowded railyard back to our company.

"Pack as much as ya can in your sacks," Hemphill ordered. "No tellin' when we'll be resupplied next."

I packed my knapsack and every pocket full of rations and looked around at the circle of soldiers who had become my brothers — admirable men. Jack, with energy enough for three; Oldham, wise and careful; Amos, an extraordinary sense of optimism; and Dallas, the best friend a man could have. We had been through a few battles together, fought bravely and protected each other, but now we were to meet the enemy in force for the first time.

A sense of awe and devotion fell upon me like a fog after a summer shower. We'd spent our young lives working farms, swimming and fishing in muddy rivers, and hunting for food. Most of us had never been outside of Mississippi before. We had traveled hundreds of miles together on foot and by rail, farther from home than I ever imagined. We were on an adventure that was way bigger than any of us, caught up in a great and noble purpose, like nothing before.

Oldham told us we had a long march ahead, so I put on a pair of dry socks and laced my boots tightly. Our company assembled four abreast and our captain led us into the dark countryside. Men stumbled occasionally, but we soon settled into a steady pace and it felt good to be moving again. After an hour, my boots loosened, socks slipped down and my ankles rubbed leather. I stopped and re-laced, fearing new blisters would appear, then double-timed it back to our company. Toting gear and food weighed me down considerably.

Conversation ceased entirely after eleven o'clock as we tromped along the road, made dusty by thousands of boots. The jovial mood I felt at the station was gone. At midnight, the column of men was halted, and Dallas and I buttoned the halves of our tent together.

"Not so quick, men," Colonel Patterson said. "Just a short stop. Rest your legs and take some water 'fore we set off again."

I stared at Dallas and he said, "They must have big plans for us."

In half an hour the whole tired army was back in formation and moving. The moon rose behind us and leafless trees stood like sentries alongside the road. Exhausted men dropped out of the column and lay by the roadside. We covered about twenty-five miles and crossed Mud River at six o'clock as the light of day grew. My canteen ran dry and an hour later we came to a halt. The cold weather had passed.

I was powerfully hungry and thirsty after the forced march and never so glad for food. Both feet were badly blistered. My socks dried in the sunshine and my bare feet enjoyed some air. We ate and rested a few hours and then the order came to pack up again. I greased up my feet and ankles and put on two pairs of socks. We resumed our march, this time heading for Clarksdale, Tennessee, a distance of forty-odd miles according to Lieutenant Oldham. The plan was to go halfway, then spend the night. Our column plodded along that day, worn out after marching all night, each carrying about sixty pounds. Most of us didn't weigh over a hundred and thirty naked.

"They tryin' to kill us?" Dallas said, half joking.

"What da ya mean, tryin'?" Amos replied with a grin.

My feet throbbed and the thought of the miles ahead made it worse. Looking at the countryside became the best diversion. We trudged by farms and grazing cattle.

Occasionally we saw civilians, mostly women, children and older men. Sometimes they waved and offered food. Others stared at us. I wondered if their menfolk were fighting with the Yankees. From newspaper accounts, we knew that some Tennesseans fought for the Union and others were on our side. We crossed Whippoorwill River in the morning and then Elk Fork Red River just after noon. Both were flowing high and muddy. Finally, in late afternoon, we camped.

Doc played cards with Dallas, Walker, and me, and after supper we exchanged news and stories.

"What da ya hear from home?" Walker asked Doc.

"Last letter from the missus was back at Laurel Creek. She said everyone's doin' fine, but I know she's puttin' on a brave face. I heard from Pastor Small that Molly and Jacob have been ill. From what he described, it sounds like measles."

"Yep," Dallas piped up. "Mamma Lou said the same in her last letter."

After a pause Doc said, "I should be home takin' care of the young 'uns." His voice was somber. "But I need to be here with y'all too. Lord knows what hardships lie ahead."

He looked off in the distance at the last glow on the horizon.

"Don't ya think we'll be goin' home soon?" Dallas asked.

"No idea," he said, still looking away. He got up to leave. "No idea."

Doc disappeared in the dusk. I'd never seen him so low-spirited. We gave up card-playing and disbanded for the night.

"Ya think Doc's okay?" Dallas asked me.

"No idea."

I went to the woods to be alone. Doc's words whispered in my dreams and haunted me that night. *Lord knows what hardships lie ahead.*

I awoke the next morning to the sound of a light rain, with sore legs and blistered feet. The rain soon turned the road to mud, mules struggled, and wagons slipped. We stopped often to get wagons back on the road and to wait for stragglers. Progress was so slow that our commanders gave up and let us camp and rest for three days. Cavalry rode ahead to reconnoiter and sent messengers back to report on conditions. At the West Fork Red River bridge, the river was swollen beyond its banks.

"We're goin' ahead!" Patterson shouted.

I worried that my boots might come completely apart being submerged. Some men were already without boots and I feared I would soon be joining them. We crossed through knee-deep water at the bridge and sloshed on, arriving in Clarkesville mid-afternoon, just as the rain stopped.

The town was situated north of a great C-shaped bend in the Cumberland River on a bluff two hundred feet above the water. We camped for the night, ate and rested. One boot heel was missing and my blisters had popped. Captain Patterson rode through our company and spread the word.

"Only two more days, men … just two more … then we'll be at Fort Donelson."

The mood was a bit more festive that night, knowing our long march would soon be over.

"Play your fiddle tonight?" Dallas asked me. "The men'll be much obliged."

"Okay. Long as I can play sittin' down."

After supper, I played a few favorites around a bonfire, then a fellow named David Cornett from Tupelo joined in. With two fiddles going we attracted a crowd and had a splendid time for a couple of hours before taps. As the men clapped and sang, I realized they were my family. All that lay ahead, the dangers, the boredom, and my life itself, was in their hands. I was powerfully afraid of dying but honored to be among such loyal men.

February 5, 1862

Dear Sister,

We've not received mail now for two weeks but will soon be at our destination. Hopefully the mail will catch up with us there. Other than blistered feet and sore shoulders, I'm fine. Hope you and Henrietta are doing well.

When the war is over, one thing I shall never miss, are the long marches carrying all our supplies and guns. Now I know what a pack mule feels like. The weather has been unusually mild the past few days. No doubt a cold spell is around the corner and we shall soon be complaining about the cold.

We're heading to Fort Donelson, in the northwest part of Tennessee and it seems that a big battle is ahead. We have good leaders and have been trained so we know what to expect. Two men in our company have been wounded, but both are recovering. No one I have known well has been killed in battle, thankfully. I say my prayers every morning and every night and ask for protection from the enemy and illness. And I say a prayer for you and Henrietta too.

Your loving brother, Anderson

Later that night, the howling wind woke me. Clouds partially blocked the moonlight and the yellow firelight bowed in the wind. A cold front was moving in and my clothes were still wet. Men covered their heads, trying in vain to stay warm and rest a little more before dawn. To a man, we were tuckered out. I couldn't sleep so I scooted closer to the fire and read from my Bible. "They that wait upon the Lord shall renew their strength; they shall mount up with wings as eagles; they shall run, and not be weary; and they shall walk, and not faint."

The next day we got an early start. We trudged headlong into the wind as the temperature dropped. Both my knees ached powerfully. Since leaving the train station, our company had lost four men. George Kendal broke his leg when he fell down an embankment. The fellows close by said he walked right off the edge, might have been sleepwalking. He was left in the care of the medical corps. Three other Mississippians were missing, and no one saw them leave. Maybe they deserted or maybe they just fell behind. Considering the grueling journey we made with little sleep and not enough food, Captain Patterson was lucky to have most of his company present and standing. Seeing the quandary, Conway commandeered a wagon that was not full, and we loaded our guns, knapsacks and accoutrements in it. This was a great relief because it meant lighter steps and fewer blisters.

Chapter 12

BATTLE IN A BLIZZARD
February 1862, Fort Donelson, Tennessee

On the last day of the journey, we departed mid-morning and marched all day without a break. The sky was solid gray and a northwest wind numbed my ears. As we marched into the night the road broke into a series of long, rolling hills, and the cold wind carried a fishy, river smell.

At the crack of dawn on February 13th, our column halted. Captain Patterson led our company off the right side of the road, and we moved double-time up the side of a gradually sloping hill stumbling over embankments and gullies.

"Over here," shouted Lieutenant Conway. "Man these trenches. The fort's west of us and the river's about a mile north," he said, pointing. "Get some rest."

Exhausted, I slid into an earthen pit, pulled my hat over my face and fell asleep. In an hour or two I grew cold and awoke to discover that a blizzard was upon us. A brutal wind swept through the valley and snow blew sideways, stinging my eyes. I wrapped my blanket around my shoulders and found Conway.

"Lieutenant, we need rations bad. Ate everything on the march. Won't be much good for fightin' 'less we get food soon."

"Wish I knew when food was comin'," he said. "In the meantime, it's fine to light fires."

The blowing snow woke everybody, and we staked canvas sections across the top of the trench and built fires. As luck would have it, our trench ran north to south and funneled the wind and snow right along through it, like water flowing down a narrow gully. We covered ourselves as best we could and played cards and told stories to keep our minds off hunger.

Boom, boom, boom came a furious series of cannons shortly before noon, shattering the sounds of the blizzard. I readied my rifle, looked over our breastworks for Yankees and waited. There was no sign of life in the snow-swept fields. A huge blast nearby shook the ground. When the smoke cleared, just five paces from our position, white smoke rose from a hole about six feet wide. Conway rode up.

"Enemy gunboats firin' on the fort!" he yelled.

"The ground's shakin'!" Will said.

"Naval guns and mortars! Some of those big guns throw thirty-two-pound shot and heavier!"

The firing stopped after five minutes, and a gust of wind blew more snow down our trench. In the early afternoon we received a modest supply of rice, coffee and cornmeal. We cooked up the best meal we could, warmed by the fires, and then news came from the fort. One Union gunboat had engaged and retreated. In another hour, the firing between the fort and gunboats resumed. Again, it lasted only a few minutes. Dallas, Amos and I huddled around our tiny fire in the driving snow. In midafternoon, Captain Patterson gathered the company and showed us a map of the battlefield.

"The Cumberland River runs northwest here ... the Tennessee runs parallel," he said. "The rivers are twelve miles apart at this point. A few days ago, Union gunboats stormed Fort Henry on the Tennessee. Our forces were outnumbered, so they withdrew and came here. Fort Donelson is about a hundred feet above the river and has twelve big cannons ... it's well-fortified."

Walker handed a cup to Patterson and he paused to sip coffee.

"Donelson is all that stands in the way of Yanks gettin' to the railroads at Nashville. And they're critical for movin' our troops and supplies."

He pointed to the map.

"The town of Dover is by the river, about a mile and a half over here. That's where our generals are headquartered. We're positioned here … the outer works east of the fort. These lines are the rifle pits. Our regiment is defending about a hundred acres."

"When'll the fightin' start?" Sergeant Dodd asked.

"Today or tomorrow, most likely. The Yankees'll surely be steamin' up the Cumberland to attack the fort again. Our job's to protect against Grant's army tryin' to surround us."

He pointed his sword to the snow-covered fields south and east and continued.

"Supply wagons are delayed by the storm. Make the best ya can of it tonight. Should get food tomorrow."

The four long days of forced march, and the unforgiving cold and lack of food, left me miserably weak and stiff. The blizzard continued into the night and I was unable to sleep for uncontrollable shivering and fear of frostbite.

The morning of the 14th was cold and quiet. The wind had stopped, only a light snow fell, and everything was white. Dodd assigned me to picket duty about three hundred yards east of our earthworks. I hid behind a clump of trees at the edge of a bog and watched. Standing still hour after hour my feet, fingers and ears grew numb and lost feeling. Suddenly there was movement across the bog, and I readied my rifle, but it was only a gray fox running toward the river. *Good idea, buddy. Better get outta here now.* By the time my shift was over, supply wagons had arrived, and we got a decent meal.

I spent the rest of the day in our trench and slept fitfully that night. An hour after daybreak, naval cannons rumbled to the west, *Boom, boom, boom.* Conway pointed to the sky. Columns of black smoke rose from the river.

"Union gunboats!" he shouted. "This may be a full attack!"

The artillery battle roared on violently for an hour and a half and I counted over two hundred booms. Then the big guns fell silent and we heard joyous yelling. In half an hour, a runner arrived bringing us news.

"Union gunboats, four ironclads and two timberclads, moved in close to the fort and our big guns shot 'em up good. Damaged three of 'em and they're driftin' back down the river. I seen it with my own eyes."

A cheer went up from our men. Across the valley other regiments outside the fort took up the cheer as they too learned that the river assault had been turned. The night was cold, but I managed to get a few hours of sleep.

Before daybreak Sergeant Dodd woke up our squad.

"Yanks brought up more troops overnight," he said. "Extending their lines toward the river. If they're successful, we'll be pinned in and have no escape."

I roused myself and limbered my arms and legs. My boots and socks were wet and my feet numb. In the darkness, I felt the presence of the company of men from Mississippi and heard them getting ready for battle. Soon Patterson appeared on horseback in front of our works. Our standard bearer stood beside him holding our purple and white flag. Our captain spoke in a loud voice.

"Men, we're going to assault Grant's army. We are fifteen regiments strong … ten thousand loyal soldiers of the South!"

Dallas pulled his hat low over his ears and winked at me. My heart beat fast.

Patterson continued, "Our enemy is positioned at the edge of the woods about a quarter-mile south of our works. The plan is to attack at daybreak and drive 'em back. We need to open more ground between us and the river."

He spit a load of brown tobacco juice in the snow, looked up and down the line of men, and then spoke slowly in a solemn voice.

"Good men of Mississippi … this day will try all souls! If any man cannot face the music, go to the rear now."

No one moved. I rubbed my eyes, checked my cartridge pack, and laced my boots tight. I took a few deep breaths as the line of men readied for the assault. I was hungry, weak, and fearfully cold, not a good way to start a day of fighting. What I longed for most was a pair of dry, wool socks. Just as daylight came, we moved out in front of the breastworks that had been our home and protection for two days.

In line between Dallas and Amos, fear welled up within me and I couldn't make my legs move. *Could be my last day on earth.* Sounds of the other men around me became muffled as if cotton had been stuffed in both ears. I heard Dallas call my name, but when I turned his mouth was shut. My heart thumped heavily.

Somewhere across the field of snow thousands of enemy soldiers waited. The evergreen trees bearing snow and the bare branches of the hardwoods appeared in brilliant detail as if my vision had improved greatly. A voice came from inside, *I am here, I am here*, and a recollection from childhood returned. I had slipped off a log while playing in the river and went straight down. I was panic-stricken but saw light above through the brown water. A strong hand had grabbed my arm and pulled me up. I spit out water, rubbed my eyes and saw Father's bearded face smiling at me.

All along the eastern perimeter of the fort, our soldiers formed lines in the open. A two-mile band of riflemen ascended the gentle slope toward the enemy. Our regiment was near the extreme left of the advance, closest to the river. We crossed through a hollow and my boots broke through ice-covered pools. Cold water soaked my socks. Around seven o'clock, scouts on horseback reported that the Union lines were just over the next rise.

As we neared their lines our army commenced firing and we made rapid progress across the field, yelling and shooting. A wave of euphoria came over me like an almighty wind from behind and vigor flowed through my whole body. Some Yanks retreated, leaving rifles and ammunition behind. Most stayed and fought, but we managed to drive them back from their forward positions. At the crest of the next ridge we halted, knelt in defensive lines and were joined by reinforcements from behind.

We were winning the day, rather easily it seemed, but then the Yanks stepped up their rifle fire. We shot back, reloaded and fired again to match the pace. A white-tailed deer ran out of the woods and bounded across the battlefield about halfway between the great armies. Rifle fire on both sides lessened and the deer leapt over a rail fence and came to a sudden stop. The doe stood petrified in the drifting smoke. Abruptly she bounded toward the tree line. Just as she got to the edge of the woods, she fell flat and lay dead. The armies resumed firing lead at each other with renewed earnestness.

To my right, a tall man fell in a heap and lay limp, one arm at an unnatural angle. I had never seen a man shot up close before. He had taken a terrible blast in the face, but I recognized his coat and a frightful chill surged through my soul. It was Jack and there was no question that he was dead. I'd talked with him just an hour before. His blood melted the snow and turned it the color of velvet.

I don't know how long I stared at Jack. It could have been two seconds, or it could have been two minutes. My insides turned hot and tightened up, and then the sounds of the raging battle returned. Mississippi Jack was dead, and an overpowering rage possessed me. He would never again enjoy the feel of soil under his bare feet or the joy of warming by a fire on a cold night. I hated the enemy soldier who killed Jack. I hated all Yankees and vowed that every shot I took would be aimed true.

I was dog-tired and hungry, but kept moving, firing, reloading and firing over and over. I fell through loose snow into a depression. My watch slipped out of my coat pocket, but I found it under the snow. It was nine-fifteen. Time passed slowly and my heart thumped in my ears. I reached for my canteen, but it was missing. I scooped up a handful of snow and it melted immediately in my mouth. I took another and another and, in a few minutes, I was revived and stuck my head up out of the hole.

The enemy put up steady fire, but our forces still advanced across the open ground. I rammed home another bullet, inserted a firing cap, and shot at the nearest

Yankee. A crazy, uncontrollable rage took over my mind and body — the devil. I was no longer afraid. My thoughts bounced wildly from one side of my head to the other. Load, aim, fire. When my target stumbled or fell, a rush of satisfaction surged through me and I craved for more. *Is this really me?*

A blast nearby knocked me down and I dropped my rifle. I lay looking at the gray sky and heard bullets sizzing overhead. More reinforcements arrived along with servants bearing ammunition. A young soldier stopped to check on me. His uniform was new, and he had just a few whiskers on his baby-white chin. His clear, brown eyes gazed into mine.

"Are ya alright?" he yelled.

The horror of Jack's destroyed face flashed through my mind and my throat clogged with emotion. I nodded yes and the young soldier moved forward out of sight. I got back up and saw that Patterson was redirecting our attack to the west. I came upon the bodies of two dead soldiers, one of ours and one enemy. Both lay flat on their backs side-by-side, their arms overlapped. A dusting of snow obscured the details of their faces and muted the uniform colors. Numbness set in upon me and I didn't care a whip. They could've been dead rats.

We crossed a road and pressed our enemy. By ten-thirty we had pushed them a mile backward. My right leg cramped so badly it folded up and I fell. A man I didn't know helped me straighten it and, in a few minutes, I rejoined the fight. Firing and moving forward took all the will power I could muster, but a crazy cheerfulness in victory kept me moving. The devil was alive and well inside.

Fighting became routine, like shucking corn one husk after another. *Boom!* A cannon shell exploded in front and dirt splattered in my eyes. Smoke choked my lungs and I fell back, grasping my throat. *I'm gonna die!* A man helped me wash out my eyes. In a minute, I was better and saw that it was Dallas.

"Let's get goin'!" he yelled. "We're whippin' 'em!"

I reloaded and we moved forward side-by-side. The first blue soldier to show his form was crouched to shoot. I aimed at his chest, squeezed the trigger, and he fell over. Maybe I hit him or maybe someone else did. Bullets flew thick like sleet blown sideways. There was no way to know who shot who. I found a loaded rifle in the snow then spotted another Yank. He was propped up behind two trees, both shortened by cannon fire, aiming at us. I fired and he disappeared behind his protection.

The fighting continued and we advanced without rest. More Yanks dropped their guns and ran. I pushed beyond what effort I thought possible and by one o'clock I had emptied my cartridge case four times — a hundred and sixty bullets. Each time I fired I took deadly aim, just as I had vowed.

"Andy?" I heard a voice from behind.

I turned and was surprised to see Brantly, the boy who was my runner at Sewell Mountain.

"More ammunition," he said. "Patterson's lettin' me help." He had a gleeful look in his eyes.

"You shouldn't be out here!" I yelled back.

He left a full case, ran back from the shooting, and disappeared in the haze of smoke and falling snow.

"Push ahead boys!" a booming voice came from behind. It was our captain on his horse. He redirected our advance, this time to the south.

We had opened a wide gap between the enemy and the river, plenty of space for our army to escape if we needed to. I was thrilled and couldn't believe our success. Our first big battle and we were routing the Yankees. I shared cartridges with Dallas, and we fired like mad men. The eyes of my comrades were alive and wild. The devil had gotten inside all of us.

A cannon shell exploded behind. Cold, wet dirt and snow peppered my hat and slipped down the back of my coat. We rose and charged the Yankees again. The sharp crack of rifles filled the air. Our men fought as though we had always been soldiers, not farmers. On the next charge, a canister shell packed with lead balls from an enemy cannon cut down several men to my left. They fell flat at once and lay motionless. An overwhelming sense of danger clutched my bones. *Better not to think*. I kept moving forward to stay ahead of cowardice.

Our advance continued, but at a heavy cost and the Yankee resistance stiffened. At three o'clock there was a lull in the shooting. Our company was low on ammunition, exhausted and thirsty. Orders came for our regiment to retreat to the trenches where we had begun the day.

"Why're we givin' up this ground?" Sergeant Barnes asked Patterson.

"There'll be enough to hold it. We've been ordered to retreat and that's what we're doin'. Get movin'!"

He was angry at being questioned.

I was considerably run down and not sure I could make it all the way back. We'd been fighting continuously for eight hours with nothing to eat. Wounded men and dead bodies lay about. Dallas and I came to one of ours writhing in the snow.

"Oh God, I'm hit," he said. "Who'll tell mother?"

We stopped and grabbed his shoulders.

"Leave him!" shouted a stern voice from behind. It was Lieutenant Oldham. "Our litter corps'll be along soon."

"But we can carry him!" Dallas screamed.

Oldham looked hard at us and we moved on, leaving the man behind. I hated obeying his order. It was far from certain that anyone would come back and save him. If it had been Dallas who was down, I would have disobeyed Oldham and faced the consequences.

There was hardly a spot where the once pristine snow was not trampled or littered with bodies and articles of war. Velvet stripes colored the brilliant white ... spilled blood. A dismembered leg caught my boot. It was naked except for the sock and boot, tied neatly in a double bowknot. Later I picked up two Yankee haversacks.

When we got back to the earthworks, it was around four-fifteen. My legs quivered and cramped again, and Dallas helped me straighten them. I found a full canteen, drank it all, and puked on myself. Sounds of gunfire moved closer.

Dallas sat next to me calmly reading out loud from his Bible. "My God is my rock, in whom I take refuge, my shield and the horn of my salvation, my stronghold."

"I'm not dyin' am I?" I said.

"No buddy. Just thought Bible readin' might calm your nerves."

Rifle fire continued and the battle between the gunboats and the fort rocked the ground. My head spun and I drifted into a perplexed state and couldn't see distinctly. For several minutes, I sat in the trench with my eyes closed trying to remember people I knew ... to picture my dear Sister and Mary Ann. Finally, a peaceful scene of sitting by the fireplace at home came to my mind.

When my head stopped spinning, I noticed the sole of one boot had separated from the upper and my sock was showing. I opened one the haversacks and found hard biscuits, about three inches square.

"What's this?" I asked Walker.

"It's hardtack. Where'd ya get it?"

I pointed to the haversacks.

"How much do ya have?"

"Two sacks. Have one."

I gnawed on the cracker for a while, but it was too hard to break. Walker told me to soak it in hot water till it softened up. It tasted awful, but I was desperate. In a short while the sacks were empty and our bellies full.

Around five o'clock, all shooting ceased, but the ringing in my ears persisted. Patterson sent several of us on burial duty. We found wounded close to our lines and pulled them back to safety. Those most gravely injured were put in wagons and taken up the hill to the hospital inside the fort. When the living were recovered, we gathered the dead, dug up clods of earth and lay the bodies three and four side-by-side in shallow graves. We covered them as best we could with earth and snow.

Across the way in the failing light, the Yankees pulled their dead and wounded from the fields. The rules of war called on both sides to refrain from firing when the battle was over for the day. Honor and respect for the enemy was drilled into us at Iuka. I hated the enemy as never before and was tempted to shoot the closest one.

Back in our trench, I covered my head with a blanket and tried to block out the sounds of suffering men. Each time I closed my eyes, Jack's butchered face reappeared.

"Captain's gonna address the company," Dallas said near my ear.

Several men had to be helped to their feet. Patterson's left arm was in a sling and his uniform wet and muddy.

"I have sad news," he bowed his face. "Doc Perry's dead."

We stared at each other in disbelief.

"I saw him at the breastworks," Dallas said.

"He took a bullet in his shoulder but he kept working in surgery and lost too much blood. Died an hour ago."

Patterson paused and caught his breath. It was evident he was suffering from his wound.

"David, Columbus and Jack were also killed, and Issac's missing. Will, Dodd and Pyrrhus are wounded."

Patterson turned and left, so Lieutenant Conway dismissed us. Dallas and I returned to our position in the trench, both devastated. Doc was the most beloved of our officers.

After dark, I walked along behind our lines and came to Patterson's command tent. The flap was open, and he looked up at me.

"May I come in, Captain?"

"Yes," he replied in a strained voice.

He sat at a fold-up table, writing, and had a wad of chewing tobacco in his mouth.

"Do ya have a sheet of paper and a pencil ya could spare?" I asked. "I wanna write my girlfriend."

He handed me what I wanted.

"Writin' your wife?" I asked.

"No. Families of our dead."

"How do ya find the words?"

"Better get some rest."

"Yes, sir," I saluted and left.

Doc, Jack, David, and Columbus dead. Issac missing ... could be dead. Five comrades in ten hours. I prayed for their spirits and asked God to calm my mind.

Across the fighting field, light from enemy campfires danced. I cupped my ears and heard a man crying in agony.

"Help me die … help me die."

I returned to our trench, wrapped up in a blanket next to Dallas and tried to sleep. Jack's mangled face appeared each time I closed my eyes and the sound of the man begging to die echoed in my head. The devil hardened my heart with hatred, and I burned for revenge. I would fight Yankees till they were all gone, or I was dead as a brick. I was mad at God for not protecting us better, so mad I couldn't pray. Dallas snored while I lay awake, my ears ringing unmercifully. The longest, most hazardous day of my life would not end.

Chapter 13

DEFEATED

February 1862, Fort Donelson, Tennessee

The sound of excited voices woke me the next morning. Standing to shake off the stiffness, I remembered that it was Sunday and longed for a hot bath. My rifle lay beside me in the melting snow. The sky was cloudy, but the snow had stopped falling, and the air was noticeably warmer.

"Leave your firearms and assemble!" Lieutenant Oldham shouted.

I climbed the forward trench to look at the battlefield. A solid line of soldiers in blue stood just outside our breastworks, guns crossed at their chests. While sound asleep and without a shot fired, General Floyd surrendered our army to General Grant and we became prisoners of war. The enemy stood and watched as we stacked our rifles, pistols and knives. Northern forces were three times as many as ours. They surrounded us on three sides, and the river, guarded by Union gunboats, was at our backs. The two miles of ground we had fought to claim were forfeited. Oldham spent the night among us knowing of the surrender but waited till morning to tell us.

Generals Floyd and Pillow escaped with a small force in the night. Captain Patterson, Dodd and a few badly wounded men were sent out with them. This wasn't the first time we were kept in the dark. The men muttered about our leaders being too quick to capitulate, but as the situation became clearer, most accepted the news. If we'd continued to fight against the overwhelming odds, many more would have been killed and the Yanks would have eventually taken the fort.

Soldiers stood in groups by campfires and a deep sense of regret filled my being. We fought well and with great courage, I thought. In fact, we whipped the Yanks, but our generals didn't take the escape we fought and died for.

"Where's Brantly?" Dallas asked Oldham.

"He went out with Patterson and Dodd last night. Prison's no place for a fourteen-year-old."

The enemy allowed us to keep our personal gear and cooking utensils. We walked downhill to the town of Dover and assembled with thousands of men from the fort and outlying defenses. The melting snow and tromping soldiers turned the hillside into such a muddy mess, some fell and slid downhill.

"That's where our generals surrendered," Oldham said.

He pointed to the Dover Hotel, a double-story, unpainted building about sixty paces uphill from the Cumberland.

A Union gunboat straddled the river. It was like nothing I had ever seen. It had black, metal-covered sides that slopped upward ten or twelve feet. Four huge cannons peeked out of slot openings on the side, and three more pointed out the front. A metal-clad command station stood in front and the paddlewheels were under cover of a shell near the rear. Amidships, two black smokestacks stood tall with a wisp of black smoke rising from each. Green stripes were painted near the tops. One man stood on the command station with his hands clasped behind and a silver pistol tucked under his belt. Inside, no doubt, gunners were standing by the big cannons ready to fire at us if we rioted.

A Yankee commander standing beside the hotel called out.

"Officers over here! All soldiers to the boats!"

Our lieutenants joined the group of officers and were led away.

"Wonder when we'll see 'em again," Amos asked.

"Look," Dallas pointed up.

A gaggle of forty or so geese flew underneath the heavy clouds. Their loud honking quieted the chatter of the prisoners. As the geese gained height, they flew above the fort and circled around the huge battlefield. A second group of geese from the river rose to join the first. The combined group stretched out in a loose V-formation and they circled again, gaining altitude and entering the wispy under-clouds. They crossed above us prisoners once more as they turned west and climbed into the clouds. I lost sight of them but heard honking for a couple of minutes as they receded into the distance.

We were led to the river and walked a gangplank onto a large steamboat tied to the dock. Three paddlewheelers floated side-by-side as thousands more prisoners waited on the muddy hillside. A Yankee guard was stationed at the top of the stairs. He had a whisper of brown whiskers on his chin and looked at me with a curious expression.

"Ya fought well," he said.

This caught me by surprise because I assumed the enemy would treat us with distain.

"We had ya whipped," I said and ducked below deck.

The boat stank to high heaven and was so crowded below deck I feared no one would survive if it sank. Dallas and I stuck close together.

"Think we're all finished with fightin'?" I asked him.

"I don't think so. This is gonna take a while to settle. I wonder where they're takin' our officers?"

I shrugged. There was hushed talking among the men. We were demoralized and dumbfounded that our fight was over, and prisoners of war after our first big affair!

"I was jis gettin' good at shootin'," Amos said.

"Maybe you'll get good at bein' a prisoner too," Dallas replied.

"Oh, I don't intend on bein' a prisoner long."

The paddlewheels engaged and our flatboat backed into the river and headed north. As it picked up speed, water swashed along the hull and spewed through tiny cracks. We were cramped together in almost complete darkness and the boat's boilers kept the inside warm. At daylight our captors let a few dozen men at a time exchange places with prisoners on deck. A whole day passed before my turn came. When I finally got out, my eyes hurt even though the sky was overcast.

I struck up a conversation with one of the guards, a man of twenty-one like myself. Robert was from Chicago, eldest of four brothers and two sisters. He had worked in a broom factory before enlisting. Robert talked about his brothers back home and how he hoped they would not have to fight. His mother sent him a letter most every day. While we talked, the steamboat came to the end of the Cumberland and turned up the Mississippi. We watched the riverbank slide by, and I found it hard to think of Robert as my enemy. The wide, rolling river connected his state with mine. In other circumstances, we might have been friends, or fished, or sung hymns together in church.

He told me that we were going to a prison in Chicago named Camp Douglas.
"When'll we get our officers back?" I asked.
"Don't know. Think they're goin' to another state."
My time on deck was over and a new set of prisoners came up for fresh air.

Chapter 14

RECOLLECTION
February 1862, Mississippi River

Below deck again, Dallas challenged me to a game of chess. My mind was elsewhere, but I didn't want to disappoint him. Although his opening attack was weak, he managed to capture my bishop straightaway. Already down a major piece and with no opportunities for counterattack presenting themselves, I resigned, blamed my loss on the dim light, and we called it a night. I covered my head with a blanket to muffle the voices of comrades and a memory returned.

On a warm day when I was nine, I was helping Father get a field ready to plant. We moved a mound of rotting corn stalks and disturbed a nest of bees burrowed in the pile. A bee stung my leg and I ran fast to get away from the swarm. A bee stung my father's nose and he slapped it off, scratched it a bit, then took up the plough harness again and furrowed the rows.

At suppertime, his nose was so red and swollen that Momma and I had fun kidding him about it. We got to laughing so hard he laughed too. The next day Father worked till noon, then came back to the cabin to rest. His nose and cheeks were red and swollen and Momma put wet rags on his face to cool the fever. The next morning, he was up early plowing again. On the following day, he did not get up, his body racked with fever. Momma sent my sister to fetch Doc Perry. He came that afternoon and said Father had erysipelas and there was no medicine to treat it, but he'd most likely get better on his own. He stayed in bed day after day, but got worse instead of better, and folks came around to visit.

After a week, Father stopped eating the soft food Momma fixed and could only sip a little water at a time. One night he talked wildly in his sleep and it frightened me something fierce. A few days later, Momma didn't come out of their room in the morning, so I knocked on the door and heard someone stirring. She came out, closed the door, and sat in the rocking chair. Momma gathered the kids around her.

"Your father's gone to be with the Lord," she said in a quiet voice.

I was the youngest but remembered hearing words kind of like that at church before. I sat at her knees and held on tight. Bugs buzzed, a scant breeze passed through the cabin, and Momma cried softly. I closed my eyes and pictured Father's figure ahead of me, plough straps over his shoulders and the mule pulling ahead. I saw my bare feet leaving little prints in the freshly turned earth following along behind. I leaned on Momma and sweated through my clothes.

Father lived fourteen days after the bee sting. He was in the full of life, a strong and active man. I couldn't believe something as small as a bee killed him. I couldn't even remember which one of my legs was stung.

Floyd Shirley, a family friend and carpenter, made a coffin out of pine boards for Father and a lot of folks gathered at Old Lebanon Church, including people I didn't know. My father was well-known and admired. He was Justice of the Peace for Beat Four of Attala County and held his courts at Attalaville, about a mile south of Sallis. When I was little, I rode with Father on his horse sometimes when he went to hold court. He tried to get people to settle their differences by agreement and heal their hard feelings. Some of the people he helped became friends.

After the service, they nailed the lid shut and loaded the coffin onto a wagon for the trip to the graveyard. Momma sat me on top of the coffin, and I watched the horses ahead and looked around at the people walking slowly behind. Everybody was quiet the whole way. I guess everything that needed to be said had already been said. When the men shoveled red clay in the hole, I cried because I'd never see Father's face again.

Back home, Momma sat in her rocking chair and gathered us close. She talked about how we would get along and keep the farm productive. My oldest brother Jesse had already married and moved out. My sister Pernecia was seventeen, and brother John, eleven. Everybody called Pernecia — Sister, even though that was not her given name. Momma was delicate and sickly and there were many tasks she couldn't do. She knew we couldn't keep the farm up to the level of when Father was alive and she said we would ask Uncle Willie to help out, especially with the cotton harvest.

Sister and I went to visit Uncle Willie the day after the burial. He put on his hat right then, walked home with us, and stayed for six days. We all worked hard to get the planting finished. On Sunday we went to church and afterward, we had quail, rice, and biscuits with butter and scuppernong jelly for dinner. Momma thanked Uncle Willie, then John and I walked him home. We took cane poles with us and fished the Big Black in the afternoon, because we wanted to catch a big one for Momma. When we got back home, she was asleep in her rocker on the porch. She looked mighty tired, so we were careful not to wake her.

We cleaned the two blue cats we caught and fried them for supper. While we were cooking, Momma slipped up behind and hugged us. She cooked up some cornbread and peas for a good supper. We accomplished a lot together in the first week without Father. Working hard was one of the things he loved most.

Chapter 15

THE BELLY OF THE FISH
February 1862, Mississippi River

I awoke in the night hearing voices on deck and noticed that the ship had stopped. A single lantern hung in the middle, casting dim light over us. It was our third night in the belly of the fish. Smells of rot, wet clothes, and wood smoke filled the air. Sprawling bodies covered the floor, a mass of tired, defeated soldiers, trying to make it through another night. The air was heavy and humid from the ship's boilers.

A rat ran up on my britches and I kicked it away. Sometime later I woke again as a man having a nightmare yelled, "Retreat, retreat!" We were little more than rats ourselves — hungry, powerless, and humiliated; nothing I had imagined a soldier's life would be.

Dallas was still sleeping when the light of day filtered through the deck boards. His face was drawn and dirty. There were lines around his eyes like he had aged years in the eight months we had been soldiers. I probably looked much the same.

91

We'd had nothing to eat on the journey except a few hardtack biscuits. My stomach growled, my limbs were weak, and my bones ached. I shut my eyes to block out our misery and tried to remember pleasant smells and the warmth of our fireplace.

Sometime later, a hatch at the top of the stairway was opened and colder air poured inside. The men began to stir and talk. When all were awake and standing, one man lay on the floor, his hat covering his face. Someone touched him on the shoulder, and he didn't budge. I knelt and pulled his hat off. His mouth was closed, and I touched his cold forehead, realized he was not breathing, and fell backward.

"Who is this man?" I asked.

"I don't know," a man answered. "He's not from our regiment. Told me yesterday he got lost durin' the battle."

"Help me," I said.

Three men close by helped me grab his arms and legs. We took him to the stairway and I called for an officer.

"One of our men has died. We need to bury him proper."

The officer looked stunned, then he said he would check with the captain. We stood and waited, holding the dead man's body. His wet clothes smelled of piss, tobacco and dirt. Soon the officer yelled down and a multitude of hands joined and passed the dead man's body up the stairs and handed him to other prisoners on deck. Dallas handed me my Bible and I climbed the stairs and stepped on deck.

"Follow Sergeant Evans," the officer said. "He'll show ya the way."

I was among the group of five prisoners who carried the dead man off the boat and onto a loading dock in the shadow of a city. A row of warehouses stood along the river, with two-story buildings on the street behind. A light rain fell from the ash gray sky. Sergeant Evans led us uphill to a muddy graveyard beside a Methodist church. I sat in the mud and my comrades lay the dead man's head on my lap. I covered his face with his hat and the Yankees gave out shovels.

Our captors stood around us, rifles at their sides. Except for their blue uniforms, they looked much like us, in their twenties. They stood silently and watched as the hole got deeper. Water puddled in the bottom and the pile of mud grew higher beside. A knee-high, white board fence surrounded the graveyard and a small gate stood open toward the church.

Inside the dead man's pockets, I found a crumpled photograph of a family and a page torn from a Bible. A name was written in pencil at the top.

Dallas stood with a shovel at his side. "We're ready." He motioned toward the grave.

We lowered the dead man's body into its final resting place and then stood for a moment looking down, each one alone with his thoughts. I covered him with my coat, then took a shovel and put the first scoop of mud back in the grave. Others took turns till we had finished. One of the Yanks brought a plank of wood and Dallas borrowed a jackknife to carve the marker.

"Our brother's name is Lester Stillman," I said.

The others looked on in silence as Dallas carved the letters L and S and tamped the plank into the mud.

I looked up through the rain at the church steeple and turned to the Book of Matthew. The men on either side of me held their hats over my Bible to keep the rain off. I read the Lord's Prayer out loud and said my own prayer too. When finished, I tucked the photograph and torn page in my Bible and closed it. As the guards led us back toward the river, I wondered if Lester's mother and father would ever know what happened to him. I felt my heart beating. *Do souls really live on?*

Dallas was by my side as prisoners and guards walked down the hill and across town. The rain grew heavier and the steamboat whistle blew three times. Dallas put his hand on my shoulder. By the time we reached the steamer, I was wet to the bone and shivering.

Chapter 16

PRISONERS OF WAR
February 1862, Chester, Illinois to Chicago

Our burial crew rejoined the other prisoners aboard the steamer, and we spent a waterlogged night in the belly of the fish docked at Chester. The next morning, we resumed the upstream journey and around noon, I heard blustering winds above deck, like a strong winter rainstorm. Streaks of light filtered through the deck boards and water dripped on us. The rhythmical splashing of the paddlewheel and muggy, stale air made for a miserable journey.

To make matters worse, Dallas and I had run out of things to talk about. I passed hour after hour with my eyes closed, wishing there was no war and that I was home. That time of year, I'd have been at the Big Black, stalking wood ducks and mallards. My winter coat and dry socks would keep me warm, and at the end of the hunt a hot supper would be waiting for me. After supper, I'd read by lamplight and warm my feet by the fire. Sister might ask me to play Father's fiddle. I'd protest a little and then play a hymn and she'd sing the verses. She knew them all by heart. Even with both parents gone ahead to be with the Lord, the goodness of our lives would fill our souls and we would be happy together.

I looked over the horde of tired, defeated soldiers confined below deck. Dallas was asleep. *Is this what it feels like inside a casket?*

The following afternoon our boat stopped, and we heard men and ropes moving on deck. The hatch was removed, and frigid air poured in upon us.

"Time to unload," an officer yelled down the hatch. "We're at Alton. Bring everything ya got."

I made sure my Bible was in my haversack, checked Father's pocket watch, and took a deep breath. The trip from Fort Donelson had taken six days. During the journey, we had eaten only hardtack and a handful of dried beans soaked in water. The Yankees were no better prepared to hold us than we were to be their prisoners.

I winced as we emerged from the dank darkness. Freezing wind whipped the heat out of my clothes and stung my nostrils. We walked in columns through the dockyards and uphill into town. The sky was overcast and I couldn't tell north from south. A handful of people were on the streets and they stared at our procession. After a few blocks a crowd began to form and follow along beside us. Some in the crowd grew rowdy.

"You bastards got what 'as comin'," a voice jeered.

Kids threw rocks at us. We far outnumbered the guards, but they were well-armed. Our clothes were inadequate for the cold and we were weak from the long journey, lack of food, and cramped conditions. Many were sick and wounded, a ragtag bunch if ever there was one. Walking got my blood moving and although the weather was freezing, for the first time since leaving Fort Donelson, I felt alive inside.

In twenty minutes, we came to a rail line where a long row of box cars was waiting. Snow began to fall as we were packed into cars. The door on our car was rolled shut and locked, and soon I was cold to the bone again. As the train rolled out of the station, the late afternoon sun broke through the clouds and stripes of light flickered over the men in our car. I knew some faces well, others not at all; brothers facing an unknown future together.

The wind whistled through the car as the train rolled on into the night. My body grew cold and stiff, and men moaned as they tried to sleep. My fingers and toes ached deep inside and I longed for a mug of coffee. *Will I die in prison?* Fear gripped my mind and I was unable to stop the flow of terrible thoughts. I imagined waking in the morning with my feet frozen, as good as dead.

My shivering became uncontrollable so Dallas wrapped his arms around me and after a while the shaking subsided. Later, lights outside the car woke me and I stepped over others to the sidewall. Through a knothole I saw that we were passing through a station. A couple of inches of snow covered the train yard. Boxes and supplies were stacked along the tracks — materials of war. *Weapons to kill us, no doubt.* The station was deserted except for a few guards. I returned to my place beside Dallas and spent the rest of the night worrying about everything.

When morning came, the train stopped, and all was quiet for fifteen minutes or so. Then we heard shouting outside, and the door slid open. Sacks of hardtack and jugs of water were tossed inside, and the door was shut and locked again.

"We need a doctor!" one prisoner yelled.

The men passed out hardtack and took turns drinking from the jugs. With a jolt, the train got underway. Stronger men helped the weaker ones and we suffered through another day as a family.

Several hours later the train slowed and came to a stop. The doors rolled open and we got out in the gathering dusk. We were in a station with many tracks and warehouses. Comrades carried prisoners who couldn't stand, and we assembled beside the tracks. A fat older man dressed in a fine Yankee uniform and fancy hat came through the rail station on a brown and white horse. A guard raised his rifle above his head and told us to be quiet. Then the officer addressed us from atop his mount.

"I'm Colonel Madden. Commander of Camp Douglas, your new home."

There was no reaction from the prisoners.

"If you all cooperate, we'll be there in an hour and out of this cold."

He rode his horse up and down the line looking at the prisoners.

"You may be wondering where your officers are and when you'll see 'em again."

No one spoke.

"They've been taken to camps in other states," he said.

Men shuffled in the cold as the last light of day faded in the west.

"You'll see 'em after the war," Madden said. "When the uprising's defeated!"

We followed Colonel Madden and trudged along the gas-lit streets. A few people stepped out of their houses to watch us go by. We were met with expressions of curiosity and pity. We walked away from the city for two or three miles and then came to an enormous walled enclosure. Two large wood doors swung wide open and we filed inside. Lanterns lit the prison entrance, but beyond that it was hard to see.

We were counted off in groups of a hundred, sent to wooden barracks and locked in for the night. I lost track of Dallas in the dark. The building I was in had windows along the length and one woodstove in the center. The temperature was just a mite warmer than outdoors. I found a straw mattress on the floor, covered myself with a thin blanket and settled down for the night. I heard two men talking about escaping. I thought they were a bit ahead of themselves as we had yet to even see our surroundings, but I surely admired their passion.

Chapter 17

CAMP DOUGLAS
February — March 1862, Chicago, Illinois

In the morning, the barracks door was unlocked, and I stepped outside. A cold wind cut through my light coat. Hundreds of men stood in the prison yard, many facing the entrance under a cloudy, gray sky. A ladder was leaned up against the wall and a man was perched on top behind a box camera. Yankee guards stood nearby lest any prisoners use the ladder to escape. The photographer yelled out, "Stand still!"

After he took an image he yelled, "Okay."

"We're gonna be in the newspaper!" one prisoner joked.

The soldiers nearby laughed. I asked a guard about food and he shrugged his shoulders.

Dallas found me and we walked through the place. It was a huge expanse of identical buildings laid out in rows. There must have been forty or fifty in all.

There were no trees, bushes or grass, just bare ground and a tall, gray stone wall. We heard sounds of the city beyond, but couldn't see anything outside, the surrounding land being flat. It was good to know that Dallas and I would be together through whatever happened.

At each end of the camp were trenches about ten feet long, two feet wide and six feet deep. A pole was laid from the ends of the sink and that's where we sat to shit. About every other day a layer of dirt was added to cover the vile stink. The sinks were not shielded so there was no privacy at all, and the cold wind added to the discomfort. The lack of privacy caused some to shit on the ground behind the barracks, instead of using the sinks. As the days passed, the prison yard became filthier and disgusting.

When we had been at Camp Douglas for a week, Thomas Victor, a buddy in our regiment, was badly injured when a guard smashed his knees with a rifle stock. I asked to talk with an officer about his mistreatment but was refused. The next day a more sympathetic guard agreed to pass my request along. That morning Frank Rook got into a fight because they gave us nothing to eat. The guard beat him about the head and shoulders till many prisoners surrounded them and the guard fled.

"I'll kill him, next time I see him," one of the men fumed.

Frank lost three teeth and had a bloodied head. We patched him up as best we could and got him to bed.

During the second week, we ran out of firewood and the barracks were unbearably cold after sundown, the only warmth coming from our being crowded up together. We grew weaker by the day and many came down with smallpox. The men were brimming with anger and ready to lash out with their bare hands at any provocation. Fights with the guards were common and among prisoners as well.

Finally, I was allowed to speak to Lieutenant Burnett. I told him about the beating the guard gave Thomas and the fight with Frank.

"Tensions are gettin' high," I said. "If we don't get more food, I'm afraid the men'll rise up."

Burnett did not answer.

"There's not enough firewood to keep the stoves going," I said. "I'm sure ya don't want things to get out of control and neither do I."

"Are you an officer?"

"No. I'm just appealin' to you man to man. We deserve food, clothing, and decent treatment."

He noticed me looking around the officer's quarters.

"We're undersupplied," he said. "Don't have enough guards. This is the first time we've held prisoners."

"At least ya could treat us with respect. Is that in short supply too?"

"What's the guard's name? The guard that hit your man?"

"I don't know his name. What Thomas needs now is medical treatment, sir."

"I'll see what I can do." He dismissed me with a backhanded wave.

On my way back to our barracks, a tall, clean-shaven guard stopped me at gunpoint.

"Where've ya been?" he demanded and I told him. "Get your redneck ass back to your barracks! And mind your own business, or else."

He pointed his rifle at my chest. Several prisoners gathered around, ready to come to my defense.

"There's nothin' we can do," I said. "He's the boss dog."

A redheaded prisoner yelled at the guard, "We got ya outnumbered!"

"Yeah, but I got this!" he shouted back, swinging his bayonet-tipped rifle toward the man. "And I'd be happy to blow a hole in your chest!"

"Leave him alone," I appealed to the men and they dispersed reluctantly.

The next morning, I awoke to the crack of rifle fire, two shots in rapid succession. Dallas and I ran outside and saw guards dragging a prisoner by his arms.

"Where're ya takin' him?" Dallas asked the guards.

"Detention. He was tryin' to escape."

Near the wall lay the body of a fallen prisoner. Dallas and I ran to his side. There were two holes in the back of his coat stained dark with blood. We turned him over and he was dead. We carried his body back to our building and asked our chaplain to say words for him. Some of the men had been talking about escape, but these two were our first to try.

As the days went by, my heart grew harder. Like the others, I was angry and schemed ways to get back at the guards. Once men start killing each other, revenge keeps it going. A few days after the shooting, our group was especially quiet and sullen after lock down.

"Why don't ya play Grimes' fiddle?" Dallas whispered.

"I don't much feel like it."

"That's exactly why ya should. Boost our spirits!"

He was right, so I tuned the fiddle up and a man yelled out, "Play Mississippi Sawyers!"

"Yeah, play it," another shouted.

I started the tune, Will played his harmonica and the men tapped their feet. Dallas sang and others joined in. After two tunes, even the dourest souls in our building came back to life. Suddenly, the door burst open and in came the tall, clean-shaven guard who had threatened me before, followed by two others.

"Up against the wall!" he yelled, and they pointed pistols at us. "Whadda ya think you're doin'?"

No one answered.

"Gimme the fiddle," he demanded, staring at me.

"We're not hurtin' anyone," I said. "Jis havin' a little fun."

"Gol-derned idiots! This ain't no party. Give it to me now!"

I motioned the other men aside and handed it over.

The guard shouted, "Open the stove!"

Amos, who stood in the center of the building, opened the metal door. Only a few coals glowed.

"Burn it, ya little fart."

Amos took the fiddle and glared at the big guard. Amos, no more than five feet tall with his boots on, looked so angry he could have taken down a bull. He stood firm with the fiddle in his hands. The devil welled up in the prisoners and rage showed in every man's face. A few quiet seconds passed, then the guard started toward Amos.

"I'll do it!" I said, stepping in between.

I grabbed the fiddle, tossed it in the stove and clamped the door shut.

"There," I said. "Ya got what ya wanted. Leave us alone or I'll talk to Lieutenant Burnett."

The clean-shaven guard started toward me, but the other guards pulled him to the door and outside. Our men were angry as hornets.

"Why'd ya do that?" Dallas screamed at me. "We coulda killed all three!"

I put my hands on his shoulders and said, "To live another day, good buddy."

It took a good while for me to settle down that night. As the cabin got quiet, a violin string twanged as the tuning pegs burned, the last note of the night.

Conditions at Douglas became unspeakably unsanitary. Our drinking water was often frozen and when we thawed it out it was dirty. One man made filters out of threadbare shirts to remove the larger bits of debris. The prison yard was a field of mud frozen in a thousand boot prints. The food was terrible and there was never enough to fill our stomachs. Our pigs at home had far better prospects. I had camp itch and so did everybody else. The last time I had had a decent bath was before Fort Donelson, eight weeks earlier. My clothes smelled to high heaven and my hair was long and tangled.

From time to time there were rumors that prisoner exchanges were being arranged. I looked forward to the day when I returned to the fields of battle and I vowed to make every shot count if I ever got back.

Near the middle of March, I was summoned to Lieutenant Burnett's office. He sat behind a table covered with stacks of papers with an empty chair opposite.

"Have a seat," he gestured with his open hand.

"Thank you, sir."

Sitting in a chair in a well-heated room was a luxury.

"Flowers, I'm assigning you responsibility for Thomas and Frank. We're sendin' 'em to a hospital in Mound City."

Neither was recovering well.

"You're lettin' me outta prison?"

"Oliver Middlebrook will accompany you. He's my personal aide … a gentleman. He'll tell ya the details. You'll leave tomorrow."

Burnett stood and walked to the window facing the yard. Prisoners moseyed about, taking advantage of the first good sunlight we'd had in weeks.

I thanked him, returned to our barracks and told Dallas the news.

"That's not what I'd call sticking together," he said.

"I'll be back in a few weeks."

"You have no idea what'll happen in a few weeks!"

"What was I supposed to do? Tell Burnett no?"

"Of course not. I'm sad you're leaving, is all … and afraid. I don't wanna rot away here."

"You're my best buddy, ya know, and I'm afraid too," I said.

"Yeah, this ain't the kind of adventure I 'as lookin' for!"

"Me neither. We just gotta keep goin' a day at a time and pray for the best."

"Okay, buddy." Dallas patted my shoulder. "You be careful."

Chapter 18

PRISONER OUT OF PRISON
March — April 1862, Mound City, Illinois

The next morning, Dallas helped me get Thomas and Frank into an ox-drawn cart. At the train station, we met Oliver Middlebrook, a slight man, about thirty years old, with a neatly trimmed mustache and thick spectacles. He was unarmed and didn't look like a warrior in any regard except for his uniform.

We boarded a passenger car and got the injured men situated, each in a full seat and covered them with blankets. *WOOooOOOH, WOOooOOOH, WOOooOOOH,* the whistle sounded, and the train got underway.

"They'll get good treatment in Mound City," Oliver said in a quiet, gentlemanly voice.

"How far is it?"

"About four hundred miles. At the southern tip of Illinois, where the Ohio joins the Mississippi."

105

Oliver was talkative and relaxed. I learned that he was a teacher from La Crosse, Wisconsin.

"What do ya teach?" I asked.

"History. English history."

"I can read and write. Went to school two months in the summer after first harvest and two in winter. And my parents made me study the Bible every night."

"You a farmer or tradesman?"

"Farmer."

"How many slaves?"

"None. We do all the work ourselves."

"What do you grow?" he asked, genuinely interested. I could see him as a teacher.

"Corn, peas, beans, pumpkins, peanuts … you name it. And cotton for sale. We raise chickens, pigs, cows and goats too."

"I thought slaves picked the cotton?"

"On the plantations they do. There's a family over near Yazoo City that has a large place and forty slaves. They sell hundreds of bales each year. We harvest five or six, use some for makin' clothes and blankets and sell the rest."

Oliver looked out the window for a few seconds and then leaned toward me.

"Why doesn't your family have slaves?"

"My father was a county judge and he believed every man should be paid a fair wage for his labor."

He looked surprised and I continued.

"When I was eight, Father took me with him to Yazoo City to buy supplies. When we got near the city I heard a woman screaming and it scared me. I asked Father what was the matter and he said, 'you'll see.' He tied up the mule and wagon and we walked toward the center of town. The woman's screaming got louder and we came upon a crowd. Father put me on his shoulders so I could see. A negro woman was standing on a platform and a white man was holding up her arm. Another white man stood nearby holding a baby. I asked Father what they were doing and he told me the woman was being sold and her baby was being taken from her. The mother fell to her knees and cried as the man with the baby walked away. On the way home Father told me that slavery was a great wrong and should be abolished. The memory has stuck with me since."

"Then why are you fighting?" Oliver said.

"To protect Mississippi and do my duty." Oliver shifted in his seat and I continued. "About a quarter of the men in my company own slaves. The rest are poor farmers like me. Some hope to save money enough to buy a slave one day … they see it as the best way to increase their livelihood."

"Are they fighting for the same reasons as you?"

"Lots of reasons. Lookin' for adventure … sense of duty. A bunch in my county volunteered. Some boys even lied about their age to get in. No one wants to be called a coward."

"And your officers?" Oliver asked. "Do they own slaves?"

"Some do."

"But you fight even though you believe slavery is morally wrong?"

"Wouldn't you fight if an army invaded your land?"

We looked out the windows as the countryside slid by. The trees were bare and there was a lot more snow on the ground than I had ever seen. It was great to be outside the prison walls away from the hostile guards. Being with Oliver was like having a talk with Jesse, my oldest brother. After a while the rocking of the train put me to sleep and I dreamed of Mary Ann, Sister and home.

When I awoke, Oliver was reading a thick book with gold lettering on the binding. He lay the book on the seat, removed his spectacles and rubbed his eyes.

"What're ya readin'?" I asked.

"*The History of All Nations*, by S. G. Goodrich."

"Interesting?"

"Yes, it is. There's quite a lot to be learned. Humankind's been making the same mistakes over and over."

"In the last few years our minister's been preachin' that the Bible allows owning slaves. And our politicians are singin' the same tune."

Oliver chuckled. "Preachers here tell us God's absolutely on our side!"

"By the time the cannons fired at Fort Sumter, our preacher had the congregation whipped into a frenzy 'bout God ordainin' the war and white Southerners bein' the chosen ones. He had more people comin' to church than ever. Thinks he's top rail."

The train slowed and passed through a station yard. Rows of cannons and supplies waited to be loaded as sentries stood guard. I shuddered at the sight and looked back at Oliver.

"Seems God's gettin' credit on both sides for fannin' the flames," I said. "That's gotta be flim-flam."

"You could be on to something there," he laughed and touched the side of his head.

"I'm thinkin' men are responsible for this conflict," I said "And maybe God's just lettin' us fight it out among ourselves."

He nodded.

"Does your book talk about religion and how that figures into wars?" I asked.

"Indirectly, yes."

"Maybe if they put you and me in charge, we'd come up with a better way out than fightin'."

We discussed serious and frivolous subjects and fed off each other hour after hour. I laughed till my cheeks cramped. The journey took three days, so we had lots of time to talk.

When we arrived in Mound City, Oliver arranged for a horse and carriage to take us to the hospital. The town was rightly named. A number of dirt mounds about thirty feet high lined one side of the river.

"Where'd the mounds come from?" I asked.

"Indians."

At the hospital, we turned Thomas and Frank over, and they were helped inside. Oliver told me the hospital had been a warehouse and foundry just a few months earlier. He directed the driver to an address on Ashley Street. Three- and four-story brick buildings lined both sides, and many appeared to be recently built. A few blocks along, the carriage stopped.

"I'm leaving you here," Oliver said.

"Alone, unguarded?"

"You're trustworthy and a man of honor. And you wouldn't abandon your comrades."

I stepped down from the carriage and noticed that Oliver had a letter tucked in his pocket.

"I'm going back to Chicago now," he said. "You are to check on your comrades each day and you'll get orders by telegram in a few weeks."

"Where will I stay, what'll I eat? I have no money."

"Relax. I reserved a room for you." He pointed behind me. "That's your boarding house. There's twenty dollars in the envelope for food and necessities. And there's a letter too. If any authority challenges you, just show 'em the letter." He tapped the envelope.

I couldn't believe the Yankees would leave me unguarded.

"You're free to mail letters home, if you like. Sister and Mary Ann will appreciate your attention, I'm sure," he smiled.

"So you're the one who censors the mail."

"All of yours were mailed without mark outs." He smiled again and signaled the driver. "I must bid you farewell now. I'll tell Dallas where you are."

"Thank ya for your kindness and conversation. I wish …"

He waved me off. "Me too."

As the carriage moved away, the hard, sharp sound echoed off the buildings and I turned toward the boarding house.

Inside, the clerk led me upstairs to room number four and unlocked the door. It had a window, desk, chair, and a bed. A neatly folded stack of clean clothes sat on the bed and a coat hung on the back of the door. I sat at the desk and looked out the window at the city below. It was strange to look down at a street. I had never been in a two-story building before. Civilians walked about as if times were normal … no guards … no guns. The envelope contained four 5-dollar greenbacks and an official letter from the U.S. Army signed by Colonel Joseph H. Tucker.

In a few minutes I returned to the front desk.

"What's the arrangement for gettin' a bath?" I asked.

"Just let me know when you're ready and I'll have hot water brought up," the clerk said.

What luck!

"I'd like to bathe soon."

"Fine. It'll be ready in half an hour. Here." He handed me soap and a towel. "Middlebrook said to tell ya there's a barber nearby if you'd like a haircut and shave."

The mirror on the bathroom wall reflected a face I hardly recognized and a thick brown beard like my father. My hair was long and tangled. I took full advantage of the bath, scrubbed over and over and stayed till the water cooled. I emerged a new man and put on the clean clothes that had been left for me.

"Where's the barber shop?" I asked the clerk.

He pointed through the front window to a building right across the street. When I stepped into the air of the city, I felt almost like a free man. The barber gave me a shave and haircut and then held a mirror to my face.

"That's more like me," I said. "How much do I owe ya?"

"Nothin'. The officer took care of it."

"Thank ya very much, sir."

Both sides of the street were lined with brick buildings side-by-side. The air was hazy and laden with soot and it reminded me of the pungent smells of battle.

Women dumped pails of wastewater in the dirty street. Two blocks down toward the river I found the café the clerk had told me about.

Inside I asked, "How does this work?"

"What da ya mean?" the man replied.

"I've never eaten in a café."

"Oh, new to the city, are ya?"

"Somethin' like that."

He handed me a list of meal choices and pointed to an empty table. I read a copy of the <u>Chicago Daily Journal</u> while I waited. There were several accounts of the war, including one about Union prisons in Illinois. Camp Douglas and Alton were both mentioned. In a few minutes the waiter brought a plate of steaming beefsteak, potato, and hot rolls. It felt odd to eat at a table, I was so used to squatting on the ground. The food was delicious, and I felt guilty. My comrades in prison were, no doubt, getting thinner by the day.

After eating, I walked the streets and thanked God for delivering me from prison, if only for a few weeks. The whole day was strange and surprising. *Why did Oliver treat me generously? Why aren't the Northerners unfriendly? Surely, they know I'm the enemy.* I returned to my room, lit a candle, and found writing paper, ink and quills in the desk.

March 20, 1862

Dear Sister and Mary Ann,

A miracle has happened! I am a free man, nearabouts, sitting at a desk wearing clean clothes, looking out a second story window of a boarding house in Mound City, Illinois. It's nighttime and the city is lit by gaslights. Since arriving I've had a bath, shave, haircut, and a hot supper! I'm as snug as a bug.

How, you must be wondering, has this come to be? I assure you that I am of sound mind. The prison commander entrusted me to take care of two wounded comrades who are here at a Union hospital. I'm unguarded and allowed to walk the streets like a free man. I have no idea where I'll be sent next, but for now I have money for food, and a dry, warm bed to sleep in.

My soul is weary from all that has passed since leaving home, so I will end this letter now and blow out the candle. I shall post it first thing tomorrow and hope that it makes its way to you quickly.

I miss you both! Anderson — P.S. the next page is for Henrietta.

Dear Henrietta,

I imagine you're a couple inches taller than when I last saw you. I'm a couple of inches shorter — just kidding. Your mother's going to need extra help this season with planting and weeding. I know those aren't your favorite things, but it's especially important that you help more while your father and I are away. Think of yourself as Mama's special helper. You can do that because you have a heart of gold!

I am still in Illinois. Have your mother show you on the map. I'm tending to two comrades who are sick. When I return, I'll read to you at bedtime again and things will be back to normal.

Love, Uncle Andy

In the morning, I left the letter with the clerk along with one that Dallas had given me to mail to his mother.

At the café I had breakfast of eggs and ham, biscuits with gravy, and flapjacks with butter, sorghum and coffee for twenty-five cents. About mid-morning, I went to the hospital to check on Frank and Thomas. They were most interested to hear about my adventures in the city and they appreciated the newspapers. Both said Doctor Andrews was kind and they were getting better food.

A daily routine was established. Andrews and I had worthwhile conversations after I checked on the men. In the afternoons, I walked the city streets and took advantage of the newspapers. I spoke as little as possible, for I was afraid that my Mississippi accent would make me stand out like a peacock in a pigpen.

I read an account of an unusual naval battle in the James River near Hampton Roads, Virginia. The South salvaged a steam frigate from the Norfolk navy yard and renamed it the *Virginia*. They removed the wooden upper hull and covered it with iron plates. The *Virginia* attacked the Union fleet off Newport News and destroyed two warships, the *Cumberland* and the *Congress*. The *Congress* was a powerful fifty-gun frigate that would normally have been more than a match for the ten-gun *Virginia*. But the *Virginia*, with its new metal sides, was able to withstand the cannon shots while pouring fire into the wooden ships.

A few days later the Union ship *Monitor*, an entirely new type of ironclad that sat low in the water, intervened in the battle. The *Monitor* had a revolving two-gun turret. The newspaper showed a sketch of it. Neither ship was able to destroy the other, so the encounter was inconclusive. The battle of the two ironclads symbolized the whole war effort so far, it seemed to me, fighting but not getting anywhere.

March 28, 1862

Dear Mary Ann,

I do hope you're well and getting along okay under the circumstances. I still find it hard to believe that I'm free to go wherever I want. Today I walked to the place where the Cache River joins the Ohio and found a place to take my lunch. The Ohio was muddy, flowing fast, and busy with boats. About fifteen miles downstream, the Ohio flows into the Mississippi and then it keeps on rolling toward home. There's no fighting here, but the city is alive with signs of the war. The Union repairs their damaged gunboats here.

Thomas and Frank are lucky to be here at the military hospital, even though most of the patients are Yankees. Sickness and war wounds have made ward-mates out of enemies. Sisters from the Order of the Holy Cross at Notre Dame do most of the work of caring for the soldiers and they treat all the wounded alike. Doctor Andrews says the Sisters are the main reason the hospital runs well. I have deep respect for Andrews, taking care of wounded Yankees and Confederates alike. He is truly a Christian it seems to me, being able to forgive and care for others, even his enemy. I am surely not as good a man as he.

I saw a woman today who looked a little like you. She was pulling two children along and they didn't want to be going wherever she was taking them. I'd like to talk to the people I meet but am reluctant to do so for fear of being challenged. On my walk back from the river this afternoon, people passed me left and right. A wise-looking older woman looked me straight in the eye. I think she knows I'm an enemy soldier.

I'm closing for now. I miss you so much and look forward to an extra-long walk in the woods together upon my return. I shall write again tomorrow.

Fondly, Anderson

On the eighth night in Mound City, I dreamed I was picking cotton alone on a hot, cloudless day. Sweat streamed down my forehead and trickled under my clothes like little streams, all the way down to my socks and into my shoes. I stood up to stretch my aching back and heard a faint rumble of thunder in the distance. A waft of cool air rolled across the field. Then a wall of dark blue clouds approached, and rapid lightning strikes peppered the horizon. The wind whipped around me and I was startled by the speed of the approaching storm. The blue wall rolled over itself like the leading wheels of a great locomotive the size of the sky. Leaves were torn from trees and the ground moved under my feet. Bright streaks of lightening knifed the field close by and monstrous thunderclaps hammered the earth one right after another. The wind blew me off my feet and I struggled to get back up.

A brilliant streak of lightning struck a large tree just a few feet away. It was so close the boom of thunder reached my ears the same time as the flash and big strips of bark drifted slowly down to the ground. The thunder rattled my teeth and bones, and cold rain swept over me.

I awoke from the dream quite fearful and found I was sweating profusely and had thrown the covers off. I washed my face in the basin and returned to bed.

The morning after the dream, I checked on Frank and Thomas, but didn't linger to visit with Andrews. Instead, I walked the city to fill my mind with sights and sounds. In the afternoon, the sun finally came out. The foreboding sense of fear from the dream stayed with me all day. That night I read for an hour from the Book of Psalms before sleep.

April 1, 1862

Dear Sister and Mary Ann,

I got a telegram from the Union today. My time as a prisoner out of prison is drawing to a close. I'm to be at the train station a week hence and Frank and Thomas will be coming with me. We're being sent to prison, this time in Alton, Illinois.

I'm grateful to God for the respite, but so dreading what's next. Prison is a harsh and lifeless existence. Frank's injuries are much better, but he's not right in his head. He mumbles to himself at times and can't keep his eyes from shifting around. I'm afraid he may never be as he was before.

On the walk back to my room this afternoon, I passed a factory. Big doors on rollers were open, so I stopped to look inside. There were rows of steam-driven sewing machines and an army of women workers. Children folded canvas tents and loaded them onto pallets for shipment. If only we had this kind of industry in the South!

Last Sunday I attended a Presbyterian Church. The congregation meets in a two-story, red brick building with a white steeple. I sat at the back hoping not to be greeted. The service was much like those at Old Lebanon, but there were way more people than would fit in our church. The sermon was about the special place of the United States in the history of the world and how a Union victory would be a prelude to the millennium. The preacher said that God allowed the heavy Union losses at Bull Run as punishment for the North till slavery was ended for certain. He got himself all worked up trying to convince the congregation. His sermon went long and my mind wandered off, and I got out when they started the closing hymn.

Down at the Ohio, I tossed sticks in the water and watched them float out of sight. I wonder how God can be on the side of the Confederacy and the Union at the same time. Could it be that the preachers on both sides are mistaken?

I'd give anything to be home right now. Blazes, I'd even be glad to pick cotton all day and have my fingers all cut up from sharps. I can see now that I took just about everything that was good for granted. If I'm lucky enough to return, I shall never fret about everyday troubles ever again.

I miss you both, Anderson

On the appointed day, Frank, Thomas and I met Sergeant Baker at the station, and we traveled north by train. Unlike Oliver, Baker was not talkative. The only thing he told us was we would stop in St Louis for a meal. I watched the scenery go by, leafless trees and empty fields. Occasionally the train stopped to let passengers on and off. No one said anything to us, but surely it was obvious that we were Baker's prisoners.

It was dark when we got to the station in St Louis. The smell of factories and smoke from coal fires filled the air and made me cough. The station and streets were lit by gaslights just like in Chicago. Men were going about their business and there were a few horse-drawn carriages. We ate in a café near the station and returned to our car.

Though the surroundings were unfamiliar, I recalled peaceful times at home and drifted off to sleep. I dreamed of being with Mary Ann in the woods at Big Black. She put her hands on my shoulders, pressed her body next to mine and kissed me. I was swallowed up in her warmth and it felt like we were flying. Then suddenly she vanished, and I was left with a great fear that I'd never see her again.

A jolt of the train woke me.

"We're here," Baker grumbled.

He looked bored. I would gladly have talked with him if he had asked, but he seemed altogether content not knowing anything about his prisoners. Frank, Thomas and I walked side-by-side and Baker followed behind.

"Turn here," he commanded.

We turned down a steep cobblestone street and I smelled a river.

"Is that the Mississippi?" I asked.

"Hurry up!" Baker kicked my boot from behind.

We turned east and walked beside a stone wall about fifteen feet high till we came to a gate. The sign over the big doors read — Alton Federal Prison. Baker handed a letter to the guard and turned the three of us over. Knowing the great river was just a few paces away was solace for my soul. *If I escape, I can steal aboard a flatboat, float downstream and be home in a few weeks.* As the guard locked the doors behind us, the sun dropped below the horizon.

Chapter 19

ALTON PRISON
April — September 1862, Alton, Illinois

Unlike Camp Douglas, Alton was a former penitentiary, block buildings with holding cells. I was separated from Thomas and Frank and led down a dark hallway. The nauseating smell of stale piss was overpowering, and I covered my nose. The guard shoved me into a cell, slammed the metal door, and the clang echoed along the hallway. I heard others but couldn't make out the surroundings in the dark and someone pulled me down to a straw mattress.

In the morning, four prisoners sat staring at me.

"What's your name?" a tall man asked, accusingly.

"Anderson ... Anderson Flowers, Mississippi 20th."

"You don't look like a soldier. Where'd ya get those clothes?"

Before I could answer, another man said, "Bet he wrecks Union trains."

"I suspicion he's a spy," another said. "See those fancy shoes. He's a city man."

A guard brought four plates of vittles.

"I guess you ain't havin' breakfast," the tall prisoner glared at me.

117

"Guard," one of the others yelled. "There's five of us now. Got a new one in the night."

There was no answer from the guard, but in a few minutes, he returned with another plate. Over cold beans and a moldy biscuit, I got acquainted with my cellmates. The foursome looked much the same except for height. Each was thin, pale and hollow-faced. I must have looked fat by comparison. They were all from the 13th Tennessee and had defended the breastworks south of Fort Donelson.

"Last week one of the guards beat a boy from Alabama so bad his face is cattywampus," Hank, the tall man, told me.

"Yeah, ya better look out for Buster, he's the worst of the lot."

After eating, we were let out in the yard. The prison ground sloped down toward the river and we could see part of the town in that direction, even with the high walls. The bell tower of a church was visible. Alton was crowded like Camp Douglas, but worse in some ways. Being locked in a cell allowed less freedom of movement and the air was always sour.

More prisoners arrived each day, even though all the cells were already full. The Yanks built more bunk beds, three levels tall, and arranged them along the sides of the hallway. Soon they were full too. I tried to trade places with a newly arrived prisoner in the hallway, but Buster wouldn't let me. He was mean like they said, and he took a particular hostility to me right away. I wondered if he too thought I was a spy.

May 7, 1862

Dear Sister and Mary Ann,

Our bonds are strong and will endure these times apart, I pray. I arrived at Alton prison ten days ago. Two men from the 20th arrived here yesterday from Camp Douglas. They both have dysentery and are thin as fence posts. They told me several from our regiment died after I left Douglas. There are many sick prisoners here too. The Yanks have a quarantine hospital on an island in the river a mile from here to separate the sickest from us healthier ones. I pray I'll never know what the view is like from there. There are women prisoners here too, and men caught spying, burning bridges, and wrecking trains, but most are infantrymen like me captured at the fall of Fort Donelson.

I learned of the terrible battle at Shiloh Church from a newspaper dropped by the guards. The account listed the 5th Mississippi as being among the Southern forces. Have you heard from brother Jesse? I sure hope he was not among the casualties.

We've heard rumors that the generals are arranging for prisoner exchanges. I fervently hope that's true and that I'll be back home soon. In the meantime, I pray that this letter reaches you. Anderson

Piles of shit were scattered around the prison yard and along the sides of the sinks. Hordes of flies feasted on the excrement and lighted on us as we squatted. I gagged every time I used one. As the weather warmed, the stink became unbearable. One sink was filled in with dirt before it was full because black sewage was oozing out of the ground downhill.

In May, a few men from the 14th Mississippi led by a wiry man named Roger, started digging a tunnel under the wall. The crew dug for over two weeks and dropped the dirt in the sinks before a traitor spilled the beans. He turned out to be a young soldier from Alabama named Garrett. I had noticed that he hobnobbed with the guards and seemed to be getting extra food. When Roger and the other tunnel diggers found out it was Garrett, they vowed to hang him if he was ever caught on the outside.

In summer, the cells got extremely hot in the afternoons and men passed out. The prison commander, Colonel Fox, adjusted the schedule and let us stay out in the prison yard longer. We crowded in the narrow shade of the buildings and the prison walls, but there wasn't enough shade for everyone. To make things worse, water ran short. Some days I didn't get enough water to even pee.

Anger grew inside me, but I had no energy to defend my comrades. I learned it was best to obey orders and take the cursing and hard knocks from the guards. I placed my hope in God to deliver us. My Bible was stolen, and I missed finding comfort from it. The best verse I could remember was from Second Peter. "The Lord will reserve the unjust unto the Day of Judgment to be punished." My problem was, I wasn't at all sure I could wait till the Day of Judgment. If I hadn't been so weak, I might have killed a guard to get even.

Buster continued to harass Roger and the other tunnel diggers. Buster was tall and thin, with a brown birthmark on his forehead, and he was meaner and more vicious than the other guards. His most irritating characteristic, however, was his powerful, high-pitched voice. He screamed insults at prisoners, seemingly at random. He even startled the other guards. I think he was not right in the head. I knew in my heart if I ever had a chance at Buster on the battlefield, I would shoot him between the eyes and not feel a thimbleful of remorse.

One evening in early July when we were counted before lock down, Roger was missing. Colonel Fox threw a conniption fit and sent the guards searching everywhere. I was tickled at the idea that Roger might have escaped. He was clever and had a rebellious spirit. At mid-morning the next day, Colonel Fox assembled the whole population, about a thousand prisoners. He addressed us from a stand a few feet higher than the crowd as sunshine bore down upon us.

"A prisoner has escaped," he announced. "Roger Murray. I believe you men from Mississippi know him."

Excited chatter and cheering erupted among the prisoners, then a gun fired from the platform. The men ducked and got quiet. A puff of white smoke rose slowly in the heat. Buster stood with his pistol held up high.

"Any man found to have helped Roger escape will be hanged!" Colonel Fox shouted.

His face streamed with sweat and spit came from his mouth. I felt like laughing at his buffoonery, but dared not. There were no sounds within the prison walls as we stood silently in the blistering sun. We waited to hear what Colonel Fox would say next, then a steamboat on the river let loose a noisy blast of steam and a group of pigeons flew from the roof of the officer's quarters behind the stand.

"I don't think that'll be necessary, Colonel," a loud voice said.

Roger stood in the open doorway of the officer's quarters and stepped smartly down the steps. His hair was combed and he was wearing clean clothes.

"I'm right here Colonel!" Roger said. "No one's escaped, so no one need be hung."

The colonel's face turned red. "Punish this man!" he yelled, his voice cracking with strain. Then he marched off like a pissed off peacock, stomped back to his quarters and slammed the door.

Buster and another guard took Roger by the arms and led him away.

"Jis wanted a good night's sleep in a decent bed!" Roger shouted. "Too much to ask?" The prisoners roared their approval and then dispersed.

I stayed to see what would happen. The guards tied Roger's hands and feet to a pole in the sunshine and took his hat away.

"No one talks to him!" Buster shouted at the prisoners standing nearby. "Anybody talks, I'll strap ya up too."

It was cloudless day and by mid-afternoon Roger's face was burned red.

At twilight, the guards untied Roger, and Buster whacked him with his rifle stock knocking him to the ground. Roger picked himself up and brushed the dirt off his clothes. As a guard took him to his cell, they passed near me. Roger's cheeks and forehead were blistered, and his lips cracked and bleeding, but somehow, he managed to wink at me. I couldn't believe he still had fighting spirit after the beating and a day in the sun.

I was brimming with hate for Buster. I'd never met such an evil soul. He was so vicious and unpredictable even the other guards hated him. That night I recalled a story from the Book of Matthew, the question asked of Jesus about how many times to forgive a brother when you've been sinned against. Jesus told them, not until seventy times seven.

My blood boiled as I schemed ways to get back at Buster. I decided I'd steal a knife, slit his throat, and leave him on the ground to bleed out. I prayed for Roger's healing and asked God to tame my anger before it got me in the same trouble as Roger, or worse. The next morning, God had not relieved my anger one bit and I couldn't forgive. More than anything in the world, I wanted to kill Buster. *Dear Jesus, your instruction is too difficult.*

By the end of July the prison population had swelled to twelve hundred. Green flies feasted on excrement and landed on our heads, faces and food. The hallway echoed with coughing each morning. When I arrived at Alton, rats were seen in twos and threes. By summer, dozens shared the cells with us, so I slept with my boots on and my hat over my face.

July 25, 1862

Dear Sister and Mary Ann,

My heart is filled with anguish and my burdens are too heavy to bear. I'm not sure I'll make it out of here alive. Last week, two men from Mississippi died from smallpox. My trousers no longer stay up even though my belt is as tight as it will go. I doubt if I could drag a bale of hay in my present condition.

I'd rather be fired at by a whole company of Yankees than to spend one more day in this hell hole of filth and sickness. My heart has become hard with hate. I'm going to find a way to get out of here ...

I stopped writing and tore up the letter. There was nothing to write about that wouldn't frighten the women to death. Besides, our letters were probably not leaving prison headquarters. From that point on, I quit writing letters and kept notes for myself instead.

Life as a prisoner gave me much time with my own thoughts. Not having Dallas or Amos to talk with made the hours drag on. It may seem strange to hear, being cramped in a cell with six others, but I felt utterly alone during the months at Alton. The men like Roger who plotted escape by hook or crook were the most hopeful among us. I couldn't bring myself to join them, but their courage and resourcefulness inspired me to hang on.

Prison helped me learn to concentrate my thoughts. I thought a lot about what I had been taught in church and at home and how that squared with my war experiences. The guards searched our cells regularly, so I kept my notes hidden in my pockets. I tried hard to shake the feeling of defeat and worried about spending the rest of the war rotting away in prison. My goal, to get out alive and unhurt, was foremost in my mind at all times.

In late August, my cough got worse. Instead of getting out in the yard with the others, I spent two days in the cell sleeping. In the afternoon of the second day, I heard thunder nearby and then a rush of rainfall on the roof. Later I awoke from frightful dreams and my cellmates were back inside.

Finally, a ray of hope came upon us. In early September, Sergeant Lewis, a Yankee I'd befriended, pulled me aside.

"I hear tell there's gonna be an exchange of prisoners," he whispered.

"When? I gotta get outta here."

"Two hundred names will be picked."

"Can you get my name on the list?"

"Jis be out here early tomorrow mornin' at the platform."

"You're not pullin' my leg, are ya?"

Lewis looked at me and winked.

"Much obliged to ya, Sergeant."

The next morning my comrades and I went to the yard in front of headquarters. At nine o'clock, Sergeant Lewis gathered the prisoners around the headquarters stand and read two hundred names out loud. Roger and I were among the lucky ones, along with my mates from Camp Douglas. Lewis announced that we would be going home on flatboats and two hundred Yankee prisoners being held in Belle Isle, Virginia would be released at the same time and transported back North. That's how the exchanges worked. After seven and a half months as a prisoner, my prayers were finally answered. I went to thank Lewis, but he turned his back and walked away.

I lay awake for hours that night as my mind raced about. The nightmare of prison would soon be over.

Chapter 20

OLD MAN RIVER

September 1862, Alton, Illinois to Jackson, Mississippi

The next morning, two hundred lucky men lined up to leave for the river. Buster came over to me and my heart sunk.

"Gimme your watch!" he screamed.

"You have no right."

He slapped my face.

"Now!" he demanded and pressed his pistol against my forehead.

A Yankee officer stood by, but did nothing to intervene, so I gave Buster my father's pocket watch. He dropped it to the ground, stomped it with the heel of his boot, and screamed, 'you bastard, you bastard,' over and over. The lid broke off and the glass was crushed to smithereens. Pieces lay scattered in the dirt. The column began to move, and Frank pulled me back in line. I bit my lip and followed the man in front of me, praying that Buster wouldn't pull me out. I vowed to take out my anger when I had a loaded rifle in my hands again.

Frank, Thomas and I boarded a southbound Yankee flatboat. Several hundred men were crowded below deck sharing stale air. I was fuming mad about Father's watch, but jubilant about going home. Everybody was eager to see their families. The rush of joy after months of misery was stronger medicine than a shot of red eye.

During our first night downriver, I heard a woman squealing. It was impossible to see in the dark, but from the sounds I guessed what was going on. Somebody had smuggled a hooker on board and she was being passed around.

My mind raced and I couldn't get back to sleep. *Will there be news about Dallas, Eugene or Jesse?* The pulse of the steam-driven pistons and the steady thrashing of the paddlewheel finally calmed my mind and I fell asleep.

In the morning, the guards let prisoners trade places with those above. It was drizzling, so I took a place on the downwind side and watched the riverbank slide by. We passed fields of corn and beans, and grazing cows. Boys fished from the bank and some waved. I took the clean air deep in my lungs and promised God and myself I would never again take freedom for granted.

I went on deck each morning and viewed our progress down the Mississippi. The muddy, swirling water couldn't go fast enough for me. On the third day, a large river joined from the east.

"What river's that?" I asked a guard.

"No idea."

Only then did it occur to me that he might be as far from his home as I was from mine.

"I reckon you're all juiced up about bein' set free," he said.

"You're sure as shootin' right about that!"

The next day I shouted at some townspeople, "Where are we?"

"Wickliff, Kentucky," an old man hollered back. "Where you men headed?"

"Mississippi. Goin' home!"

This was how we kept track of progress.

On the morning of the twelfth day on the steamboat, I heard the peal of church bells, *bong-bong, bong-bong, bong-bong,* and then the cheers of prisoners on deck.

"Must be Vicksburg," one soldier yelled. "Ringin' bells for us!"

The boat came alive with excited voices and the guards looked nervous and ready to react if rushed. The serpent had awakened. I asked an officer what date it was.

"Sunday, September 21st," he said. "Hope ya enjoyed the journey."

"Beats hell outta prison!"

"Hope we don't meet again."

"That makes two of us."

We were met at the dock by Confederate officers who told us we would be rejoining the army at Jackson.

"Surely they'll give us furlough," I said to Frank and Thomas.

"I'm goin' home," Frank said. "I don't care what the officers say, I'm leavin' as soon as my boots touch solid ground."

The two friends split off and headed home.

"See ya in Jackson," I yelled.

I followed the officers through the crowded dockyard to a warehouse packed with soldiers. The sweet smell of tobacco drifted from the doorway. The warehouse was full of lighthearted chatter, men playing poker and twenty-one, and telling stories.

"Company K?" I yelled out.

Amos stood up and yelled back, "That you, Andy?"

I joined a group of thirty or so men sitting together in a corner, laughing, eating, and passing around a bottle of joy juice.

"Do ya know where Dallas and Eugene are?" I asked.

"They weren't on our boat," Amos said, "but there's more a comin'."

"Herbert, James, and John Terry didn't make it," Will said. "Died from illness."

I left the warehouse and returned to the dock to be alone. The flatboat that brought me home turned around in the river and started its journey north. Without a thousand men on board, the hull sat three feet higher in the water. No southbound ships were in sight. I stared at the muddy water and recalled a time when Herbert and I duck hunted together at Apookta Creek. *Never see him again.* My hatred was aroused, and I renewed my vow to get revenge.

An hour later I returned to the warehouse. Men were gathered in groups, reading newspapers. Everyone was hungry for news about the war or anything interesting. The Vicksburg Daily Citizen had an account of a great battle in Virginia, at Manassas Junction, the same place where one of the first battles of the war was fought in the summer of 1861. One hundred twenty thousand men were engaged over three days. It was hard for me to imagine a battle that large. There were massive attacks and counterattacks, and at the end, neither side had managed to dislodge the other.

A soldier threw his newspaper in the air and I caught it and went outside to read by myself. Confederate casualties were estimated at eight thousand, and thirteen thousand Yankees. I slumped beside the brown brick warehouse on the rough deck beams and buried my head in my hands. I remembered the words of Jesus, "For the hour is coming, in which all that are in graves shall hear his voice, and shall come forth; they that have done good, unto the resurrection of life; and they that have done evil, unto the resurrection of damnation." *Surely, we're all goin' to hell.*

127

A hand touched my shoulder. It was Will.

"We're boardin'," he said excitedly. "Come on!"

When we arrived at the trainyard, Lieutenant Oldham stood in the open boxcar door, in full uniform, smoking a cigar. We climbed in and the train headed east toward Jackson. Oldham and our other officers had been in two prisons, Camp Chase in Columbus, Ohio first and then Johnson's Island in Lake Erie. They had been released in an exchange a month earlier and waited in Vicksburg for our return.

Oldham addressed us. "Welcome home, my fine soldiers!"

Cheers went up from the men.

"I know you've been through hell since Donelson and lost friends along the way, but I'm awfully glad to see you fellows."

"Glad to see you too, sir!" Will yelled out and the men cheered again.

"I have somethin' important to tell ya," Oldham resumed.

The men settled down.

"Back in April when we were all prisoners, our government adopted a conscription law. The law makes all men between eighteen and thirty-five subject to military draft. Since y'all volunteered, you're under no obligation to fight. You are free to return home if you choose. Those who do reenlist will be part of Loring's division in Joseph Johnston's army."

The train went round a bend and the men held on to each other to keep from falling.

"I hope you'll reenlist because the Confederacy needs ya. The plan is to gather in Jackson for a few days while the rest of the 20th returns."

"Lieutenant," Will asked. "What'll we do while waitin'?"

"That's where the good news comes in. Every man who reenlists today will be issued ten-day permits to visit families!"

The men cheered.

"Anyone who does not return on time will be considered a deserter," Oldham said sternly. "And ya know what happens to deserters, right?"

The men nodded.

"When'll we be resupplied?" Amos asked, holding up his bare foot.

The group laughed again.

"When ya get back we're gonna get ya all fixed up, I promise. You'll have new shoes, uniforms and rifles ... Springfield 1861s!"

The news stirred great excitement among the men. Springfields were the latest long-guns with rifled barrels. A good marksman could hit a target at five hundred yards with a Springfield and the Yanks already had them. The smoothbores we'd been using were accurate only up to about seventy yards.

"Where'd ya get the rifles, Lieutenant?" Amos asked.

"You can thank our raiders. They stole a whole train load from the Yanks in Virginia."

There was more laughter among the men.

A tall man in the back yelled out, "The uniforms aren't stole too, are they?"

Oldham chuckled along with the group and then continued.

"When we get to Jackson, go see the orderly sergeant for your back pay and permits. I hope to see ya back in ten days."

He saluted smartly and we returned the salute.

Two hours later, I had reenlisted for the duration and had ten months pay in my pocket. I caught the next train to Durant, arrived late afternoon and started the walk home under a blue sky.

Chapter 21

TEN DAY PERMIT

September 1862, Mississippi

On the walk home, a towering cloud formation approached from the east and thunder rumbled in the distance. I passed a farm where two slaves were picking pole beans in a hurry. The wind grew cooler and thunder more distinct. I imagined my homecoming. Henrietta would run to greet me, and I'd pick her up and swing her in circles till we got dizzy. Sister's hug would bring tears to my eyes and I'd be lost in Mary Ann's warm touch.

A dole of doves kicked up from behind a fencerow and darted off toward the piney woods. My boots stirred up dust and I recalled the day Dallas and I walked to Kosciusko to join up. Fifteen months later, I was returning as a fighting soldier and former prisoner of war without my best friend. A wave of fear crashed over me knowing I'd be back in the hornet's nest of the war soon. I sat in the dirt and covered my face. More than likely I'd killed men. *Will anyone find me honorable with blood on my hands?*

The clop of horseshoes stirred me out of my worries. A boy on horseback came toward me, slowed and stopped a few feet away.

"Hey, Mister. You a soldier?"

"Yep. Just outta prison."

"Where's your rifle?"

"I've been in prison, silly."

"Why aren't ya wearin' a uniform?"

"Never had one."

"What kinda army is that?"

"Good question."

"Are ya a shirker?" he said. "You sound like Freddy. He tells people things that ain't true."

"I'm no shirker! I've been fightin' the Yanks and let me tell ya they're armed to the teeth."

"Okay then," he said. "Are ya hungry?"

"Sure am. Got somethin' to eat?"

"My momma's makin' supper right now. Why don't ya come eat with us?"

"I don't wanna be any trouble."

He waved his arm. "Get on."

He turned the horse around and patted its hindquarter.

Along the way, the boy told me his name was Tommy.

"I'm fourteen," he said proudly. "Man of the house. Three more years and I'll be a soldier too."

"Your daddy off to war?"

"Yep. Gone more'n a year now."

"Bub and sis?"

"Nope. Just Momma and me. Did ya shoot any Yankees?"

"Yep, I did."

"Did y'all win?"

"Nope. We lost. Our force was surrounded, and our generals surrendered us while we were sleepin'. The Yanks put twelve thousand of us on paddlewheel boats and took us up North to prison."

We rode along in silence for a while. I prayed that the war would be over and done with way before Tommy was old enough to fight. *It couldn't possibly last that long, could it?*

We arrived at a house with vegetable gardens on both sides and a barnyard with noisy chickens and pigs out back. Tommy's mother came out to meet us.

"Who'd ya bring home tonight?" she said, sheltering her eyes from the late afternoon sun.

"This here's Andy Flowers. Comin' home from a Yankee prison."

"Welcome, Mr. Flowers. I'm Cecilia Nichols. Come on in and join us."

She was short and pretty like Mary Ann, with a bounce in her step and clear-cut confidence.

"Take off your boots and wash up," she said. "Tommy'll show ya the washroom."

Being inside her house reminded me of the confines of Alton prison, but the smell of supper cooking settled me down and got my mouth to watering.

"Tell me about the fightin'," Tommy said eagerly.

"Now don't pester him," Cecilia said. "Let him say what he wants to."

"I'd really like to hear about how life's goin' here at home, tell ya the truth," I said. "How're y'all faring?"

"You saw the gardens," she said. "We're keepin' up purty well. Just a lot more pickin' and chores without menfolk. And can't get no money for cotton anymore, so we're not plantin' much next season."

"Are ya really a soldier?" Tommy asked, looking me over. "You got no rifle … ya got no uniform … and ya don't wanna talk about the war. How do I know you're a real soldier?"

"Tommy," Cecilla said. "I told ya not to pester him!"

"It's okay, Ma'am. I'd be curious too if I was fourteen and my daddy was away."

"Jis tell me one thing about soldiering," Tommy demanded.

"Okay, I'll tell ya two. The thing a soldier does most is hoof it from place to place. And often when ya get where you're going, the generals decide they want ya to go back where ya were before. And the second thing a soldier does a lot of is wait for somethin' to happen."

"That's not very excitin'. Tell me one more thing."

"Okay, but ya might not like what I have to say."

"Tell me anyway."

"War is bad business. Not enough tents and blankets to go around and I've been wearin' these same clothes for months. We drink dirty water, eat stale bread, and rarely take a bath. Ya wanna hear more?"

He nodded yes.

"We sleep in the rain, burn up in the sunshine, freeze in the winter and go hungry most days."

He looked disappointed, but I continued.

"I recommend ya forget about ever bein' a soldier!"

Tommy sat quietly and finished his supper while Cecilia and I talked. It was good to hear a woman's voice.

When we finished, I said, "Thank ya, Ma'am. You're so kind to feed me. I'll be on my way now."

"Nonsense," she said. "It's gonna rain."

"Home is only an hour away."

"You'll sleep here tonight and go home in the mornin'. Tommy'll show ya the barn."

She waved the two of us outside, making clear it wasn't going to be any other way.

Tommy took me to the barn and rustled up a nice pile of straw.

As he turned to leave, I said, "I've got somethin' for ya. Close your eyes and hold out your hand."

I placed a scratched-up three-ring bullet in his palm and he opened his eyes wide. "Where'd ya get it?"

"That was fired in a battle at Gauley Bridge, a place in Virginia. It came to rest by my boot. I figured it might've been meant for me, so I kept it for good luck. It's about the only thing they didn't steal from me in prison."

Tommy put the bullet in his pants pocket.

"Thanks, Mr. Flowers."

"Do me a favor. In the mornin', tell your momma thank you for me. I'm gonna get an early start."

"Will do."

"And one last thing, Tommy. Don't daydream 'bout bein' a soldier. It's better to stay and help your momma. I'm sure your daddy'll be proud of ya when he gets home."

Tommy walked slowly toward the cabin. He paused at the back door and saluted, and I waved back. Rain began to fall as I settled in the straw.

Chapter 22

HOMECOMING

September 1862, Attala County, Mississippi

A rooster woke me and all was quiet at Cecilia's house. I gathered my things and walked into the early light. The storm had passed, and the air was moist and cool. A half hour down the road, the morning sun touched my shoulders and I felt renewed and hopeful.

Near Sister's cabin, I hid in the woods and whistled a phrase of *Camptown Races*. The screen door propped open a bit and Henrietta poked her head out. I whistled again and she came out on the porch.

"What're ya waitin' for?" I yelled.

"Uncle Andy!" she screamed and ran to me.

I swooped her up in my arms and we swirled around and around.

"You're home! You're home!" she squealed.

Sister met us at the door and we hugged while Henrietta danced about the cabin singing, "Uncle Andy's home! Uncle Andy's home!"

"Where's Eugene?" Sister asked, fear in her eyes.

"He's fine."

"Has he been exchanged?"

"I'm pretty sure. I was released from Alton and he was still at Camp Douglas as far as I know, but the Yanks are lettin' the whole bunch go."

Henrietta hugged my leg.

"Daddy's comin' home?"

"I'm not sure when he's comin' home, but I b'lieve he's okay."

"Ya hungry?" Sister asked.

"Sure am. Been eatin' locusts and honey for days."

She laughed. "Good to see ya haven't lost your humor."

I followed her to the new kitchen and told them about the visit with Cecilia and Tommy while she started fixing food.

"The army's reorganizin' at Jackson," I said. "I've gotta be back in nine days."

"Then let's make the most of each one. I wanna invite Mary Ann over. You'd like that too, right?"

"I'd be mighty glad to see her!"

"And invite her mother, of course," Sister continued. "We'll all go to church and everybody'll be there. They'll be so glad to see ya! Emily has a new baby boy, about four months now. She'll be happy to see ya too. And next week we'll invite everybody over and have a big dinner out in the side yard. You'll help me get things ready, won't ya? And we should roast a hog. You'll butcher it, right?"

"Slow down Sister. Your mind's runnin' like a racehorse. I've only been home five minutes."

"Can I go invite Mary Ann now?" Henrietta asked, jumping up and down.

"Yes, you may," Sister said. "Tell her to come for supper tonight, but don't tell her Uncle Andy's home. Let's make it a surprise."

"I wanna tell her, I wanna tell her!" Henrietta pleaded.

"Alright, that'll be okay."

Henrietta raced out, banging the door behind.

"Sit down and catch me on the latest," I insisted.

We sat in rocking chairs on the porch and talked non-stop for half an hour. She did most of the talking and her voice was music to my ears.

"Tell me about the war," she said. "And prison, 'fore Henrietta gets back."

I swallowed hard and tears came to my eyes. She took my hands in hers and rubbed the backs.

"I have nightmares every night and a froze-up stomach. At Fort Donelson, a man I knew got shot in the ..." I stopped short.

She got up and walked into the sunshine in the front yard and faced away with her arms crossed. The way she stood reminded me of Momma.

"It was good to have Dallas with me," I said, "but we've been separated since March. I found men from the 20th in Vicksburg when we got off the flatboat and they told me he's bein' released."

She turned around and faced me. Tears streamed down her cheeks.

"When will it be over, dear brother? When will it be over?" she pleaded.

"I don't know."

We held each other close till calm returned.

"Why don't ya take a nap on the porch swing?" she said, "while I get things ready."

"Sounds splendid, dear Sister."

"Let's play." Henrietta tugged my arm, waking me.

"How long did I sleep?"

"Two hours," Sister answered. "And ya snored like there 'as no tomorrow."

"Did not! You're always the clown … always teasin' me."

"I only tease people I love," she said, smiling broadly.

"Okay young 'un," I said to Henrietta. "Whadda ya wanna do?"

"I'm not a young 'un anymore. I'm eight now! Let's go swimmin'. It's scorchin' hot."

"Okay, we'll be back in a couple of hours," I told Sister.

She smiled over her shoulder.

"I'll get some nice duds out for ya. You wanna get gussied up for Mary Ann, I'm sure," she tossed me a lump of soap. "Take this with ya. You need a real good clean up! I'll have some hot water ready when ya get back so ya can shave."

"Got it, Sister. Always lookin' out for little brother. Appreciate ya."

"Let's go, Uncle Andy! Time's wastin'."

Henrietta grabbed my hand and pulled me outside. "I know how to swim good now. Momma taught me."

Henrietta and I splashed and played, and then I got all scrubbed up in the creek. Back home I got a good shave.

"Well you look right smart," Sister said.

"It's amazing what hot water, soap and a razor will do. Help ya set the table?"

"No. You may not!" she winked. "You need to start over to Mary Ann's. Henrietta'll help me."

The dirt road looked wavy in the bright sunlight as I passed our cotton field, half-picked. Sister hadn't told me there was more to be done. I hugged the shady side trying to stay out of the sun. Dragonflies buzzed up and down the lane and honeybees tended the flowers along the sides. Where the lane turned into the woods, the crickets got going and the breeze carried the sweet smell of pine. I felt at peace for the first time in a long while.

At Brice's Corner, Mary Ann carried a basket. She wore a blue dress and had pink ribbons in her hair. My stomach was full of butterflies and I was on fire.

"Just who I've been waitin' for!" she smiled as we came together.

I pulled her up close and said, "You're beautiful!"

I kissed her lips, then her neck and started down her shoulder.

She whispered in my ear, "Happy to see me?" I felt her hot breath and asked, "Still feel like a girl?"

"What da ya mean?"

"Now that you're seventeen, you look like a woman to me."

She flashed an inviting grin, then reached up and touched my ear.

"What happened?"

"A bullet nipped me," I laughed and thanked God once again for the good fortune of a one-inch difference.

We held hands as we walked back and had just a little time to catch up before we got home. As we neared the cabin, I finally asked, "I want us to go for ..."

"A walk in the woods?" she finished my sentence.

"Yep." I said. "Got some things I wanna ask ya."

"Let's do that tomorrow," she said with a seductive smile. "It's family time now."

Henrietta ran down the lane toward us.

"I took Uncle Andy swimmin' this afternoon!"

"Did ya now?" Mary Ann said.

"Yeah and I showed him how I can swim all the way across and back."

She beamed and her pigtails bounced.

Our foursome had corn on the cob, turnip greens, fried rabbit and biscuits with butter and jelly, a great supper.

"You sure are eatin' slow," Henrietta said to me.

"Tastes too good to hurry."

"Didn't they feed ya in the army?"

"Not very often, to tell ya the truth."

We managed to keep the conversation mostly about life in Mississippi instead of the war. After dinner, Mary Ann pulled a pumpkin pie out of her basket.

"I haven't tasted pie in a coon's age," I said.

"Well ya wanna just look at it or eat it?" she asked.

We all laughed, dug in and enjoyed the sweet pie together. As the women cleared the table, I lit candles and we sat in rocking chairs and talked.

"You know when Eugene and Dallas'll be home?" Mary Ann asked.

"They should be back soon, if not already. Most likely they're headed to Jackson."

"Wouldn't it be great if they could be here when we butcher the hog?" Henrietta asked.

"That'd make things just about perfect," Sister added.

We talked a little bit more and then Sister asked me to play the violin.

"Been keepin' it right here for ya," she said, patting the wood chest.

"I'm a bit rusty."

"Now don't go tellin' me that. Your letters said you'd been playin' in camp. Play that first tune Father taught ya."

"Please, Uncle Andy," Henrietta pleaded. "You play and I'll dance. And Momma and Mary Ann'll sing."

"Sounds like you've got it all figured out, Miss Henrietta."

We played and sang, and Henrietta danced circles around us in the yellow candlelight. I felt like the luckiest man in the world to be home enjoying an evening with my loved ones, without a thing to worry about.

"I'd better get home," Mary Ann said.

"I'll walk ya," I said.

"I'll walk ya too," Henrietta added.

"I need ya to help clean up," Sister told Henrietta.

"Do I have to?"

"Yes. We'll be seein' a lot more of Mary Ann the next few days, I'm sure."

Sister winked at Mary Ann and me.

The next day I helped Sister pick cotton, clean the barn and cut firewood. There was much to do around the farm, and it felt real satisfying to work with my hands again.

About noon Mary Ann arrived with a package under her arm.

"What ya got?" I asked.

"No questions allowed," she said. "Are ya keepin' your promise, or not?"

She put the package on the table.

I turned to Sister and said, "We're headed for …"

"I know where you're goin'," she interrupted. "See y'all when ya get back."

As we headed off, I took Mary Ann's hand in mine. It felt delicate and warm. As soon as we were out of sight from the cabin, I took her by the waist and pulled her to me. She put her arms around my neck, and we kissed deeply.

"I've missed you so much, Mr. Flowers."

"How much?"

She pressed her body into mine and pushed us up against a fence post. In a few minutes she pulled away and studied me. Her neck and ears were pink and her lips shiny.

"That much!" she said.

I was speechless.

Our favorite place was just west of the Big Black, a section of tall oaks with dogwoods underneath. Two years before, we made chairs out of pines we sawed up and lashed together. When we came nigh, our chairs were leaned up against the twin-trunk oak tree right where we left them. We sat in the deep shade of the woods for a couple of hours, enjoying the cool and each other's company. After a while I got up my courage.

"There's a nice little parcel of land over by Sallis," I said.

She looked at me. "Since when you been lookin' for land, Mr. Flowers? I thought ya were fightin' a war?"

"Just 'cause I've been gone, doesn't mean I'm not plannin' ahead, is all."

"What kinda plans ya talkin' about?"

My throat was choked up, so it took me another minute before I could speak.

"I think it'd make a right nice family farm. It's close to Apookta Creek."

Mary Ann sat looking toward the river as a squirrel hopped along the ground. Her loose hair curled around her face.

"Are ya askin' what I think you're askin'?"

I moved to my knees in front of her and held both her hands.

"I'm very fond ... when we're together ... I feel butterflies ..." I couldn't finish a sentence.

"You'd like me to marry ya?" she asked.

"Well, yeah. That's the question I'm leadin' up to."

She pulled me up and we stood face to face.

"Will you marry me?" I asked.

She waited a few seconds and then said, "Oh, I'll have to think on that."

She let go of my hands and looked down at the ground. My heart dropped. It took more courage for me to ask her than to walk into a hailstorm of bullets.

I turned her face up. Her dark brown eyes were wet with tears. She stood on her tiptoes, kissed my lips, and rested her head on my chest. Her arms encircled me and she squeezed so hard my breath went out.

"I guess that means yes?" I said.

"Yes, it means yes, you bull!"

She smiled and we kissed again. Tears ran down her cheeks.

"Why are ya cryin'?" I said.

"Because I'm happy, ya silly man."

I picked her up and swung her around till we got dizzy and fell to the ground. I had never, ever been happier to hear the word yes.

"When did ya decide to ask me?" she said.

"Remember the first time I walked ya home after church?"

"I was twelve!" She laughed.

"I'm tellin' ya the truth."

We rolled in the leaves and came to a stop. A cardinal lit close by, saw us and then flitted away. Mary Ann's pink lips were just inches away.

"When did ya start havin' feelings for me?" I asked.

"Remember that time we were swimmin'? And others were around, but you were chasin' after me?"

"No, I don't remember that at all."

She popped me on the shoulder.

"You do too!" she insisted.

"Of course I remember, girl. I knew ya cottoned to me. I've been sparking ya a long time and you know it!"

Knowing that Mary Ann felt the same about me as I felt about her was heavenly. We lay in the leaves, sweet talked and pressed our bodies close. After a half-hour she got quiet and looked sad.

"What's wrong?" I asked. "Have ya changed your mind?"

"No, but I don't want ya to go back. Why don't ya jis stay?"

"If I stay, they'll come after me. They shoot men for desertin'."

"Well that don't make any sense at all," she said, pounding my chest. "Shootin' a man for desertin'? Either way the army's got one less soldier!"

I pulled her close and took in her fragrance.

"You're right," I said. "You're right. There's a lot about war that makes no sense."

I looked up and saw clouds that took the shape of a cabin.

"Look," I pointed. "There's our new house."

She looked at the clouds and then back at me.

"You better promise me you'll keep safe and come home in one piece. You promise?"

"I'll do my best, woman."

We squeezed together so close there was no space in between and rocked back and forth. I felt her warm breath in my ear. *Dearest Mary Ann.*

When it was time to head back, I took out my pocketknife.

"What do ya need that for?" she asked.

"Come with me."

We picked a beech tree on a high bank of the river and carved our initials in the smooth, gray bark.

Back home, Henrietta asked Mary Ann, "What's in the package?"

"It's for Andy. He'll open it."

She smiled and I opened the brown paper and unfolded a red, brown and green shirt made of flannel, a beautiful shirt for cold weather. I held it up to my chest to show the ladies.

"Thank ya, Miss Mary Ann! You're quite the seamstress. The fellows in Company K will be right jealous."

On Sunday, Mary Ann and her mother Miriam came to Sister's and the five of us walked to Old Lebanon Church, about two miles. Preacher Small greeted us at the door.

"Good to see ya, Andy. Keep up the good fight."

"Not sure I'd call it good," I said.

Preacher Small either didn't hear me or pretended he didn't hear me. He'd already turned his attention to others.

John and Ellen appeared in the distance and I ran to meet them.

"Mighty good to see ya, little brother," John said.

"Let's see who ya got there!"

"You can hold her," Ellen said as she handed me their six-month old daughter Lilly.

"I wanna talk with ya later," John said, sounding serious.

Thomas and Elga were the only other grown men at church that day. They were both too old to fight but were good about helping on neighbor's farms. Dennis was there, too, and he thanked me for letting him use my shotgun. All the ladies and children swarmed around me. I was the first of their soldiers to make it home from prison and was treated like a hero. I was not used to that much attention and certainly didn't feel like a hero.

Elizabeth, the preacher's wife, played the piano and the congregation got settled in. We sang all the verses of three hymns to get started. Preacher Small took his text from Ephesians 6:5. "Servants, be obedient to them that are your masters according to the flesh, with fear and trembling, in singleness of your heart, as unto Christ."

His sermon was about how the South was an uncommonly Christian nation. He talked about Southerners recognizing their dependence upon God and contrasted that with what he called the godless government of the North. I hadn't heard him take that perspective before the war, but it sounded similar to things our chaplains were saying. Small's sermon also reminded me of a speech by the governor of Mississippi I read in the Jackson newspaper and I wondered if he had read it too. Small went on too long and my thoughts drifted to what war was actually like. I missed Dallas, Eugene and my comrades, and hadn't seen my brother Jesse since he left to join the 5th Mississippi a couple of months before I volunteered. They'd been fighting over in Virginia.

Preacher Small concluded his final prayer with the words, "Lord, protect the Confederate States and give us victory over our enemies. Amen."

After church the little kids joined us under the shade trees, where we drank tea and lemonade and talked. John stood beside me, unusually quiet. Suddenly Dennis walked away from the group and ran down the lane a ways.

"Eugene?" I heard Dennis yell. "That you?"

"None other!" a familiar voice shouted.

Eugene, in dirty, torn clothes from prison, walked slowly toward the church. Sister and Henrietta hugged him, and everybody welcomed him home. He looked thin and tuckered out, but happy. It was mighty good to see him unhurt and in decent spirits.

I asked Eugene about Dallas. He told me that Dallas was in the last group to be released. The Yankees exchanged all prisoners from Camp Douglas and there were not enough boats to bring them all home at once. After visiting a while, we agreed we would all gather at Sister's on Tuesday for a family dinner. On the walk home, Eugene handed me a newspaper. The headline read, *Major Engagement at Antietam: Twenty-Two Thousand Casualties.*

"Bad news?" Mary Ann asked me.

"Just more fightin'," I said. "More fightin'."

At home, Eugene got cleaned up and took a nap while Sister put the rest of us to work getting things ready for the feast on Tuesday.

"Can I help Uncle Andy with the hog?" Henrietta asked her mother.

"If it's okay with him, it's okay with me."

"You sure ya wanna help?" I asked.

"Yep. I'm learnin' how to do everything."

"Okay then. Go get the big washtub, a bucket, the butcher knife and saw. I'll call ya in a few minutes."

I loaded Father's pistol, went to the woods behind the house and called the hogs. They hurried up to me like it was feeding time. I slipped a rope around a brown sow's neck, led it over behind the barn and the others wandered away. The bullet severed its spine and death was instant. The hog lay still on the ground at my feet, a dark hole in its neck. I closed my eyes and Jack's blasted face appeared. It took a minute to steady myself.

"Henrietta ... time to help!"

She came running out the back door with the knife, saw and bucket.

"Where's the washtub?"

"Oops. Forgot."

In a minute, she returned.

"Ya ever seen this done?"

"No, but I'm not skerry of blood."

I lashed the hind legs together, ran the loose end of the rope through a block and tackle pulley that hung on a large limb, and pulled. The furry, brown body swung back and forth a bit.

"Do pigs have souls?" she asked.

"I don't rightly know. Maybe that's a question you should ask Preacher Small."

"I think they do," she said.

She took the knife and started cutting.

"Looks to me like you've done this before."

"I watched Dennis clean a deer last winter and he let me help."

Soon we had the hog skinned and then we sectioned the hams, tenderloins, and other cuts, and put the meat in the washtub. We dragged the tub over by the well, rinsed the meat off good with clean water and took it to the kitchen.

"Looky what we did," Henrietta announced proudly.

"Stay and help your mother and I'll go finish cleanin' up."

I took a shovel from the barn and dragged the remains of the hog into the woods. A pair of cardinals flittered away. I dug a three-foot deep hole and buried the waste. A memory flashed back. I looked up from the muddy grave of Lester Stillman, the soldier who died in the flatboat. I saw the church steeple in the rain and heard the steamboat whistle blow three times. *Will these memories haunt me always?*

The sun filtered through the treetops. A gray squirrel in a tall pine barked and fanned its bushy tail in the breeze. I threw a stick in its direction. It ran down a limb, leaped to the next tree, then another and disappeared.

Back at the cabin, I soaked a few hickory sticks in a bucket of water and got a fire started in the smokehouse. Henrietta and I took two pails from the barn and worked the garden rows. We turned enough sweet potatoes for the homecoming celebration. The earth felt warm and good in my hands. Once the fire had settled, we hung the hams and other cuts, added the wet hickory and shut the door tight. Smoke poured through cracks in the shed and the fragrant smell of hickory enveloped the woods and yard.

"Henrietta," I said. "Wanna go campin' tonight?"

"Sure. Can we take poles and fish in the mornin'?"

"Great idea."

Henrietta told her parents about our plans.

"Can I go with Uncle Andy?" she begged.

"That'd be mighty fine with us," her father said. He stood with his arm around Sister's shoulder.

We gathered up our stuff and waved goodbye.

"Y'all have fun now," Sister said.

"Y'all have fun too."

Henrietta and I got back home about eleven the next morning. The air had turned cooler and Eugene and I worked the fields, cut firewood, and repaired the barn roof. It was our next to last full day at home so we tried to get as much done as we could. Working up a sweat felt good.

About two o'clock on Tuesday, John, Ellen and Lilly came over, along with Mary Ann, Miriam, and Dennis.

"Thanks for hostin' the family, Sister," John announced. "It's wonderful to be with all y'all again."

He hugged Sister tight and held on longer than you might expect.

We enjoyed ham, sweet potatoes, green beans, carrots, okra, corn and cornbread together. Normally Christmas was the biggest feast of the year, but that one topped it. Dennis and Henrietta ate quickly and then played kick ball in the lane. When they got good and hot, we sent them swimming, leaving the grownups to talk.

When questions about the war came up, the answers were short and sanitized. Both Eugene and I wanted to put it out of our minds.

Later, when the sun touched only the treetops, John looked over at me.

"When ya headin' back?" he asked.

"Wednesday. My permit's good till Thursday. What about yours Eugene?"

"Same. All permits have the same return day."

I wished John hadn't asked because I didn't want to think about going back. While the women cleaned up and put the food away, we agreed to meet John at the church on Wednesday to say our goodbyes.

"What da ya think?" Eugene asked me. "Any idea where they'll have us fightin' next?"

"I reckon we'll be close to home. With Grant's riverboats threatenin' the Mississippi and all."

"We can fight 'em good here. Our territory."

"Problem is, Grant's got the warships and the blockade in New Orlinz is chokin' us."

"Grant may be the best they've got. Or else he's especially after us Mississippi boys."

John listened but did not speak.

"Come to think of it, you're right," Eugene said. "He captured us at Fort Donelson, he's slippin' up and down Old Man River now like he owns it, and he's tryin' to run us outta our own state."

"Better make the most of the time that's left," I said. "We'll be in a swarm of bullets soon enough."

After that exchange, the conversation turned to more pleasant things, but my mind had moved back to soldiering and the dull ache in my stomach returned. Henrietta and Dennis reappeared from the river and Sister pulled out peach and blackberry pies.

After dessert, Henrietta asked, "Now can we play music and dance? Please!"

Sister went inside and brought the fiddle and bow. John went to the barn and came back with a box for a drum.

"Got your harmonica?" Henrietta asked Dennis. He pulled it out of his pocket and polished it up.

"Play Lorena," Henrietta demanded.

She was attached to songs with sentimental words and "Lorena" was the one she set store by.

We played while the kids danced and the olders clapped and sang.

> *The years creep slowly by, Lorena*
> *The snow is on the grass again*
> *The sun's low down the sky, Lorena*
> *The frost gleams where the flow'rs have been*
> *But the heart throbs on as warmly now*
> *As when the summer days were nigh;*
> *Oh! the sun can never dip so low*

Adown affection's cloudless sky
The sun can never dip so low
Adown affection's cloudless sky.

The lyrics made me laugh and cry at the same time, as always. After a few tunes, the tree frogs cranked up for the evening and the sun melted behind the pines. For one night, our family was filled with peace.

Dennis pulled out a letter from the post office in Durant. It was addressed to Sister from our brother Jesse. Everybody gathered around and she read to us.

August 23, 1862

Dear Sister,

I'm writing from somewhere in middle Tennessee, not exactly sure where. Our army has not been engaged in serious fighting since Shiloh and I'm unhurt. I'm missing all of you terribly and want to be home more than anything.

Very sad news. Bill ...

Sister dropped the letter to the floor and hurried outside, and Eugene ran out after her. John picked up the letter, looked at it and said, "Bill was killed." Bill was our cousin. Our good time together was over.

After clearing the table I walked Mary Ann home.

We lingered at Brice's Corner and a mockingbird kept us company.

"Still keepin' those plans, Mr. Flowers?"

"What plans you talkin' 'bout, Miss Hughes?"

"These plans," she said.

She kissed me full on the lips and pressed her body into mine. I held her tight to my chest where she couldn't see my tears and I felt her heart beating close to mine. I was hard with desire for my lovely Mary Ann. Luck had been with me so far, but once back in the fight, my life would belong to the army again and I'd do whatever the commanders asked. The promise of Mary Ann's love and the hope of our future together overwhelmed me.

"Are you cryin', Mr. Flowers?"

"Tears of joy, Miss Hughes. Tears of joy."

The trill of cicadas buzzed in the woods as we walked down the lane and I wanted to taste her again.

"Wish I could say when I'll be back," I said.

"Pray it'll be real soon. And I'll pray every day God'll protect ya."

Around the corner from her mother's farm, we lingered again. The smell of her hair and skin was magic. I locked my arms together behind her, lifted her up and spun us around. She laughed and looked right in my eyes. I set her down and kissed her again.

"I'll keep my part of the bargain," she said. "Waitin' for ya."

"I'll keep my part too, like I promised."

"What did ya promise, Mr. Flowers?"

"To keep my head low and come home in one piece!"

She laughed again as we stood on the porch. In the lantern light, I saw that her face was streaked with tears.

"Wait here," she said softly and disappeared inside. In a minute, she returned.

"Close your eyes and hold out your hand."

I did as told.

"Okay, open."

A glint of lantern light reflected off the silver pocket watch in my hand.

"I want ya to have it," she said. She squeezed my hand shut. "It's yours now, sweetheart."

She pushed me into the night and shut the door. The watch had belonged to her father.

On the walk back, a pair of hoot owls got to calling back and forth. *Hoot, hoot, hoot, hoot, whoall. Hoot, hoot, hoot, hoot, whoall.* I leaned against a tree and wondered if the owls were courting. The cool of evening settled in the woods and I breathed deep to keep the goodness in my soul.

The next morning Eugene and I said our goodbyes. I stooped down and whispered to Henrietta.

"Got somethin' fer ya. Pick a hand."

She picked the correct hand and I dropped a small pocketknife in her palm.

"It's for carving. I know you'll be careful 'cause I've seen ya handle a butcher knife."

"Thanks Uncle Andy," she said and ran off.

I took Sister in my arms and squeezed her tight.

"There's somethin' for ya in your top drawer," I said. "I'll write as often as I can."

Chapter 23

BROTHER JOHN

October 1862, Jackson, Mississippi

The next morning, Eugene and I met at the church. John sat on the steps with three rolled quilts beside him.

"Thanks for comin' to see us off," Eugene said. "What are those for?"

"For the three of us," John said. "I'm goin' with ya. I'm enlisting!"

"You'd best stay here," Eugene said, "take care of Ellen and Lilly!"

"Nope!" John said as he stood up. "Made up my mind. I'm joinin'!"

I protested too, but John shoved a quilt in my hands and headed off down the road.

"Come on," he yelled impatiently and waved his arm. "Let's get this over with."

The three of us walked toward Durant without further ado.

I was quite stirred up inside about John going to war. Ellen was pregnant when I enlisted, and I was proud of John for staying home. Too many able-bodied men had already left, and conditions were getting worse at home. A sense of foreboding filled me, and I didn't join in the conversation.

"How's Sister doing with you away?" John asked Eugene.

"She's puttin' on a brave face and Henrietta keeps her busy."

We walked along in silence for a while. A cloudbank drifted in from the west and kicked up a little breeze. Eugene stopped and looked at the clouds.

"What's on your mind?" John asked him.

"Rememberin' my first day of trainin'."

"Cannons?"

"Yep. Sergeant Grace poured a pile of black powder on a flat stone and touched it with a smoldering stick. It burned like the dickens and put off furious white smoke, and the air turned sour right quick."

"Was he tryin' to scare ya?" John asked.

"Guess ya could say that. Wanted us to respect the danger. Then he had an experienced crew demonstrate how to load a twelve-pound brass Napoleon."

"How much powder does it use?" John asked.

"Two and a half pounds each shot. We watched 'em load and fire twice, then Sergeant Grace assigned positions and we did the job."

Hearing Eugene talk about cannons stirred up the rumbling in my head and my stomach ached.

He continued, "Our number two man, a fellow named Johnson, cleaned out the barrel with the wormer stick. It's a simple job, but he made one mistake. He gripped the stick with both fists instead of twirling it only with his fingers. The

149

wormer touched some leftover powder and ignited. The stick blew out of the gun and took Johnson with it!"

"Was he hurt?" John asked.

"Broke fingers on both hands! And burned whiskers off his face too!"

Honeybees buzzed the sides of the lane gathering nectar from wildflowers. A thick cloudbank covered the sky and cicadas in the woods cranked up. Doves darted above and stray leaves blew along the lane.

"You had any close ones?" John asked me.

"At Fort Donelson," I said, " an exploding shell blew a six-foot hole right beside our trench."

"What happened?"

"I got a mouthful of dirt and couldn't hear anything for a minute."

We got to Durant in time to catch the afternoon train to Jackson and as soon as we boarded, it started raining. When we arrived, John enlisted. The next morning Lieutenant Oldham gathered the company. Fifty-two of the original seventy-eight were present, plus John and three other new men.

"More palefaces'll be joinin' us later," Oldham announced. "Captain Patterson's home recovering and I've been promoted to take his place."

The men cheered. Oldham was well liked and respected.

"I'm appointing two new sergeants," he said. "John Barrett and Andy Flowers. Sergeant Barrett, your first assignment is to take the four new men under your wing and teach 'em to fire properly and the drills. The quartermaster'll issue rifles and uniforms this afternoon. Be sure ya get all that's comin' to ya. We'll reassemble here at six to meet the other new men."

After he dismissed us, I approached him, surprised to be a sergeant all of a sudden.

"Congratulations, Captain," I said.

"Congratulations to you too, Sergeant. I'm gonna need your help trainin' the other new men."

"You can count on me, Captain."

He smiled, put his hand in his coat pocket, and pulled out a pair of blue sergeant chevrons. "Sew these on your new uniform coat, Sergeant Flowers."

"Thanks, Captain. Is Dallas back?"

"Yep. He got back last night. I sent him to the railyard to escort the new men. Should be back in a couple of hours."

I stood in the quartermaster line with Will and in a half-hour we both had new Springfield rifles, uniforms, caps, and boots. I didn't like the cap, so I gave it back and kept my wide brim.

Will put on his uniform, grinned proudly, and said, "By jiminy! Now we're ready for the Yanks."

We oiled up our new boots inside and out.

"Much better," Will said. "Nice to have soles again, huh?"

"We may as well been barefoot."

We laughed and enjoyed the light moment.

"I'm headin' to the railyard," I said. "Wanna come along?"

"Nope. I'm stayin' here. Goin' to meet Dallas?"

"Yep. Been seven months since I saw him."

I walked slowly, breaking in the shoes and thinking of my dear friend. Soon a group of eight men approached, Dallas leading. We ran to meet each other, hugged mightily, and the men cheered our reunion.

"I 'as worried ya got lost in Mound City," Dallas said.

"I figured your temper got loose and ya whacked a guard!"

He popped the back of my head. "No more worry now. I'm back to make sure ya get through the war in one piece."

"How'd ya get that scar?" I asked, touching his forearm.

"Remember the big, clean-shaven guard at Camp Douglas?"

"The one that didn't like fiddles?"

He nodded. "Yeah, that's the one. After ya left we took to callin' him Skunk behind his back. Skunk and I had a little altercation."

The recruits listened intently as we walked along.

"You had a little what?" I asked.

"A quarrel. Skunk stole our chess set and then a few days later the guards found his pistol in our barracks."

"Did you steal it?"

"I'm not sayin' I stole it and I'm not sayin' I didn't, but Skunk took it out on me."

Dallas held up his arm for all to see. A dark red scar a quarter-inch wide extended the full length of his forearm.

"That's what a Yankee sword'll do if'n ya don't get outta the way quick enough!"

Dallas was a bit of a braggart, so I wasn't sure his story was completely true, but it sure got the attention and respect of the new men.

After supper, we caught up on the last seven months of our adventures and laughed till the wee hours.

"Looks like ya been eatin' more'n goobers lately," Dallas said.

"Yep. I had ten days leave at home."

"Land sakes, buddy. You one lucky dog! I haven't seen my momma in over a year."

"I was fixin' to tell ya, but ya been hoggin' the time with your stories about prison. Hey — 'bout the scar … is that a tall tale?"

"I thought ya knew me better'n that, ole buddy. You know I wouldn't tell a fib." He winked. "Got a question for ya, Sergeant. Do I have to be in your squad?"

I jabbed him in the ribs.

"You're takin' orders from me now, Private Townsend. How else can I make sure ya stay outta trouble?"

I slept well that night and woke the next morning with renewed optimism. I knew nothing of what lay ahead, of course, but believed that whatever happened would be more bearable with Dallas by my side. The next day two letters came for me.

October 10, 1862

Dear Brother,

Your visit home was wonderful for me and it was especially good for Henrietta to be with her father again. It's not fitting for a girl to grow up without her father. After you left, she told me you are her other father. I appreciate the way you encourage her and teach her new things.

The weather's turned a little cooler and the squirrels are non-stop gathering for winter. The work you did to patch the barn is keeping them out of our supplies.

I found the note you left with the money. That's very generous of you! It'll help out a lot next time we buy supplies, but I'd much rather have you here than the money.

Big news! Elizabeth is pregnant again. Since the war started there's not as many children being born for obvious reasons. This one will be her fourth, all under eight. Sure hope she can keep up with them. She's not the most organized, you know. Lucky for her, she gets extra considerations, being the preacher's wife. Old man Wilson brought her a wagonload of firewood, all split, dried and ready to burn.

Henrietta's taking up more chores since y'all visited and acting more grown up. She told me that with y'all away, more of the work needs to be hers. I worry that not having her father all these months is making her sad inside. She spends more time alone reading than before and goes for long walks in the woods by herself. I can only pray that everything will balance out somehow.

Ellen is missing John sorely. He didn't tell her he was going to join till the night before y'all left. He should have at least prepared her better. Surely the army doesn't need every single able-bodied man to win this fight. I worry that the war is changing everyone, soldiers and homebodies. Do be careful. I pray for you every day and trust that it helps.

Love, Sister

P.S. Mary Ann is all smiles and giggles since you left. Are you two making plans?

October 9, 1862

Dearest Anderson,

I've been powerfully lonely without you. Having you and Eugene home perked everyone up. Henrietta was here earlier today and brought over the latest newspaper. It's just awful to read the war accounts. I hope you are keeping your head down like you promised.

Momma gave me the envelope you left. My, my you're a fast mover — once you make up your mind! Before you enlisted, I thought you might ask me, but then when you didn't, I had doubts. Now I'm getting secret notes and we're saving money together for a down payment! By the way, how did you sneak that envelope to mother without me noticing? I thought I had you in my sights the whole time.

It's tempting to tell mother about our plans, and Sister and everyone, but I guess it's best that we keep it between us till you get back for good. I think Momma suspects, but she's good at keeping a secret. If she knew we were planning to marry, she might worry even more. I guess you know this, but Momma thinks you're handsome and I do too.

Since your visit the big news here is that Ned got caught stealing tools from Mr. Simon's store. He broke in on a Sunday, but a traveling salesman who happened to be passing through that day saw Ned and reported to Sheriff Dawson. Once the salesman described Ned, Dawson knew exactly who did the stealing and went over to Ned's to confront him. Ned claimed he hadn't even been to Durant that day, but four new shovels were leaning up against the front of his cabin. He never was the brightest fellow. Dawson locked him up overnight. Mr. Simon decided he would not press charges, so Dawson let Ned go on home with a warning that he was not to set foot in Mr. Simon's store ever again.

I'd better finish up this letter now and get to making supper. I miss you already. We're praying for you from here, but don't forget to pray for yourself. I don't think God would find that selfish in any way, especially since you're in a shooting war.

Love, Mary Ann

October 20, 1862
Dearest Mary Ann,

Thank you for your letter. Your words place me back at home under peaceful circumstances, and home is the oasis every soldier seeks.

My mind is fixed on our plans and that makes me feel like a kite up high. I can picture our new house in my mind, starting our own farm with one mule and building up step by step each year. The dream of being in your arms and living our lives as one is the star that leads me through these trying days.

Some surprising news from here. Oldham is now our captain and he appointed me second sergeant. I'll be paid $17 a month now instead of $11, so that will come in handy for our savings. I'm in charge of a squad, about twenty-five men, depending upon the situation. Dallas is in my squad and John isn't. Oldham trusts me and that helps bring out my best.

We've not engaged the enemy so far but have covered a fair piece looking for them. The scouting reports say Grant is moving forces by land and sending gunboats down the Mississippi toward Vicksburg. Suspect we'll be seeing blue uniforms soon enough.

All my love to you, Anderson

After Dallas and I both caught up on letters, he pointed to his coat collar.

"Ya need to tell the new men," he said.

I shrugged, called the new ones together, and showed them how we wrote our names and hometowns and pinned the paper inside our coats.

"I'm not doing that," Barry said. "Might bring bad luck."

"Do it. Do it now!" I said. "If you're killed, I want to write a proper letter to your family and tell 'em what a brave soldier you were."

He looked forlorn but did as ordered.

Chapter 24

WINTER CAMP
October 1862 — January 1863, Mississippi

Our army moved several times over the next few weeks to block Union forces under General Grant as they advanced upon Vicksburg and not once did we see the enemy. On November 13th, we arrived in Tippah Ford just as a cold front rolled in from the northwest. We camped in the pinewoods bordering the road to have some shelter against the wind.

Most men, including Dallas and me, needed winter coats. Fortunately, we did have new Yankee tents captured by our cavalry raiders. Dallas and I gathered up a good pile of wood and got a hot fire going. That evening we sat by the fire and talked way into the night.

"Reminds me of our huntin' trips," Dallas said.

I looked over and remembered a time when we were eleven, camping in winter when freezing rain fell.

"Remember at Apookta Creek when I showed you my father's watch and …"

"I pulled out my father's stones?" Dallas completed the sentence. We laughed and looked back at the flames.

"Ten years ago," I said. "We're gettin' old." We laughed again.

At first light, the camp was deathly quiet, and my boots were cold and as stiff as boards. The ground and tent were covered with a thin coating of ice and my backbone felt like a cold, iron rod.

Dallas crawled out of the tent and joined me. The pine needles were coated with ice and limbs sagged under the weight. Freezing rain had come quietly in the night. Luckily, we had covered our woodpile with a tarp and were able to get a fire started. We sipped hot coffee and looked at the strange glistening scene. The first breeze of morning stirred the woods and a crinkly sound came from the ice-coated limbs.

We ate our corn biscuits and bacon in a hurry. Other men began to stir, including Irvin whose tent was nearby.

"What's your hurry?" he asked.

Dallas glanced up at the bent tree limbs. There was a sharp crack like rifle fire and a limb broke off and fell heavily to the ground. Then another limb popped and fell, covering the ground with thousands of tiny ice shards. More limbs broke and fell, and we all scrambled to get out from under the frozen pines. Enoch ran back to untie his dog, which he wasn't supposed to have, and got caught under a fallen limb. His buddies rushed over and rescued him. Over the next half hour, dozens of falling limbs doused fires, smashed tents and reduced our encampment to rubble.

Captain Oldham rode up on his horse, joining the men gathered along the road. We heard someone yelling from the woods and two men went back to see. They came back holding James between them.

"What happened to ya?" Oldham asked James.

"Trapped in my tent," he said, clearly in pain. "Limb bruised my leg bad."

"Better get it looked at. And next time, don't oversleep."

The men howled and James forced a smile.

When the bombardment of limbs was over, we packed up and followed Oldham to Canton, Mississippi for the winter. We felled trees and built log huts big enough to hold eight men each. Stones were laid out in rectangles for the foundations. Walls of notched timbers were built up about six feet high, then we stuffed mud between the logs and inside the chimney. We made the roof of sawn boards, and made mattresses by stuffing sheet bags with pine straw. The finished huts were far more comfortable than dog tents. The main drawback was smoke built up inside because the chimneys did not draw well.

We ate fresh meat, walnuts, and boiled acorns from the forest, and occasionally got potatoes, salted beef, cornmeal and peanuts from our supply lines. We would have been fine there all winter, except for lack of proper clothes.

As a sergeant, I led a scouting patrol about every other day, looking for signs of the enemy. About twice a week we got mail and newspapers. There were reports of heavy fighting in Fredericksburg, Virginia in the middle of December. The battle was a Confederate victory, but casualties were in the thousands. I figured I'd met about a hundred and fifty people in my whole life including the soldiers surrounding me. It was difficult to imagine thousands dead, wounded and missing in a single engagement. Being close to home and camped for the winter, we got mail more often. I wrote home most days and got several letters each week.

December 18, 1862
Dear Brother,

Henrietta has been asking about you, so I told her she could put a note in with my letter. She's getting pretty good at writing. Winter has set in hard. Good thing you were here to help with the firewood because we're burning through it fast. Christmas will be sad without you and Eugene. Mary Ann and Miriam are coming over to spend Christmas day with us. When you left to enlist, you promised you'd be home before Christmas. I believed that was folly then. Now I wonder how many Christmases will pass before peace is settled.

Dennis is doing mighty well with your shotgun. He brings us meat about twice a week. Last week he killed a big doe and brought it here on a skid and Henrietta helped him butcher it. We fried some to eat that day and smoked the rest.

Elizabeth is getting bigger. Her baby is expected in March. Some of the ladies at church gossip about her after services. Last Sunday I overheard (I won't say who) saying Elizabeth couldn't handle the children she has already. I put a stop to their yapping and told them to think about how they'd feel if other people were talking about them behind their backs. Some people have a lot of nerve.

I'm going to finish up this letter now. Don't worry on us, we're doing alright. Lord knows you have enough on your heart already. I pray that the good Lord is watching over all of us.

Write when you can. Always good to get your news.

Love, Sister

P.S. Mary Ann, Henrietta and I have been making bandages for the war since you were home. Women from all over are doing this now. When we get a few boxes ready, Dennis takes them over to the train station at Durant where the army collects.

Dear Uncle Andy,

I am writing this letter all by myself. We are doing fine this winter. Staying warm by the fire. One night ice covered the house and garden. Everything. The whole world was covered with glass. I needed to feed the chickens. Momma told me to take little bitty steps. Taking care of them is one of my jobs now. Momma says I am e-centtual. I'm not for sure what that word is, but I think it means important. Of course, I already knew that.

When January comes, I will be back at school.

I miss you, Henrietta

One day in mid-January, after we finished late afternoon drills, the clouds blocked the sun once again and it was hard to warm up. A supply wagon arrived and that perked me up. An orderly handed out the mail and gave the Vicksburg newspapers to Captain Oldham.

"Gather 'round men!" Oldham called out. The company assembled around a big fire in the central space surrounded by our huts.

"Gentlemen," Oldham said. "President Lincoln issued a proclamation and I want everyone to hear it."

A hush settled over the men and Oldham cleared his throat and read aloud.

"That on the first day of January, in the year of our Lord one thousand eight hundred and sixty-three, all persons held as slaves within any State or designated part of a State, the people whereof shall then be in rebellion against the United States, shall be then, thenceforward, and forever free; and the Executive Government of the United States, including military and naval authority thereof, will recognize and maintain the freedom of such persons, and will do no act or acts that repress such persons, or any of them, in any efforts they may make for their actual freedom."

The company stood still and quiet under the gray sky as the light of day weakened. A cold down wind blew smoke among us. I covered my eyes and coughed.

Oldham continued with Lincoln's words.

"And I hereby enjoin upon the people so declared to be free to abstain from all violence, unless in necessary for self-defense; and I recommend to them that, in all cases when allowed, they labor faithfully for reasonable wages. And I further declare and make known, that such persons of suitable condition, will be received into the armed service of the United States to garrison forts, positions, stations, and other places, and to man vessels of all sorts in said service."

The wind calmed and the smoke drifted upward again. Men shuffled their feet and looked at the bare ground.

"And upon this act, sincerely believed to be an act of justice, warranted by the Constitution, upon military necessity, I invoke the considerate judgment of mankind, and the gracious favor of Almighty God."

Oldham threw wood on the fire, pulled a burning stick and lit his cigar. After a few deep draws, he tossed the stick back in the fire and walked down the lane out of sight.

"Lincoln's an ape!" one soldier yelled, veins standing out from his neck.

"A savage," another screamed.

"Kill 'em all," yelled a third.

"Now we'll be fightin' the slaves too!" another screamed.

Quite a ruckus erupted among the men, brimming with anger and disbelief. Lincoln had made a similar announcement four months earlier, right after the Union victory at Antietam, but slaves hadn't been set free yet. I believed that slavery should be ended, but felt the heavy weight of the proclamation nonetheless. I feared that the war would then go on till one side was defeated.

A few minutes later a cannon fired to the northwest, followed by another.

"Get your guns," Lieutenant Hemphill yelled. "Assemble here in two minutes."

When we had gathered, Oldham spoke.

"Sergeant Flowers pick eight men. Reconnoiter the road to the northwest. Send a runner back and don't shoot unless ya have to. Retreat if ya encounter substantial forces."

The wind swirled the campfire smoke among the company.

"Everyone else take defensive positions around the camp perimeter and wait. No talking, no smoking. Understood?"

The men nodded and dispersed quickly.

I was glad to be sent on assignment. Being under threat tempered the spell of defeat I felt upon hearing Lincoln's words. The North was intent to end slavery once and for all.

The road led toward the Big Black River. We covered about eight miles in three hours and I sent Dallas back with our report. When we got close to the river I went out ahead. Smelling tobacco smoke, I left the road and moved cautiously through the woods till I heard voices. I saw two campfires and counted eighteen Yanks milling about. Their talk was about Lincoln's proclamation, but nothing about their plans, so I returned to our squad and we hightailed it on back to camp in darkness.

Amos, Dallas and I ate beef jerky, cornbread and radishes with our hut mates. Later, Dallas and I borrowed a stack of Vicksburg papers from Oldham to read. In one, dated near the end of December, there was an account of a gunboat battle.

The U.S.S. *Cairo* was clearing Confederate mines from the Yazoo River as part of Grant's approach to Vicksburg. The *Cairo* came under rifle fire from Confederates on the bank, so the Yankee captain brought the gunboat into position to fire back. It turned out to be a trap. Confederates on the bank detonated two torpedoes in the river with an electric charge. It took only twelve minutes for the *Cairo* to sink in thirty-six feet of water. The boat sat on the river bottom with its two green-striped smokestacks sticking out of the water.

"Hey, didn't that gunboat at Fort Donelson have green stripes?" Dallas said.

"Sure did!"

"Those stripes … that's how they tell 'em apart, ya know. Bet it's the same boat!"

"Well I'm glad they sunk it. They're killers, that's for sure!"

January 16, 1863

Dearest Mary Ann,

I miss you so much it hurts and when I think of you I feel warm inside. I am so pleased that you agreed to marry me. I was afraid you'd say no, because I'm a poor farmer and have little money. And now, I'm not even that.

The army is not reliable in many ways — pay is one. Food too. Our cavalry scouts tell us the Yankees have enough supplies for both armies. Last week one of our scouts returned from patrol with a sack of coffee beans. He must have traded with the enemy. Our officers have told us not to have any friendly contact with the enemy, but they don't complain when coffee, whiskey or sugar appears out of nowhere.

I've been thinking more about the land near Sallis. From recollection, I made a drawing of the layout, stream and the road, and I have ideas of where our cabin could be. Planning for our future brings encouragement to my heart and gives me something important to dwell upon.

Please check in on Ellen and Lilly and let me know how they are. John is doing okay here, but I worry a lot about them.

I have to end now, about to go on patrol. Please give my love to Miriam and tell her thanks for keeping our secret. You are my first thought upon awaking and last before I fall asleep, dearest woman.

Love, Anderson

Chapter 25

CAPTAIN DORIAN BROUSSARD
Late January 1863, Natchez, Mississippi

One evening about midnight, Able, Captain Oldham's slave, woke me.

"Sergeant Flowers. Captain wants to see ya."

"Right now?"

"Yes, sir, right now."

"Okay, puttin' on my boots."

Able waited outside our hut. I followed him through the bitter cold to our Captain's cabin, lit with two oil lanterns.

"Secret mission, Sergeant," Oldham said.

"Certainly, sir."

"I need ya to travel to Natchez to meet an old riverboat pilot named Broussard. Need ya to leave tonight. Ever been to Natchez?"

"No, never have. How'll I find him?"

"On Jefferson Street, just off Canal, in view of the river, there's a tavern with three bells above the door. He's always there. Either downstairs drinkin' or upstairs sleepin'."

"How da ya know him?"

"He was a friend of my father's. Piloted steamboats from St. Louis to the Gulf for years. He smelled the wind and heard the river better'n anyone."

"What's my mission?"

"Deliver a letter to him and stay overnight. The next day he'll give you a letter and you bring it back to me unopened, understood?"

"Yes, sir, unopened. Is he a spy?"

"That's all ya need to know. Able'll fix ya up with civilian clothes. Don't want ya lookin' like a soldier."

"Yes, sir. Anything else?"

"If ya get questioned, tell 'em you're in the shippin' bidness."

A chill went up my spine as I stepped back into the dark. I was barely awake and about to leave camp as a civilian. I poked my head back inside.

"Captain, may I take one man with me? Safer if there's two of us."

"I agree." He smiled. "Think Dallas would be good for the job?"

"Thanks, Captain."

I hurried back and woke Dallas. Able took us to a supply tent and opened two trunks packed with clothes.

"Change here and leave your uniforms with me," Able said.

Dallas looked at me, puzzled.

"Adventure," I said. "Goin' on an adventure."

I put on a ruffled white linen shirt and black tie and found a pair of black boots that fit well. Dallas wore a pair of checked pants and a thick, gray wool coat.

"How do we look?" Dallas asked Able.

"Like you're ready to hobnob with gentlefolk, Mr. Townsend. And Mr. Flowers, ya may as well go whole hog. Wear this fine hat."

Able grinned and led us to the edge of camp where two saddled horses waited. He handed me two envelopes and I slipped them inside the lining of my coat.

"Y'all be careful now," he said as we took off. "Shippin' bidness can be tricky."

We walked the horses past our forward pickets and then mounted. The moon was not up, and we covered a half-mile in silence before Dallas pulled up and stopped.

"You gotta tell me where we're goin'."

I told him what I knew and his eyes grew wide. "So we're spies now?"

"Messengers might be more like it."

"Let's be spies!"

"Okay, fine."

We rode along through the shadows. The night was hard case cold and there was just enough light to see the contours of the forests and farms. My heart beat fast and I wondered if we could pull off the mission without getting caught.

"I think my father worked with Broussard," Dallas said. "I remember Momma sayin' his name."

"Well, you're gonna meet him soon if we're lucky."

"What's in the envelopes?"

The unsealed one was stuffed with money.

"Here," I handed half the bills to Dallas. "For food and lodging. Gonna be sleepin' indoors for a few days."

Dallas' disposition brightened. We headed on through the cold, still night, and didn't see another soul. Around first light we accidentally stirred the interest of some dogs at the edge of a town named Carlisle. We took a room, slept and ate, and resumed our journey in the afternoon. We rode through another cold night and arrived in Fayette the next morning, just as it began to rain. We ate and stayed overnight.

The next morning we enjoyed warm sunshine on our shoulders on the short ride to Natchez and encountered no Yankees, at least not in uniform.

"What do I say if questioned?" Dallas asked.

"Just let me do the talkin'. The Union controls the river from Natchez to the Gulf and Oldham said the Yanks have spies in town."

"How we gonna know what a Yankee spy looks like?" Dallas asked.

"They'll look like us, I guess."

As we entered Natchez on Saint Catherine Street, the town clock chimed eleven. Two-story brick buildings lined both sides of the street. Some had narrow second floor balconies with ornate iron fencing. They were the fanciest buildings I had ever seen. We turned onto Jefferson and headed northwest toward the river like our Captain said.

In a few blocks Dallas pointed. "There's the tavern!"

"Good. Let's find a room nearby and eat before we go meet Broussard."

"Sounds good to me. I could get used to bein' a spy. Traveling on horseback, rooms with fireplaces, and hot meals cooked by somebody else."

"You complainin' 'bout my cookin?" I teased.

We paid the clerk for our rooms and to board our horses, then sat down at a table in the dining room.

"You men travelin' through?" the clerk asked.

"Just got here," Dallas said. "Shippin' bidness to tend to."

"Friendly with the Yanks, are ya?"

"Enough to get what we need," I answered.

"You have a newspaper?" Dallas asked.

"Yeah. I'll get one fer ya."

The clerk returned shortly with a New Orleans Daily Picayune and we read while we waited for our food. I hadn't seen a newspaper for at least a week.

There were several articles of interest including a report on the Battle of Murfreesboro, Tennessee and one about reactions to Lincoln's Emancipation Proclamation. There was also an account of President Jefferson Davis's message on the state of the Confederacy at the third session of the Congress in Richmond.

At Murfreesboro, thirty-four thousand Confederates under General Braxton Bragg battled forty-one thousand Yanks under General William Rosecrans. They fought over the Stones River for three bloody days and both armies suffered heavy losses before Bragg withdrew.

After eating, we walked to Broadway and sat on a bluff overlooking the Mississippi. On the lowlands both upriver and down, were large plantations with mansion houses. A few flats and a gunboat under a Union flag passed by. There were no steamers packed with cotton bales or other commerce bound in either direction. Along the wharf, cotton presses sat idle. Men rolled carts and wagons laden with army stores. War-making was the commerce of the day.

"Blockade's shuttin' us down," Dallas said.

He was right. It was hard not to worry what life would be like if the Union won. After an hour at the river, we walked to Three Bells. Coming out of bright sunshine, the tavern was quite dark. I'd never been in a tavern before and did not know what to expect. Our religious upbringing strictly prohibited drinking and the other kinds of things that usually went along with drinking. We took a table and looked around the room. We were the only customers and the innkeeper came over.

"What to drink, gentlemen? Hard cider?"

"Nothing, thanks," I said. "We're here to meet someone. You have a newspaper?"

"Got a Weekly Advocate, ten cents."

He brought us a paper and it had an article about the pre-war period in the South. A number of Mississippi and Louisiana citizens opposed secession including a majority of the people in Natchez and Vicksburg. They predicted that war and ruin would happen if their states seceded, but in January 1861, secession was approved in both states nonetheless.

Louisiana put out a call for volunteers and raised an army of five thousand quickly. Some believed there wouldn't actually be a war. Most were in a hurry because they figured if fighting did break out, it would be over in a few months and they didn't want to miss out on the adventure.

They set up a training camp north of Lake Pontchartrain and right away a measles epidemic broke out. Hundreds of soldiers died before the army was sent off to fight. After the war started and the reality of death from disease and fighting sunk in, fewer men enlisted.

About three o'clock an old man with a long, white beard came down the stairs hugging the rail. When he reached the bottom, he touched his cane to the floor and wobbled slowly over to the bar.

"Afternoon, Broussard," the innkeeper said. "The usual?"

Broussard nodded. He finished a glass of rum right quick and the innkeeper gave him another.

"There's some fellows here to see ya, I b'lieve."

Broussard turned around and looked at us.

"What you boys drinkin'?"

"Nothin'," Dallas replied.

"Hmm?" he mumbled to the innkeeper and tottered over to our table in the corner.

"What's your name, young man?" he asked.

"Dallas Townsend."

"And you, young fellow?"

"Anderson Flowers."

"Pleased to make your acquaintance," he said in a scratchy voice. "Captain Dorian Broussard ... famous for takin' boats up-down the River and gettin' a few men killed."

"You know J.R. Oldham from Attala County, right?" I asked.

"Sure do. His old man ran boats with me for years."

"Oldham sent us to see ya. Said ya could float a flat boat in a good rainfall."

Broussard chuckled. "I've heard that one before, but admiration's always appreciated."

I handed the sealed envelope to Broussard and he tucked it in his coat pocket and kept on talking. "Tell me 'bout yourselves."

We talked about being Mississippi boys, the battle at Fort Donelson, prison camps and re-enlisting. He sat back, listened and drank from his mug.

"Mighty interestin'," he said after we'd caught him up.

"My father worked the boats," Dallas said.

"Is that right," Broussard replied.

"He left for a job on the Mississippi when I was six and never came back."

Broussard looked curiously at Dallas. "What'd ya say your last name is?"

"Townsend. My father was Ben Townsend."

"Thought ya looked a little familiar," he said. "Ben worked with me a good bit."

His eyes became teary and he reached for his handkerchief. He took the last swig of rum and looked out the window. His deeply wrinkled face, brown from years of sunshine, wind and rain, showed in the light.

"Will you fellows take me out to the river? I don't get around well by myself, as ya can plainly see."

"Yes, sir," Dallas replied.

We helped Broussard up and held one arm while he used his cane. He stepped gingerly down the steps into the cold air.

As we eased down Jefferson Street, he blurted out, "Mahogany!"

"What's 'at?" Dallas asked in a loud voice.

"Mahogany! This here cane's made of mahogany."

He stopped and held it up above his head. The crooked old cane was reddish-brown with a tarnished copper handle.

"Got it from a Mexican in 1813, the year I started on the boats," he chuckled. "Traded a straight knife for it. Got the best end of the deal." He laughed.

When we reached the edge of the bluff, Broussard sat on a log, looked toward the late afternoon sun, and pointed his cane to a gunboat heading downriver.

"That used to be the *Amelia Watts*, a mighty fine boat. Took her on a trip or three."

We sat in silence as the gunboat rounded the bend.

"Yankees captured her last year, sons of bitches. Made her into a gunboat!" Broussard caught his breath. "I'd like to beat the hell outta the men who tore her up … put guns on her!"

We watched as the boat went out of sight.

Broussard continued. "I can't hardly take care of my own self now."

"Tell me 'bout my father," Dallas said.

Broussard wiped his eyes with his handkerchief again.

"Ben made a number of runs to St. Louis and back with me. One of the finest boatmen I ever knowed. Had a keen eye for floatin' logs. Spotted 'em a quarter mile 'fore me."

"What was he like?" Dallas asked.

"Your old man was a joker. Once we was runnin' a sidewheeler down to Vicksburg carryin' some highfalutin' folks from New York City. They was havin' a weddin' on deck … nice afternoon. Right in the middle of the weddin', Townsend blowed out the mud drums and it let out such a roar the New Yorkers went to runnin' off in all directions. They musta thought the boilers were blowin' up or somethin'. The funniest scramble of over-dressed rich people I ever seen. Laughed so hard my sides hurt."

"When was the last time ya saw my father?" Dallas asked.

"Let me think on that a bit."

A thick bank of clouds blocked the sun and the wind off the river chilled us. In a minute Broussard continued.

"I guess it mighta been about '47 when we was takin' a load of cotton to New Orlinz."

"Do ya know if he's still alive?"

Broussard shivered and pulled his jacket close.

"Do me a favor, will ya?" he asked Dallas. "Go get my heavy coat from Three Bells. I'd be much obliged."

"Sure."

"Ask Isaac. He'll get it for ya."

Dallas looked puzzled.

"The innkeeper."

After Dallas left, Broussard turned toward me and tears moved slowly down the wrinkles in his face.

"I'll tell ya what happened to Ben ... and you decide if ya want to tell your friend or not."

"You know what became of him?"

"Yeah. I was by his side when he passed."

I sat close to Broussard so I could hear his weak voice over the wind.

"We were carryin' a load of cotton from Natchez on the *Lady Mars*. We'd been underway 'bout two hours when there came an explosion from the furnace room. Cotton on deck caught fire and we were in trouble fast. I steered the boat toward the bank and some of the crew swam to shore and others got away on john boats. Luckily we had no passengers that day. They'd a panicked for sure. Townsend went below to help the boiler men, then there was a second blast and the boat started sinkin'."

Broussard stopped and caught his breath. The wind cut deep lines across the brown river.

"A farmer pulled me out of the water. The ones of us who made it to shore went lookin' for Townsend and the others but didn't find a soul. I figured they 'as trapped in the boat and drowned. Darkness came on and we couldn't look no more."

Broussard paused and wiped his nose with his handkerchief.

"In the morning we found Townsend hangin' on a patch of willows about a half-mile downriver. His head and shoulders was badly burned, and he was just alive enough to hang on. A doctor treated his burns and bandaged his head. He told me Townsend was blind and would probably live only a few days."

Broussard paused and then continued in a trembling voice.

"Ben didn't want his family to see him all burned up and blind. He made me promise and I've honored his final wish all these years."

"Did he talk about his family?"

"No. He had me describe the clouds, the trees and the river. Said it helped him picture what he found most peaceful. I stayed with him for three days, then he died."

Broussard looked at me, tears spilling from his eyes.

"You're the only person I've told the truth." He began to sob.

Dallas returned and we helped Broussard put on his coat.

"Take me back, fellows. I'm feelin' puny."

We helped him back to Three Bells and upstairs to his room.

"Come back tomorrow at noon," he said. "I'll have what ya need."

"Thanks, we will," I said and closed his door.

"Why was he sobbin'?" Dallas said. "And what was he talkin' 'bout?"

"I don't know. He got to mumbling. He 'as worn out, I guess."

We left the tavern and walked down Jefferson toward the river. The sun peeked through the moving clouds and the wind chilled me.

"Did he say anything more 'bout my father?" Dallas asked.

"All he said was last time he saw him was in '47. Let's get back to the inn. I'm cold and hungry."

After supper, Isaac asked, "You fellows need anything more for the night? Anything?"

"No. Thanks," Dallas said. "We're both fine."

I felt bad not telling Dallas about his father and we went to our separate rooms. I stoked the fire and crawled under the blankets. *What luxury.* About the time I got the covers warmed up, a knock came on the door. I opened it and there stood a pretty young woman about eighteen years old.

"Want some company?" she asked softly. "One dollar ... for whatever ya want."

The way her brown hair curled around her face reminded me of Mary Ann and I was sorely tempted. The money Oldham gave me lay on the nightstand by the bed.

"Oh, no thanks, miss. I'm ..."

"Maybe tomorrow night," she smiled and shut the door. I heard a knock on another door down the hallway and wondered if Broussard or Isaac had sent her.

Back in bed, I lay awake for a long time feeling all-overish about lying to Dallas. *Maybe tomorrow.*

In the morning, we had a late breakfast and read more newspapers. Snow was falling and I could hardly see the river.

"Wait here and I'll go see Broussard," I said.

"Nope. I'm goin' with ya. I wanna ask him 'bout my father!"

When we arrived at Three Bells, Isaac told us Broussard had left a letter for us. I took the sealed letter addressed to Captain O. and stuffed it in the lining of my coat.

"Will that be all?" Isaac asked.

"Yep, that's all," I said. "Thank ya for your hospitality. And please thank Broussard and tell him we're leavin'."

The day was miserable for traveling. The snow was wet and heavy, and the horses labored. The trees stood like skeletons against the gray sky. I thought about the letter in my coat and the importance of getting back quickly. I hated lying to Dallas but had decided to honor his father's wish and stick with the lie.

After we'd traveled a mile or so, Dallas stopped his horse and looked at me in anger.

"Don't you piss on my leg and tell me it's rainin'!"

"Why'd ya say that?"

"I know you're lyin' about Broussard. He told ya somethin' 'bout my father!"

My ears turned hot and Dallas rode ahead. We made about twenty miles before we stopped for the night and not a word passed between us.

The next day was sunny, the snow had melted, and we made better time. When we were about ten miles from winter camp in Canton, Dallas stopped us and spoke.

"I have a mind to see my mother."

He caught me by surprise.

"It's only one day past camp," he said. "I could get there tomorrow, visit with her overnight and be back the next day."

"But we're supposed to get the letter right back to Oldham. It's important."

"Or it could be worth a shit!" he spat back. "Why don't ya come with me and visit Mary Ann?"

I thought for a few seconds and then said, "We're under orders to come straight back."

"All creation, buddy! You got the heart of a hollow log!"

"I don't have authority to give ya leave," I pleaded.

He glared at me and then moved ahead. We rode the rest of the way to camp without speaking.

Chapter 26

FORT PEMBERTON
February — April 1863, Tallahatchie River, Mississippi

February was cold and rainy and I lay awake many nights, thinking of home and Mary Ann. In mid-month a cold wind swept in from the northeast and the temperature dropped in a hurry. We gathered firewood for the night as snowflakes drifted through the bare trees. While Dallas got our fire going, I laid pinecones and sticks under his bedroll. After supper the snow turned to rain and we went in the hut for a game of chess. Dallas kept squirming around trying to find a comfortable place to sit, till finally he caught me grinning and picked up his bedroll.

"Blowhard!" he said and punched my shoulder.

It was great to be back on friendly terms.

February 24, 1863

Dear Sister,

This morning, a bit before sunrise, I was on watch. It reminded me of early mornings at home when Father got us up to milk the cow and feed the chickens. Who knows how long we'll be here? We could get orders to move today or we could be here the rest of winter. Deciding what to do with the army seems to be an everyday dilemma for our commanders. It was so foggy and humid this morning my clothes were about as wet and cold as if I had dunked them in a washtub. Knowing that campfires would be roaring, and hot food ready kept me going till my picket duty ended.

Oldham lets me pick squads and lead patrols, and sometimes he has me write company reports that go to headquarters. I'm sure glad I did my homework for Miss Williams and our parents made me read the Bible every day. Who would have thought that knowing a lot of words and having good handwriting would be indispensable in the work of war?

Wow, it sounds like Henrietta's growing up in a hurry — making soap and learning how to sew. Don't let her grow up too fast because I need someone to dig arrowheads with when I'm back. The other day Sergeant Barrett told me John is a fine soldier. Please relay this praise to Ellen. Knowing John, I bet he won't tell her himself.

Thanks for your letters and news from home. They calm my soul and give me something worthwhile to dwell upon. I've got to finish up and post this letter now. There's talk we'll be going to Greenwood soon to defend a fort. I'll write again when we get where we're going.

Your loving brother, Anderson

The next morning, the 20th Regiment boarded a steamer named *Sharp* and traveled up the Yazoo River. General Loring had gotten word that Grant was planning to attack Vicksburg by coming down the Tallahatchie River, connecting with the Yazoo and then on to the Mississippi.

We arrived in Greenwood on February 28th. It turned out there was no fort there to defend; instead, it was our job to construct one. We were joined by the 46th Mississippi and 2nd Texas regiments. All together we made a force of three thousand under the command of General Loring. We were given shovels and wheelbarrows and got to work digging. Under the direction of engineers, cotton bales were arranged in rows and covered with earth. In the space of the next ten days, we built an earthen fort to protect our cannons. The engineers named the fort after General Pemberton, a Philadelphian who was a trained military man. He sided with the South because he believed our cause was just and his wife was a Virginian.

Riflemen were positioned in trenches just ten feet from the river's edge. Behind us, on elevated mounds, the fort had eight cannons including six four-inch rifles, one eight-inch Columbiad, and a single eight-inch Parrott rifle. The fort faced north up a long, straight section of the Tallahatchie River just before it made a hairpin turn to the east. To make things more difficult for the Union, the engineers sank a Southern steamship, *Star of the West*, in the middle of the channel. Once all this was done we sat and waited for the Union navy. General Loring learned from spies that Grant had cut the Mississippi River levee two hundred miles upstream. The floods made several bayous between the Mississippi and Tallahatchie navigable.

A few days after the fort was finished, Oldham sent me to scout the riverside.

"Grant may send foot patrols in advance, so be careful ya don't get caught."

"Yes, sir," I saluted.

I told John about my mission.

"If I don't come back," I said. "I want ya to tell Mary Ann and Sister what happened."

"Why're ya tellin' me this now?" John said.

"Just in case. Anything can happen."

"So far I haven't seen much happen at all."

I moved up the west side of the Tallahatchie through thick brambles. The river had flooded the woods fifty yards past the bank and at times, I was wading up to my waist. A mile upstream there was a tree at the river's edge that leaned out over the channel. I climbed out on a long limb and found a good spot to view the next stretch of river. It seemed impossible that foot soldiers could mount an attack on Fort Pemberton because of the floodwaters. Being on scout was a good rest from shoveling and hauling dirt and my rifle felt light in comparison.

Suddenly the opposite side of the river was alive with noisy, red-winged blackbirds swarming by thousands from tree to tree. As a child, I wondered where they came from and why so many appeared at the same time. Father told me all about them. Multitudes flew through each spring. Then one day they were suddenly gone. In October and November here they came again, heading south.

After a half-hour, the whole flock of blackbirds suddenly crossed the river and filled the trees around me; their cries – *conk-la-reee, conk-la-reee, conk-la-reee* – overwhelmed my ears. That was an excellent day! No enemy, only blackbirds and the swollen brown river flowing beneath my feet.

On March 11th, we were dumping wheelbarrows of dirt to strengthen the forward earthworks when a call rang out.

"Yanks on the river! Positions!"

I dropped the shovel, ran to the forward trench and looked through my field glasses. Two ironclad gunboats, side-by-side, steamed full speed toward us. Men swung open hatches and three hefty black cannons appeared from inside. Black smoke poured from the boat's smokestacks. Rounding the bend other boats followed.

"Must be the troop ships behind." I handed the glasses to Dallas.

When the ironclads were about a thousand yards from the fort, our cannons, just thirty yards behind us, commenced firing without warning. *Boom, boom, boom!* The concussions shook my jaws, set my ears to ringing and started a headache in a split second. Waterspouts erupted around the gunboats, and cannon smoke curled over the trenches, burning my eyes and stinging my nose.

The gunboats came closer and I saw three red flashes in quick succession. A second later the blasts reached my ears, *Boom, boom, boom*! A shell exploded in the river in front of us and others screamed overhead. Dirt and water rained down upon us. The roar was louder than thunderclaps.

"If they keep this up we'll be buried alive," I yelled at Dallas.

"What?" he shouted back.

"Nothin'. Keep your head down!"

I waved, covered my ears and slumped down to the bottom of the trench. The gunboats lobbed shell after shell raining shrapnel all around and our cannons answered back. The roar overpowered my ears, smoke filled the trench and I gasped for air. More explosions came from behind. Aside from staying low in the trenches or burying ourselves in holes, there was nothing except luck and the protective hand of the Lord to save us.

The ironclads delivered a continuous bombardment for a quarter hour then stopped suddenly. I watched through the field glasses as the gunboats steamed back around the bend. We were ordered to stay in position and an hour later the gunboats attacked again. Our cannons hammered back and one of the gunboats caught fire and turned around. The Yankees made three more attacks before giving up for the day. I never saw a Yankee or fired a shot, but I sure had a bird's eye view of the battle.

Two days later the gunboats attacked again. This time their exploding shells started a fire in one of the fort's magazines. A tremendous explosion followed when the powder kegs ignited. Dirt and burning timbers flew high in the air. I covered my head and lay on the ground as debris showered the fort. Our artillerymen stopped firing as they realized what had happened. Officers and men scurried about. The cannoneers soon resumed firing using ammunition from a second magazine. We lay in our trenches with handkerchiefs over our mouths trying to breathe.

"Help!" Captain Oldham shouted.

Dallas, John, Amos and I left our rifles and crawled into what remained of the magazine, an underground storage room about ten yards square. It had been covered with beams and a plank roof with three feet of dirt piled on top. A large part of the roof had collapsed, and the ground was littered with wounded. Smoke rose from the loose dirt and the stink of burned hair filled my nose. I puked till my belly was empty. John and I carried a man who was missing an arm and bleeding badly. His face and neck were blistered pink and his eyes glowed like blue stars.

"What happened?" he asked.

"The magazine exploded," John said.

"Am I okay?" he asked, apparently unaware he was missing an arm.

"You'll be fine."

We hurried him to the hospital.

"Put him over there," the doctor said when we entered a tent some distance behind the fort. He pointed, we obeyed, and then stood watching him work.

"Go see if there are others! Hurry," he shouted and waved us out.

We returned to the magazine and helped another man get to the hospital. One of his legs was badly burned and he screamed incessantly. Oldham arrived and sent us back to our positions. Melted skin was stuck to my hands, jacket and trousers. Both ironclads and two wooden gunboats were still blasting away at our fort. Fire and smoke erupted from the black barrels, but I no longer noticed the booms. We stayed at the ready for the rest of the day, but the Union troop boats never got close enough to unload infantry. I peeled burnt skin off my hands and clothes and the smell haunted me for days. Later, we learned that sixteen men were wounded in the battle and five killed.

John and I talked that night about the devastation.

"I'm gravely afraid of being burned," John said. "If I get burned all over I want ya to end it."

"From the looks of it, some of those men won't make it."

"What's it like?"

"What da ya mean?" I said.

"Battle."

"You got a taste of it today!"

"No," John said. "I mean when soldiers attack, rifle fire."

"For me everything slows down. Sometimes I see farther and better."

"Aren't ya afraid?"

"Terrified is more like it. My insides tighten up something fierce."

"I'm afraid all the time," John said, "but don't want anybody to know."

"Some show it, others don't. But any man who tells ya he's not afraid is lyin' through his teeth. Now Amos — he's different. He gets extra calm in battle."

"I'm definitely not like Amos," John said.

"The trick is to concentrate on what ya have to do," I said. "The next step. The man on your right and the man on your left. That's who you're fightin' for."

Union gunboats attacked two more days that week and our cannons hammered them hard. Then four days passed without contact. On the 1st of April, we repulsed another attack successfully and our scouts on horseback rode upriver to reconnoiter. On the 2nd they reported that the enemy had headed back where they came from. The fort and the flooded river were too much for our enemy to overcome. Our company suffered no deaths or serious injuries at Fort Pemberton. We were awfully lucky.

That afternoon we learned we would soon be leaving for Jackson to help in the defense of Vicksburg. After supper, I started letters to Sister and Mary Ann, but it began to rain, so I crawled in the tent with Dallas. We talked about our parents and swapped stories from childhood. In my prayers, I thanked God for keeping me alive.

Chapter 27

AMBUSH ON THE ROAD
April 1863, Mississippi

In April, our regiment and others boarded steamers and traveled down the Yazoo River toward Jackson. We took turns above deck because the boat was packed like when we were prisoners. I used my sergeant rank to stay on deck much of the time. The river smelled familiar and fishy, and pink azaleas were in full bloom. Families waved to us and yelled out questions and encouragement.

After two peaceful days on the river, we disembarked at Yazoo City, had a cooked meal and marched twenty-odd miles east to Vaughn's Station. We spent the night there in the railyard and the next afternoon, traveled south in boxcars with the doors open. Pine pollen swirled in the strong breeze and left a coat of yellow on our clothes and equipment.

I had been asleep for a few hours when the train came to a sudden halt and everyone woke up. We were in Jackson. I pulled out the pocket watch Mary Ann gave me. It was one o'clock in the morning.

April 18, 1863

Dear Mary Ann,

Last night I dreamed I was sleeping in a pile of yellow straw in a barn. You came to me in the night and kissed me. I held you in my arms and we rolled over and over. You got to giggling and that got me laughing and pretty soon we couldn't stop laughing. My cheeks ached and you cried and said you were happy. When the sun came up you were asleep beside me. We were both covered in straw and some stuck in your hair.

I'm still unhurt after suffering under several days of cannon fire at Fort Pemberton. John, Eugene and Dallas are okay too. General Grant seems to have taken a special dislike to our regiment. He's been on the other side of the line from us just about everywhere we've been so far.

A few days ago, one of our scouts was returning from a mission and two of our pickets fired at him. Luckily he wasn't hit. Oldham gave the pickets a good telling off in front of the whole company, so it served as a lesson for all of us. The Yankees all wear blue uniforms. Our men are wearing all kinds of garb. Some gray uniforms, others butternut colored. My uniform was ruined in a fire, so I'm back in clothes I brought from home. In the dark and rain, it's nearly impossible to tell friend from foe.

The health of our company has improved some since winter, but about a third are still not ready to fight. As usual, supplies are not keeping up with our needs. When we are supplied, we eat well for a couple of days then we're back to gathering roots from the woods and hunting rabbits. Sometimes we have money and can pay farmers for food, but it still feels like stealing from my own family. A few days ago, near Vaughn Station, Rufus took some shotgun pellets in the buttocks from an angry farmer. He's going to be okay, I think, but I doubt if he'll try stealing chickens again.

Good news for you and me! When we arrived in Jackson we got paid for the last six months. I used some for food and am hoping to buy a new hat and trousers, then I'll send the rest to you. Please split it halves with Sister and use yours for our nest egg or whatever you need to buy.

If you have time, please make me two new pairs of socks. They wear out fast with all the marching. When I get home, I'm going barefoot for a few weeks to let my feet heal up. They are a wreck right now.

Each time I check my watch, I'm reminded of our fathers and mothers and all the souls who've come before. We are surely joined in love and fate with our forebearers. I hope and pray I'm worthy of carrying the family name forward. I think of you often, my dear, and long to be by your side.

Love, Anderson

The next evening John joined Dallas, Amos, Will and me for supper. John contributed a chicken and sweet potatoes he bought in Jackson. We had a lively conversation about the Federal Draft Act. Draft quotas had been set by President Lincoln for each district to enlarge the Union army. All men between the ages of twenty and forty-five, except those who were feeble in the head or physically unable, were eligible. If a man found himself drafted, but could come up with $300, he could pay the government and buy his way out.

"I hate to hear that," Will said. "They already got more'n we do."

"Aw, don't ya worry," Amos replied. "They'll be lined up so thick we can kill 'em without aimin'."

I did not see any advantage to facing more Yankees, but Amos was head and shoulders above us all for finding a silver lining.

Afterward, John and I took a walk along a stream that ran just west of our camp. Willows bordered both sides of the stream. The sky was cloudless, the moon high and almost full. When we got out of earshot from camp, I spoke.

"What's on your mind big brother?"

"I'm worried about Ellen. I got 'nother letter from her today."

"What's wrong?"

"Nothin' big really. Lilly's sick, but it'll probably go away."

"You look like you're carryin' a mule on your shoulders."

"Ellen's overwhelmed. I really oughta be home with 'em."

A gray possum scurried out of our way.

"You've been writin' her, haven't you?"

"About twice a week," John said.

"Maybe ya should write more often."

"What good's that gonna do?" He was angry.

"I don't know," I said. "But if she's anything like Mary Ann or Sister, I bet she'll worry less if ya keep writin'."

"I've run out of things to say and I don't wanna write about fightin', that's for damn sure."

"Ya might try tellin' her camp stories, especially funny ones."

As we walked, the night cooled, and the owls began hooting and hunting.

After camping in Jackson for two nights, orders came to move west toward Vicksburg. Our regiment marched ten miles to Clinton and set up camp again. Oldham joined our squad for supper.

"Captain, do ya know when we'll be fightin' again?" Dallas asked.

Oldham gave him a questioning look and then spoke.

"You know, Colonel Russell doesn't tell me much. And I'm pretty sure he doesn't tell me much because General Loring doesn't tell him much either."

The men laughed.

"So we're all kinda in the dark?" Amos opined.

"That's a good way 'a puttin' it. Soldiering is mostly doin' what you're told."

"That's for sure," Dallas added.

"As a matter of fact," Oldham said, "we've been ordered back to Jackson in the mornin'."

"You're jokin', right?" Will said.

"Nope. Colonel just told me. Don't tell the others. I want the company to get a good rest. I'll tell everybody in the mornin'."

After Oldham left, Will complained.

"They're using us up traveling back and forth and gettin' nowhere."

"If they'd let us face the Yankees and fight 'em," Amos said, "we could git this over with."

"I've heard all this before," Dallas said as he got up from the fire. "Goin' to sleep."

After breakfast, Oldham gave the orders and we marched and bellyached back to Jackson and set up camp on a farmer's field. Late that afternoon, I borrowed a fiddle and went to the edge of the encampment. Doves kicked up, flew a short distance and lit in a sprawling live oak. After tuning up, I played slow tunes for a while and it made me real homesick. In a while someone approached. It was Oldham, so I stood up and saluted.

"Sergeant Flowers. Got a mission for ya."

"Yes, sir. What do ya want me to do?"

He picked up a stick, cleared the leaves on the sandy ground and drew a map.

"General Loring thinks the enemy may be moving troops from the southwest to create a flank against our army, here."

"That's along the creek we crossed when we came in, right?"

"Yes. And we have no reinforcements or supply lines, so we'll be exposed if the Yankees move troops there."

I nodded, coming fully alert and Oldham continued.

"Want ya to head in this direction, get as close to the creek as ya can, and scout upstream. There's a road just south of the creek right about here." He made an X in the loose soil. "When ya reach this point, observe overnight and return after daybreak. We expect if they move, it'll be durin' the night."

"Yes, sir. When do ya want me to leave?"

"Right now."

He handed me his Colt Navy revolver, a canteen and knapsack.

"I'll take your fiddle," he said. "Keep a cool head and you'll do well. Captain Patterson trusted ya and so do I."

"Yes, sir."

Hugging the tree line, I paused to look back at the farmer's field. Dozens of campfires burned, and smoke drifted up. A thousand brothers talked, played cards, and wrote letters home. *This is my family for now.*

I passed through our picket line heading west and turned into the thick woods, the setting sun my guide. A light breeze stirred the top leaves. In an hour I heard bullfrogs, *jug-o'-rum, jug-o'-rum, jug-o'-rum, jug-o'-rum,* and reached the creek within a couple of minutes. It was no wider than a horse length and the water was clear and undisturbed, like springtime at home. I took a good drink and filled the canteen. Suddenly water hit my face and I jumped up, expecting to see the wrong end of a rifle, but it was only a little green frog. I crossed over and moved slowly, came to the roadbed and checked for tracks. There were no signs of foot traffic or wagons. To be safer, I slipped back in the woods and kept a course parallel to the road about twenty yards in, moving from tree to tree, pausing often to listen.

The wind died down and the night was quiet. About midnight I reached the place where I reckoned Oldham made his X on the ground and sat by a beech tree with a view of the road. The sky was clear, and a half-moon provided good light. *Hoot, hoot, who whoooo,* came the call of a hoot owl up ahead. *Hoot, hoot, who whooo.* The sound drew my thoughts to Mary Ann. *We'll get married when the war's over and have children. And one fine evening years from now, our son or daughter will hear hoot owls in the woods, too.* I longed to be home, plant fields, and build a house for Mary Ann and me. My heart beat strong and I prayed for God to bring us together again soon.

When the hoot owls went silent my watch said half past three. Oldham's pistol lay in my lap and a raccoon wandered by. When it got close, it rose on its hind legs, sniffed the air and moved off in a different direction. The night passed without incident.

As the light of the new day touched the forest canopy, I peered into the gray morning, pistol in hand. A herd of deer ran toward me and stopped suddenly. I counted twelve, including four fawns, nostrils' steaming. My heart beat fast. The lead deer looked around and turned its ears back down the road. Suddenly, the whole bunch bounded off as quickly as they had arrived.

I heard muffled voices and took cover behind a wide oak. A line of uniformed soldiers with rifles on their shoulders moved down the road. I counted a hundred men; a probing patrol. In a few minutes a second rifle company passed, then no more.

I took a course directly to our encampment. In a half-hour, I came to the edge of the farmer's field and our picket lines. I tucked the pistol in my belt, raised both arms, and walked slowly out in the open, hoping our sentries had been told of my mission.

"Stop right there!" a voice came from behind a bush.

"Sergeant Flowers. 20th Mississippi. Captain Oldham sent me on scout."

A soldier came out, his rifle aimed at me. He took the pistol and my headquarters' pass.

"Come with me, then."

He followed with his rifle touching my back.

"You can put that gun down, soldier," came Dallas' voice. "This man is our scout."

Dallas accompanied me to Oldham's tent where he was sipping coffee from a tin cup while Able polished his boots. I made my report and he called our company together right away.

"We've got a mission, men. Enemy troops are movin' to flank us. Sergeant Flowers knows the way, so he'll lead. Load up, you're leavin' right now."

It was the first time our captain had called on me to lead a large patrol.

"Here's your pistol," I said to Oldham.

"Keep it. It's yours now."

I led our group quickly through the woods and we crossed the creek. When we got near the road I had the men hold up. Seeing no fresh tracks, I gave instructions.

"About an hour ago I saw two hundred riflemen on the move west of us. We're gonna set up along the sides … half here with Sergeant Barrett and I'll take the other half about a quarter mile west. Understood?"

They nodded.

"If the enemy's movin' this way, my group will see them pass first. We'll hold our fire and stay hidden in the woods. When the Yanks reach your point, Sergeant Barrett will give the order to fire. Form two firing rows and let 'em have it. When Barrett's squad fires, I believe they'll retreat back down the road."

The men listened intently.

"When they pass by my group, we'll give them a double volley just the same. That oughta send 'em back down the road for good. If they decide to stay and fight, stay in cover of the woods and pick 'em off one by one. Captain Oldham's sendin' another company to reinforce us, just in case."

"Good plan," Sergeant Barrett said.

"Okay, let's get going," I said. "Remember, no smokin', no talkin' … quiet as a mouse. Surprise is our advantage."

I led my group, about thirty-five, through the woods and we hid behind trees fifteen paces off the road. Soon Yanks approached and passed without seeing us. It seemed to be the same group I'd seen earlier, and they had no cannons. Two minutes passed then we moved to within a few yards of the road, formed a firing row ten yards long, double deep. A volley of rifle fire crashed through the woods to the east. A second volley followed a half minute later. After that we heard a few scattered shots then all was quiet. The plan seemed to be working.

"Don't fire till I lower my pistol," I said.

The men nodded and waited at the ready. Directly, a powerful rage came over me the moment I saw the Yankees running up the road toward us. It seemed that I heard each footstep distinctly and saw the details of their uniforms, caps and faces. I lowered my pistol and squeezed the trigger. Our squad let loose a furious volley and enemy soldiers fell in the dust. Our second volley broke them down more and the Yanks ran scared. We fired at the stragglers and then the shooting was over, no more than a minute from the start. My heart raced and my mouth was dry. The men followed me toward our other group and counted the fallen enemy soldiers along the road.

Sergeant Barrett reported. "We killed ten and took two prisoners."

"We got eight," I said. "Let's get back to camp."

"Shouldn't we take their guns and ammunition?"

"No, let's get back quick and report. The prisoners may have information."

In an hour, we were back and reported to Oldham.

John and I talked that night.

"So how was your first shootin' battle?" I asked.

"A little like huntin'. They didn't have time to shoot back. Good plan ya cooked up."

"Wish they were all like that. Luck was ours today."

Chapter 28

CHASING GRIERSON'S RAIDERS
April — May 1863, Mississippi

About a week after the successful ambush, John and I went for a late afternoon walk. A white-bellied cat squirrel hurried out of our path and scooted up the far side of an oak tree. It popped out on a limb twenty feet up, barked and fanned its tail. John raised his arms, pretended to shoot a shotgun and yelled, *Pow*!

We both laughed. It was a game we played growing up before we were allowed to use guns.

We reached a point where the creek made a big turn to the west. Orange streaks of light glowed off a patch of high clouds on the horizon.

"I'm glad we're together again, big brother," I said.

"Like old times."

In late April, Oldham assembled the company and announced a new mission.

187

"A Yankee cavalry force under command of Colonel Grierson is moving south through Mississippi, tearin' up railroads, cuttin' telegraph lines, and freein' slaves. We're going to be part of a mounted infantry force to stop him. Colonel Richardson will be leading us."

"Captain," Will said. "Does this mean we're gonna get carbines, pistols and sabers too, like real cavalry?"

"No. Each man will get a horse, that's it! We're mounted infantry. Any more questions?"

There being none, Oldham proceeded.

"Lieutenant Hemphill's gone home to recover, so we need to elect someone to fill his place. I nominate Sergeant Flowers." He paused and looked at the men. "Any other nominations?"

I was elected second lieutenant by unanimous vote and Daniel Woods was elected sergeant to replace me.

"Lieutenant Flowers."

"Yes, Captain?"

"See me in my tent in half an hour."

"Certainly, sir."

After the gathering broke up Dallas spoke to me. "Lieutenant? Will you be ridin' a big, white stallion?"

"Probably not, Private Townsend. I'll be ridin' a plain, brown gelding just like you."

The men around us chuckled.

"Less marchin' for the company," Amos bragged. "Can't wait to tell Father we're cavalry now."

"Mounted infantry," Dallas reminded him.

"Soldiers on horses sounds like cavalry to me."

Able let me in our Captain's tent.

"You wanted to see me, sir?"

"Yes. Please sit down." He motioned to a stool. "I'm pleased to have ya as my new second lieutenant and I know you'll do a good job."

He handed me two gold, single-bar second lieutenant's chevrons.

"Thank you, sir. I'll do my best."

"You know about the chain of command. General Johnston commands the army, Colonel Russell commands the regiment, and so on. At every level, we carry out the commands from the rank above to the best of our abilities."

"Yes, sir, I understand."

"Officers often do not know the whereabouts or strength of the enemy. In the heat of battle, officers often don't know where all their own soldiers are."

I nodded and he continued.

"I may be missing or killed when ya need me. The sergeants and men who report to you may be killed or captured. Men get confused."

"Yes, sir. Fairly often, I'd say."

"Someday commanders may have a bird's eye view of the field, but for now a lot is left to chance. Once the fightin' starts, the chain of command can't always be depended upon fully."

"Yes, sir, I understand. You're gonna say a lot depends on the lieutenants and sergeants."

"That's right. I expect ya to make decisions based on your own best judgement and your own view and knowledge of the facts on the ground as you see it. You are the commander of the soldiers around ya."

"Yes, sir. I understand."

"In a sense, every soldier is a commander and must be ready and willing to make smart decisions if separated from others."

"I see what ya mean."

"Remember. It's your job to instill confidence in your men, so they are confident themselves."

"Yes, sir. I'll do my best."

"I'm glad we had this little talk. Now go be with the men, Lieutenant."

The next afternoon hundreds of horses arrived, stirring up quite a cloud of dust. Lieutenant Conway took care of assignment of horses for Company K. Later a second wagon train arrived carrying hay and grain.

"You got a mount for me?" I asked Conway.

"Yep, I saved ya a nice hoss, about fifteen hands high ... over there."

He motioned to the edge of the woods where the last few horses were tied.

"Thanks," I said. "Hope we can keep the horses fed better'n we do ourselves. By the way, you know how much they paid for 'em?"

"$100 a head," Conway said. "That's what I hear."

"That's almost ten months pay for a soldier and payday's about as rare as Christmas."

Conway shrugged his shoulders.

Dallas and I took our horses for a ride. At the creek we let the animals wade and drink their fill.

"What ya gonna name yours?" Dallas asked.

"Suggestions?"

He grinned. "Yep. I got the perfect name. See his eyes? Don't he look sleepy?"

I looked at my horse. Water dripped from his mouth. "You're right."

"Sultan!" Dallas howled and slapped his leg. "He always looks like he's been nappin' or sippin' booze."

"Okay then, it's settled," I said. "Ya got a name for yours?"

"Nope. But I got a feelin' you do."

"See how your little feller is 'bout a hand shorter than Sultan?"

He leaned way over and looked.

"Maybe a tad."

"Call him Shorty!"

We both laughed again and for a while I forgot we were in a shooting war.

April 25, 1863

Dear Sister,

I'm surprised and proud to report that I've been promoted to second lieutenant. That means a lot more responsibility and a little more pay. Our company is about to leave on a special mission, so I'll probably not be able to post letters for a while, nor receive.

Two of our newest recruits disappeared yesterday. They were both seventeen, best friends, from Holly Hill. We've not been in contact with the enemy, so it's not at all likely they were captured. Oldham, Conway and I talked about going after them, but decided against it since we need the whole company for what lies ahead.

Are you getting any letters from John? I'm worried about him. He's been acting like he's snake bit this whole year and he's told me more than once he wishes he'd not enlisted. He certainly won't shirk his duty or desert, but his mind isn't on the job of soldiering. I don't like worrying about him in this way. How are Ellen and Lilly getting along?

Captain is asking for me, so I must end now. I'll write again as soon as I'm able. Your loving brother, Anderson

P.S. Please share this letter with Mary Ann.

We rode two days southwest to Union Church and rested the horses. On April 28th, Colonel Richardson called a meeting of officers.

"Flowers, you'll be leadin' a detachment of one hundred men northwest to look for Grierson. Oldham said you're just the man for the job."

Richardson directed two more patrols to scout other areas.

"The raiders have been splittin' up their forces, so there could be a few hundred, or a thousand, we don't know. It's our job to find out."

"What do we do if we find them?" Lieutenant Conway asked.

"Retreat if you're attacked by superior numbers. Let 'em have it if you find 'em in small groups. And one more thing. Grierson's outfitted some of his cavalry in Confederate uniforms, so be careful."

I mounted Sultan and led the detachment along the road toward Hazelhurst. Forty minutes later we spotted enemy pickets, dismounted and fired as they retreated into the woods.

"Dallas," I said. "Follow 'em. See if ya can get a look at the main force."

Shortly after he disappeared among the trees, we heard bugles.

"Attack call!" Will said.

"Form a double line here!" I yelled.

Dallas returned in a hurry; his eyes wide with excitement.

"I saw about three hundred horses!"

"Okay men, tie your horses back in that ravine and get back in firing position. Wait till ya get clear shots."

Soon Yanks on horseback began filtering through the trees toward us. The thrill of battle returned, and my heart beat fast. We fired and white smoke rolled through the trees. Two enemy horses went down and the other raiders turned back. Three minutes later a second wave of attackers came racing through the woods.

"Make it count!" I yelled.

Lead crashed through the trees snipping off limbs.

"Back to the horses. Let's get outta here!"

We galloped back to our main force at Union Church and Dallas rode up beside me.

"Think they'll pursue?" he asked.

"Sure do! We just stirred up the hornet's nest!"

Colonel Richardson called his officers together.

"How many Yanks did your scout actually see?" Richardson asked me.

"We saw about thirty," I said. "But he saw three hundred horses tied up."

"That could be Grierson's main force. One report we got said five hundred. Another said two thousand. Get ready to be attacked."

Oldham's uniform was clean, and his beard neatly trimmed. His fingers toyed nervously with an unlit cigar and streaks of sweat rolled down his forehead.

An hour passed and a light rain fell. On the back of my watch, the initials J.E.H. were engraved, Mary Ann's father. I pictured how she looked that last night on her front porch, tears running down her face.

The rain slowed. *They'll attack now.* The stomachache that always accompanied battle returned and my left hand trembled till I tucked it in my pocket. *The devil again.* I opened my Bible to Second Timothy. "For God hath not given us the spirit of fear; but of power, and of love, and of a sound mind." I tucked it back in my haversack and closed my eyes. The verse ran over and over like an echoed voice. My mind was a race of thoughts — fear, excitement, and uncertainty. Rain soaked through my coat, shirt and britches. My heart beat like I'd been running, though I'd been sitting still for over an hour. *No man of sound mind would put himself in this perilous situation!*

Hot fear pounded in my ears and my chest tightened. The thought of death came, as it always did before battle. *I hope it's fast.* An image of Henrietta popped into my mind. She stood with a big, bloody knife in her hand, smiling.

Galloping horses brought me back to the present. Enemy cavalry emerged in the gray rain, riding fast, firing into our ranks.

Oldham raised his sword and shouted, "Fire!"

A mounted enemy soldier was almost on top of me when I pulled the trigger. Mud splattered my face and coat. The enemy assault was fast, and our forces were instantly overrun and disorganized. Some of our regiment were surrounded. Oldham called out, "Retreat, retreat!" and waved his sword to the rear.

I scrambled in the mud, found my pistol and retreated to the woods. In the rain and smoke, I lost track of my men. Sultan's eyes were wide with fear and he pranced nervously and yanked the reins.

I rode back to the line of encounter. A comrade grabbed Sultan's neck and we dragged him back to the woods. Forked lightening lit the sky. The ground was strewn with rifles, equipment, and bodies. I came upon a fallen horse, one of its legs shattered. It looked at me with dark, panicky eyes, and I put my pistol behind its ear and fired. It lay still and steam rose from its wet, brown body.

I got back on Sultan and caught up with other retreating soldiers. Then suddenly, the firing ceased. *Heavenly rain, the great equalizer.* Wet gunpowder is useless.

Our group took the road south out of town and traveled about four miles till we came upon others of our own including John who was unhurt. In the rain and confusion, there was no way to know how many had been captured or killed.

"Let's keep on to Mendville," I said. "We'll regroup there."

"Those Yanks mean business," Will said, shaking his head. "I got off one shot and didn't hit nothin' but raindrops."

We gathered in the town of Mendville as the storm passed and sunshine broke through the clouds at intervals. I looked Sultan over. A streak of blood on his hind quarter turned out to be just a skin tear.

"Are ya hit?" Barrett asked me.

"No. Just a little blood from my hoss."

"There!" he said, pointing to my shoulder. "There's a hole shot clean through."

I took off my coat. It had two holes at the shoulder, one entering and one exiting.

"If that don't beat all!" Barrett said. "You should have a bullet hole in your shoulder!"

I rubbed it. There was no blood, no wound at all.

"Good Lord 'as lookin' out fer ya!" he said.

"Either that or I moved so fast my coat couldn't keep up."

We laughed.

"Horses comin'!" Barrett shouted.

"Load up."

The horses slowed to a walk.

"It's our captain," the picket called out.

Oldham, Dallas, and four soldiers doubled on horses rounded the corner into the sunlight carrying our purple and white regimental flag.

"That's everybody," Oldham said. "How many here?"

"Seventy-three, sir," Barrett reported.

"Damn!" Oldham swore. "Nineteen missing! Grierson's one relentless cavalryman! You've gotta give him that."

A few high clouds drifted eastward reflecting the orange sunset and I breathed easily for the first time that day. Yellow black-eyed-Susans shone brightly along the roadside and in the fields. Many farms had stands of crepe myrtle at the lane turnoffs. Songbirds filled the air with peaceful sounds.

I opened my Bible and read the first verse my eyes landed on. "Ye shall know them by their fruits: Do men gather grapes of thorns, or figs of thistles? Even so every good tree bringeth forth good fruit; but a corrupt tree bringeth forth evil fruit. A good tree cannot bring forth evil fruit, neither can a corrupt tree bring forth good fruit." I pondered the words of Jesus and prayed for my captured comrades and the souls of all who were killed.

Over the next three days we chased the raiders through Summit, McComb, and Magnolia, and all the way to Greensburg, Louisiana. When horses and soldiers could take no more, we stopped to water, feed and rest.

A courier from General Loring intercepted us with a message. After reading it, Oldham called his officers together.

"New orders, men. We're headin' back to Jackson. Rest the night and we'll start back tomorrow."

"What about Grierson?" Sergeant Woods asked.

"We did our best. He was faster than we were. General Pemberton needs us back now to protect Vicksburg."

After studying Oldham's map, I figured we had traveled about one hundred twenty-five miles over three days. After supper, Able told me Oldham wanted to see me. His tent flap was open so I went on in. Oldham sat at his desk, a smoldering cigar in the ashtray and a bottle of whiskey in his hand.

"Care for a drink?" he asked.

"B'lieve I will, Captain."

He smiled and said, "Have a seat."

He poured a shot into a tin for me and I downed it. Then he took off his spectacles, rubbed his eyes, and put his elbows on his knees. I'd never seen him so tired.

"You must be curious about the envelope," he said.

"What envelope?" I asked.

"The message you and Dallas brought back from Broussard."

"Yes, I am curious."

"I'm not at liberty to tell ya exactly what it said, but I can tell ya it saved the lives of many soldiers."

"That's good to know. Alright if I tell Dallas?"

"Sure. That'll be okay."

He picked up the bottle and said, "How about a little more?" He added a shot to my tin.

"Thank you, Captain."

"Take it with you," he said. "I've got a report to write. Goodnight Andy."

I stepped back outside. The stars twinkled in the moonless night and a breeze brought the smells of campfires and tobacco. Soldiers talked and a fiddle played a love song.

"Beautiful night," came a voice beside me.

It was Able and he was gazing at the stars too.

"Makes me think of my woman," I said. "She's waitin' back home for me."

"My Mabel, she's waitin' in heaven for me."

We stood together looking up for a few minutes.

"Why do ya stay?" I asked.

"Stayin' till the end."

"But you could be free now."

"My Mabel's gone and my children's lost."

"I'm glad Lincoln freed the slaves," I said.

"I knowed that already. And I knowed your father was a judge. A man's reputation precedes him."

"I'll be glad when this is all over," I said.

He nodded, "When it is, we'll all be free."

We shook hands and parted.

May 3, 1863

Dearest Mary Ann,

I'm writing from Greensburg, Louisiana. Two days ago, a bullet went clean through my coat, but my shoulder was not touched. I've never been one to believe much in miracles, but in this case, I can't figure anything else. The miracle, or whatever it was, strengthened my resolve to return to you soon.

In your last letter, you mentioned that Dennis is talking about joining the army. The next time he brings meat, please tell him I believe it's better to stay at home and support his family. The mess we're in is no place for a boy his age. I don't know how to explain it to him or anybody who hasn't been in the shooting but fighting changes men in bad ways. At first every soldier was excited about fighting. Now some have to be prodded to obey orders — even something as simple as gathering firewood. There's one man in Company C who stays to himself all the time and mutters things that make no sense at all.

A good many are tough on the outside, seeming not to be bothered by bloodshed and death, but I don't think they're being honest. So far I've not gone feeble or become too hardened, but it pains my heart every time I think of shooting at other men. I have to tell myself I'm doing my duty. My prayer for all soldiers is that our tender feelings are still somewhere deep inside and will, with God's help, someday rise again.

I apologize for this gloomy letter. There's nothing that brings peace to my heart more than reading your sweet words.

Love, Anderson

Chapter 29

SPIES

May 1863, Mississippi

On the journey back to Jackson, a detachment of ten men from company K were pulled out and sent with others under the command of Lieutenant Hale, Company A, on a scouting mission to Edwards Depot.

"Don't like it one bit," Captain Oldham told me after the squad left.

"Is Hale a problem?" I asked.

"I wouldn't walk across the street to piss on him if he 'as on fire!"

"What do ya know about him?"

"I'd better leave it at that," Oldham said and he stomped off.

The 20th resumed the march toward Jackson. Along the way we saw loose livestock, burned barns, and found a young boy wandering around. His family name was Tarbutton and he was lost.

"Can we take 'em with us?" Dallas asked me.

"No, but ya can help find someone who'll take him in. Catch up with us as soon as ya can."

Late that afternoon we camped for the night. About two in the morning, the sound of horses and angry voices woke me. The detachment under Lieutenant Hale had returned. Oldham was huffed and all hell broke loose.

"What da ya mean ya don't know what happened to 'em?" Oldham screamed at Hale. "What the dickens were ya doin'?"

Spit flew from Oldham's mouth and he paced back and forth and then shouted in Hale's face.

"I'm gonna have you court-martialed. Get outta my sight you son of a bitch!"

Hale hung his head and walked away. Oldham pulled a burning stick from a campfire, threw it at Hale and almost hit him. The commotion woke the whole company, and everyone gathered around.

"What's the problem?" Lieutenant Conway asked.

"Hale lost five soldiers!" Oldham screamed as he threw his cigar in the dirt and ground it to shreds with his boot. "That piece of crap Hale is responsible."

He stomped off and ducked into his command tent, pulling up a couple of stakes.

"Good thing Captain didn't have his pistol," Barrett said. "I think he mighta shot Hale on the spot."

"Able'll get him a drink," Conway said. "He'll be better in an hour."

I went back to sleep and a while later Dallas returned from his mission and woke me. He looked distraught.

"Did ya find the boy's family?" I asked.

"Yeah, no problem," he said, "but there's bad news."

He led me a ways from the camp under a quarter moon.

"John's missing," he said. "He was in Hale's patrol!"

My chest tightened like a vise and my heart raced. I ran to our tent, grabbed my pistol, and sprinted along the road toward Company A's encampment. Dallas chased after me.

"Where're ya goin'?" he said.

"To kill Hale!" I yelled.

Dallas caught up with me and grabbed my shoulders.

"I won't let ya do that," he shouted. "You're comin' with me."

He took my pistol and hauled me down a hillside in a trot. We came to a river and fell in. The current drug us along and I gasped for air. He pulled me up and screamed in my face.

"Calm down, man!"

The water swirled around us.

"Lemme go, asshole!"

He dunked me under again and then pulled me to shallow water. A booming voice called out from the woods.

"You two goin' for an early mornin' swim?"

Colonel Russell, the commander of the 20th, stood tall in his saddle on the creekbank, his cigar glowing in the dark.

"I need all my men rested and ready to fight," he said calmly. "We've got a mission tomorrow."

We sloshed up the bank.

"Get some sleep!" Russell commanded and rode off into the darkness.

I beat the ground with my fists, angrier than a hornet, then lay in the grass, catching my breath while Dallas stood nearby.

"What'll I tell Ellen?" I said.

"The truth."

"But she'll be devastated!"

"John'll be alright. If he 'as captured he'll probably be in prison for a while and then exchanged like we were."

"You know they're not makin' exchanges now!"

"Then he'll sit out the war in prison."

"Dog gone ya Dallas! I just lost my brother and you're tellin' me he'll be fine. Prison's as dangerous as fightin'. You know that!"

He took my pistol and left me by the riverbank, wet from head to toe, worried and confused. My knuckles were torn and bleeding from pounding the ground.

When I crawled out of our tent the next morning, Dallas was cooking our breakfast. He handed me a tin of coffee and patted my shoulder.

"I'm sorry, Dallas. I ..."

He cut me off. "That's done. Forget about it. We're in this together, remember? Your loss is my loss, buddy."

After breakfast the company packed, mounted and headed north again. At sunset on May 11th, we arrived at Jackson and I posted my letters, including one to Ellen. Dallas made me rewrite it three times before he said it was okay. We resupplied and rode all night on Utica Road and arrived at Edwards Depot as the sun came up.

"Leave your rifles with the horses. Get axes and shovels from the wagons," Oldham pointed. "The last quarter mile of the road ... make it impassable."

"But won't that block our retreat?" Conway asked.

"We're blockin' Grant's advance on Vicksburg!"

We felled trees and lay them crisscrossed on the road. Skinny pines were sharpened into spikes and fixed within the roadblock. It reminded me of Sister's pin cushion. We worked furiously hour after hour in direct sunlight and by mid-afternoon the company was exhausted, hot, and powerfully hungry. We'd not eaten in over a day.

When we returned to camp, Walker had a mouthwatering supper ready for us. By a stroke of luck a foraging patrol had found an enemy wagon in a barn. It was full of fresh potatoes, flour, rice and honey. They also found ammunition and three-dozen pairs of new boots. That evening was the first time my stomach had been full in weeks.

Around four o'clock the next morning, Oldham woke me. I hoped he had good news about John, but he did not.

"Get up," he said. "Goin' to battle and I want ya to lead."

In fifteen minutes our company was ready and mounted. A local man led us along a backwoods road under a sliver of moonlight. In a half hour, we intersected a bigger road leading southwest.

"There's a church about a mile on down," the man said. "Chapel Hill."

I sent Sergeant Barrett to scout while the rest of us waited along the sides of the road in the morning dew. Low clouds crossed the sky moving east.

"Smells like rain," Dallas said.

An old man on a mule came up the road from behind.

"Ya can't go this way," Conway told him.

"But I've gotta get home to my wife, she's sick and I've got her medicine."

"I'm sorry, but there's gonna be shootin' up ahead in a bit. You'd best sit here a spell and rest. We'll come back and let ya know when it's safe."

Barrett returned and reported that the church was all clear, so our company advanced and set up a defensive perimeter around the church, cemetery, and a burned barn.

"The men want to build fires and cook," Barrett whispered.

"Not now," I said. "Expecting Yanks any minute. Gotta stay ready."

The first light of day touched the treetops. About a half hour later, Amos, one of our forward pickets, ran back to the church grounds.

"Men marchin' this way!" he said.

"Take positions," I commanded.

Directly, two columns of enemy soldiers emerged from the mist and moved along the road toward us. I fired at the officer in front, then a volley of rifle fire shattered the morning quiet. The smoke blew back among us and filled my nostrils. Most of the Yanks broke and ran to the cemetery and the field beyond. A handful continued toward us, firing, and were cut down in a hurry. Five minutes later the enemy regrouped and attacked up the road, but our position on higher ground and better cover gave us the advantage. Several Yanks fell and the others retreated.

"Barrett," I said. "Take twenty men and pursue 'em. Everyone else spread out and hunt 'em down. Take prisoners and guns."

Our men gathered up the wounded Yankees who could walk and we heard shots coming from Barrett's direction.

Barrett's squad returned a few minutes later with three more prisoners. They sat on the ground and I circled them with my pistol drawn.

"I want information," I said. "What units are ya from?"

A man with a bushy, black beard spoke up.

"20th Illinois."

"A full regiment?" I asked.

He hesitated and then said, "I'm not required to tell ya more."

"Don't make me ask more questions!" I yelled. "Tell me what you'd want to know if you were the one holdin' me prisoner!"

"About eight hundred, I think," he said.

"What are your orders?"

"Movin' north on Utica Road. There're more behind us."

"How many?"

"Don't know, sir. I'm not an officer and they don't tell us much."

"Well that's one thing we've got in common."

I recalled how defeated, hopeless and afraid I was when captured at Fort Donelson.

Away from the prisoners, I told Barrett, "Have 'em dig graves and bury their dead."

That afternoon Oldham told me our generals were not sure if Grant would direct his army toward Vicksburg or Raymond.

"We need two scouts behind their lines to find out. Who should we send?"

"How 'bout Harrison?"

"Haven't seen him since Edwards Depot. I'm afraid he's been captured."

Harrison was our best scout.

"How 'bout Bob Waddell?" I said. "He's as good at bluffin' as any man I know."

"You're right about that. Slicker'n owl shit. Who should go with him?"

"I'll go."

"Okay but be careful. I need ya back in one piece."

It was treacherous to go deep behind enemy lines, so Bob and I laid our plans carefully. We looked over the map and talked to an old man who lived in the area. Late that evening, we rode through our forward picket lines, traveled for an hour and saw no Yankees.

About midnight we came upon a two-story mansion with white columns. A sliver of the moon lit the night. It was as quiet as a tomb and we approached slowly. An old negro man sat in a rocking chair on the front porch smoking a pipe, so we showed ourselves fully.

"Who's y'all?" he asked.

"Name's Anderson. Lookin' for a place to stay the night."

"I's the only one left, so we got plenty of room. Master's off to war and the rest of the family left last week."

"This is my business partner, Bob. We're travelin' through to Tennessee."

"My name's Henry."

"Will ya tend our hosses?"

"Yes, sir." Henry showed us inside. "You can sleep here," he pointed.

"One more request, Henry," I asked. "Will ya wake us up in four hours?"

"Sure, but the family took the clock with 'em and I don't have no watch."

"Here, use mine." I handed him my pocket watch and two dollars.

"Thank ya kindly, Mister Anderson."

He took the horses around back.

"Think we can trust him?" Bob whispered.

"We have to. Let's get some sleep." I slept with my hand on my revolver.

Henry woke us as promised and we rode cautiously along the road toward Port Gibson. We hitched our horses in a skirt of woods near what we supposed was Grant's picket line and proceeded on foot. It was still dark when we spotted a picket pacing back and forth over a thirty-yard span with his rifle on his shoulder. We slipped through the picket line and proceeded toward the light of campfires.

About a quarter mile along we hid in a large clump of bushes on a little ridge and waited. In half an hour, the light revealed a great field below us, packed with Grant's army. I counted eight regiments, about eight thousand men. We observed for two more hours and then after they ate breakfast the enemy began to break camp. The pickets returned to their units and we retreated to the woods. Bob stood guard while I climbed a tall tree to get a better view.

Up high, through my field glasses, I made out the farthest reaches of the encampment including a signal corps with a large tent, which I presumed to be the

Union command. Troops and wagons started lining up on the road heading northeast, the road to Raymond. Back on the ground, I found Bob sound asleep.

"Wake up, man. They're headin' to Raymond. Let's get goin'."

We expected our return trip could be hazardous. It was not uncommon for scouts to be accidentally shot by comrades. We walked the horses across the road into a thick pine forest. Suddenly, Bob's horse broke loose and headed back toward the Yankee camp. He took off running after his horse, but I caught up with him and told him we had to get back. He paid me no mind and disappeared into the woods chasing the horse. A few minutes passed then a pistol fired twice in quick succession. Bob did not return, and I decided it was best to get back to headquarters and report.

Near our lines, a picket arrested me and had two men escort me to army headquarters. As we approached the command tent, Oldham stood with a group of officers, smoking his ever-present cigar.

"I see ya got yourself in trouble again, Flowers," he said, laughing. "Soldiers let this man go. He's my spy."

"Where's Bob?" Oldham asked.

I told him what happened.

"General Loring's here."

I made my report to Loring and he sent messengers on horseback to notify other regiments. Oldham and I rode to rejoin our company.

"Any news about John?" I asked. He shook his head no.

When we reached camp Oldham spoke to Walker.

"You got the doings for a good meal? Our spy has returned and he's hungry."

"You've got food?" I asked.

Dallas walked up and greeted me. "Yep. Got a nice resupply early this mornin'. Fresh Union provisions." He pointed to wagons.

"Seems we get food every time I go on a mission," I said.

"Sure does," Dallas said. "I wish you'd leave more often."

I enjoyed a good meal then lay down and took a nap, being unusually fatigued from the mission. In midafternoon, a hubbub woke me.

"Get up, we're movin'," Dallas said. "By the way, Bob's back, and he's got a cockamamie story."

We packed, mounted and headed north with the regiment.

"Where's Bob?" I asked Barrett.

"He's ridin' in a wagon at the rear. Injured." He rolled his eyes.

I slipped Sultan out of line, let the column pass and found the wagons for the wounded. Bob's head was propped up on a sack of corn and his feet dangled over the edge, still in his civilian clothes. He didn't look hurt to me.

"What happened?" I asked.

He told me he surprised two enemy pickets in the woods and killed them both.

"You disobeyed orders!"

"I needed my hoss!"

"You killed both with two pistol shots?"

"Nope," he said. "Killed one with my pistol and slit the throat of the second."

He held up a long knife with blood stains on it and went on to tell me he found his horse but was caught and taken to General Grant's headquarters.

"How'd ya get away?"

"Convinced him to lemme go."

"You met General Grant?"

"Yep. It took some fast talkin', but it worked. Looky here."

He held out a letter. I took it from him as the wagon train ambled along. It was a well-written document releasing Bob on the condition that he not fight again unless he was formally exchanged. It was signed, General U.S. Grant. Bob was a well-educated man, so I figured he had written the parole letter himself.

"That's a rip-snortin' story, but I'm glad ya made it back. Ya hurt?"

He grinned and pointed to the side of his head. "Touched!"

We both laughed.

"Hey," Bob said. "Want some coffee?"

"Sure. Where'd ya get it?"

"From Grant!"

I took the bag of coffee beans, rode back to the front of our column, and relayed Bob's story to Sergeant Woods.

Chapter 30

DEFENSIVE ENCOUNTERS
May 1863, Mississippi

In May our army was sent northeast of Raymond to a place called Fourteen Mile Creek to help stop the Union advance. A round of cannons boomed in the distance. We'd not seen the enemy, but judging by the sounds, the cannons had to be about a mile away. Sporadic cannon fire continued for half an hour and then a runner arrived.

"Message for Captain Oldham," he said, panting.

Oldham arrived with his map.

"Yanks are advancing up Utica Road," the messenger said. "They have artillery. The 15th Tennessee is holding here. Your company is to reinforce them on the double."

"Do we know the enemy strength?" Oldham asked.

"No. I've gotta get back. Any message in return?"

"Tell 'em we're on our way."

We followed Oldham down the road and came to a large, treeless valley. Enemy cannons were placed along a ridge overlooking the valley where they could support an infantry advance. I counted puffs of smoke as the cannons on the ridge fired in order. *Boom, boom, boom!* Twenty-two in a row! Cannon fire was my worst fear, next to being burned alive. We joined the Tennesseans and formed long attack lines, two rows deep, our purple and white colors out front. Blue-clad soldiers by the hundreds poured down the rise on the other side of the valley and formed battle lines perpendicular to Utica Road, four rows deep.

As we waited, sharp pains shot through my stomach, and Dallas noticed me wincing.

"You okay?" he said.

"Yeah, I'm fine."

"That's bull. The Devil's got ya! Happens every time, right?"

"Whadda ya mean, every time?"

"Before battle. The pains ya have."

I didn't know he knew. A minute passed as we waited for orders to advance.

"You have it too?" I said.

"Sure. Sometimes my innards seize up for days."

"How'd ya know I call it the Devil?"

"You talk in your sleep, buddy."

"Strange. We've fought side-by-side for two years and this is the first time we've talked about it."

"There's a lot of things we don't talk about."

I wondered if he was referring to our visit with Broussard in Natchez.

Drum corps on both sides began their cadences and both armies marched across the field to engage. At a range of a hundred and fifty yards rifle firing began. Volley after volley, we exchanged lead. Clouds of rolling smoke obscured the valley between the armies. Enemy bullets ripped through us in multiples and cannon shells exploded in the chaos. A man fell next to me, instantly dead. The devil's rage boiled within me. My pistol was useless at that distance, so I took the dead man's rifle and cartridge box and joined in the shooting.

After firing and reloading once, impulse took over. As the armies drew closer my ears rang and my stomach ached unmercifully. *My final battle.* We fought over the field for three hours and then fell back to the road to regroup and resupply. The smoke and dust made it hard to assess the strength of the enemy and our losses.

Oldham found Lieutenant Conway and me.

"What's the report?" Oldham asked.

"All soldiers accounted for, sir, except Attison," Conway reported. "No one's seen him since we left the woods."

Attison's mother, Aliza, had been my school-ma'am.

As we resupplied, the road clogged with soldiers returning from the battlefield … many without guns or shoes. Comrades held each other upright. Dazed expressions were on many faces and some looked frightened out of their minds. The stream of stragglers kept coming like a spring of water from the ground. Hundreds passed by in the space of twenty minutes.

Conway pulled a man aside.

"What regiment ya with?" he asked the man.

The soldier stared back, his mouth open and bleeding. His eyes were pink like wild sweet potato flowers and he pointed at his ears. If he had seen the Devil himself, he couldn't have looked more afraid. He tried to answer Conway's question, but no words came out of his mouth, only blood. A buddy grabbed his arm and pulled him back into the flow of retreating men.

"Cowards!" one of the Tennessee soldiers near us shouted. He was tall and had overly large, bright blue eyes.

"Maybe not," Conway said. "They're comin' from the front! You don't know what they've been through."

"They's cowards," the blue-eyed man repeated.

A few other onlookers hissed at the stragglers. Conway stepped toward the Tennessee soldier, but Barrett held him back. Company K fell in with the Tennesseans again and both armies started massing lines for another attack. Dallas was beside me and he looked exhausted.

"Good luck, Lieutenant," he said with a sigh.

"Double good luck to ya, my friend."

My stomach seized up in pain like a solid block of ice and it was all I could do to stand up straight. My right eye was swollen almost shut from loose gun powder. Our company was in the second wave crossing the field as bullets zipped through our ranks, some hitting flesh.

This time our advance went farther. I lost count of my shots, but my rifle barrel became scorching hot. Halfway across the field we came upon a ditch three feet deep with just a trace of water in the bottom. We crossed quickly and reformed our attack lines. Enemy fire quickly overwhelmed us, and we fell back to the ditch. Scores of men were struck down. Wounded men who could still load and fire did so. *Amazing what a loyal soldier will do.* I soaked my hands in a muddy spot in the ditch to cool the blisters. Suddenly men around me began shouting. A company of enemy cavalry charged our position. We returned fire, but they got perilously close to us and raked the ditch with their repeating rifles, before retreating. Several men were hit. My luck held and then I realized I'd pissed my trousers.

"Captain," I yelled. "We've gotta get out of here! We're way outnumbered."

"Must wait for orders," he said, looking unnaturally calm for the chaotic circumstances.

"Look!" I motioned to the place we had begun the charge two hours earlier. The dusty field was littered with bodies, guns and dead horses. Canister shells exploded overhead with regularity.

"No one's gonna come through that to give us orders. It's up to us to decide what to do."

Oldham stared at me.

"You think you're smart enough to decide what to do?" he asked, frustrated.

"Sir, I feel it's wise to retreat and fight another day. I've heard you say that before."

He hesitated and bit his lip.

"Okay, get the men ready."

"Thank you, Captain."

Orders were passed along. In a few minutes, I told Oldham the men were ready.

"Let's wait jis a bit," he said, glancing at the enemy. "I think they're 'bout to call it off."

He handed me his field glasses. Streams of Yankees were flowing out of the field and up the ridge where they came from before the mass battle began. Cannon fire slowed, then ceased. We waited a few more minutes, then retreated without being fired upon.

"Anybody seen Attison?" I asked.

"No," Woods said. "Olive and Lampkin were killed, and three others hit … Miles in the gut."

"Make your report to Oldham."

Bodies of the dead and wounded lay in the ditch on both sides of the road. Soldiers lay in the fields, exhausted and nursing wounds. A shoeless soldier begged me for water. His forehead was blackened, and his shirt tied in a sling to hold his arm. I poured water to rinse his face and he opened his eyelids for a moment. He was the tall, blue-eyed Tennessean from earlier. Shortly after dark, word came that our whole army was to retreat to Raymond. The enemy outnumbered us, and we were short of ammunition and out of food. A sane commander could make no other choice.

A fair number of our men walked because their horses had been killed or lost in the confusion. Dallas' horse disappeared, so he doubled with me on Sultan and our procession moved slowly north toward Raymond.

Amos rode up beside and handed me a haversack.

"It's Attison's," he said.

I thought about Attison's mother, Aliza, and what I would tell her if I made it home. I worried about Ellen and what she'd do when she heard about John.

We passed through Raymond and arrived back in Jackson early on the morning of May 13th. Company K and several others under the command of Brigadier General John Gregg were assigned the task of defending Jackson while the bulk of the Confederate forces evacuated westward to reinforce Pemberton's garrison in Vicksburg. Soon after we set up defensive positions, a light rain began. I rested with my men while pickets kept lookout.

At daybreak Oldham called an officer's meeting.

"Scouts just reported Grant's army two miles away, headin' toward us. We're to set up defensive positions along here." He pointed to a map. "Baker's Creek runs here. The bald crest … Champion Hill. The road from Raymond comes in here. The road from Clinton … here. The town of Edwards is behind us. This crossroads is what Grant needs to advance on Vicksburg. Questions?"

"Will we have cannons in the fight?" Sergeant Woods asked.

"Yes. Fifteen batteries, about sixty cannons. Should hold 'em back." Oldham looked each officer in the eyes. "We're not gonna let Grant take the crossroads!"

After we readied for battle, I ate the last of my peanuts, drank from my canteen and watched the sun rise over the treetops. Behind us, magnolia trees lined the lane to the Champion's house. Big white blooms glowed brightly in the sunlight against the dark green leaves. The breeze carried the fragrance of lilacs and water beads glistened in the dancing tallgrass. Dozens of meadowlarks sang joyfully from the rain-soaked fields. A yellow-breasted meadowlark lit on the fencerow near me. *Soon this'll be chaos. Where will the larks go to hide?*

Bugle calls echoed across the peaceful meadow, followed by cannon booms to the east. It was seven forty-five.

"Here we go," Dallas said with a grimace.

Enemy divisions came up from the south and we reoriented our defenses as they marched en masse up the gradual incline. At two hundred yards the enemy charged and began firing.

"Brave men," Dallas said to me, motioning toward the enemy.

"Plenty brave."

"And plentiful."

Our cannons flung shot and canister upon the charging Yankees and every rifle joined the defense. Despite our full effort, enemy soldiers advanced to our lines and a few crossed the lane and got behind us.

Oldham appeared on his horse and ordered a retreat. He rode up and down the line to make sure every soldier heard. He made a tall, open target and it was a miracle that he was not cut down by the withering fire. We mounted and headed west down the road toward Vicksburg and halted a half-mile along.

"Regroup here!" Oldham shouted.

The men gathered around him, about one hundred and fifty, a half-dozen without mounts.

"We're going to counterattack," he said. "Get loaded and ready."

At two o'clock, we attacked and drove the enemy back past the crossroads and up past the Champion house where we had started the day. Before long the enemy sent forces against our right flank, attempting to cut off our path to retreat. We withdrew once again and moved toward Vicksburg. Two more of our men were missing.

"We're outnumbered, as you well know," Oldham said. "In another eight miles or so we'll come to the Big Black. Six companies of the 20th Mississippi will be joining Tennessee forces already there. We're to protect the bridges while the wagon train and army crosses. It's certain that Grant's forces will attack us. He's not cautious! He means to kill us all!"

At midnight we arrived at the river and joined the Tennesseans. Our horses were taken across the bridge to be fed and kept away from the battle for the bridge. Each man was issued forty cartridges, a half-pound of smoked pork, two carrots and a loaf of bread. I ate my whole portion and fell asleep straight away.

In the morning I heard footsteps, muted voices of men, and the rumble of wagons. Hundreds of our soldiers, some on foot and others mounted, along with wagons and cannons, were crossing the bridge in a flurry. Thick clouds had moved in overnight, so daylight came on slowly. Rifle trenches had been dug along the east side of the Big Black and fortifications of felled trees erected still farther east.

"When do ya think they'll attack?" Dallas asked me.

"As soon as they're able. They must know they have us on the run."

I handed my rifle to Dallas and walked back to the bridge. The Big Black was muddy and the current swirling. Sultan's ferry was less than a hundred miles upstream and home just a few miles beyond. *Henrietta might swim in the river today. Sure hope the fighting never gets near home.*

My musings were interrupted by cannon and rifle fire from the east and I hurried back to the front line. Suddenly the column of retreating soldiers approaching the bridge rushed forward upon itself like falling dominoes. Men fell and some were trampled.

An officer raced up on horseback and yelled. "Prepare to be attacked!"

When the press reached the bridge, soldiers fell into the river and screamed for help. They shed their rifles and equipment and swam to shore. Others slipped under. Horses panicked in the commotion and fell into the river. Another officer ran toward us.

"They're attacking our column a quarter mile back," he screamed. "You've gotta come help us."

"Our orders are to protect the bridge!" I said. "Keep the crossing orderly."

He ran back to save his men.

The enemy was closing fast toward the bridge from both the east and south when one of the Tennessee scouts returned, his clothes wet to the waist.

"We're protected by a bayou over there," he pointed. "I just came through it."

"We've got eighteen cannons that cover that sweep," a Tennessee officer said. "That oughta hold 'em."

Fire from our cannons signaled that the Yanks were getting close.

"Ready, men?" the Tennessee officer yelled. "Give the fools hell!"

Enemy soldiers appeared at the edge of the open ground and charged across in large numbers. When they reached the swamp they waded through without slowing, bayonets fixed. We fired, reloaded and fired again, striking some, but not slowing their advance. I fired nine shots and the Yanks were upon us. They'd closed the gap in less than five minutes.

"Back to the bridge," I hollered.

Our forces fell back and set up another line of defense about seventy yards from the bridge.

"A lot of our men are cut off," the Tennessee officer yelled.

"Too late to save 'em," I screamed above the shooting, waving him back. "Get everyone ya can across."

Oldham rode up. A hail of bullets slapped into a stand of trees beside us and a willow branch fell on his horse. A bullet popped my coat and fell to the ground. I ducked behind a tree and noticed blood on Sultan's neck.

"Hold out as long ya can," Oldham shouted. "Then burn the bridge."

"But that'll doom the rest of our army," I screamed.

"It's what we have to do!" He turned his horse and shrugged his shoulders. "General Pemberton's orders."

Back at the front I yelled to Sergeant Barrett. "Consolidate the company along both sides of the road and step up your fire. I'll be at the bridge."

A tall officer with a silver-barreled revolver tucked under his belt stood straight-backed in the middle of the bridge with his hands on his hips. Retreating soldiers ran past him. He looked like a statue among the escaping men.

"Major Lockett," he said calmly. "Engineering Corps."

"Lieutenant Flowers."

"I need you and your soldiers to burn the bridge."

"Yes, sir. Tell me what to do."

"The wagon?" he pointed. "Coal oil. Empty all the barrels on these timbers. When you're finished, bring the last of your men over."

A dozen men helped me soak the bridge good with five hogshead barrels, then I returned to our firing line. Yankee gunfire intensified and the nearest enemy soldiers were only fifty yards away. Streams of our soldiers ran toward us, many without rifles.

"We're leaving now!" I yelled as loud as I could.

I motioned to Barrett and Woods as enemy fire cut down more Confederates along the road.

"Leave ten men to keep shootin' … ten men who can swim. Everyone else, cross now!"

Five minutes later the last of Company K was across, except for the swimmers.

"Lieutenant Flowers?"

Major Lockett stood holding two burning torches. He handed one to me and walked downstream on the riverbank.

I crossed the bridge and touched the soaked timbers on the east side. Within a minute flames roared eight feet high, a fearsome firestorm through which no man could pass alive. The heat scorched my face and hands. The rising inferno seared the leaves off nearby trees, and they floated up and away and then back to the river as ashes. A cloud of noxious black smoke rose in the afternoon sky. Through the heat waves and smoke, I saw wavy images of our last men racing for the river. Farther behind, other Confederates ran toward the bridge.

Major Lockett stood on the west bank twenty yards downstream by a pontoon bridge. He tossed his torch on the bridge and it burst into flames, and then we saluted each other. *How strange the deeds of war — destroying works of God and man.*

Thick smoke rose through the trees as our men swam across and crawled up the bank. I counted as they emerged from the muddy water. Some were shoeless, but all ten were alive. The last man from the river was Dallas. He ran down the road after the others and I hurried to catch up.

Suddenly the firing at the bridge ceased and I turned around to look. Confederate soldiers stood with their hands above their heads, waiting to be taken prisoner. I felt like a failure.

Chapter 31

SLOWING THE ENEMY
May — mid-June 1863, Jackson — Vicksburg, Mississippi

We rode a few miles west on the Jackson-Vicksburg road in the afternoon and stopped to rest and feed the horses. Captain Oldham gathered the men, took off his hat, and addressed the company.

"I'm proud to lead such brave and determined men. I asked you to give the fight to the enemy and you exceeded my expectations! Wish I could give each one of you a medal for valor!"

He raised his hat to us, and we basked in our captain's praise. Our trust in him was an indispensable part of our loyalty and willingness to risk our lives over and over.

"Your fierce defense allowed thousands to cross the river and escape. I know you'd rather have stayed and fought head on, but this day the wiser choice was to retreat."

He paused and wiped his forehead with his handkerchief. He looked tired and his voice trembled, but his words inspired nonetheless.

"Captain ... we goin' to Vicksburg?" Lieutenant Conway asked.

"We're the last across, so our job is to keep an eye out for enemy cavalry. The Big Black is our rear guard for a few hours at least."

"Captain," Barrett said. "It's been two days since we had a decent meal."

"Food's on the way so start your fires!"

Cheers went up from the starved and weary men, and Oldham put his hat back on.

"We're goin' to rest here till dark and then move toward Vicksburg. Need to put some distance between the enemy and us."

Oldham saluted the company.

"You are the pride of the South!" he shouted with all his might. He smiled broadly and dismissed us.

"Captain," I asked. "Permission for a couple hours off?"

"Sure. Where'll ya be in case I need ya?"

"Cotton patch on the north side of the road a quarter mile back."

I tied Sultan with the other horses, left my guns and headed back down the road. Smoke rose in the distance. The factories and machine shops in Jackson had surely been burned to the ground, and telegraph lines and train tracks destroyed.

A fencerow knotted with trees broke at the cotton field. I lay on my back and looked at the sky, clear and blue from horizon to horizon. The air was warm and humid. My eyes burned from gunpowder and coal oil smoke. Tears ran off my

213

cheeks and my thoughts ran fast. After a while on solid earth my head slowed down.

A hawk and two crows passed over the field. The hawk sailed along just ahead of the crows and perched in a gumtree in the fencerow. The crows screamed and circled, then one nose-dived and struck the hawk. It let out a shriek and flew away with both crows in pursuit. They passed out of sight and hearing distance and I fell asleep. Soon here they came around a second time and five crows followed the hawk, not just two. They mobbed the hawk then backed off. The hawk hollered out and changed course. The crows screamed *caw, caw, caw* and the fight continued into the distance as I dozed off again.

Boom! Boom! Boom! The deep sound of naval cannons far to the west woke me. *Vicksburg.* An oval-shaped white object tipped the horizon and I climbed a tree to get a better look with my field glasses. It was an observation balloon. I'd seen sketches in newspapers. As it rose, I barely made out the basket hanging underneath as the sun drew closer to the earth.

After a good supper, Oldham addressed the company again.

"We're to return and rejoin General Loring to the east."

"I thought we were here to defend Vicksburg?" Conway asked.

"These are our new orders! What do we do when we get orders?"

"Obey!" the men answered together.

"We're in a bit of a bind going back," Oldham continued. "The Yanks have us tight from the rear. We're gonna need some luck and cunning to break through. Cook up your food and get some rest. We'll leave later tonight."

At midnight, our company and five others from the 20th Regiment headed north in two columns on a narrow lane. We covered about five miles and then turned east. Miraculously, we slipped around the Union lines near Rocky Springs Church without arousing their attention and just before dawn arrived at the outskirts of Jackson.

Two days later I led a patrol of twenty men along the east side of the Big Black. While taking a rest in a shady acorn flat, we were ambushed by two-dozen enemy cavalry. It was a blustery day and we didn't hear them approaching till they were almost upon us. I suspect that our picket fell asleep. The Yanks surrounded us so quickly I told the men not to fire.

The Yankee lieutenant leading the patrol took me away from the group while his men held the others under arrest. He said he was under instructions to capture as many Confederates as he could, but they were far from their lines and he didn't want to take all of us back, preferring to advance instead. I suggested that he keep me and let the rest of our men go, and after consulting with his sergeant, he agreed. The Yankees took our guns, ammunition and horses and I told my men to walk back to camp and not try to rescue me.

The officer had me blindfolded and placed on a horse. My hands were tied to the saddle and we rode for what seemed like several miles before stopping. I was left alone for about half an hour, then the lieutenant returned. He helped me off the horse, took off my blindfold, and told me I was near the Big Black. I thanked him and he rode off. I sat on the bank and after considerable effort I got the ropes loose.

I headed upstream until it got dark and then slept in a hollow cypress stump. In the morning, I set out again and soon came upon the carcass of a dead horse. I recognized the place where our patrol had been captured and found my pistol under the leaves. Just as the sun was setting I came to a farm and was welcomed by an old woman who took me in for the night and fed me. The next day I found my company and reported to Oldham.

"You got real lucky Flowers," he said. "Thought we'd lost ya for the duration."

"I even managed to keep this," I said, holding up my revolver. "But I lost Sultan."

"See the quartermaster. He'll find ya a new mount."

The 20th Regiment camped at Beattie's Bluff for the next three weeks and sent patrols out on the roads in Hinds County leading to the Big Black. Occasionally we encountered enemy soldiers who had been separated from their army, but otherwise we enjoyed a respite from the fighting. Food was again more plentiful and the mail that had accumulated at Jackson was delivered. I got a letter from Sister.

May 13, 1863

Dear Brother,

Guess who I saw at church on Sunday? Attison! He told us about being captured, hit in the head and knocked out. He's got a scar across his forehead about two inches long, but otherwise seems okay. The Yankees paroled him a few days after he was captured and sent him home. He's waiting till he's called back up when the next parole-exchange happens. Of course, Aliza is overjoyed to have him home.

Lamkin's mother broke down in church on Sunday. She'd just learned the news of his death. Elizabeth and I tried to comfort, but she was beyond help. That makes three families that I know who have lost men in this dreadful war. We live under a dark cloud of uncertainty. Even if the war ended tomorrow our lives would never be peaceful again. Our losses are too great.

Please be careful, dear brother.

Love, Sister

I put the letter in my pocket and went to see Oldham.

"Is Captain in?" I asked Able.

"Sure is," he said. "Go on in."

I told Oldham the news about Attison.

"That's great, Flowers," he said with a smile of relief. "I was worried he'd been killed."

He found a list on his worktable and scratched Attison's name off.

May 29, 1863

Dear Sister,

I'm writing from Jackson again and send greetings from Dallas. He saw me writing Mary Ann a while ago and he's jealous because he doesn't have a special girlfriend like I do. He knows Emma likes him, but says he's not written her.

War is a hazardous occupation to learn on the job. At first I felt completely swallowed up in the troop movements and especially the battles. Now as an officer, I have a little bit of control over the lethal elements and can sometimes make decisions on behalf of my men. Only one thing is for sure in this deadly enterprise — we are all in it together. The life of each soldier depends on wise generals and the lives of the generals depend upon the discipline of the soldier and the faith he has in leadership. My aim is to be a trustworthy officer and do my best to protect the lives of our men.

The longer the war goes on, the farther away home and normal life seems. I wonder how much longer it will be before I'm back home again.

Your loving brother, Anderson

Orders came on June 12th that the 20th Regiment was to report to Vernon. We rode hard, arrived on the evening of the 13th, and Oldham called the company together.

"Men, we're givin' up our horses tomorrow. Goin' back to regular infantry."

There was a murmur among the men and a voice from the back yelled out, "Captain, my feet are fixin to hurt."

It was Amos, and everybody had a good laugh.

"I know you'd rather ride than march, but these orders are from General Johnston. We're now part of General Adam's Division and our horses are needed for the cavalry."

"Where're we goin' next?" Sergeant Woods asked.

"Headin' for Canton. About five miles. Leavin' first thing tomorrow. Hope y'all remember how to march."

The men laughed again and dispersed.

The next morning, after a good brush-down, I wished my new horse good luck and turned him over to the quartermaster.

Chapter 32

VICKSBURG FALLS
Mid-June — July 1863, Mississippi

After setting up camp northwest of Canton, our company passed the next few days in peace. It was the first time in many weeks we had enough food to get our fill. Within a few days, a dozen sporting women had slipped in among our regiment. This often happened when we camped in one place for a while. Early one morning, I saw one of the hookers, an Indian woman, come out of Oldham's tent and hurry away. I was severely tempted to make a woman friend too, but it was contrary to what I'd been taught in church. The war caused many men to throw off the rules of civilization.

On June 22nd, our company was sent out, this time to Bear Creek, a distance of twenty-odd miles. The weather was broiling hot and humid and the sun bore down on us unmercifully. We moved along a powdery dirt road, coughing in the dust we kicked up. Oldham sent Will on scout and then went over the map with his officers.

"On this ridge," he pointed, "Hill's Plantation. The ground falls off gradually down toward the creek. Three roads intersect here. Chances are good the Yanks are comin' down either this one here, or this one, so we're going to set up along this ridge. Most always better to have the high ground."

Oldham lit a cigar and we waited in the shade of a pecan grove. After a while Will returned and reported.

"About two hundred riflemen on the way, sir."

Oldham gave orders and the company moved double-quick toward the intersection. We set firing lines along the ridge and waited in the sunshine. My canteen was empty. Some men had scooped water from mud puddles in the road, but I wasn't that desperate yet. Our company, eighty-two strong, waited, rifles loaded.

Directly a column of Yanks came along the road and we opened fire. Several enemy soldiers dropped, and others took up defensive positions along the fencerow bordering the road. We exchanged fire and neither side advanced.

"Fire only when you've got clear targets," Oldham ordered. "We don't know how long we'll be here. Can't afford to run out."

"Captain, let's send a patrol to block their leading edge," I suggested. "So they can't cut off our retreat."

"Good idea. Do it."

"If the Yanks don't advance in the next half hour," I said, "we'll attack 'em from that end. That'll either drive 'em back where they came from or out in the open."

I led a squad of ten down the backside of Hill's Plantation where the enemy couldn't see our movements. We circled back to the road and waited at the fencerow. I checked my watch. Twenty-seven minutes had passed.

"Fix bayonets and get ready to charge," I said.

We stepped out into the road one by one and proceeded quietly along the inside curve where we couldn't be seen till the last moment. After covering about a quarter mile, we saw an enemy soldier who stood facing the plantation house, his back toward us. Our squad ran down the road firing and hollering, and the startled Yanks broke and ran. We fired and followed them for another fifty yards.

"Our main force is right up there," I pointed. "Our job's done. Let's get outta here."

By the time we got back around to the plantation all shooting had ended.

On June 26th, mail arrived along with reports from Vicksburg. The city had been under constant bombardment for over a month from heavy mortars on barges and

Grant's land artillery. Food was in short supply and families dug caves in their yards to hide from the relentless bombardment.

I had one letter from Mary Ann.

June 15, 1863

Dearest Anderson,

I got four letters from you last week. Wonderful! That's an amazing story about being captured and let go. I'm deeply grateful to God that you're safe. He must be looking out for you. After all the months apart, your letters are music to my ears. I miss your touch and the way you pick me up and spin me around. Can't wait to lie with you as your wife!

Two more soldiers came home with injuries. Isham is missing an arm and Lewis has one leg amputated at the knee. Maggie's glad to have Lewis home, but he's crestfallen because he can't take care of his family as he did before. He told Maggie it would have been better to be killed on the battlefield. The cost of the war is going to be with us the rest of our lives, I'm afraid.

The gardens are producing well. We have good crops of beans and potatoes, and the corn looks like it's filling out well. We'll have enough cotton for our needs. I told Momma about our plans and it was no big surprise to her. She knows we write letters like crazy. You are my heart's desire, Mr. Flowers. Remember — home in one piece!

Mary Ann

P.S. still have the pinecone?

Several days passed without incident, then on June 27th around noon there was a commotion west of our lines. A procession of two-dozen unarmed Confederate soldiers in ragged clothes approached and our soldiers helped them through the lines. A mother and two children were among the stragglers. Her dress was torn and dirty.

"Where'd y'all come from?" Sergeant Woods asked.

A man with hollow eyes said, "Vicksburg … escaped … two days ago."

We got water and food for the weary survivors and then one fellow who was in better shape than most told their story.

"The bombardment goes on day and night. Our cow used to give five gallons a day and helped keep us alive, but she was blown to bits two weeks ago."

I moved to check on the mother.

"What happened?" I asked her.

"I was workin' at sewin' when there came a great explosion outside and the wall fell in. Hanna and I got to lookin' for April, my youngest, and her girl Carol. We couldn't find 'em, so we looked outside." She sobbed and continued. "We found 'em in the flowerbed side-by-side."

Her tears flowed uncontrollably. Dallas gave her cornbread and she gave it to her children and continued.

"Hanna wouldn't leave. I begged her to come with us, but she wouldn't hear of it."

Midmorning, Oldham gathered his officers in the shade of a spreading hickory. He looked beat and his voice was weak.

"We're headin' back to Vicksburg. General Johnston's assembling a few companies to leave tomorrow and I volunteered us. We're leavin' at seven so go tell the men."

We marched twenty-five miles in full sunshine the next day, encountered no enemy soldiers and camped on open land near Edwards. After set up, Dallas and I walked a half mile west to the Big Black. A fallen bird nest lay in the sand. We bathed, washed clothes and cooled off.

On the first of July, Oldham rode ahead while we stood in full sun. In twenty minutes, he returned with new orders.

"We're turnin' back around," he said. "Too late to help."

At three o'clock in the morning we arrived at the fortified lines protecting Jackson and were placed in reserve well behind the trenches for the night.

At first light, I walked through the city. Train tracks were destroyed and a line of boxcars were burned down to the iron chassis and wheels. I passed a burned foundry. A broken sign on the ground read: Jackson Metal Works. Stores of grain, potatoes, and dry goods were strewn in the streets, trampled by boots and mixed with horseshit. A two-story building was collapsed into a pile of bricks and charred timbers. Leafless trees stood here and there, some broken off from cannon fire. I sat in front of an empty store with broken windows. Smoke arose from smoldering buildings, turning the morning sunlight amber. Jackson was ruined. My heart, already filled with gloom, hit rock bottom. *Dear God, must our country be destroyed to bring this war to an end?*

On the afternoon of July 4th, we received news that General Pemberton had surrendered Vicksburg. The Union army took complete control of the city and Old Man River. It was hard to fathom the loss.

"Officers," Oldham called. "This way."

We followed him to a barn filled with fresh hay. Inside, he took off his hat, ran his fingers through his hair and spoke slowly.

"This news is most distressing." He paused to swat a horse fly. "We've all known for some time that we had to hold Vicksburg."

"We coulda whipped 'em!" Conway interrupted.

"You may be right," Oldham continued. "But that's behind us now. We're outnumbered and have nothin' to be ashamed of."

He paused and took a deep breath. I did the same and the smell of fresh hay filled my head.

"The surrender will no doubt dampen the spirits of our men and some may be tempted to give up and desert. As officers, it's our job to carry on with strong minds. The best soldier is one who is unwavering in his commitment to the cause."

He paused again, took in a deep breath and let it out slowly.

"You know what to do. Lead by example. If ya have any doubts in your mind … if ya aren't up to the task … tell me now."

Oldham looked at each of us one-by-one and no one spoke.

After a moment of silence, in a stronger voice he said, "Officers of Company K of the 20th Mississippi Voluntary Regiment, men of Attala County … brave, determined and loyal men … we move forward together!"

We all saluted, cheered and followed our captain back to our men. For the remainder of the day, I felt eager and determined, like two years before at enlistment in Kosciusko. Once again, I felt as though we were embarking on a great and noble adventure.

July 4, 1863

Dear Sister,

The yellow and black checked shirt Mary Ann made was burned when my haversack caught fire recently. I was able to save some clothes, but not my favorite shirt. It's impossible to keep clothes in decent shape while soldiering.

I've been right sad lately and find it harder to touch the tender part of my heart. I fear that blood and death has overwhelmed that which is good within. When I first looked upon a dead man, I was as sad as I had ever known. I am embarrassed to admit it, but now when I see a dead body, I look upon it much as I would the carcass of an armadillo. That's not right, I know. It's immoral and un-Christian. I'm afraid that my soul is mangled.

Sorry for being so cheerless. I'd hoped to comment on more interesting topics, but this is the state of my heart. Hopefully, someday real soon, we shall be reunited.

Your loving brother, Anderson

On July 7th, our raiders captured a column of Union supply wagons filled with rifles, ammunition, and a load of mail and newspapers. Our men quickly took up the papers and read about the engagement at Gettysburg, Pennsylvania. The battle was fought over three consecutive days by massive forces and ended in the retreat of General Lee's Army of Northern Virginia. Many thousands were killed, wounded and captured on both sides. I threw my newspaper in the fire and it burned in a hurry. Bits of black ash drifted up in the draft. In the beginning, I hungered for news of the war. Two years later, I wanted to hear nothing more.

In mid-July, Attison rejoined us. The men gathered around and he told the story of being captured, held, then paroled. He had a nasty scar on his forehead.

"Mighty fine to have ya back, Attison," Oldham said. "Bullet nick ya?"

"I have no idea. Jis remember wakin' up with a rifle pokin' my ribs."

After dark I heard some of our men arguing around their campfire and I slipped up behind a tree to listen. Ben Beauchamp was standing up close to Attison and getting loud.

"That scar looks like ya coulda made it yourself with a knife," Ben said. "That don't look like a bullet wound."

The onlookers stood back.

"I think you're a coward and ya let yourself get caught," Ben said.

I stepped from behind the tree into the firelight.

"Ben," I said. "What's your beef with Attison?"

He fumbled. "Well I jis, ya know. I don't believe his story, is all. He's a coward!"

"Sergeant Woods," I said. "Bring me a rifle, will ya."

I stared at Ben and then Woods handed me a rifle. I held it by the barrel and stepped up close to Ben.

"How'd ya think you'd remember right now, if I slapped your head with this stock?"

Ben's eyes grew wide. "You wouldn't do that, Lieutenant."

I moved right up in his face. "Don't try me!"

His eyes were bloodshot, and his breath smelled of whisky.

"Don't ya ever call Attison a coward, again! Ya hear me?"

"Yes, Lieutenant."

"Tell Attison you're sorry ya doubted his word! Now!"

Ben moved reluctantly toward Attison, apologized and shook his hand weakly.

"From now on, you're tent mates!" I said to the pair. "Any fightin' to be done is with the enemy, not between yourselves. Ya got that?"

Both men nodded.

On the morning of the 18th, new orders came. We packed up immediately and left Jackson as quietly as thousands of soldiers can, moving east.

"How far we goin'?" Dallas asked me.

"Brandon, 'bout eighteen miles."

"Tonight?"

"Yep. General Johnston wants every soldier outta Jackson 'fore the sun rises."

When we arrived in Brandon we set up perimeter pickets and rested. After many days of expecting an assault any minute, it felt as though something essential was missing. I fell asleep that morning in the shade of a magnolia tree at the edge of a field.

I dreamed I was sitting at my father's knees and he was cutting sugar cane chunks small enough for my mouth and handing them to me one at a time. I chewed the cane and swallowed the sweetness. When I'd gotten most of the goody, I spit the fibers in a tin pail on the floor by his rocking chair.

My father grinned at me and said, "How much sugar cane ya gonna eat?"

"Till ya run out," I said and I squeezed his knee for another bite.

A bee buzzed near my ear and I slapped it away. Someone laughed and I opened my eyes. Oldham stood over me smoking a cigar and laughing to beat all.

"Musta been a good dream, Flowers!" Oldham said. "You've been laughin' in your sleep." He kicked me lightly with his boot. "You can get back to dreamin' later. I need ya now."

I carried out Oldham's orders and then crawled in our tent. My jaw was aching, and I had no idea why.

July 22, 1863

Dearest Mary Ann,

A few days ago a doctor pulled one of my back teeth with a pair of pliers and before I knew what was happening, he poured in a shot of whiskey. The stuff burned something terrible and I coughed it out and got out of there. The good news is — with the exception of a plenty sore jaw, I'm still in one piece!

Our generals conceded Jackson to the enemy and we are now camped near Brandon. We've been in a few skirmishes since I last put quill to paper, but nothing earnest.

The Yankees burned Jackson and destroyed the stores of food. I've asked myself the question several times — would I burn Northern towns if our army invaded their territory? Suppose in the end it would come down to what orders I was given. I guess I'd do what I was told but would certainly not feel good about it.

The war has my mind in a quandary. My upbringing as a Christian, especially the ten commandments and Jesus teaching us to love our neighbors as ourselves, is the source of my pondering. I look to God each day and believe that all is under his care, but I wonder if he decided to sit this one out and then come help us again when we're finished fighting. I'm not saying I've lost faith in God, but I am saying that what we're all caught up in is a mighty far stretch from any idea of heaven on earth I ever imagined. I look forward to the time when I'm watching for flying ducks instead of bullets.

I think of you each day when I awake, each night when I go to sleep, and as often as I can in between. I hope I'm home by next spring so we can walk in the woods and taste sweet honeysuckle together.

Love, Anderson

Chapter 33

RESPITE
Late July — September 1863, Central Mississippi

After a few days' rest near Brandon, our regiment marched twenty-odd miles east to Morton and set up camp at the edge of a forest. My socks wore clean through and both feet blistered. We saw no signs of the enemy, and it appeared that the Yanks were not going to pursue us further, at least for the moment. Fighting and movements of the prior months left our army tired, hungry and hurting. The surrender of Vicksburg and the defeat at Gettysburg were heavy, heavy blows. Some men requested leave to go home to help with harvest. Unfortunately, General Johnston granted furloughs only to a few sick and injured.

For two solid weeks we hunted and bought vegetables from local farmers. Their crops were plentiful and they were happy to sell. We rested, wrote letters, and healed, and that boosted our spirits considerably until we had to start rationing food again.

I proposed to Oldham that he send out a hunting party under my command toward the Strong River, six miles east of our encampment. He agreed and the next morning the quartermaster had horses, guns and supplies ready for us. The party was Dallas, Woods, Will and me, plus Ira and Joey, boys from the drum corps.

"Are ya good at scoutin'?" I asked the boys.

"Yes, sir," Ira said proudly. "My daddy's a trapper. I travel with him a lot."

"Is that right. How 'bout you Joey?"

"I'm good in the woods too. I 'member landmarks, creeks … everythin'. I won't get lost, I promise."

We rode about two miles under a towering forest of pin oaks, the ground thick with acorns. Dallas tied a flag between two willows to mark the rendezvous spot, and we split into two groups and moved east in the direction of the Strong River. Dallas, Joey and I moved a half-mile south and tied up our horses.

"Joey," Dallas said. "You stay here."

"I wanna hunt too," he said, looking eagerly at both of us. "What's the point of me stayin' with the hosses when we could have three guns firin' 'stead of two?"

"Can ya handle a shotgun?"

"Yes, sir. Most surely can!"

"Okay, you hunt between Andy and me. And don't wander off."

"I won't!"

With a double barrel shotgun over his shoulder Joey looked like a toy soldier.

"Don't forget this," Dallas said, tossing him a game bag.

We spaced about a hundred yards apart and walked slowly through the woods scanning the trees for squirrels and watching for rabbits. Joey was twelve years old and not much taller than the shotgun. When I was twelve I was already hunting too.

Occasional shots came from the north. With no breeze, it was easy to spot squirrels feeding in the leafy trees. *Boom*, a blast came from my right.

A good number of shots were fired that afternoon, and we hunted until dusk as agreed, then returned to our horses. Our first day was profitable. Dallas and I laid our kill out on the ground. Together we had twelve squirrels and five rabbits.

Joey returned a few minutes later.

"How'd ya do?" Dallas asked.

"I did alright," he said, looking down at the ground.

"Well let's see," Dallas prodded.

He took the heavy game bag off his shoulder, put it on the ground, and took his kill out one by one. First he pulled out a swamp rabbit, then a fox squirrel, and then another squirrel. By the time he'd emptied his bag he had fourteen kills and grinned at us like he'd won first prize at the county fair.

"That proves it," Dallas said. "You are good with a shotgun!"

We loaded everything on the horses and returned to the flag where the others were already waiting. We built a large fire, gutted and cleaned the game and cooked it on four spits. Ira took the meat back to the army overnight.

The second days' hunt was also prosperous. By mid-afternoon, Dallas, Joey and I had killed two white-tailed deer and a good number of small animals. We gutted them and sent Joey back heavily loaded to the camp at Morton. Ira returned and we moved our base camp two miles closer to the river and hunted till dusk. The weather was hot, but bearable under the tall shade trees.

After supper on the third day, our hunting parties packed up and traveled under good light from the moon. We arrived at the regimental camp about midnight and woke Walker up. He and a few others got busy cutting and cooking the meat. A letter from Mary Ann was waiting for me.

August 5, 1863

Dearest Anderson,

We miss all our men, but I especially miss you and want you home. Now that the fighting has died down it seems like a perfect time for furloughs. Why can't Colonel Russell let the regiment come home? Seems to me he could easily do that by releasing a company at a time. We need help getting the cotton in. It's just too much work and the old men are worn out from helping everybody. An old man's worth about a third of a young, healthy one, it seems to me.

There's been some trouble here lately that I want to tell you about. Lewis has been home for three months and has taken to liquor in excess. He had that bad habit before the war, but now he's much worse. He gets around slowly on crutches but will never be able to do the work of a farmer. Two weeks ago, Preacher caught Lewis stealing money out of the offering plate while we were singing Nearer My God to Thee. Then last Thursday he was found sleeping in the church.

He's such a burden to his mother now. He can't do anything to help with the farm and he refuses to snap beans or cook. Lord knows you don't need both legs to use your hands. He says it's women's work and beneath him. He's a stubborn fellow and not willing to roll with the punches. Not all the wounded men are like Lewis. Isham, he's missing his right arm below the shoulder, but he works about as fast with one arm as most men with two. And at church, he passes the offering plate, of all things. Now there's a fellow who's making the best of life in spite of his misfortune.

Momma's doing better this summer than last. Pollen makes her sneeze like crazy, but nothing more than that, thankfully. She's taken to complaining about rheumatism in her hands, but she still knits as fast as ever. I hope my spirits are as bright as hers when I'm old. Of course, that's a long, long ways off because I'm still a girl.

I'm missing you a lot, Mr. Flowers. Do you remember the night we stayed out really late by the river and watched the stars shine? That was the first time I knew for sure I wanted you for my man. I don't mind saying I need you to come home and settle these yearnings inside.

I am yours, Mary Ann

A week later, Oldham sent the hunting parties out again. This time we traveled two miles farther east before we set up our base camp. The weather was cooler and game plentiful. We settled in for the night and owl calls filled the woods. It had been weeks since the terrible thunder of cannons, but my dreams were still filled with explosions, soldiers screaming in agony, and burning bridges.

Joey took the kill back the first night and the next morning I put Ira with the other party. Dallas and I rode east till we smelled the Strong River, tied up the horses and walked quietly under the trees to the water's edge. The water was considerably clearer than Big Black, and rocky in places. We both got a good drink and then started hunting.

Dallas picked his way along the riverbank downstream and slowly disappeared in the woods. The setting reminded me of our boyhood hunting trips and a sense of rightness and peace swelled within. Living with a constant sense of danger had worn me down. We hunted for a few hours and met back where we split up. Dallas had a gleam in his eyes.

"Bear scat 'bout a quarter mile down!" he said. "Let's come back tomorrow!"

"Most definitely!"

Dallas and I left early the next morning and reached the river before sunup. Moonlight gave the water a gray-green look. Water swirled over the shallow rocks and underneath a fallen tree; its leaves still dark green. We inched along, taking care not to disturb the bushes and lower tree branches. In a half hour, Dallas motioned with his arm to a pile of scat on a flat rock.

"Let's go to that bend," he whispered near my ear. "And wait there."

We eased along the bank, then Dallas signaled to the ground. I crouched behind a bunch of elderberry bushes, pulled my hat down to cover my forehead, and sat as still as a dead man. Dallas moved two dozen paces downstream and stopped where we had a clear line of sight between us. A kingfisher suddenly swooped down, touched the water lightly and vanished. My heart raced and I sensed that a bear was near. First rays of sunlight filtered through the trees on the opposite side of the river and a momentary breeze stirred the leaves. The air was cool for late August and no mosquitoes bothered me.

Splash, splash, splash came sounds from downstream. Dallas raised his gun to the ready. He held an over/under shotgun loaded with buckshot. I carried a Springfield rifle with a single lead slug. The splashing grew louder. Through the bushes a shadowy form moved our way, searching the dark, moving waters for food. It was a big one, about two and a half feet tall and six feet long on all fours, black fur with a brown muzzle. Dallas winked at me. The bear was within range, but he waited for it to get closer.

When it was ten paces away, he aimed. Seconds passed and I felt my heart pounding.

Boom! The sound rocked the early morning quiet and rolled through the woods. The bear stumbled and kept moving upstream.

Boom! Dallas fired a second time. The stunned bear stood on its hind legs.

Bam! I fired into its chest.

White smoke filled the bushes in front of me and seconds passed before it cleared. The bear took a step, fell backward and came to rest in the river, half submerged, its front paws stretched toward the sky.

Yeeeeeee! Dallas let out a yell. We left our guns and waded across the river, knee-deep and cool. When we reached the bear, it trembled, let out a long breath through its nose, and then lay still. The horrible image of Jack lying on his back came to my mind, his face destroyed, and life gone. Water ran through the bear's fir, turned dark red and flowed away. A light-colored patch of fur on its chest shone in a spot of sunlight and water dripped from its claws into the flowing river.

Together we pulled the bear by its front legs, warm and flexible. The claws scratched my forearm and drew blood. I slipped and fell in the river and Dallas laughed.

"Wow, she's a big 'un," he said. "Over two hundred pounds, I bet."

"Let's get her to the side, then go get the horses."

It took us ten minutes, but we managed to drag the bear up on the bank and fell exhausted beside its wet body.

When we got back to our camp, Woods' hunting party had already returned and there was great excitement over the bear. Joey showed off four arrowheads he found that day and gave two to Ira. That night we had roasted rabbit with rice and cornbread and enjoyed each other's company. Hunting, camping, and sleeping in the woods was salve for my ailing soul. The smiling faces of my comrades in the evening firelight helped me feel whole inside again.

August 15, 1863

Dearest Mary Ann

I'm writing to wish you a happy eighteenth birthday. Wish I was there to help celebrate! My heart grew warm when I read your last letter. Hot is more like it. Sometimes I read your letters out loud to Dallas, but I skip over the parts that are just between you and me.

Colonel Russell has been sent home due to illness and our new commander is Colonel Brown, from Claiborne County. Oldham says he thinks Brown will be a trustworthy leader.

We get newspapers occasionally but have no idea what lies ahead for us. Morale among the men has taken a beating since Vicksburg and Jackson. On the positive side of the ledger, the men are getting healed up and we've had enough to eat for a change. The place where we're camped has ample game.

The forest here has some of the tallest pin oak trees I've ever seen. This would be a perfect place for us to walk under the trees. We could walk just about forever and not come to the edge. I know you'd love that!

The break from fighting is giving me more time to think about the war and the rightness of our cause. I believe it's wrong for one man to own another and that every man should be paid a fair wage for his labor. In Jeremiah the Lord says 'Woe unto him that buildeth his house by unrighteousness, and his chambers by wrong; that useth his neighbour's service without wages, and giveth him not for his work.'

I would never own, though I could see hiring, a negro, if I could afford him, to help clear the land for our farm, but only if he got to keep the wages. I tried to explain this to the men last night when we were kicking words around after supper. Dallas agreed with me but a man by the name of Albert got red in the face angry and cussed at me. His ears were plugged up and he stomped off in a hissy.

After Albert left, Dallas brought up an interesting point that I'd not considered before. He explained that when a slave-owner hires out a slave to someone else, the owner determines the wage, so the slave-owner is in control. You can either hire a slave at the wage the slave-owner sets, or you can do without. There is no negotiating. The slave-owner commands the situation entirely.

So when you want to hire a helper, you have a choice between hiring a slave or a freeman. If the freeman asks for a wage that's higher than what the slave-owner asks, most employers will choose to pay the lower wage. So this situation keeps the freeman from earning any more than the rate a slave owner sets. So once again, the slave-owner controls the situation.

If you follow Dallas' logic, then it's clear that slavery is bad not just for slaves, but for freemen as well. Only the slaveholder profits, at the expense of both the slave and the freeman. It seems to me Dallas is exactly right. I'm convicted that owning another person is not moral and I'm still haunted by my childhood memory of the negro woman's baby being taken away from her at the slave auction in Yazoo City.

Forgive me for going on and on. I'd give anything to be back with you now. The dream of living together as man and wife is the hope that lights my path!

Your devoted man, Anderson

From time to time we learned of events in other theaters of the war. In mid-September, there was an interesting account of fighting along the Louisiana/Texas border. Four Union gunboats moved into the Sabine Pass as part of their effort to control Houston and Beaumont. Forty Confederates, under the command of Lieutenant Dowling, held an earthwork fort with a few light cannons. Two Confederate cotton-clad gunboats guarded the river, a weak force against the Yanks. When the Union gunboats fired on the fort, Confederate cannons struck the two lead gunboats and they were both grounded. The Yankees were forced to surrender, and their other two boats withdrew. The victory was unexpected and a big boost for morale to our western forces.

Near the end of September I received this letter from Henrietta.

September 13, 1863

Dear Uncle Andy,

I am good at handwriting now, as you can see. Miss Rivers has been working us hard at school. I don't see the point of writing a whole page of capital Ss and then a whole page of capital Ts. Wouldn't it be better if she just had us write letters to our fathers and uncles and cousins that are off at war?

Momma said tell you we are doing fine. What I want to tell you is about hunting. Last Saturday Momma gave permission so Dennis and I went to that good squirrel hunting place by the big curve. I leaned against a tree and waited real still. Two squirrels got to chasing each other up one side of a tree and then back down. Finally they stopped on a limb to rest, I guess, and Dennis helped me hold up your shotgun and aim it. When I pulled the trigger my shoulder took a beating. Dennis picked up the dead squirrel and brought it back. It was warm in my hands. I told Momma all about it. That was three days ago. My shoulder still hurts a little and has turned blue.

I go to Mary Ann's house pretty often. Fun to be with her and Miriam. They tell stories I have not heard before and they like hearing my stories.

I hope you are getting enough to eat. Momma tells me things from your letters. I need to stop writing because Momma needs me to help can corn.

I miss you, Henrietta

Newspapers brought news of a considerable engagement in Tennessee at Chickamauga Creek. It was a victory for us, but ten of our generals were killed or wounded, and there were twenty thousand Confederates casualties!

In spite of some victorious battles, the war was going badly for us. Letters from home mirrored the discouragement the soldiers felt, but rarely spoke about. Without more men, supplies and luck, it did not seem possible to avoid defeat. Discouragement showed in every soldier's eyes, but I did not speak a word of my own doubt, not even to Dallas. *We must keep on. Our honor's at stake. I'll not be called a coward.*

Chapter 34

BACK TO THE FIGHT
October 1863, Mississippi

One morning in early October, Captain Oldham called me to his command tent.
"I've got a mission. Need ya to reconnoiter the Strong River."
"Do Yanks have troops east of us?"
"Not that I know of," he said, smiling. "That's why I need you and Dallas to take horses and go see."
I was still puzzled.
"Flowers, I'm givin' you and Dallas permission to go see the river again. Sometimes ya take things too seriously. We've got orders to move out tomorrow. Now get outta here!"
I fetched Dallas and told him to saddle up.
"Where're we goin'?" he asked.
"Not sayin'. Just ride."
When we were beyond our pickets he spoke.
"Another spy mission? Are we in the shippin' bidness again?"
"Nope. Even better. We've got the whole day to ourselves."
The forest was dry and a few leaves already on the ground. As we rode through the woods, the wind picked up and the treetops came alive, and orange and brown leaves drifted down. By noon we reached the Strong and found a good place to stretch out. We ate cornbread, bacon and peanuts and watched the river run clear.
"Think we'll make it home?" Dallas asked.
"Colonel's not givin' furloughs."
"That's not what I mean, buddy. I'm talkin' 'bout survivin' the war."
"Don't want to talk about it."
"Well, I think it's high time we did!" He was clearly irritated.
"Can't we jis enjoy bein' in the woods?"
"You always whitewash things over."
I walked away and he caught up with me.
"I'm sorry," I said. "You're right."
"Chances are at least one of us isn't gonna make it."
"You have no way of knowin' that!"
"Right, I don't. But I know if one of us gets killed, the other'll have regrets."
We sat quietly for a few minutes and watched the wind brush the surface of the river. A kingfisher swooped low above the water, snatched a fish and flew off.
"You're my best friend," I said. "I don't think I'd wanna carry on without ya."

"Looky here. I'm tellin' ya, you'd better carry on! Carry on for both of us! You'd better be a double-good man. You'd better marry Mary Ann and have kids and love 'em up good. And comfort my mother too."

"Alright, alright, I promise. And I expect the same from you if I don't make it."

"Ya think Mary Ann would marry me?" He grinned and I swatted his shoulder.

"You'd have to see 'bout that your own self. I'd be in heaven with the angels. Besides, I thought ya liked Emma best."

"I do, but when the war started I backed off. I didn't want to … I'm not tellin' ya anymore."

He pushed me in the river, and we tussled and laughed. After we tuckered out we crawled out on flat rocks and napped in the midday sun. When I awoke, Dallas was lying beside me, gazing at the sky. He looked relaxed and younger. It was our last peaceful day in the woods.

The next day our regiment moved out after several weeks in camp. We made a short trip west to Brandon on the Southern Railroad. About an hour along the train came to a full stop and we rolled the doors open on both sides. The air was cool and pleasant and the sky free of clouds. The trees and undergrowth by the tracks were so thick a man couldn't take one step inside without becoming tangled in briars. A blue jay swooped out of the trees toward us and veered upward just before it got to our car. Suddenly rifle fire broke out near the front of the train, then all was quiet again.

"Let's just hold tight," Oldham said. "Probably sympathizers makin' trouble."

The birds were silent. In twenty minutes the train lurched back into motion. The next two hours passed slowly, and tension returned to my body. My time as a hunter was over. It was time to be a soldier again, and an officer.

Just after noon we unloaded in Brandon, formed columns immediately, and marched north without a bite to eat. We put about twenty miles behind us that day and stopped at the Yockanookany River at dusk, tired and hungry. Both my feet were badly blistered again. In spite of the hard and uneven ground I fell asleep quickly. Several hours later I popped wide awake. The campfires were out and no stars were visible through the thick cloud cover. A steady wind came from the east.

After breakfast, we crossed the river on a pontoon bridge. My boots rubbed my blisters so much, I walked barefoot the rest of the day. We arrived at our destination a little after noon joining other regiments already settled in near Canton.

Our first full day in the new camp was spent gathering firewood and digging sinks. We got fresh rations and the first real coffee we'd had in a while. The dry, rusty smell of fallen leaves reminded me of agreeable times back home after the crops were in. It seemed that fighting might be over for the season. That night a heavy rain came.

Early the next morning we got new orders. Our regiment marched southwest to Brownsville where we joined General Jackson's cavalry and continued south searching for the enemy. Our cavalry found two regiments of Yanks north of Clinton and reported back. Oldham sent a third of Company K under my command due east to ascertain the extent of enemy forces on our right flank. About a mile along we came upon an empty enemy camp. Debris was spread over the ground and campfires still burned.

"Go through the papers," I said. "See what ya can find."

Sergeant Barrett returned shortly with a pile of letters addressed to soldiers in Ohio and Illinois regiments. The enemy had left in a hurry and it seemed that their force might have been as large as a brigade. By the time we rejoined the main group it was almost dark. In our tent I pulled out one of the letters to a soldier in the 37th Ohio and read it out loud to Dallas.

August 9, 1863

A.G. Christopher,

Respected sir, I undertake to answer your letter that I received one day after we left Vicksburg. We were fifteen days making it to this point and had little fighting. We found the country to be swamps and slews for the last sixty miles. Run out of rations and had to live on half rations the last seven days. Last night our lines advanced to about eighty yards from the Rebs without exchanging a shot. They fell back a few paces and dug new holes at the same time we were advancing and sinking ourselves in the earth. The men that were in the siege of Vicksburg say that the Johnnies are more stubborn here than they ever were. I think a few days more and they will be as lame as we wish.

We are losing some men though no more than we expected. There is heavy artillery drilling today, as the Boys say — more homemade thunder. More than is pleasant while the lead hail rains as thick as it did this morning for a couple of hours.

We drawed four days rations of tobacco this morning which will revive some of the Boys considerably. There is a fort six miles below here and they are going at it pretty strong. Uncertain when it falls. I think we can get these fellows out of it in a short time though we cannot do it till then. Our Company has been in the rifle pits twelve hours longer than the last group. I guess we will say nothing about it.

Well as I cannot write nothing and only something about ourselves, I will quit. Hoping to hear from you. Give my respects to all.

Remain as ever, T.W. Gaddis

Excuse mistakes for the air is in such a bad condition that sentences will not flow readily from mind to pen.

Later, a touch on my shoulder woke me. I stumbled out of the tent and looked at my watch in the firelight. It was three-fifteen in the morning.

"Captain's called an officer's meeting," Able said. "Now."

After we gathered in his tent he spoke.

"New orders, men. We're going chasin' again. Cavalry spotted Yanks breakin' camp an hour ago. Gonna run 'em down."

"Now?" Conway asked.

"Now! Pack rations for two days, full ammunition. Assemble the men in thirty minutes. You are dismissed."

The 20th, 13th and 24th regiments followed the retreating Yankees south toward Clinton. Locals informed us that the enemy passed through three hours earlier headed towards Vicksburg. After a couple of days, our generals decided we had chased them far enough, so we turned around and headed back toward our winter camp. The road was nothing but dry ruts, some as deep as my knees.

After two hours of rough walking, the heavy gray clouds that had been shadowing us for several days let loose. The ruts filled up quick and the wagons and mules slowed to a stop. The rain kept on coming and soon we were all wet to the bone. I lost one boot in a mud hole and walked on without it.

The downpour became so heavy the column was halted and we moved into the woods for cover. Dallas and I found a wide beech tree on a modest rise, sat next to the trunk and pulled the tent sections over us. As the rain pelted our canvas, we gnawed on some hardtack we'd found at the enemy camp. Water ran down the tree trunk wetting my backside and I couldn't fall asleep.

In the morning, we stumbled out of the woods and resumed the march. At the roadside, my bare foot struck something in the mud. I picked it up and found that it was a bare human leg and foot.

"What're ya doin'?" Dallas asked. "Better left alone."

I dropped the leg back in the mud. "Get me a spade."

I shoveled mud from the road, covered the leg, and stood over the pile of mud as the column marched by. The rain quickly melted the mud away and the leg was exposed again. *Where's his spirit? Or is this all that's left when men die?*

I followed at the rear of the column till we stopped and camped for the night. A day later we reached Canton at nightfall. The next morning, the rain had stopped, and the sun came up in a cloudless sky. Warmer air followed and we began to dry out.

Chapter 35

WINTER COMES EARLY
Late October 1863 — March 1864, Mississippi

On October 25th, winter arrived early and my canteen froze overnight. Company K was relocated a mile up Bear Creek and we set about the work of making huts. Tent tarps were sewed into mattresses and stuffed with leaves. Men who were not building gathered wood from the forest, stored it in piles and covered it with canvas. No sooner had we finished our huts when a fierce sleet storm swept in. The wind found weak spots in the walls and blew a few chinks open. We stuffed leaves in the holes. *If only we had enough food.*

The next day we took shovels and pickaxes to the task of digging latrine trenches. Unlike in prison, we were able to provide privacy by locating the sinks behind evergreen bushes, and the cold weather kept the odors from ruining the air around camp.

October 28, 1863

Dearest Mary Ann,

I'm very cold tonight. So cold my shoulders ache and my feet are swollen. In the morning I'm afraid I'll not be able to get up without help. I just told my toes to wiggle and can't tell if they're moving or not.

Closing my eyes brings back the rumble of cannons at close range. I brace to take the blast in my chest. There are no cannons pointed at me now. You should see the terrible carnage a chain shot does to a row of soldiers. A cannon is loaded with two half-balls connected by a two- or three-foot chain. It comes careening through the air whipping off necks and tearing men and horses to pieces. Cannister shot is equally terrifying. Cans filled with metal balls, nails, or other pieces of metal are loaded into the breach of a cannon. In flight the can opens, and the pieces go flying through flesh. Once, a man near me vanished in the blink of an eye. I fear a lone cannon more than a row of fifty trained riflemen standing shoulder to shoulder.

Fear pins me to the ground like a fallen tree. I think my teeth will shatter the next time a cannon shell detonates near me. I cover my ears with both hands, but it makes no difference because the roaring is inside my head. I want to scream and run ...

In the morning, I awoke alone in the hut and found the pages of the unfinished letter lying in the dirt. I ripped them to shreds and stuffed them in holes in the walls.

November 2, 1863

Dear Sister,

We are settled in for winter near Canton, not more than forty miles from you, but they won't let us leave. My cough has started up again. Everybody in my hut has a cough or the shakes, and spirits are low. Our scouts captured Yankee supplies including a crate of stout whiskey. Oldham tries to keep us busy with hours of drills each day. Shipments of food arrive irregularly. We've eaten more radishes and onions here lately than a hog loose in a barn.

How's Miriam faring this winter? I pray that everyone has enough food and firewood to stay warm and in good spirits. No doubt you're having the same frigid weather that we are.

Do you have any word from brother Jesse? A newspaper account said the 5th Mississippi was in the battle at Chickamauga where losses were terrible. I pray that he is safe from harm.

Oldham wants to see me now. I'll write more later.

Your loving brother, Anderson

Captain Oldham sent a twelve-man hunting party north to the Big Black. The men were all itching to do something besides drill, so there were more than enough volunteers. Conway led the men including Dallas, and the whole company gave the foraging party a rowdy send off. They moved out on foot with two mule-drawn wagons.

"Bring 'em back full!" Oldham shouted and the men cheered.

While they were away the weather was cold and the sky was solid overcast. Oldham reduced drills to every other day with Sundays off. My Bible, newspapers, and letters kept me occupied. Men played poker and gambled their pay. Dominoes and chess were my favorites. After supper some nights, I played the fiddle and the men sang and danced.

Two weeks later the foraging party returned with wagons loaded with game, fish, potatoes and onions. Walker cooked a feast for the whole company that night and we celebrated. The foraging party had met an old fellow living alone in the woods near Pickens. He couldn't get around by himself any more, but in his younger days he had been a fisherman. He went with our men, let them use his nets, and showed them the best places to fish. They caught more than a hundred catfish, some as heavy as forty pounds.

December 28, 1863

Dear Sister,

Thanks so much for the package! It arrived two days ago. Here lately, we're getting regular deliveries of mail and newspapers for a change. I hope you're getting my letters. The wool socks and sweater are making this cold winter a few degrees warmer!

I started one of the western novels you sent and loaned the other one to Dallas. It brings great comfort to imagine myself in another place and circumstance. Winter life has become so monotonous that some of the men are itching for spring fighting — but not me. The perils are still fresh in my mind.

Colonel Brown gathered the regiment together on Christmas morning and gave a speech to rally us. It was hard to hear him for the constant coughing. If the enemy is in our area, they can probably hear us a half-mile away.

A few days ago, our men cut a twelve foot cedar tree and tied it up in the middle of camp. Having no cakes or oranges to deck it, we tied strips of colored cloth on some of the branches. For presents, we tied our package wrappings back up with string and put them under the tree. Compared to home, it's a pitiful sight, but it reminds everyone of better times. On Christmas, after supper, we sang Deck the Halls just like at home. Singing brightens our spirits, at least for a while.

Two men in Company D got in a yelling, fist-throwing fight the day after Christmas and had to be separated. Their captain had them tied up on opposite sides of the camp, but the next morning both were missing. A search party found one at the edge of Bear Creek face down in the water, drowned, and the other fellow hasn't been found. None of the soldiers knows what happened, or if they do, they aren't telling. Christmas seems to have brought out the best and the worst in us.

Sorry to have ended this letter on a sad note. Dallas, Eugene and I are all doing as well as can be expected. I promise not to get in fights except with Yankees. I think of you and Henrietta every day and pray earnestly for John's return.

Your loving brother, Anderson

After supper on New Year's Eve, our regiment assembled at Colonel Brown's headquarters. The sky was clear and air cold, but there was no wind. Company C had stacked wood for a bonfire in the middle of camp. Brown gave a speech about honor and bravery and then lit the fire with a torch. The wood burst into flames instantly because the fire-builders had poured on coal oil. In a couple minutes the blaze reached thirty feet high and sparks flew up in the night air. Eugene and I visited again that night.

January 2, 1863

Dearest Mary Ann,

I got your package and letter today. My, my … you've been busy. I am most grateful for the new shirts!

It's good to hear Elizabeth and the twins are doing well. I am sure she appreciates your help a great deal. And it's great that Henrietta is taking an interest in the babies too. Elizabeth may be in a pickle if Small doesn't get well soon.

Two nights ago, in a dream, I was standing in bright sunlight by a creek, shaving in a tin basin. A tiny mirror hung by a string on a tree trunk. When I leaned over to see my picture, Momma's face looked back at me. Instead of being surprised, it felt ordinary, as if I often saw faces of people who have passed on to the next world. She said I looked tired and ought to take better care of myself.

Then the dream was over, or at least that's all I remember. I've been turning it over in my mind. I'm trying to keep my mind fastened on life after the war and praying that peace will come soon. Love, Anderson

Our struggle to find food continued in January, so Oldham asked for volunteers for a raiding party. Scouts reported Union supply wagons traveling the road between Clinton and Jackson regularly. The party left the next morning headed for Jackson. A couple of days later, about midnight, the sound of horses and heavy wagons woke me. The men got up and lit torches to greet our returning raiders. Five mule-drawn wagons came to a stop in the middle of camp and Oldham emerged from his tent in full uniform.

"Did y'all do any good, Sergeant Woods?"

"Yes, sir, we got a right smart load. Salt pork, flour, molasses, condensed milk, and coffee!"

"Did I hear ya correctly? Did you say coffee?"

"Yes, sir."

"Excellent work, Woods! Everybody make it back?"

"Yes, sir, and we didn't fire a shot. Found these wagons abandoned on the road and commandeered the mules from a farmer."

"What do ya mean, commandeered?"

"We paid him."

Oldham chuckled. "Good work. See if Company C needs food. This is more 'an we can use in the next few days."

"We also found blankets. I know ya told us to only bring food."

Oldham laughed. "Sergeant, I'll let ya get by with this one."

January 15, 1864

Dearest Mary Ann,

I hope you can make out my words okay. We have no ink, so pencil is the best I can do for now. I received two delightful letters from you yesterday (December 13th and January 5th) and have read them over and over. Though we are apart these many months, I hear your voice in your words and feel your warmth. By the time spring comes, I hope I'll be kissing you under the flowering dogwoods.

Not much new to report. Shivering through winter, coughing and remembering home fondly. I have a new wool blanket, courtesy of the Union. The old one was so thin and shredded I cut it into strips for bandages.

Last night in a dream I saw your face in the moon, smiling at me. When I awoke, I remembered your rosy cheeks and sparkling eyes. The thought of being with you brings a smile to my face and helps me fall asleep at night.

Regretfully I must stop for now because this is my last piece of paper. Please know that my heart is with you every moment.

Love, Anderson

PS Please write your letters on one side from now on, so I can use the blank side to write back.

In February, the weather was a mix of sudden snows followed by warmer air and rain that turned our camp into a rubble of mud. Nearly all the trees within a half mile of camp had been cut for huts and firewood. Our drinking water came from Bear Creek which was also where we bathed and washed our clothes. The creek became a mess of mud and waste, and illness was rampant. If the Yankees had come calling, only half of us could have mustered to fight.

General Polk had his companies make more reconnaissance missions beginning in February. On the 10th, I led a patrol of twenty-five to probe Union supply lines between Clinton and Jackson. We saw a number of abandoned farms, and cabins stripped of furniture and tools. One farm we came to looked empty. Upon further inspection, however, we found an old man and his wife, both sitting in chairs covered with blankets. Two pans of waste sat near the door, not emptied in quite some time. Only a few sticks of wood remained in the bin and there was no fire burning.

"Bring in more wood," I ordered the men.

"There's no more," the old man mumbled.

"Check outside. And check the barn too."

"Who takes care of ya?" I asked.

"No one," the woman replied. "Our sons are off to war and we've got no daughters."

"Seen any Yanks?"

"Not since November," the man said. "They was through here lookin' for deserters."

We stayed with the couple for a half hour, restocked their wood supply and left a pouch of hardtack. Then our patrol headed south again and shortly, we came upon a wagon heading north. In it were three wounded soldiers, each missing a leg. A boy about fifteen was driving the mules.

March 18, 1864

Dearest Mary Ann,

We're breaking winter camp tomorrow and heading to Meridian, Mississippi. As much as I hate to enter a new season of fighting, right now it seems preferable to drilling, coughing and freezing. Oldham says we're headed for the town of Laurel in Jones County, about eighty miles south of Meridian. I have no idea why we're going there.

I like the way your face looks in firelight and the gleam in your eyes when you greet me on the lane. Your love has sheltered me these many months apart. I'm determined to return and walk in the woods with you again. I promise.

Love, Anderson

Chapter 36

RENEGADES
March — April 1864, Jones County, Mississippi

On March 19th, the 6th and 20th Regiments boarded trains at Meridian southbound for Laurel. Colonel Robert Rainey was assigned to lead our force of about one thousand. After three hours, our train stopped, and Rainey convened a meeting of captains and lieutenants in the woods.

"Our mission is out of the ordinary," Rainey began. "We're going to Jones County to arrest deserters."

Captain Oldham glanced at me as Rainey continued.

"We'll unload at Laurel, 'bout sixty miles south where a number have congregated."

Rainey told us that the renegades, led by Newton Knight, had taken over the county and refused to pay taxes to the Confederacy. The people of Jones County were mostly cattle-raisers and farmers who didn't own slaves and they had been against succession but enlisted to fight for the South anyway. After the war was underway, the Confederacy took their cattle and horses, so some men deserted and came home. Knight's company had taken over the town of Ellisville, raised a Union flag, and declared Jones County a free state, independent from Mississippi.

"Our mission is to catch these men and put down the rebellion," Rainey said.

"How many in Knight's force?" Oldham asked.

"Don't know for sure. Seven hundred, possibly. They've harassed tax collectors and killed local people loyal to the Confederacy. They've raided supply trains and killed conscript officers."

"Do we know where they are?" Oldham asked.

"No. It's our job to find 'em. I don't want our men favorin' Knight and his bunch just 'cause they're Mississippians. They're Yankees now! Understood?"

"What do we tell the men?" Oldham asked.

"Give 'em a short version of my speech and remind 'em that orders are orders. Any man who refuses to obey will be shot."

We returned to our boxcar and briefed the men as the train got underway. No questions were asked, but the men looked uneasy. Like me, most did not own slaves and had grown wearier of the war since the defeats at Vicksburg and Gettysburg. We had serious doubts we could win and wanted to get back home and take care of our own families.

We unloaded at Laurel and Oldham went to meet with Colonel Rainey. The men were issued rations and cooked supper. The air was cool, and the smell of lilacs sweetened the air. Springtime was at hand.

As soon as we'd eaten, we packed up and moved west along a narrow road as darkness fell. Two Jones County men led the way with pitch torches. Around midnight we came to the bottomlands beside a river, set out pickets and slept on the ground. A light rain came in the night.

Before breakfast I walked along a slough bordered by Cypress trees. In a huddle of cypress knees beside the still water, I watched the first light illuminate the forest. Early birds flitted about and the wet, woodsy smells put my mind at ease.

One of my earliest memories as a child was a walk by a river with Father. We had come upon a ring of cypress knees, about chest high on me, and I asked why the short trees had no leaves. He laughed and explained that the knees were part of the tree's roots sticking above ground. Then I asked him where the cypress feet were. He laughed again, hoisted me on his shoulders and we forded the river.

I wished John was beside me and we were duck hunting on the Big Black. Perhaps he was in a Yankee prison at that moment. The North and South had stopped prisoner exchanges, so my brother would most likely spend the rest of the war in prison. Ellen had to be worrying herself silly, in spite of the brave front she put on, and Lilly would not see her father in her second year of life. *A waste.*

After breakfast, our company pulled away from the main force, forded the Leaf River and searched for Knight's group on the west side downstream. We'd been told that Knight had a swamp hideout called the Devil's Den. We came in contact with farmers and cattlemen occasionally during the morning and asked about Knight. Nobody reported seeing him, but we couldn't be sure they were telling us the truth, as there were many Union sympathizers in the area. For that matter, we might have been talking with the renegades themselves. A thunderstorm came in the night, a gully-washer. In the morning, the rain was over, and we were able to start fires and cook a decent breakfast.

Colonel Rainey brought two-dozen bloodhounds in wagons. Teams of dogs and men were let loose on both sides of the river. The howling dogs raced into the swamp pulling the men behind. About four o'clock, we heard men approaching and got ready in case. One of our pickets came running back all excited.

"They caught some of Knight's men!"

A few minutes later our soldiers appeared with a group of ten renegades tied together in a line. They looked much like us, mostly in their twenties and thirties.

"What do we do with them, Captain?" Sergeant Barrett asked.

"Turn 'em over to Rainey."

Rainey interrogated the prisoners himself and to a man they refused to give their names or betray Knight's whereabouts. This angered Rainey so much he had them tied to stakes in an open field. The next day, Rainey ordered the 20th Regiment to Ellisville with the prisoners and sent the rest of the force back into the swamp with the dogs to search for Knight.

Rainey picked a fine house at the edge of Ellisville, forced the owners to leave and occupied it himself. He had the prisoners interrogated again, and the result was the same, no squealers. Rainey stormed out of the house, shot a horse in the head with his pistol and left it dead in the street. The horse's owner ran up and screamed at Rainey and he had the man arrested. Rainey was a Mississippi man, a slave-owner, and he held himself in high regard.

Able woke me that night.

"Captain wants to see ya now."

I went to his tent where he sat at his desk. He put down his pen, removed his spectacles and stroked his chin.

"Rainey's ordered us to build a gallows tomorrow."

"He's gonna hang the prisoners?"

"That's right. He aims to make a public display for the townspeople and our soldiers."

"Aren't deserters supposed to be shot?"

"Yes. But he's made up his mind."

"Hanging's for criminals, not soldiers."

"You're right, Flowers." He put his spectacles back on. "But he's made his mind up. In the mornin', choose a team and build the damn thing."

I wanted to say more but thought better of it and left straightaway. I couldn't get back to sleep that night, thinking of the effect on the men and worrying about the reaction of the townspeople. After breakfast, eight men volunteered including Danny Ellard, a carpenter from Kosciusko. We felled several longleaf pines and got to work. My stomach was in knots the whole time. Word had gotten around, and soldiers and townspeople came to watch us build. By one o'clock we had a sturdy structure wide enough for five men side-by-side and tall enough to snap their necks.

I walked west along the road toward the Tallahaha River to be alone. The war was hard enough without having to execute men from my own state. Military rules specified that deserters be shot, and most times officers settled for lesser punishments. *Hanging?* Colonel Rainey was going out of his way to make an example. A blue jay swooped low across the road, rose suddenly and lit in a cottonwood tree. From there it gave me what for, *Jeer-jeer, Jeer-jeer, Jeer-jeer.*

As I walked back toward town, a freshly plowed field was alive with robins hopping up and down the rows, pulling worms. I closed my eyes and remembered walking behind Father plowing our field, careful to keep my little bare feet in between rows. When the field was plowed, Father had me cup my hands. He gave me a few dried butterbeans and showed me how to press my finger in the loose dirt, place two seeds in each hole, and push a bit of dirt on top.

I prayed with all my might for God to save the souls of the condemned men and for fortitude for myself to hold up at the executions. At the river I washed my face and lay on a flat stone. The sun and the breeze dried my skin. Buzzards circled high above; gray-tipped wings caught in an updraft.

At half past four, our company assembled in a square around the gallows as ordered. Townspeople had been rounded up and forced to attend. All in all, about a hundred and fifty witnesses were present when the prisoners were marched into the square tied together. A town minister huddled with the men and read from Psalms as the crowd stood quietly. Some children were among the witnesses.

Five men were led to the scaffolding and their hands untied. Each climbed the ladder as the hangman, a local fellow, waited on top. He tied their hands behind their backs, slipped nooses over their necks and bound their feet. Then he stood back and nodded to Rainey.

The Colonel raised his sword and spoke.

"Confederate Orders of the War Department directs men convicted of desertion to be killed at such time and place as the commanding officer may direct. You men have been found guilty of desertion and murder. Do you have any last words?"

The Colonel waited a few seconds, and no one spoke. The hangman covered the men's heads with corn sacks and Rainey said, "May God have mercy on your souls."

He lowered his sword and the hangman pulled the lever. The footboards dropped and the hooded men fell ten feet in an instant. The ropes popped taut, necks snapped, and the scaffolding rocked under the weight. The crowd gasped and mothers covered their children's eyes. The dead men's bodies swung back and forth, feet kicking for a few seconds.

Oldham stepped forward and several soldiers followed. We removed the bodies, lay them on the ground underneath the scaffolding and returned to positions.

The second set of deserters climbed the ladder. When they were tied up and ready, Rainey repeated their conviction.

"Do you have any last words?" he asked. The man in the middle, older than the others, with a thin, clean-shaven face spoke up.

"I have somethin' to say."

"Go ahead."

The condemned man looked out over the crowd.

"I fought against the Mexicans and I volunteered and fought for the Confederate States from the beginning through the end of '62. When I found out my cattle were stolen to supply the Confederate army, I came home. The tax agents robbed my family and neighbors and left them without food, so I chose to stay and protect 'em."

He paused, fixed his gaze on Rainey, and then continued in a strong voice. "Yes, I deserted, but my duty is to my family first. Do what ya have to do, Colonel. My conscience is clear. That is all I have to say."

His words settled among the silent crowd. The hangman covered their heads and took hold of the lever.

"May God have mercy on your souls," Rainey said and lowered his sword.

I closed my eyes tight, but in my mind's eye, the five fell and their bodies rocked back and forth. I'll never be able to erase that memory.

When it was over, Oldham and I took down the body of the man who had spoken.

"Burial detail?" Oldham asked.

Dallas and a few others came forward. As the crowd slowly dispersed, a massive, dark cloud blocked the sun and the wind turned cooler. After burying the bodies, we returned to our company. Rainey had paid the hangman handsomely and given him a horse. I reckoned that he'd be dead before he could spend his earnings.

That night, I challenged Dallas to a chess match to get my mind off the executions.

"Sure," he said. "I'll see if we can borrow Bob's."

In a few minutes Dallas returned with a chess set.

"No problem," he said. "Bob's on picket tonight."

Dallas outplayed me the whole game, but I managed to avoid checkmate and we played to a draw.

The next morning Bob didn't return from picket duty. Oldham sent several men out to look for him, but they found no trace. I suspected he was killed in retaliation by Knight's followers. The hangings soured the attitudes of local folks, even those loyal to the Confederacy.

Our company kept guard at Ellisville, while other squads continued to search for Knight and his men. A few nights later distant thunder woke me. The wind whipped our tent, blew one half loose, and I retied it. Dallas didn't stir. He could sleep through anything.

"You awake?" I asked him.

"Am now," he grumbled.

A bright light lit up the tent, followed by a heavy clap of thunder.

"That was close!" he sat up.

"No bull!"

A sheet of rain swept over the tent and water dripped on my head.

"Ah," Dallas said loudly. "The glooo-ree-us life of a soldier!"

The way he strung out the word reminded me of gospel preachers and we both laughed.

"Everythin' about it is glooo-ree-us, glooo-ree-us!" he said, continuing his imitation. "Goin' for days without eatin' … sleepin' on wet bedrolls in thunderstorms, all for the glory and honor of soldierin'!"

Laughter came from tents nearby. Thunderclaps hammered the camp and then the bottom dropped out of the clouds. I lit a candle.

"Good to laugh," Dallas said.

"Ya got that right!"

Suddenly he turned angry and tears came to his eyes, and his shirt dripped at the elbows.

"I'm a cold-blooded killer!" his voice trembled.

He shivered all over and then lay still for a few minutes. After a time, I spoke.

"I'm afraid I'll not be able to love Mary Ann as before."

Dallas opened his eyes. "I know what ya mean. I feel as empty as a hollow tree." The downpour had stopped, but the leaves continued to drip.

"I've learned one lesson," Dallas said. "Don't ever get drawn into a damned war!"

"You're right about that! The choice is, join or not. After that it's obey orders or else!"

He blew out the candle and the dreadful memory of the executions returned to my mind.

Our company held Ellisville for two more weeks without incident, then the 20th Regiment prepared to leave Mississippi to travel to Georgia to reinforce the Army of Tennessee. There were still no clues about Bob's disappearance.

Chapter 37

DEFENSE OF ATLANTA
Late April — June 1864, Georgia

April 26, 1864

Dear Sister,

A train of empty boxcars arrived today from Meridian. Tomorrow we're heading to Georgia and we'll be back with General Johnston again.

I thank God each day for sparing me from death but worry about how much longer I'll last. Though I have no more damage that shows than a short ear and a few scars, my soul is wounded deeply, I fear. It's hard to put in words. My faith in God is firm, but the waste of life seeds honest doubts in my heart. Perhaps we can talk about these things when I return, if you will hear it.

*I'd give anything to have an hour or two to sit and talk with you. Please keep
sending the news from home. I look forward to reading a whole pile of your letters
when we get where we're going!*
Your loving brother, Anderson

The 20th and 6th Mississippi regiments boarded trains for Georgia and traveled
for six days doing nothing but taking naps. At Demopolis, Georgia, the train pulled
into a freight house where we took on supplies. Oldham told us we were nearing
Atlanta and showed us a map.

"The Yanks are approachin' from the north. It's a massive campaign to take
Atlanta."

On May 11th, having gone as far as we could by rail, we gathered our gear and
formed up columns. As we marched along Dallas said, "Been soldiers almost three
years now, old buddy."

"Three long years," I said. "And I'm dad-blame tired of your snorin'!"

"Is that so? Well I'm doggone tired of your uppity ways!"

He slapped me on the back. It was great to be laughing and carrying on again.

We marched five hours till dark then continued up a hill under torchlight. Soon
we came upon a deep entrenchment, already packed with riflemen. The 20th moved
along behind the trench for a half-mile more before we were positioned.

The morning light gave us our first look at the territory. To our front lay a great
valley and a town was visible in the flat, a mile or so away. Oldham called his
officers together as the men started fires for breakfast.

"The town is Resaca," Oldham said. "Our lines stretch four miles along this
ridge. We're part of Adams' Brigade now."

The sweet smell of fresh-cut pines filled the air. Light clouds passed high above
and swarms of buzzards sailed in the westerly winds.

"We've got to be ready for an enemy assault up this ridge. And I want timbers
placed over the trenches. They'll certainly bombard us. If there's one thing they've
got plenty of it's artillery!"

On the 15th, thousands of enemy soldiers crossed the valley and cannons on our
left flank commenced firing at the Yanks. At two hundred yards separation,
Oldham gave the command to fire. Up and down our line smoke rolled from rifles
and men reloaded swiftly. The distinctive aroma of gunpowder filled my nose. I
loved and hated the smell.

"What a fine group of soldiers," I said out loud to no one in particular.

"The finest!" came a forceful voice behind me.

Oldham stood smoking a cigar and smiling. There was a gleam in his eye. He felt the vitality of the fight too. A surge of pride and satisfaction flowed through my veins and warmed my ears like a hot shot of whiskey.

On the 16th, the Yankees attacked the Confederate center, a mile north of our position. In late afternoon, orders came for our withdrawal.

"Why are we leavin'?" Conway asked Oldham.

"The Yanks have us flanked to the south. There's just too many of 'em. If we stay, they may surround us."

Our army marched toward Atlanta for twenty-four hours without a break and rested the night in the Allatoona Mountains.

The next day we continued south. A dozen buzzards picked over something beside the road and they flew away as we approached. The stench in the air grew stronger, then we came upon a row of bodies that had been thrown in gullies and covered lightly with dirt. Hands, heads, and feet were exposed. The innards of more than one man had been torn open and multitudes of green flies feasted on the remains. I covered my face with a handkerchief and passed by as quickly as I could. The smell of rotting flesh cannot be forgotten.

On the evening of May 24th, we were positioned in a deep trench. The night sky was clear and moonlit. At daybreak Oldham summoned his officers.

"Just returned from a meeting at headquarters," he said.

"Where are we, Captain?" Sergeant Woods asked.

"New Hope Church."

The first Confederate forces had arrived at New Hope two days before and constructed two miles of formidable earthen, log and stone parapets to protect soldiers and artillery. A graveyard lay a hundred yards in front of our section. We hurried through our morning meal and then waited for the Union assault. That afternoon a fierce thunderstorm broke and there was no fighting that day.

The next afternoon the sun bore directly in the muddy trenches. Sweat stung my eyes and my clothes were soaked through. We sat tight behind our wall of stones three feet high and ate what food we had and talked. Dallas read his Bible and Barrett pulled out the packet of letters he kept in his breast pocket. Distant cannon fire lulled me to sleep.

"Lieutenant Flowers," Woods called. I awoke from a dream, dazed. "Yanks are comin'!"

Soldiers in blue poured out of the woods by the hundreds. They assembled in three rows and began surging toward us. The rows looked like long, blue serpents, writhing toward our entrenchment. *What brave men!* Bugles sounded and enemy artillery opened on us. Shells exploded near the stone wall, knocking out chunks and stirring up dust.

When the Yanks were two hundred yards from us, they raised rifles in unison, fired and fell back to reload. A hail of bullets slapped into the stone wall and zipped over our heads. A second blue row fired as our enemy climbed the hill toward us. When they were a little closer Oldham signaled and forty rifles fired in the space of a second. Then our second line stepped up and fired. The Yankee charge thinned but kept on coming.

A shell exploded nearby, and I was knocked to the ground and dropped my rifle. A vice-like force gripped my head and battle sounds suddenly ceased. My head throbbed and I couldn't see. When my sight returned, I got back to the stone parapet and my cartridge box was missing. Woods handed me another box. His lips moved, but I couldn't hear him. A few Yankees reached our outer works but were shot down. My eyes burned from the smoke and my stomach turned to steel. *The devil.*

Our cannons poured canister into the onrushing Yankees and they were cut down dozens at a time. Fierce fighting continued for two hours before the enemy retreated. Many Yanks lay dead or wounded on the field and few of our men at the wall were down. Litters were brought up and our wounded were carried to hospital tents in the rear.

"Woods," I said. "Take charge of burial detail."

He looked at me stone-faced. "My brother's wounded. I'd like to …"

"Go take care of him," I waved him away.

I called the men around me, about a dozen.

"Leave your rifles and follow me."

We got shovels from the wagons, found a flat area a quarter mile behind the lines, and began digging.

"Dallas, Will, Columbus. Come with me." We went back to the battlefront and gathered bodies. I penciled names on a folded sheet of paper. Marcus Malone, Berry Green, and Uriah Lewis. Berry took a bullet in his head.

"Does anybody know this man?" Will asked.

We gathered around a crumpled body. The back of his head was blown away.

I wrote 'unknown brave soldier' on my list and tucked it back in my pocket. We loaded the bodies on a skid and dragged it back to the makeshift graveyard. We covered their faces with hats and shoveled dirt on top. Columbus made markers from boards of a ruined shed and I said a prayer for all four at once.

"Our heavenly Father receive the souls of our brothers Uriah, Marcus and Berry, and this brave man who fought alongside us. Comfort their mothers and fathers, wives and children. Amen."

Back at the battlefield the shadows grew longer. Through my field glasses I spotted a Yankee officer on a horse at the edge of the woods far beyond the graveyard. He might have been making a list of dead soldiers too.

I went to Oldham's tent and handed him my list.

"Our losses, sir."

He took the paper and placed it on his desk with other notes. "Get some food and rest, Flowers."

May 26, 1864

Dearest Mary Ann,

There is nothing good about war. Dead bodies left in the sun grow bloated like pigs and smell like dead, rotting rats. The smell gets in your throat and you can taste it for days. The stink of burning hair plagues me. War is destruction and starvation. We steal crops from the people we are supposed to protect and rob them of their livelihood. We turn seasons into one long, bloody day after another. War has no proper season. It is disease, butchered forests, burned buildings, and slaughtered horses. We leave dead bodies half buried, crawling with worms. They rot in the sun and are picked apart by wolves and buzzards. Wounded men lie in fields screaming for help and no one comes, so they die alone. Dead men's heads swell up like melons and maggots feast on their eyes. Everywhere we fight we leave ghastly sights and the shameful stink of man.

Only the Lord knows how many mothers I have robbed of their beloved sons. I am damned to hell. I'm not worthy of God's love, nor yours. For what I have wrought of my own hands, I don't deserve to live another day. I've grown so tormented I desire not to think ...

Dallas yanked the letter from my hands, looked at it and said, "You're not sendin' this!"

He dropped it in the campfire. As the pages caught the blaze, I covered my face and wept. *Hell couldn't be worse.*

On the morning of June 4th, it began raining and I was sure we would be holed up for the day. Instead, orders came to break camp. We marched in the rain a good part of the day and camped on Pine Mountain.

On June 14th, Union artillery delivered fire at eleven in the morning, but our company was not engaged. That afternoon we learned that General Polk, our corps commander, had been killed in the blink of any eye by a direct hit from a cannon. Instant death was our constant companion.

At five o'clock in the afternoon on the 15th, the Yankees made an all-out, uphill attack on our position. They overtook one of our picket lines and our regiment was sent to retake it. Oldham led the attack down the hill through a pine woods that had been considerably reduced by artillery fire.

"Three groups," Oldham said. "Hundred men each. Conway take the right flank. Flowers, left. I'll command the middle. The center will advance slowly while both flanks slip down the sides. Then all three squads attack the center. Catch 'em in crossfire. Understood?"

"Yes, sir," Conway said.

"Check your watches. Flanks attack at six-forty-five. Best of luck men!"

At six-forty-five, a volley of rifle fire broke out across the hill and we heard the piercing yelps of our comrades. *Woh-who-ey! Woh-who-ey! Woh-who-ey! Woh-who-ey!*

We rose and ran through the trees, yelling and firing. The Yanks were surprised when bullets came ripping through them from both sides as well as from uphill. Bullets zipped from all directions and more of our men were hit. Bullets smashed into pine trees. Branches and needles showered the ground. *Oh God protect me! I want to see my Mary Ann again.*

Our men fought on in spite of losses and after twenty minutes of close fighting, the enemy finally retreated. We trudged back uphill, bringing our wounded as we were able. I stopped to help Jake. A bullet had smashed his kneecap and he was bleeding badly. He was a big man and I struggled to help him uphill. Dozens of men from other regiments came running through the trees with stretchers for the wounded and dead.

Colonel Brown called his captains and lieutenants together.

"I'm proud of you fine men of Mississippi. Colonel Russell told me the 20th was unwavering. Now I've seen that for myself."

When I left the gathering, I suddenly realized that Sergeant Barrett was not back. We looked for an hour in the dark till Dallas found him. He was shot through the neck, dead. We carried his body up the hill and placed it in a row with the others.

Our men lay on the ground exhausted and we had no food or water. A light wind rolled up the hill from the west and over our entrenchment. Smells of death, gunpowder, and pinesap saturated the air. Across the valley, a mile away, hundreds of enemy campfires flickered.

A mule-drawn wagon pulled up and stopped. "Water!" the driver shouted.

Every prone body in hearing distance jumped up, grabbed water barrels from the wagon, and drank deeply.

"Don't drink it all at once," I yelled. "We don't know how long it'll be 'fore we get more."

The water revived the men for a while and then all were quiet again.

I stopped by Oldham's tent. His spectacles lay on his desk; his hair in disarray. "What's wrong?" I asked.

He held a sheet of paper close to the lantern.

Twentieth Mississippi

Dead — 32

Wounded — 110

Missing — 9

Total Casualties — 151

"Eighteenth Regiment, lost even more," he said, rubbing his chin.

One hundred fifty-one losses out of eight hundred men in our regiment was staggering! Shock filled the space between us, and I left him alone. I tried to read my Bible by candlelight that night, but my mind ran from place to place too fast. The words of scripture confused me and did nothing to calm my heart.

Morning came and our men scoured the hillside gathering berries and nuts. Knapsacks were emptied of every last peanut and old potato. By noon the air was stifling, and flies irritated us to no end. In midafternoon, cheering came from soldiers on our left flank as a row of wagons made its way slowly up the road behind the trench line.

A soldier yelled, "Hardtack, hardtack!"

The men were so thrilled you would have thought we had won the war. We swarmed the captured food like bees in red clover and were soon revived.

June 25, 1864

Dearest Mary Ann,

I long to read your lovely words. Unfortunately, we've not had mail in several weeks. Even better — I'd like to hear your voice.

Our army was in a brutal hilltop battle a few days ago, but I came out unhurt. We suffered terrible losses, including John Barrett who was killed. He was a friend and I miss him sorely.

These last few weeks I am constantly weary. We set up defensive positions, are attacked, then retreat and set up defenses again. Enemy forces are always greater than ours. We're gradually being backed toward Atlanta. The heat and strain is enough to make a long, hot day picking cotton seem leisurely. I pray that my luck or God's grace or both will last to the end of this grievous folly.

Barrett's death has dampened my spirits and those of the company too. He was the most level-headed among us. He sometimes disagreed with orders, but he had a respectful way of voicing his point of view. He must have been the same man at home, a forthright husband and father. He has four children, including a daughter who was born shortly after the war began and a son who recently enlisted. He never laid eyes on his daughter.

You are always in my heart, dear woman. If I should fall and not return, I want you to know I am blessed by your love and joyful spirit. If I do make it home that will be a sure sign from God that we are meant to be as one.

Yours, Anderson

At the end of June rains finally came and cooled things off a bit. Food supplies improved and we even got a supply of molasses. One evening after supper, Dallas convinced me to play the fiddle which I had not done in a good while. I played and the others sang and danced on the top of Pine Mountain. For an hour, the suffering and loneliness was pushed to the back of my mind and a portion of joy returned.

Chapter 38

TRAGEDY

July 1864, Peachtree Creek, Georgia

On July 1st, we pulled up stakes and headed southwest. Mosquitoes attacked us persistently for ten miles in the windless summer heat. Suddenly companies K and C were peeled off from the rest of the regiment without explanation. Oldham led us through a hardwood forest, and we came upon a large field that had been recently harvested. We deployed along the edge of the trees, just out of sight, as a defensive wall in case the enemy discovered our army's retreat and tried to flank us. Two field cannons were brought in to help block a charge if it came.

It had been more than a day since we last ate and I was weak, and my head ached. We sat still in position for hours waiting for an engagement. At half past two, Amos, our lookout, signaled from his treetop and climbed down to join us. Hundreds of dark specks approached from the far side of the field. As the specks got closer we saw that it was huge rafter of turkeys slowly grazed across the field, eating the leavings from harvest.

Dallas licked his lips and smiled and the taste of roasted turkey was on my tongue. Under strict orders not to shoot, we watched hundreds of turkeys and felt our stomachs growl for another hour before they finally wandered out of sight.

That evening, we rejoined the main army moving south, hoofed it for three more hours, then camped. In the morning, Oldham went over the map with us.

"We're here at Peachtree Creek … Atlanta is two miles south." He marked an X with a pencil. "We're goin' to cross the creek, destroy the bridges and set up defensive positions along this corridor."

"What's the terrain like?" Conway asked.

"Thick woods … rolling. And the creek's bordered by dense underbrush. Should be difficult for the enemy to get through."

The breeze carried smells of bacon, biscuits, and tobacco through the musty bottomlands. Smoke from campfires circulated through the leaves. A half-hour later I spotted a man standing alone a good distance from our camp. I took out my field glasses to get a better look. It was Oldham. He had one hand tucked in his pocket, a cigar in the other, and he was looking down the tree-shaded lane toward Peachtree Creek.

After all were across the bridge, we set it on fire. About a mile south, we cut pine trees, sharpened the small ends to points, and placed them in front of our trenchworks as an extra barrier against an enemy assault. During our wait for the enemy, fresh beef, corn and flour was in good supply from Georgia farmers.

On the 10th, it began raining and continued off and on for several days. The ground grew soggy and the creek spilled over its banks. On the 18th, we learned that President Davis had replaced General Johnston with John Bell Hood. Hood was known to be an aggressive fighter. Oldham was sorely disappointed, and the men had much the same reaction. My bones felt uneasy at the news.

On the morning of July 19th, the 20th Mississippi was repositioned at Moore's Mill on Peachtree creek to prevent the enemy from crossing. The bridges there had been destroyed and the heavy rains widened the river by ten yards. Dallas was posted to my left and Frank to my right. I had fought side-by-side and suffered the hardships of prison with these good men for three years running. They were loyal soldiers and looked out for one another. We waited for hours watching birds flitting about. At four o'clock they all suddenly disappeared and enemy infantry approached through the thick woods. At sixty paces we exchanged rifle fire across the fast-flowing creek.

Smoke rolled underneath the leafy canopy and my eyes and nostrils stung. The crack of rifle fire, at first like a pattering rain, increased to a continuous roar as more enemy soldiers advanced. The smoke thickened and we kept up a steady fire as ordered. Something knocked me to the ground, and I smashed my wrist on a tree root. A handful of Yanks managed to cross the river. We poured lead into them and they dropped their weapons and tried to swim back across. The strong current swept them downstream and some went under. When the last Yanks disappeared into the woods, we rested and waited for orders. I told Frank to see if anyone was hit and I checked my pocket watch. The glass was cracked, but it was still ticking. Four-thirty.

Frank returned looking shaken. "Ray Meek's dead, Ted Chapman's wounded and Dallas is missing."

"Where did ya last see him?" I asked.

"Back near that row of trees over there," he pointed.

Oldham rode up. "Good work, men! Take cover as best ya can and keep an eye on the river. They'll be back for sure!"

I left Sergeant Woods in charge and searched for Dallas till I found a yellow bandana lying in the mud. It looked like the one Dallas wore for good luck. A rifle lay beside. The initials DT were carved in the butt. I took the rifle and bandana with me, searched the field behind us, then returned to my post. Frank recognized the bandana.

"I'll go look for him," he said.

He headed upstream to check with others.

"Amos, have any ammunition you can spare?" I asked.

He returned shortly with a cartridge box and firing caps. I loaded Dallas' rifle and resumed my position behind a shagbark hickory. The woods was unnaturally quiet for half an hour and I grew increasingly worried about Dallas while we waited for the enemy.

I remembered a time when we were both twelve, riding horses along the Big Black through a patch of thick woods. Dallas was in front and he turned around to say something. At that moment his horse went under a low limb and he was knocked clean off. I was afraid he had been knocked out and pulled his eyelids back. He laughed loudly in my face and punched me in the ribs. He couldn't stop laughing at how easily he'd fooled me.

Conway, who was directing troops east of our position, came up.

"Flowers," he said. "Come with me."

I left Woods in charge and followed Conway to our camp, about a mile to the rear. He turned me over to a negro orderly who led me to a hospital tent and pulled back the flap. Dallas lay face up on a blanket on the ground. He was attended by a woman in a black dress with brown hair pulled tight in a bun. His eyes were closed, and he looked pale and weak. A Bible lay beside him.

"You okay, buddy?" I asked.

He did not respond, and the nurse took me aside.

She leaned close and whispered, "A bullet pierced his chest. We gave him morphine."

"Is he gonna die?" I whispered.

"Your friend asked for ya. You'd better talk to him now." I felt her warm breath. She bowed her head, turned and left.

I felt swimmy-headed and I kneeled by his side. His clothes were torn and spackled with mud. His face was thin and gray, not the young man he was when we joined. The worst we'd suffered was cold and rain, blisters and cuts ... and my short ear. We had talked a few times about what we would do if the other was shot, but now that it had happened, I didn't know what to say. My mind raced. *Nothing's worth fighting for if it costs my best friend his life. What can I say that'll help?*

He opened his eyes and placed his hand in mine.

"You'll be alright," I said.

His blue-green eyes followed my lips, but without expression. I leaned down close to his face.

"No matter what ... for sure," he spoke faintly, but without his usual smile.

"We'll go huntin' this fall," I said. "Get that big buck, the one that's always eluded us."

I told him how our company had driven the Yanks back to the creek and they'd dropped their rifles in a hurry to get back across. He motioned slightly with his hand, so I leaned down close.

He whispered, "Bible."

Someone had left a blue jay feather as a marker in the Gospel of St. Mark, so I picked it up and read.

"And one of the scribes came, and having heard them reasoning together, and perceiving that he had answered them well, asked him, Which is the first commandment of all? And Jesus answered him, The first of all the commandments is, Hear, oh Israel; The Lord our God is one Lord: And thou shalt love the Lord thy God with all thy heart, and with all thy soul, and with all thy mind, and with all thy strength: this is the first commandment. And the second is like, namely this, Thou shalt love thy neighbour as thy self: there is none other commandment greater than these."

The nurse returned, saw me reading and left. She looked about the age of Dallas' mother and might have had sons in the war too. Dallas' eyes were closed and his breathing shallow. I turned to another passage and read out loud. He opened his eyes and watched me closely. When I finished, he motioned me closer and whispered to me again.

"Mother."

Tears flowed from my eyes and dripped on his shirt.

"Yes. I'll talk to her," I said.

For a second his eyes widened and then closed.

I whispered near his ear, "Dear Dallas, can you hear me? Yes, I think you can. I love you, brother."

His mouth was dry, and he whispered, "Stick with me."

I prayed to our Maker God, *Lift up my brother on angel's wings and fly him high above the treetops ... where he can't hear cannons or smell this dreadful war. Take him to heaven and fill his ears with cheerful sounds of birds in springtime and children playing.*

I stayed by his side whispering, I'm with you, over and over. His breaths became shallow and his grip on my hand loosened. I thought I heard children playing and recalled earlier times, when we played, hunted, and went to school together ... our longest, happiest days, and promised that I would never forget.

"I'm with you my friend. I'm with you."

The tension on his face lessened and his hand slipped from mine. His breaths became less frequent and I put my ear to his chest. His heartbeat was faint. A blast nearby shook the ground. His heart thumped weakly a few more times and then went still. He was gone.

After a few minutes, I folded his arms across his chest and straightened his head. The long scar on his forearm reminded me of the story he told the new recruits about Skunk, the prison guard. In his jacket were two folded sheets of paper. I checked his pockets and found two smooth, gray stones about the size of hickory nuts. One was almost as round as a marble; the other shaped more like a robin's egg. They had belonged to his father and Dallas always carried them. Deep sadness filled every part of me, and I fell into a bottomless pit. Cries of the wounded nearby blurred into one long scream. When the nurse returned, I hugged her shoulders. Her eyes were wet, and my tears spilled over again.

"I'm sorry," I said. "I promised I'd look out for him."

She pushed the tent flap open, her eyes shiny and joyless, and spoke softly.

"Grief is never just our own."

"Thank you, Ma'am."

I stumbled out of the tent into the fading sunlight. *How many men has she seen die?* Cannons boomed in the distance and the smell of gun smoke drifted south from the fight. My ears rang incessantly. I ran downhill, tripped and fell forward. My head hit something hard and white light flashed behind my forehead. When I awoke all was quiet except for sporadic cannon fire several miles away. A pair of wood ducks rose up from the creek and flew into the sunset. I watched till they were out of sight and prayed that Dallas was in heaven.

Bodies, rifles and equipment were spread through the field leading down toward the river. We had driven the enemy back, but at an unbearable cost.

I found Oldham and told him about Dallas.

"Go back to camp," he said.

"No. I want to be with my men."

He pointed east.

"'Bout two hundred yards downstream. Reinforcements are bein' brought up. There may be another assault before it's completely dark. Make sure you're set for ammunition and ...," he trailed off. "You know what to do."

Streaks of dirt filled worry lines etched in his face and sweat soaked through his hat. A bloodstained bandage covered his left hand and there was a smattering of dried blood on his coat.

"I'm afraid war's makin' old men of us, sir," I said.

He gave my shoulder a little push toward my men.

In the night, we returned to our entrenchment and were resupplied. At first light, some rested, others sat nervously. Many reread letters they kept tucked in their pockets. You could never be sure how much more time you had to live ... good men in frightful situations with no way out ... and every man knew the next assault could very well be his last.

The next morning Sergeant Woods woke me. I readied the men, took a few deep breaths, and loaded Dallas' rifle. My pistol was tucked at my waist. Hours passed as we waited for the enemy attack. My canteen ran dry and my stomach growled. At one o'clock orders came for us to assault the Yanks.

We massed four lines deep about three quarters of a mile south of the creek and waited for the order to move out. More time passed and no orders came. Finally, at three o'clock, we began striding at the drum corps' signal. A wall of blue-clad soldiers had crossed the creek, slipped through the trees, and assembled a line for battle on the south side of Peachtree.

On command our front line fired a volley of lead and the peaceful quiet was shattered. White smoke rolled out front and a light breeze pushed it on toward the enemy. A return volley ripped through our ranks, zipped over our heads and popped holes in the mud. Cannons commenced on both sides. Murderous rounds of canister flew into our ranks and theirs. The devil's rage overtook me, and I fired again and again, hoping to do damage with each shot. *I'm a soldier.* We charged. I emptied my pistol, fired Dallas' rifle, reloaded and fired as fast as I could.

I thought nothing of killing every Yankee I spotted, caring nothing for his life or my own. There was no mercy inside me. Time, distance and proportion evaporated. My cartridge pouch seemed to refill itself. The rifle hammer went missing and I searched the muddy ground, but it was lost. The light grew dim and I lay on my back and checked my watch. We had been fighting for over four hours though it seemed only a few minutes.

White flags came out on both sides. After all the smoke, fury and death, neither side had any gain to show. Slain bodies lay all around. Men with torches crisscrossed the field and among the few trees that had not been shattered or burned. We intermingled with the enemy, as both sides gathered their dead and wounded. Some bodies were so ruined it was impossible to tell who they belonged to. *Could God still be on our side?*

I felt worthless and ashamed, and wanted to be swept away. I pictured Dallas and me hunting in the Big Black bottom with nothing to fear but rattlesnakes. The sorrowful quiver of a fiddle reached my ears. It sounded quite like a woman singing but could have been my imagination.

Soldiers in reserve from the 7th Alabama took our place and our company returned to camp for the night. Our men were weary and forlorn as never before. I no longer cared if we won or lost, or if I was alive or dead. It was a tragedy that would not retreat. I ate supper alone and went to our tent. I placed the folded sheets of paper and two gray stones on Dallas' bedroll.

What will I tell his mother? What can I say that might comfort her? A raging river of resentment flowed through me — the way we were treated in prison, comrades who died from lack of food and medicine, and now, Dallas, gone. The sad memories nearly drowned me. An hour passed in a minute and I unfolded the sheets. It was a letter Dallas had started to his mother. I couldn't bear to read it, so I closed my eyes and prayed hard.

Dear Heavenly Father, I fear I've been the cause of letters to grieving mothers. Please forgive me oh Lord, for I have killed and maimed. Battle made me mad and I lost all mercy. Forgive me oh Lord, if you can.

War remade me in its image, a killing animal, not worthy to live another day. *How will I ever be able to go home?*

In Dallas' knapsack I found three letters addressed to Emma and a bear claw. He'd told me he was saving the claw to give to his six-year-old cousin Billy.

Oldham poked his weathered face inside my tent.

"You alright?"

"Yes, sir. I think so."

He knelt beside me and picked up the two small stones.

"Those belong to Dallas?"

"Yes, sir. That's all he had left of his father."

"And the papers?"

"A letter he'd started to his mother."

He looked away for a minute and then back. "You'd better finish it for him."

Oldham would be writing letters to families of fallen comrades that night, one of his duties as company commander.

"I'll write to Dallas' mother," I offered. "That'll be one less for you."

"You can have tomorrow morning off," he said. "But I need ya back here by noon."

He patted my shoulder and walked away. After he left, the clouds broke, and moonlight shone on Dallas' unfinished letter to his mother.

July 19, 1864

Dear Mother,

We're in Georgia now with our backs to Atlanta and the railroad. Thank goodness we are finally getting enough to eat again. Even had fresh beef and vegetables this week. First time in ages. No coffee, but I guess that would be asking too much.

I hope most of the crops are in now. When I think of the work at home, I think of it more favorably than I did at the time. So much about life, it seems, depends upon one's point of view. I'm learning a lot about people and the durability of the human spirit. You wouldn't believe the efforts our soldiers make to help each other. There's a bond among us that I didn't know was possible among men.

The Yanks have quite a large army and are determined to have their way. God must be looking out for me, for I have dodged bullets for three years now. At first I thought the Yankees had poor aim. But after many battles, I now know that they are just as good at shooting as we are. Divine power is the only possible reason for my wholeness.

I miss you deeply. Upon my return, I shall never again let you out of my sight.

I added on.

P.S. Captain Oldham singled me out last week for bravery in a battle at Pine Mountain. He said if there were medals to be given, he would give me one. Our company was called upon to go far beyond our lines to recapture lost ground. We won the ground back but suffered many casualties.

Next time you see Uncle Willie please tell him I appreciate the ways he took me under his wing when Father didn't come home. When he took me fishing, he listened when I wanted to talk, and he was fine when I didn't want to talk too. I'll be forever in his debt. I think he knows I'm grateful, but I'm not sure I ever told him straight out.

We're about to go out on a mission, so I must close for now. Please give my love to Margaret and Anna. When I return, I shall sing and dance with joy at our reunion! And with your permission, I shall push you high in the swing like you did for me when I was a boy. Your love is my constant companion and my heart is in your keeping.

Your devoted son, Dallas

Then I wrote my own letter to her.

July 21, 1864
Dear Miss Townsend,

My heart is heavy as a mill stone as I write these words. I do not know how to soften the news, so I'll just come right out with it. Dallas was badly wounded in a fierce battle, the worst we've been in so far. The doctor did all he could but was unable to save him. I was still in the fighting line when I heard he had been struck and went immediately to be by his side. I was with him during his last few hours in this battered, imperfect world. He had me read from the Bible and then he asked for you. I promised him I would talk with you upon my return. For now, this letter is the best I can do.

No cause is worth the loss of your beloved son and my dear friend. I assure you that he always did his best and was a brave soldier and true friend till the end. I pray that he is in heaven now with our Maker. Surely all his suffering is over and he's singing God's praises.

My prayer for you is that in suffering you shall find a glimmer of hope that will sustain you in the days ahead. May the sting of death soon be overcome by the memory of love and the joy of his life. As soon as I am able, I'll come see you. I have some things that belonged to him that he would want you to have. He loved you with all his heart and did his best to protect and honor you. I am honored to have been your son's friend. He was the best of us.

Yours in the faith of God, our Savior, Lieutenant Anderson Flowers

At daybreak, I stood under a sprawling beech tree and leaned on its smooth gray bark. The leaves waved gently in the morning air, then a shower of beech mast trickled through the leaves and peppered my hat and shirt, a squirrel feeding above.

I walked along the trenchworks and reached the southern end of our army. The men were beginning to recover from the heavy fighting. Groups of men huddled, cooking breakfast, drinking chicory coffee and talking. The morning sun touched my face and the trees and fields came to light. The countryside was busy with birds searching for food. My soul was empty and held no hope that a new day would bring an end to the misery at hand or any goodness at all.

At noon, supply wagons arrived, and mail was distributed. An orderly handed me two letters, one from Mary Ann and the other addressed to Dallas.

"This one's not for me," I told the orderly.

"Oldham told me to give it to ya … said you'd know what to do."

I put Mary's letter in my pocket, sat on the ground, and slit open the one addressed to Dallas.

June 20, 1864

Dear Dallas,

Several weeks have passed without word from you and my heart grows heavier with each passing day. These times are trying my resolve mightily.

The corn filled out right nicely this year. Bugs are eating the apples and pears, but we are still getting a good many canned. We planted only one acre of cotton this season, but that will be all we can use for ourselves. This is our third crop since the war started. Folks have fallen into new habits about how much to plant and banded together to get the harvests in. The cycle of life is harder with so many menfolk away, but we are managing.

The war news is discouraging through and through. People are reluctant to speak of it, and most have given up hope of victory. Enough of that, I will move on to more uplifting subjects.

Florence gave birth to another girl. Of course, that makes her especially busy with William away. I've been going over to help her some each week — gives her a little break. It's the least I can do.

Last Sunday Emma asked about you again. You know she's been sweet on you since school days. I know you're on the shy side when it comes to girls, but she is a wonderful cook and has a good heart. You could certainly do worse. I'm not saying she would marry you if you asked — just saying that a letter or two would warm her heart in case you did come a courting later on. A girl likes to know you are thinking of her when you're apart.

I will end this letter now. Tell that stubborn colonel to give you a furlough home!

Love, Momma Lou

The next evening Sergeant Woods approached me. "How 'bout a game of chess?" I hesitated. Dallas had been my regular chess partner. "Only if ya want to," he said.

I accepted reluctantly. We were evenly matched, and both played carefully, but just as I had arranged my pieces to put him in checkmate, he castled out of danger, and then I lost my knight. I threw the board and pieces in his face and left the camp to be alone.

Chapter 39

HEARTACHE
July 1864, Georgia

A voice broke through the cloud in my mind. "Take a ride with me, Lieutenant."
It was Captain Oldham sitting tall on his horse with another beside. My head
throbbed like I'd had too much whiskey.
"Special mission?" I asked.
He motioned me up but didn't speak. I mounted and followed him along a woods
trail leading behind our lines. In a mile or so we stopped in the shade of a tree line
a few paces from a group of hospital tents. Terrifying screams pierced the air.
We sat in our saddles and watched the surgeons and nurses work. Wounded lay
in rows, side-by-side, like a day's kill of doves. Two negroes loaded tubs filled

with arms, legs, and feet onto a wagon, and a trail of blood led back to the tents. A breeze brought the nauseating smell of blood and rotting flesh our way. I took a swig from my canteen and Oldham lit a cigar.

I heard a gruesome scream, "Not my leg!" Several men held the wounded man down and a surgeon took a saw to his leg. I turned away to keep from puking.

Finally, Oldham spoke. "There's no special mission. Need to talk to ya about your state of mind, Flowers."

I nodded.

"I only want to say this once," he continued, "so listen carefully."

"Yes, sir."

"You've been too rough on the men lately. You can't be takin' out your anger on 'em! I know Dallas was your best friend, but we're in a life and death struggle here."

"Yes, sir."

"The best way to honor Dallas and our other brothers who've gone before is to carry on the fight!"

"Yes, sir, I understand."

"I expect you to keep an officer's standing at all times. I'm countin' on ya! The men are countin' on ya. Get the point?"

"Yes, sir, I do."

"We've all lost friends and we'll lose more 'fore this contest is settled, more'n likely." He pointed to the tents. "The men'll follow ya into the hornet's nest if they respect you … if they trust you."

I nodded.

"From now on, I expect you to aim your anger at the enemy! One hundred percent!"

"I'll do better, sir."

He gave me a handful of opium pills.

"I don't need these, sir," I said.

"Keep 'em. You may someday! Let's get back."

About noon I found Amos among the men gathering firewood.

"Amos," I said. "Come with me." We walked a ways off. "I was wrong to accuse you."

"I didn't cut bait and run," he said.

"I know ya didn't. You're one of our bravest. Since Dallas was killed I …"

"It's okay, Lieutenant. He 'as my friend too, ya know." He patted my coat pocket. "I know 'bout the letters."

Oldham had granted me off-duty time till supper. A half-mile west of our encampment I found a stand of willows and lay under their shade. The long, green tassels waved in the breeze as the clouds drifted slowly eastward, and sleep came quickly. Later, the afternoon sunlight filtered through the leaves onto my face and woke me. A vivid memory returned.

When I was seventeen, Momma and I were the only ones left at home. Jesse, Sister and John had all already married and moved out. After supper one Sunday, Momma asked me to clean up so she could sit on the porch and listen to the grasshoppers. When the dishes were finished I joined her. She was sitting still with her eyes closed. I kissed her forehead, pulled my rocking chair up close and relaxed. The sun had just a few minutes to go before it slipped behind the pines. The twilight insects were in full chorus and the bullfrogs on the creek were cranking up.

Our life wasn't easy, especially after Father passed, but it was filled with goodness.

"Andy?" she said, surprising me.

"What is it?"

She looked at me, then closed her eyes, and her breath came out. It was her last.

We buried Momma beside Father in the Old Lebanon Cemetery. The carving on the grave marker read: Drucilla Walker Flowers, 1805-1858. After she passed, I lived alone in the family house for a year and then moved in with my sister and her husband Eugene. We made one full crop together and started another before the war broke out.

Amos met me under the willows.

"Lieutenant!" He was excited. "Good news!"

I couldn't imagine any news that could be good and wished he would leave me alone.

"Jesse's here!"

I jumped up and followed Amos quickly through the woods to an encampment a mile north where brother Jesse greeted me with open arms. His regiment had arrived at Peachtree a few days before. They had seen plenty of action and taken losses, but he was unhurt.

"You okay, little brother?" Jesse said. "Thought you'd be real happy to see me."

"Dallas was killed two days ago."

"No! No! No!" Jesse screamed and beat his chest. His face turned red and the veins on his neck looked like they were about to pop.

Two men in his company stepped up close. "What's the matter?" one asked.

"Our good friend was killed," I said.

Amos and I stayed and had supper with Jesse. His regiment had been in several terrible battles before Peachtree. Jesse and his buddies told stories about Shiloh, Murfreesboro, Chickamauga, and Chattanooga. I was only half listening, but it was good to be with Jesse, hear his voice, and see that he was alright.

Amos and I walked back to our company about ten o'clock. The ringing in my ears had lessened and I heard the wind passing through the leaves. A hint of rain was in the air. We passed a group of soldiers sleeping on the ground, one snoring loudly. Another man leaned against a tree smoking a pipe, and he tipped his hat to us.

I slept in the woods that night to be alone. I was haunted by thoughts of Dallas' last hours and the way his eyes followed me without expression. *What was going through his mind?* I felt split apart inside after Peachtree, as though a part of me died along with Dallas. *Was his lightheartedness what kept me level?* Father, then Momma ... now Dallas ... and brother John missing. I was consumed by anguish and felt like I was slipping away. Suddenly I panicked, thinking I had forgotten to breathe. *Hoot, hoot, hoot, a whowaa ...* Finally sleep came.

In the morning, sunlight filtered through the trees and all was quiet. I sensed animals nearby as my eyes came into focus. A herd of white-tailed deer were bedded down a few yards away. They awoke, leapt to their feet, and vanished in two seconds.

Chapter 40

OUTNUMBERED
July — September 1864, Georgia

General Hood moved the Army of Tennessee closer to Atlanta and set up defenses on the city's east side. On July 22nd, Hood attacked Union forces from both his flanks. Gratefully, our regiment was placed in reserve and did not engage the enemy. We learned later that our army suffered five thousand casualties to no gain.

Following the defeat, the 20th Mississippi and other elements of the Army of Tennessee were repositioned once again. We had gotten two hours' rest that night and had nothing to eat when word came that we were to assault the enemy. It is fair to say that we were a good deal broken down and discouraged. Men huddled in groups and talked quietly, rifles nearby. Others wrote letters or reread old ones. Sergeant Woods read his well-worn Bible.

Oldham called his officers together over a map.

"We'll attack through a lightly wooded area and across this road. The midpoint of the Union line is here, at Ezra Chapel. We're outnumbered and unfortunately, they've had time to build a wall of logs and rails."

The day was stifling hot under a bank of high clouds that seemed not to move at all. We waited, still with nothing to eat. I lay beneath a cottonwood tree and tried to ignore the pain in my stomach. A swarm of yellow butterflies played in the limbs and flittered among the men.

In an hour, a battery of six Napoleon cannons, crews and ammunition wagons from Alabama pulled up behind us. Two-dozen of our men got to work shoveling dirt. They built berms four feet high in semicircles around each gun.

At two o'clock, orders finally came. We lined up shoulder to shoulder, tightly packed, two rows deep; a quarter-mile long wave of loyal soldiers, rifles at our shoulders, purple and white colors held high. A drum cadence sounded our assault.

At two hundred yards separation the Yankees began firing at us. Our company held formation, fired two successive volleys, then advanced again. Men were cut down. Some fell silent, others screamed wildly. We moved steadily forward following Oldham's silver sword held up high. A blast in front sent dirt flying and a soldier who had been standing there disappeared. An empty shoe lay in the dirt and smoke came from the churned up ground.

We fired rapidly and our enemy did the same. More men were hacked down. The air was hot with shrapnel and thick with smoke. I struggled to breathe and couldn't see the enemy. Leaves and tree limbs fell to the ground like sleet. A thunderous concussion knocked me over and I covered my ears to stop the torturous ringing.

Our lines were fragmented, but we continued advancing and fought bravely. About eighty paces from the enemy breastworks the hail of bullets was too much and our assault came to a standstill. Men took cover on the ground and behind the few remaining trees. The clouds cleared and the searing sun bore down. My tongue was dry, and I had not a drop to drink. We couldn't take the hill and no reinforcements arrived. The stalemate lasted for two more hours before orders came to put up covering fire and retreat.

When the last of our company returned to our trenches, I checked my watch. It was half past six and all was quiet. We kept the enemy from taking the railroad, but otherwise our assault was unsuccessful.

Suddenly, a cannon barrage fell upon us. Shells exploded around and above us. Rows of Yankees massed in front of their wall of logs. Through my field glasses their blue uniforms looked unsoiled. Oldham had us fix bayonets in case. In fifteen minutes the artillery barrage ended, and the Yanks disappeared behind their defenses. Our company lost two killed, eleven wounded and one missing that day.

After Ezra Creek, portions of the Army of Tennessee, including the 20th Mississippi, moved south of Atlanta to protect the Macon and Western Railroad. Calvary scouts reported that General Sherman's troops were moving to encircle Atlanta. I wondered if Jesse was alright but had no way to find out. Our retreat was fast and disorganized.

Our regiment was repositioned west of the town of Jonesborough with responsibility for keeping an eye on a large field surrounded by trees just west of the Flint River. We took up positions about twenty paces inside the woods and slept with our rifles. The night was clear and the moon almost full.

At sunup, snare drums rattled across the field, followed by scattered rifle fire. A half hour later, Union artillery began shelling the woods from the leading edge on back. The second round of shells exploded dead-on our position. A shower of limbs, leaves, and shredded bark descended upon us. Chunks of shrapnel dug into trees and pockmarked the forest floor. Shrapnel hit a man a few paces behind me. He screamed and fell, and a comrade rushed to tend his wounds.

Oldham ordered us to the forward edge of the woods. Enemy soldiers stepped from their side of the woods by the hundreds, stirring up a cloud of dust across the width of the field as they advanced.

Oldham called Lieutenant Conway and me to meet with him away from the men. He had a map in his hand.

"We've got a mission. The Yanks outnumber us two to one. That's what General Hood believes. I think it could be even worse. The plan is to reduce the enemy forces as much as we can, then retreat to Jonesborough."

"What's our mission?" Conway asked.

"To the west there's a road that runs north to this creek and then turns back east. If the Yanks try to flank our left, this is probably the route they'll take. Our job is to guard this road and slow or stop any flanking movement. Get the men ready."

The men were assembled along with two cannons, ammunition wagons and crews.

Our road turned eastward and up a little hill. At the peak of the rise we took down a few sections of fencing and placed our cannons on either side, reinforced by riflemen. All guns pointed down the road and we waited. The sun rose higher as the heat of the day pressed upon us and horseflies took their share of flesh.

"Careful with your water supply," Oldham passed the word. "Could be here all day."

Another two hours passed in the relentless sunshine. Sweat poured down my face and redbugs attacked my ankles and crawled up my britches. Weakness set in. I wasn't sure I'd be able to raise my rifle when the shooting began.

Our forward patrols lay low in the bushes. Doves kicked up and flew over our heads. *Boom, boom,* came the roar of our cannons fifty paces ahead and men shouted. A second later a volley of rifle fire let loose; then a second volley. A few Yankees on foot stumbled toward us on the narrow road and were cut down by our fire. *Boom, boom,* our cannons fired again. There was a large explosion to the east and a cloud of white smoke rose in the air. Scattered rifle fire followed.

I rushed forward and came even with our cannons.

"Report?" I asked the artillery commander.

"We hit one of their ammo wagons and I think we've disabled two of their cannons. Hard to tell for sure in the smoke."

We ran down the fencerows stopping only to fire and reload. I climbed a fence post and trained my field glasses as our cannons let loose another round. Concentrated rifle fire erupted farther down the road. One Union cannon lay on the ground, abandoned, its wheels blown off. The other lay in the ditch beside a pair of dead mules. A handful of Yankees fired as they retreated, but no strong force remained in sight.

"Let's get outta here!" I yelled.

In twenty minutes, our patrol was all back together.

"Anybody seen Conway?" I asked.

"He walked back a while ago," Amos motioned back up the road. "I think he's hit. He was holdin' his arm."

About four o'clock we got back to the woods and found our army in pretty good shape, considering.

August 31, 1864

Dear Sister,

The sounds of drums are in my ears most every day now. It's a frightening experience to say the least. By some miracle I have survived another day of flying lead. We fought well, but there are too many of the enemy. We fight them off and then dig holes to bury our dead. Then we retreat and dig more holes to protect the living. More men have deserted and that makes it more dangerous for those of us who remain.

I'm having trouble sleeping these days. My eyes are closed, but I wake at the slightest sounds. Every night I hear voices in my head — voices of wounded crying for help. I awoke from a dream this morning thinking I was covered in blood. My mind is becoming infirm I fear, and I burst into anger often. I'm not sure I'll be able to adjust to a quiet, orderly life of husband and farmer if I am fortunate to survive.

Please do not let Mary Ann read this letter! That is all I have to say.

Your devoted brother, Anderson

At daybreak, scouts reported that Sherman's forces west of Jonesborough had been reinforced.

"Tell the men to get ready," Oldham commanded. "Expect an assault any minute."

Thirty-two men in our group were positioned and ready to fight. Four others were in the forward picket line. In July 1861 when Company K was formed, there were seventy-eight men and officers. The names of our dead, wounded and missing were my etched in memory, and names of the living on the tip of my tongue.

Oldham and I stood side-by-side looking at our line — men with beards in ragtag clothes and a hodgepodge of hats; grimy faces, worry lines and tired eyes all. Hardly the same men as when we started. Amos stood with us.

"Can we hold 'em, Captain?" Amos asked.

He put his hand on Amos' shoulder. "Don't see why not," he grinned. "Best men in Attala County. Haven't been beaten yet."

A good rifleman could load and fire three times a minute in perfect conditions, but conditions were never perfect in battle. The enemy would attack us with forces impossible to beat. *Why don't we retreat?*

Around ten o'clock, we heard cannons thundering north of us and we waited for orders. A pair of blue jays chased each other along our breastworks. A horsefly bit the back of my neck and Amos slapped it off.

"Sneaky little devils," he said, laughing.

Amos had an easy sense of humor like Dallas. I couldn't escape feeling responsible for the lives of our men, but there was little that could be done in the face of such poor odds. Amos and I shared what we had left in our haversacks — peanuts, soft sour apples and scraps of hardtack.

At two o'clock, food wagons arrived bringing more hardtack and rusty pears. We trimmed off the rotten spots and savored the wet sweetness. A woodpecker landed high up on a limbless, dead tree and slipped behind the trunk out of view. A loud, rapid *tap, tap, tap, tap, tap* echoed through the forest. *Tap, tap, tap, tap, tap.*

At three o'clock Oldham called an officer's meeting behind the lines.

"They've crossed the river and are massing. Pass the word down the line and take positions."

Our enemy moved methodically in tight formation across the field, strong sunlight on their red, white and blue colors. A volley of cannon fire screeched over our heads and exploded thirty paces behind. At a hundred yards separation Oldham yelled.

"Give 'em two rounds, men. Then hold. Need to save for when they're deadly-close."

We fired and a handful of Yankees fell, but their gaps were quickly filled. The blue wall of soldiers was solid. At eighty paces, bullets peppered our breastworks. Something tagged my forehead and blood ran in my eyes.

"Am I hit?" I asked Amos.

"Just a skin wound."

He handed me a handkerchief and I wiped my eyes clear.

"Looky here," Amos said. He held up a misshapen bullet. "Still hot."

He handed it to me. I turned it over in my fingers and gave it back to him.

"Keep it for good luck."

He slipped the smashed bullet in his pocket and reloaded.

"They're chargin' again!" Conway shouted.

I got a closer look through my field glasses. The wall of blue led by men holding regimental and Union flags moved steadily toward us. Intense firing erupted and bodies dropped. A bullet scrapped the skin off the back of Amos' hand. He wrapped a handkerchief around it and went back to shooting. The enemy got closer with each push. The sun fell lower and got in my eyes when aiming. Four brave Yankees crossed through our works. We shot one, caught the others and tied them together.

My hands were blistered, mouth dry … lips cracked and bleeding. Amos kept firing away with a satisfied expression on his face. I thought of Dallas and how his fight was over. I was so weary I was ready to join him in heaven. Around seven o'clock, the Yankees made another charge and were upon us quickly. We crawled out of the trench and began our retreat. There was no time to take our dead or wounded. When we arrived at the rendezvous point I counted heads. Thirty-three present for duty.

"Anybody see Ben, Attison or Conway?" I asked.

"Conway's with us. Bullet grazed his shoulder," Woods said.

It hadn't rained in weeks and the creeks and rivers were mostly dry. As we made our way along the dusty road, the sun slipped below the horizon and the enemy assault on Atlanta continued behind us. Our group moved south to the reorganization point at Lovejoy's Station. The high clouds in the night sky glowed from fires in the city. Over the next two days, Union troops probed our defenses repeatedly.

After a midday meal, I lay in a fallow cotton field and slept hard, dreamed deeply, and heard cannons booming. Upon awakening, the rolling sound was not artillery, it was a thunderstorm approaching from the west. The sky grew gray and blue, the air cooled sharply, and flashes of lightning illuminated the tops of the towering clouds. Broad rumblings followed, and occasionally, sharp veins of lightning knifed the ground. A few seconds later thunderclaps shook the earth and first raindrops splattered on my face.

The wind whipped, raindrops grew fatter and the cloud burst open. Lightning streaked and thunder hammered the countryside for half an hour. Then the storm calmed, and a gentle, steady rain followed. By suppertime the sky had cleared completely. All that was left was a rumble in the distance as the storm moved east across Georgia. I arose from the wet earth and returned to Company K.

September 8, 1864

Dear Sister,

We are encamped seven miles south of Atlanta, resting and licking our wounds. Yesterday we learned that the citizens of Atlanta are to be evacuated. It's sad that we weren't able to protect them. Our army is a hard-fighting bunch ... brave and dependable, but the enemy has too many soldiers and they fight hard too.

My head is full of vengeful thoughts and my dreams are often about killing Yanks. I know it's the devil in me. I've asked God to rid me of this curse but have received no relief so far. The last few days I have been holding onto one verse from Matthew. "For if ye forgive men their trespasses, your heavenly Father will also forgive you." Doc told me that he sometimes picked a single verse and let it rumble over and over inside. Said it helped calm his nerves.

My temper is getting away from me more. Yesterday I yelled at Amos again in front of the men. He'd done nothing wrong; he was just trying to cheer me up. I'm afraid that after the war I'll not be a peaceable neighbor. The acts I've committed are inhuman and vengeful.

I see that I've gone on too long about the futility of it all, so I'll stop writing now before I discourage you and me both even more. I'm going to talk to Amos now. Forgiveness is all that I can ask. Tell Henrietta I miss her and hope to be home soon.

Your loving brother, Anderson

Chapter 41

BIG SHANTY STATION

September — November 1864, Georgia and Tennessee

September 11, 1864

Dear Sister,

I hope this letter finds you and Henrietta in good spirits. We are now camped south of Atlanta awaiting further orders, resting and writing letters. It's a luxury to sleep without the rumble of war. The fall weather is quite pleasant.

Fall brings back good memories about home — playing outside and swinging under the white oak tree in the side yard. I love the feeling of weightlessness at the high point just before the swing starts back down. I pray that peace will be settled soon and we will be reunited.

Your loving brother, Anderson

September 30, 1864

Dear Mary Ann,

After almost a month of rest we are about to move. We don't know where, but we are told it will be soon. I'm mailing this letter today because I don't know when my next chance will be.

Though I have much to be thankful about, I must tell you that I'm plenty worried about coming home because I fear that normal life will be a shock. The chaos of battle arouses fierce energy inside me. The constant fear kicks my mind and body like nothing I've ever done before and blocks out other thoughts and feelings. Dallas and I used to talk about it. One time when we'd not fought for several weeks, he told me how much he missed the thrill of battle and I confessed that I felt the same.

I don't expect you to understand, but I now crave the danger of battle. I think it must be like the way some men can't get enough whiskey or their fill of gambling. I'm pulled toward what I fear most. Hard to explain, like I said, but I don't want to keep secrets from you, my dear. I know you love me, and I fervently pray that upon my return, you'll recognize me as the man you loved.

I Love You, Anderson

On October 1st, the 20th Mississippi packed up and marched around the east side of Atlanta.

"Where're we headin', Captain?" I asked.

"Can't say."

We marched all morning, stopped for an hour to eat and rest, and then continued into the night. Later Oldham pulled me aside and whispered.

"Gonna take back the railroad. We're goin' north of Atlanta to disrupt Union supplies comin' from Chattanooga."

Our target was a high point on the railroad leading north, a place called Big Shanty. About a half-hour before sunup, our regiment and two others were ordered forward. At early light, I made out the form of a water tower and rail station in the fog, then rifle fire broke out. We charged the station and overcame the enemy in a half hour of close fighting. As the sun came up, we learned that most of the Yanks had been asleep in bunkhouses and were taken prisoners by the 7th Regiment.

Around eleven o'clock we heard wagons and men coming toward us from the west.

"Ready men!" Oldham said. "Wait till they're in good view."

Cannons fired on us and then a flood of blue soldiers rushed our position firing. Ben was cut down. We retreated to the east side of the tracks and took cover behind the station house and a row of boxcars.

Attison called out, "I'm goin' back to get Ben."

He left his rifle, ducked under the train, and was gone. I watched as he drug Ben by the shoulders back to our side. A bullet ricocheted off steel and popped my shin. Blood soaked my trousers and it stung like a hornet but didn't enter the muscle.

Rifle fire continued along our line. Reinforcements from the 15th Alabama arrived and saved us from being overrun. After we pulled back, I found Attison on the ground behind the water tower. His face and neck were covered in blood, and Ben lay beside him wide-awake. Ben was wounded in the thigh and both men needed a doctor's attention.

Oldham ordered a full retreat and luckily, our enemy did not pursue.

After accounting for our men, I went to the hospital. The doctor had taken a bullet from Ben's thigh. Luckily the bone was not hit and he was sitting up, drinking water while the doctor tended to Attison.

"He should'ta come back for me," Ben said. "Now he's worse off than me." His voice was filled with anguish.

"He'll be alright," I said. "He's a tough one."

"It's my fault."

"I bet he'd have gone through about anything to help you. You're lucky to have such a loyal friend."

"What if he dies?"

"Get some rest. I'll be back to check on both of ya in a while."

The men of Company K were tired and quiet, except for Amos, who never seemed to wind down. He told stories non-stop. It was hard to know if his stories were true, but they were entertaining nonetheless.

Able's voice came from outside the circle of firelight.

"Lieutenant Flowers. Captain wants to see ya."

I followed him through the darkness to the hospital cluster. Oldham stood hatless next to a lantern pole, staring at the ground.

"Bad news," he said. "Attison didn't make it."

Attison's body lay on a bed of brown pine needles and Ben sat beside.

"He saved my life," Ben said. "And now he's dead."

Oldham spoke. "Attison was a good man and he died doin' his duty. You would've done the same for him."

Oldham knelt and put his hand on Ben's shoulder.

"Your war's over, son. I'm sendin' ya home. Your mother'll help ya heal up. She's gonna need ya on the farm next season."

"But Captain, the other men?" Ben said. "Ya need every gun smokin', don't ya?"

"You're darn right about that, but we'll get by. When ya get home and are feelin' able, go visit Attison's family and tell 'em what a fine soldier he was. Make 'em proud."

Oldham and I left the tent together.

"I'll write to Attison's family," I offered.

Oldham put his hand on my shoulder. "Remember when Attison and Ben went at it?"

"I do."

"This war made 'em friends."

On October 17th, the Army of Tennessee, comprised of thirty thousand infantry and eight thousand cavalry, abandoned the railroads we had fought over for two weeks and moved southwest towards Alabama. I nursed blisters and wished for a decent pair of boots. Five days later we had walked one hundred fifteen miles and arrived near the town of Gadsden late in the afternoon. Before we had time to build fires, a rainstorm fell upon us and we spent an uncomfortable night, hungry, tired and cold.

The next morning Oldham gathered the company and gave us some news.

"As most of ya know, Captain Patterson was our first commander. He fought bravely and led wisely. He was sent home after Fort Donelson on orders from Colonel Russell; otherwise he wouldn't have left. I just found out that Patterson died last month. We'll carry on to honor his sacrifice." He sighed and continued, "Tomorrow we're headin' for Tennessee."

On November 21st we crossed into Tennessee and kept walking. From time to time we heard scattered rifle fire ahead of us. Later we learned that General Forest's cavalry had skirmished with enemy cavalry, preparing the way for our army's movement north. Our army chased the Union rear guard, but our company was not engaged. After breakfast on the 29th, we started hoofing it again.

"Another long day?" I asked Oldham.

"Apparently. The Yanks escaped under our noses last night. General Hood's screamin' mad. He's blamin' everyone but himself."

He puffed on a cigar as we walked along together in silence for a mile.

"What'll you do after the war, Captain?"

"Go back home and try to make a livin' without slaves, I guess. Maybe I'll lease land to farmers. What about you?"

"Go back to bein' a poor farmer. Maybe I'll lease some land from ya."

"I suppose nothin'll be the same."

We walked on a while without conversation.

"Captain, I want to tell ya what an honor it is to serve as your second lieutenant. I've learned a lot from you and appreciate the opportunity."

"You plannin' on leavin' soon?" he grinned.

"No, sir. Just wanted to tell ya once again, is all."

As we marched through the afternoon I recalled a time in the woods alone near Apookta Creek when I was sixteen. I lay on my back on the forest floor. It was a cold day with a light breeze, and I watched the clouds. Suddenly, the quiet was interrupted by an urgent cawing crow atop a bare tree, cawing over and over. Four more crows appeared and flew in a circle around the one perched in the treetop. Each circling crow answered the call and more crows flew in and joined the circle, flying faster and cawing excitedly. Together they stirred up quite a racket, like a room full of people screaming at each other over some disagreement. Still more crows arrived till I counted more than twenty — all joined in the clamor circling the lone crow in the tree.

I waved my arms and yelled but they seemed not to notice me, so I sat down and covered my ears with my hands and closed my eyes. The madness continued for several more minutes and then suddenly the noise stopped. I opened my eyes and saw them flying away. The one in the treetop was still there, and he was silent and looked down at me it seemed.

Chapter 42

FIRE AND BRIMSTONE
November 30 — December 1, 1864, Franklin, Tennessee

After marching twelve miles through muddy fields and woods, our army, Loring's Division, arrived at a series of low, rolling hills and halted. It was a beautiful, sunny day, a quarter past one. Word came that the Yankees were entrenched north of us near a town named Franklin. The division received orders to form battle lines and move forward.

Captain Oldham returned from meeting with General Loring, gathered officers around and showed us a map of the area.

"This U-shape is the Harpeth River. Union lines start at the river and circle to here, by the town. The only bridge across is here and this road leads to it. The other road over here follows the river. Our attack lines will stretch from here to the river, a two-mile front."

"How far to Franklin?" Lieutenant Conway asked.

"Two miles from where we stand right now."

"Enemy strength?"

"Twenty thousand, 'bout the same as ours. Scouts said the first Yanks got here at daybreak and have been workin' all day on trenches and barriers. They have a number of cannons in place."

There was fatigue in Oldham's voice and worry on his face. We had been fighting together for over three years, survived numerous battles, and lost many comrades. Over the past year we had faced ever stronger enemy forces and been in retreat much of the time.

"What's the ground like?" I asked.

"Mostly open … low, rolling hills with a few trees. And two large plantations. See that two-story house over there?"

He pointed. "Carnton House." He turned back to the map. "There's a hill on the far-left flank. As our army attacks that'll compress the formation down to a mile."

"The enemy's had all day to entrench," Conway said. "And that's a fair piece of open ground to cover. Why move into the teeth of their defenses? Wouldn't it be better to flank 'em over here by the river, or on the west?"

Oldham looked directly at Conway and said, "Our orders are to man the extreme eastern flank, by the river. We'll move up Lewisburg Pike to about here." He marked the spot on the map. "Then form attack lines. Get 'em ready. This one's gonna be a heavyweight." He saluted smartly and we returned his gesture.

I'd become indifferent to the likelihood of death. One soldier looked like all the others to me. We were as one. "All go unto one place; all are of the dust, and all turn to dust again."

Sergeant Woods pulled me aside after the meeting.

"Where're our cannons?" he asked, looking shaken.

"Don't know. Haven't seen 'em."

At half past three we marched north, parallel to the river road. The regiments in front kicked into double-time and we rushed to keep up. The 20th Mississippi, along with others, formed attack lines about two hundred yards from the river.

As soon as we formed, we shouldered our rifles and moved toward the enemy fortifications en masse, our purple and white colors leading the way. The sun hung low in the clear blue sky. I checked my watch and it was four o'clock. A bevy of doves flew low over us heading north. Rabbits kicked up and hurried away. A child's bicycle lay in a ditch, its front wheel missing. The sounds of tromping feet rumbled over the two-mile advance and a cloud of dust surrounded us.

When we topped a little rise, I looked to my left and then to my right. A wall of brothers, four rows deep, rolled like a gray serpent through the withered straw grass, and a feeling of great pride filled my breast. Halfway across the two-mile plain enemy artillery commenced firing. There was a lesser reply from our cannons behind us. Following Oldham, we moved steadily across the field. Strings of rapid fire ripped from enemy rifles. Bullets buzzed through the air like bees, smacked bodies and hacked the ground. I lost sight of Oldham in the smoke and dust.

A succession of enemy cannons let loose. *Boom, boom, boom* ... I counted ten in a row without pause. Canisters exploded and the smell of burnt powder stung my nose. Something whapped my arm hard and I fell. My coat sleeve was torn open and a searing pain seized my arm and ran up my shoulder. A chunk of metal the size of a hammerhead lay beside me. Blood flowed from my elbow through a hole in my coat, but my arm was still in one piece. My comrades and I pushed on.

A hundred yards from the enemy defenses, we began concentrated volley fire and white smoke rolled in waves out front. As we advanced in the open, bullets zinged like sparks from a softwood fire. The enemy fired from behind a hefty wall and I couldn't imagine that our fire caused them much harm. Enemy cannons hammered away, cutting gaps in our advance. Dozens of men lay in the field and screams of agony sent shivers down my spine. Some men fired and advanced; others ran back. A half hour into the shooting an officer on horseback circled in front of us.

"Retreat, retreat!" he screamed. His red face was wet with sweat.

As we fell back I passed a man holding his mangled leg. Blood covered his hands and britches. He looked to me for help, but I didn't stop. We regrouped and were reinforced by other regiments that had not yet been in the fight just as the sun touched the horizon.

"Anyone seen Oldham?" I yelled.

No one answered. Another officer on horseback rode up.

"We'll assault and take their defenses," he yelled above the noise. "Orders from General Hood himself!" He sounded confident.

Can it be done?

"Double-time!" he shouted.

We moved rapidly across the field yelling and firing. Enemy fire was sporadic. The Yankees might have been surprised that we were foolish enough to attack again over the open ground. Our first obstacle was a ditch, then a wall of trees laid in rows. Behind the cut trees was a wall of earth and logs. At intervals, firing gaps were cut in the wall. Most enemy soldiers were behind these defenses, hidden from our sight.

Rifle fire intensified and several among us fell. I reached the ditch and dropped below the spray of bullets. The ditch was about three feet deep and dry. Up the other side we came upon a wall of hedge apple trees. My coat got tangled in the thorns and held me up. The enemy delivered deadly fire through their shooting gaps. More brothers were struck down, but we kept advancing. I emptied my pistol and kneeled to reload but was out of ammunition. Bullets zipped around me, pitching dirt and grass in the air. Exploding canister shells lacerated soldiers to my right and several dropped at once. Enemy fire was double or triple what we were giving them it seemed. *Like sheep to slaughter.*

Smoke was so thick it was hard to breathe. I took a rifle from a fallen comrade's hands and then a blast knocked me off my feet. Dirt got in my mouth and the back of my head burned. I lay still as my heart raced out of control. We retreated a hundred paces and were met by resupply runners as the sun dropped below the horizon. A frightened officer arrived and yelled, "General Hood's ordered another attack." *My final battle.*

Fear was etched on the face of every man around and they looked to me. I signaled, we reformed, and I led us back into the hail of bullets, our third assault. Our front row raised rifles and fired. It was difficult to find clear targets to shoot in the twilight chaos. The roar of explosions was deafening and smoke filled my lungs. I grew dizzy and lost balance. As soon as I was able, I got back up and fired at a gap in the wall.

My ears screamed from the exploding shells. Two men to my left were blown backward and lay deathly still in a scant patch of burning weeds, one without his head. I fired again through the smoke. The light over the horizon was quite weak. A huge blast knocked me over and I was partially buried in dirt, terrified. *This is murder! Why don't they call off the assault?*

We fell back again under the withering fire. Companies were broken and battle flags lost. Reinforcements joined and we reformed lines in the dark. Burning grass and exploding shells provided glimpses of the contested field, littered with bodies, dead horses and rifles. Wounded men screamed for help. My hands shook and my ears rang unmercifully. *Such brutality!* A man lay gulping up blood. Numb all over, I filled my cartridge case and reloaded my rifle. In minutes, we were ready for another assault across the open field, though it was too dark to fight.

We charged into a sea of red muzzle flashes and a hail of lead and smoke. A few of our men reached the wall and rushed through openings. I fell again and landed face down in a pile of brush. Thorns pierced my hands, side, and neck, and I had a fleeting thought of Jesus on the cross. A soldier came upon me in the dark and I fired my pistol in his face. Soldiers of both armies mixed together. I aimed at another man but didn't fire. *Who's the enemy?*

Two soldiers passed by me — one fighting with a pickaxe and the other, a long knife. I couldn't tell which one to help. Another man slipped and fell on my legs, knocking me over. We helped each other up.

A pistol fired into a man's head, not three feet away and blood and brains splattered on me. Another explosion knocked me off my feet and my hearing was lost. I lay face up, my mouth open and dry. A few moments later I heard a base drum thumping fast. After a few seconds I realized the thumping was my own heart, then suddenly my hearing returned. *Hell on earth!*

I rolled on my side and in the brief flashes of light, I saw feet tromping about. A man missing both arms trudged by. Another soldier led a comrade who was shot in the face. A shell exploded directly overhead and a shocking pain traveled from my head down to my toes like lightning. I was too dizzy to stand, so I crawled away on all fours. My mind was a blur of struggle, death and deafening noise.

Our situation was hopeless. I moved in one direction believing I was retreating and came upon the Union wall. Running the opposite way, I ordered the men around me to retreat and about a dozen followed me. We came upon the tangle of hedge apple trees and crawled under. Then two of the soldiers in our group turned around and crawled back. *Almighty God make this end, I beg you!*

My boots touched dead men and horses, and wounded soldiers. I tripped and my head came to rest on a dead man's bare feet. Bodies lay on top of each other. I walked, fell, crawled, and fell over and over in the darkness. I covered a hundred yards stepping on bodies all the way, acres of death and chaos. *Wake me from this nightmare, oh God!*

The firing slowed to an occasional rifle shot, then finally ceased. I dropped my rifle and fell to the ground. My ears rumbled like thunder and a strange sensation came over me. For a moment I was looking at the battlefield from above. *Am I in heaven?* I rolled over and a sharp pain shot through my arm. There was a terrifying scream close by, then I realized the scream was my own. Lying on my back, the purple-black sky filled my vision. Wisps of smoke drifted across the glittering sky. I closed my eyes and the world began to spin. *Take me away dear God! Take me away!*

Suddenly back inside my skin, I heard shrieks of wounded men. Smells of blood, piss and burnt powder overwhelmed me and I puked. I drank water and gave some to a man who begged for help. He asked for a blanket and clutched my hands.

"Mother?" he asked.

I pulled hard to get out of his grip and his blood got on me. As I moved east toward our camp, the plantation house, lit with lanterns, loomed up suddenly. I went through the house looking for Oldham but didn't find him. Every room was packed with wounded. A nurse stopped me.

"Let me help you," she said.

"I'm okay," I said.

She pulled a thorn from my neck, gave me a handkerchief, and said, "Hold this tight."

Outside, hundreds of wounded men covered the grounds and brush fires burned across the battlefield. I stumbled over a man, hands clasped in prayer, then saw that he was dead.

Away from the house, I walked toward the fires of our camp and shortly came upon a few ragged men sitting around a fire. A pile of corpses was stacked a few feet away. I called out for Company K, but no one answered.

A man motioned and said, "Sit with us."

The men sat in silence; all eyes fixed on the fire. I tried to take off my coat, but my injured elbow was swollen stiff and dried blood stuck the sleeve in place.

"Need help?" a man asked.

He helped me clean and bandage my arm. I warmed my hands and feet by the fire as the men smoked and stared at the flames. Then a familiar voice came from behind.

"Lieutenant Flowers?"

It was too dark to see.

"It's me, Amos."

"Seen Captain Oldham?" I asked.

"No."

In the firelight, I saw that his face was streaked with powder marks and dirt, and his eyes were dull. His left arm was in a sling. Never before had I seen Amos so bedeviled. We had fought continuously for over five hours, much of it in the dark, a futile fight from the start and an unnecessary waste of lives.

I woke with a start when Able shook my shoulder. His brown face looked worried and his hands shook.

"Captain's wounded," he said. "Bad!"

My legs were stiff, but Able helped me get up and steady myself. Morning sunshine flooded the field. Bodies of dead and wounded were scattered everywhere. Litter crews walked the fields and loaded bodies in wagons. They helped those who could walk and loaded others into carts. Hundreds of buzzards moved about the field. Soldiers ran about waving their hats, shooing the vultures away. Able led me through the woods to a road where wagons loaded with wounded were lining up to leave. Oldham lay next to three others in a wagon, all with closed eyes. His skin was gray and his uniform coat was ruined.

"Captain," I said.

He opened his eyes and strained to see me.

"Flowers. Good," he managed to say. "Conway's missing. Need ya to take charge."

"I'll certainly do that, sir."

"I'm goin' home for a while. Make a casualty list."

His voice trailed off.

"Yes, sir. I know what to do. You heal up quick. We need ya back."

"Able'll stay and help ya."

He closed his eyes and his head fell back. The driver whipped his switch and the two gray mules pulled. Oldham's wagon lurched, following the one in front. We stood and watched as the wagon train moved slowly south.

"He took bullets in the thigh, forearm and neck," Able said.

Suddenly a huge blast came from the woods and a plume of white smoke drifted through the bare branches. A man ran wildly from the trees screaming at the top of his lungs. Able and I caught him and offered water.

"What happened?" Able asked.

The soldier's eyes were bloodshot, his head blackened, and coat sleeves burned.

"Powder wagon blew up," he stammered. "Gotta get help!"

He pulled away and started running, then fell forward on his face. As we got to him, his body jerked once, and he died.

Scouts reported that the Yankees had built new bridges in the night, crossed the river and headed for Nashville. Able and I walked across the fields. Bodies of our dead were carried to new graveyards in the open field. Local men and boys had been hired to help dig. Three and four bodies shared shallow graves.

The ground was pockmarked from explosions and littered with shoes, rifles, and body parts. Hardly a blade of grass stood tall. A butternut-colored coat was caught in the hedge wall and a revolver and pair of field glasses lay in the dirt beneath. I picked up the gun and it was loaded. A group of buzzards flew off as we moved along, one carrying something dark red in its beak. Torn bodies lay in the ditch swarming with fat, green flies. Over a little rise we came to a horse blown in two and a thousand flies took flight. I covered my mouth but was not quick enough. I puked up breakfast along with the flies and then Able gave me a drink.

"This is where we fought," I muttered.

I picked up a blue cap and stuffed in under my belt.

"Terrible," he said. "Terrible."

We stepped through a firing gap in the wall of timbers. Dozens of dead Yanks lay where they had fallen. The ground was covered with hundreds of spent firing caps. Canteens, cartridge packs and rifles lay about. My foot kicked a leather satchel and unopened letters fell out. One was addressed to Miss Sarah Wallace in Anderson, Indiana. Another to Mr. Albert Cummings, of Defiance, Ohio. Through the field glasses I looked back east over the abandoned Yankee fortifications toward our forces. Our men moved about the field, loading bodies and picking up equipment that could be salvaged.

"They had us dead from the start," I said to Able.

"What's that ya say, Mr. Flowers?"

"You oughta leave."

Able looked at me questioningly.

"Go," I said and pointed. "Catch up with the Yanks."

"But Captain told me to help ya."

"President Lincoln made ya a free man."

Slowly, Able's face broke into a smile and his eyes gleamed.

"Ya mean it?"

"Yep. Please go. And take this."

Able put on the blue cap and we shook hands.

"Good luck," I said and handed him the pistol. "Hope ya don't need to use it."

He chuckled. "You're a good man, Flowers."

"Don't feel like a good man."

Able walked to the bridge, crossed over, and in a couple of minutes disappeared over the hill. I knelt beside the earthen wall and prayed for Able, Dallas, John, Oldham, and all our men.

I saw movement in the direction of the enemy retreat and looked through my field glasses, but it was only straw grass waving in the wind. *The spirit passes over the quick and the dead.*

Back in camp I made out a list of casualties on the blank side of a letter from Sister.

Company K, 20th Regiment, Mississippi, December 1, 1864, Franklin Tennessee

Killed — 7

Wounded — 15

Missing — 8

Total Casualties — 30

Amos came over.

"Where's Able?" he asked.

"He was with Oldham last time I saw him."

He gave me a doubting look. "Thought I saw you two walkin' in the battlefield."

"That's right!" I said. "I set him free!"

I found Colonel Brown sitting in the command tent staring at the ground.

"Casualty report for Company K," I said.

He placed the list on his fold-up desk without looking at it.

"We were murdered," he mumbled. "Lost fourteen generals, including John Adams killed."

"General Adams?"

"The Army of Tennessee is destroyed!" He waved me away.

I returned to our men and told them about Adams. We sat and tossed sticks in the fire and watched the flames. Gloom fell heavily upon us and there was nothing to be said. After a half hour watching the flames, my mind calmed and I read to myself from my Bible for a few minutes.

When I looked up Amos said, "Read to us."

The men looked to me and I read from the Book of Ephesians.

"For we wrestle not against flesh and blood, but against principalities, against powers, against the rulers of the darkness of this world, against spiritual wickedness in high places."

I lay awake for a long time under my blanket, watching thin clouds cross the starry sky. I thanked God for protecting me through another battle, though it was surely hell on earth. Wolves howled in the distance. Our assaults went over and over in my mind and I trembled in terror. Finally, my thoughts hushed, and the divine peace of sleep came.

Chapter 43

OVERWHELMED

December 1864, Nashville, Tennessee to Tupelo, Mississippi

We found out later that Hood's counselors strongly advised against his battle plans, but no one could change his mind and his bullheadedness cost us dearly. Six thousands of our soldiers were killed, wounded, or missing at Franklin. Our division of three thousand lost nine hundred. Besides Oldham, our company lost Walker, Conway, Brown, Davis, Taylor, Beauchamp and others. We were in desperate need of reorganizing and our wounded couldn't be cared for properly. Morale hit rock bottom and desertions increased.

On December 2nd, the temperature dropped, and new orders came. Our shattered army crossed the stone bridge in Franklin and moved north toward Nashville in pursuit of the enemy. It seemed beyond foolish to engage in another fight, but General Hood felt it imperative that we recapture the city and its rail lines. Scouts informed us that Union forces had taken positions along a line of hills south of the city. Our forces aligned parallel to the Union army along another set of hills.

Working feverishly, we erected fieldworks, dug trenches and built log barriers. Expecting to be attacked any hour, some stood guard while others bolstered our defenses and helped nurse the wounded.

What was left of the 20th Regiment was positioned near the center of the lines. Enemy fortifications were just a mile and a half away. A week passed waiting for the enemy to attack, but they did not.

December 9, 1864

Dear Sister,

I'm writing on the back of your last letter because it's the only paper I've got. I'm grateful to God for sparing my life once again. The battle we've just been through was a catastrophe and I don't know how it's possible that I was not shot. We're in desperate shape and facing enemy forces that outnumber us every time and we're still in dire need of food and clothing. I pray that General Sherman will overestimate our numbers and be afraid of heavy losses. Only God can save us if we're attacked.

Luckily Eugene, Jesse and I are still unharmed. If John's alive, then it's truly a miracle for our family. I apologize for dwelling on such things, but this is the state of my mind.

After I read the Bible tonight, my mind turned to Henrietta. If something bad happens and I don't return, I'd like her to have Father's violin. She's told me more than once she wants to learn to play and I'm sure if she had the chance she would not let anything stand in her way. I'll bet Uncle Willie would be glad to teach her. I think Father would be pleased if his granddaughter made music for our family. Would that be all right with you? Love, Anderson

I folded the short letter, put it in my pocket, and prayed I could post it soon. I didn't want to frighten Sister but couldn't keep my wish silent.

That night, a sleet storm descended upon us and when it was over, two inches of ice covered the ground. In the morning, men who were not on picket huddled by fires to keep from freezing.

"Lieutenant," Amos said. "Ya look thicker today. You gotta a secret stash of potatoes?"

"No on the potatoes, but I'm wearin' every stitch of clothes I've got!"

The men laughed. Amos, bless him, could always be counted on for a light heart; trivial things were all we had to smile about. The crushing defeat at Franklin devastated our spirits more than any trial we had faced before. The frigid air and ice was hard on us for five days straight. Our army couldn't move, but neither could our enemy. On December 14th, the ice began to melt, and we prepared for battle.

Sergeant Woods and I played chess that night. Although my opening game was strong, I lost several pawns in a series of poorly conceived moves, opening the board for Woods to set up his attack without serious challenge. Then my major pieces began to fall as I retreated and tried to protect my king. To no avail, as it turned out: my king was trapped. I should have resigned long before then, but I foolishly kept thinking I would find a way to press my own attack. Although his endgame was awkward, when he finally put me in checkmate, I had only one knight and a few pawns left.

At daybreak on the 15th, a dense fog settled upon our camp and the ice was melting fast. My boots broke through the ice and bogged down in mud at every step. As we started breakfast, cannon booms from the northeast broke the frigid silence. Our forward pickets reported that they couldn't see more than a few paces ahead. A half hour later, enemy cannon fire thundered through the hills from the west, much closer to us and the long-awaited Union attack was on.

Wind kicked up from the west and the fog began blowing away. A messenger on horseback came up behind our left flank.

"Main enemy force advancing on our front," he yelled. "Who's in charge?"

"I am," Colonel Brown stepped forward.

"Hood's ordered forces to defend our works at all cost."

He saluted and rode off to relay the message to other units along the line. A round of artillery shells whined overhead and blasted the woods behind us, shattering trees.

Colonel Brown shouted down the line, "Every man to the wall. Hold your fire till they're at a hundred paces, then make every shot true."

As the fog cleared from the field we saw that our enemy had brought cannons up closer to our lines during the night while we slept. They lobbed round after round of exploding shells at us. Mud and ice splattered the trees. Shrapnel smacked bodies and men screamed in pain.

"Take cover in the trenches!" Brown yelled.

Sergeant Woods and I kept watch. There was no point in keeping everyone up since the enemy infantry had not yet appeared. Our artillery command reoriented cannons and fired back. Once cannoneers on both sides were underway, the roar was so fierce we couldn't hear each other talk. Smoke from our own cannons rolled forward and settled in and around our trenches. Shells burst all around and we were pinned down by the relentless barrage. We huddled in the bottom of the trenches trying not to give in to fear and run. Sheared tree limbs fell on our heads.

An hour after the bombardment began, enemy artillery ceased, and waves of blue soldiers emerged in the wooded valley. They struggled up the grade through ice toward us.

"Firing positions!" Brown yelled.

Loaded and ready, I watched the undisturbed ice field in front of us, soon to be trampled by boots and splattered with blood. Some would take their last breaths in the field. Like many, I'd become resigned to the likelihood of death and a strange sense of peace came over me. I imagined that when hit, I'd spend my last moments on earth lying in the melting ice watching gray clouds pass overhead. I'd take a handful of ice to quench my thirst and ask God to forgive my sins. Mystery upon mystery, I would pass from a state of fear and hunger and be in the presence of the Lord in eternal life.

The enemy came within effective shooting range and the fight was on. We fired bullets by the hundreds every minute and they kept coming. Union cannon fire pounded us. The blue wave took losses, but others stepped up to fill the gaps and they got closer. Tall men, short men, bearded and clean-shaven. It seemed certain we would be overrun unless they suspended their attack. We had no soldiers in reserve and the enemy seemed to have an endless supply. Every one of us was on the line firing.

By mid-morning there had been no appreciable let-up, so only a few men at a time could slip down in the trenches to rest, drink water, and resupply. Bullets zinged over our defenses, a foot above my head. *Whap, whap, whap,* bullets hit tree trunks and shreds of bark fluttered to the ground. A stream of water ran along the bottom of the trench and my clothes were soaked. Ammunition runners resupplied us, and we directed brutal fire upon the enemy. They stalled but did not retreat.

About half past one, a solid wall of Yankees shoulder to shoulder charged us, only forty paces away. *What brave men! ... in our killing zone!* On command, we gave them a full volley. When the smoke cleared, the Union line was badly broken. Standing Yankees stepped over bodies in the muddy ice and kept firing. *Determined fighters!* I aimed at a man twenty paces out and pulled the trigger. As the recoil of my rifle pushed me back, he dropped his gun, fell in a lump, and reached up for a helping hand.

Some of our men crawled out of the trenches and began falling back from the fight. Another wave of blue soldiers reached the top of our hill and Colonel Brown called for our retreat. Stopping short of our last row of trenches, I turned and fired at the enemy once again. All our soldiers abandoned the trenches and ran. We fought in the trees as we withdrew and then followed a muddy road about a mile south. There we reassembled and dug more holes in a hurry. Companies and regiments were mixed up and I hadn't seen Eugene. Every soldier worked feverishly as we braced for another attack. We were of one mind — survival.

Darkness came and we spent another miserable night as rain mixed with snow fell on our heads. I finished a chunk of bread and sucked handfuls of snow. It was too cold to sleep, and I was so afraid of frostbite, I walked circles around a cottonwood tree all night long.

At four o'clock the next afternoon, the enemy made a massive push on our position. Their numbers were so great we were overrun immediately and many of our men were taken prisoner. A bullet nicked my neck, drawing blood. Our force moved south for several hours and I lost one boot in the mud.

Exhausted and with few supplies, we built fires and rested. Only six men from Company K were present for duty. In Kosciusko in the summer of 1861, we were seventy-eight strong. Woods and I were the only officers remaining. Amos got up and walked away.

Mary Ann and Sister prayed for me every day, but Dallas' mother prayed for him too. Doc Perry and the others, all their families believed God was watching over them. *Why have I been spared?*

Amos tapped me on the shoulder and handed me a pair of boots. I nodded and didn't ask where he got them. I slept fretfully and woke often during the night. The others lay still, and I hoped they were not frozen. I stoked the fire and a voice inside whispered, *These men are in your care.* I prayed for a quick end to the fighting.

In the morning, we headed south in full sunshine and soon came upon a town. The day was unusually warm for December and a breeze kicked up from the south.

"Whoa, that stinks to high heaven!" Amos said, holding his nose. "Franklin! We're back at Franklin."

A pungent smell with a tinge of sweetness hit me hard and I puked and trembled with fear.

"You alright, Lieutenant?" Amos asked.

I took a drink of water to calm myself. We passed along the road that ran through the battlefield. Bodies of lifeless men and horses lay where they had fallen days before. Bodies had begun to swell in the sunshine. We passed the plantation house. Hundreds of tents sheltered the wounded who couldn't fit inside. Beyond the tents stood a forest of markers, a graveyard. I promised God if I made it home I would tell my story to anyone who thought war was glorious. I promised myself that if Mary Ann and I had children, they would know full well the folly of war. The five-hour battle at Franklin haunts me to this day. Hell could not be worse.

Our army retreated ten miles south and camped by Rutherford Creek just north of Columbia. We set up a rear guard and spent another cold night without tents or blankets. To preserve heat, the men lay together, spooning. In the morning, scouts informed us that Union cavalry was pursuing us, so we crossed the creek, burned the bridge and hurried on south. We crossed Duck Creek and burned the bridge there too. Our cavalry scouts reported the enemy still in pursuit.

"They must think they have us this time," Woods said. "They're certainly not lettin' up."

The following day we marched twenty-some miles south to Pulaski, Tennessee, close to the Alabama border. I still hadn't seen Eugene, but our army was hopelessly disorganized and spread out, so I held out hope that he was still among the living.

"Too bad we aren't mounted infantry like durin' the Vicksburg summer," Amos joked.

"Agreed!"

"I bet sleepin' with a horse would be a lot warmer 'an sleepin' with you."

We both laughed.

From Pulaski, we turned west, moved eighty miles on foot over three days and reached Bainbridge, Tennessee on Christmas day. Our rear-guard reported that the enemy cavalry was no longer following.

The weather turned colder, but there was no rain or snow. We found food at times but logged more miles than meals. Many had frostbite, my older brother Jesse among them. His feet were in such bad shape he rode in a mule-drawn wagon.

At Stantonville, Tennessee we turned south and headed for Mississippi, crossing the state line on December 28th. Colonel Brown told us we were going to Tupelo to reorganize and camp for the rest of winter. Three days and fifty miles later, on the last day of 1864, we arrived at winter camp north of Tupelo. Food wagons awaited us, but still no word about Eugene. *What'll Sister and Henrietta do without him?*

Chapter 44

TAKING BROTHER JESSE HOME
January 1865, Mississippi

The new year started out so cold I slept with my canteen to keep it from freezing. After supper on our second day at winter camp, Colonel Brown pulled me aside.

"I'm givin' ya leave to take your brother home."

"Thank ya, Colonel! When can we leave?"

"First thing tomorrow. I'll have the furlough in writing and a wagon to get y'all to the station."

"Thank you, sir."

"One more thing. You'll need this." He handed me some money.

After breakfast, Amos went with Jesse and me to the railroad station in Tupelo. The next southbound train was not expected till the following morning, so I got Jesse situated next to the wall on the east side of the platform out of the wind. His feet were wrapped in burlap bags and we covered up with a blanket a stranger gave

313

us. The night was terribly cold, but it helped knowing it might be our last one outdoors.

Night sounds woke me several times. My ears were always on duty. At first light, I fed Jesse coffee and biscuits. He was in bad shape from frostbite and fatigue, and mumbled words that made no sense. At eleven o'clock the train arrived and we traveled the rest of the day to Macon where we got supper and a room. It rained that night and I prayed hard that Jesse would make it home.

The next day we hired a driver who took us on to Louisville. There, our driver introduced us to a man named Eliga Shirley, a tax gatherer for the state. He had a wagon and kindly agreed to take us on to Kosciusko, a thirty-five mile journey. We arrived in Kosciusko that afternoon, rented a mule, and set out immediately for home.

We arrived at the Big Black in the dwindling afternoon light. The flooded river made a swamp of the woods. Up to my waist in cold water, I reached the ferry landing and rang the bell over and over. Atop the bluff on the other side, there was no movement at Sultan's house. I was so furious I'd have shot a hole in a window if I'd had a rifle.

There was nothing left to do but retire for the night and hope for passage the next morning. Bone cold and with no dry wood for a fire, we huddled in a hollow tree just as it began raining. I wrapped Jesse in our only blanket and tried to sleep.

At daylight, I had a terrible sore throat and cough and Jesse was so weak I could not get him on the mule. I waded to the bells again and rang them over and over. Sultan's front door opened and he moseyed slowly to the ferry. He ferried us across and I did not pay our fee. Sultan didn't lift a finger to help as we made our way stiffly up the bluff. His wife invited us to come in the house to warm up and have coffee.

"I'm so sorry he didn't come get y'all last night," she said. "I told him he was an ass!"

"It's okay, Ma'am."

"I begged him to go down and put ya over. Musta been a horrible night."

"Yes it was, Ma'am. Thank ya kindly for takin' us in. And you're right about him … he is an ass."

She smiled and touched the side of her head. "Always been that way."

Her coffee was marvelous and we pressed close to the fire. My shoulders ached and feet throbbed.

"Don't get too close!" she warned. "Might thaw out too fast."

Jesse sipped his coffee and said nary a word. Sultan brought in an armload of wood, added to the fire and then went back outside.

After we warmed up and our clothes dried out a bit, we resumed our journey home. *Two more miles.* The west wind blew in our faces and my feet and hands grew numb again. Finally, we arrived at Jesse's house and I yelled for Martha. She helped me get Jesse off the mule and inside.

"Is he wounded?" she asked.

"Frostbite ... both feet. Hasn't been able to walk for a couple weeks."

He looked mighty poor and fell asleep immediately in a chair by the fire.

"What do we do?" she asked, worry lines on her brow.

"Doctor said wrap his feet in warm, wet washcloths several times a day. Not hot, just warm. And keep a blanket on him."

She unwrapped the burlap sacks and gasped. Both his feet were swollen and blue. She treated Jesse's feet and then poured us coffee.

"He has a wound on his upper arm, from Franklin ... but it's almost healed."

"I'll get y'all some food."

She left for the kitchen and I added wood to the fire and rubbed Jesse's shoulders. My fingers and toes ached from the inside out as they warmed. *Thank you dear God for sparing us! Thank you!*

Soon Martha brought a plate of ham and biscuits inside. Jesse managed to eat a biscuit before he fell back asleep. After the food and coffee hit my stomach, goodness flowed inside again.

"What happened at Franklin?" she asked quietly.

The memories overwhelmed me and I shuddered.

"That's alright." She touched my shoulder. "It's a blessing you're home and not hurt."

"It's been a year, probably, since I had ham."

"There's more." Her smile reminded me of Momma.

We sat together for an hour while she caught me up on news and she didn't ask more questions about the war.

"I've gotta go now," I said, "but I'll be back in a few days to check on the old boy. It's good to be with ya again, Martha."

We hugged and I stepped outside.

"Oh, can I leave the mule here, for now?" I said.

"That's fine, I'll take care of it," she waved.

Snow was falling again. As I walked along in the quiet, a whisper within said, *You have enough courage!*

Smoke rose from Sister's chimney and I scooped up snow and made a few snowballs. The icy balls burst when they hit the front door and in a second Henrietta poked her head out. I grabbed her waist and she screamed.

"You scared me half to death!"

I picked her up and swung her around in the yard. She squealed and hugged me tightly. Sister came out and we all hugged as snow swirled around us.

"Didn't know ya were comin' home," Sister said.

"I didn't know either till Colonel Brown told me two days ago. Let's get inside."

"How are Eugene and Jesse?" She looked worried.

"Haven't seen Eugene since Nashville a couple of weeks ago. The army was all strung out when we retreated."

I wasn't sure he was alive but didn't want her to worry even more.

"Colonel gave me leave to bring Jesse home. I just left him with Martha."

"You look worried," Henrietta said.

"He was wounded at Franklin." I pointed to my upper arm. "But he's healin' okay. His feet are the problem."

"Did they amputate?" Sister asked and Henrietta's eyes went wide.

"No, no. He's got frostbite. Hopefully he'll be okay in a few weeks. Have ya heard from John?"

She nodded no.

"You must be hungry," she changed the topic.

"I can wait till supper. Had food at Martha's. Catch me up while we sit."

An hour later I cleaned up, shaved and put on fresh clothes. Wearing clean clothes felt odd.

"I'd like to visit Mary Ann."

"Good," Sister said. "Invite her over for supper if ya like."

I put my ragged coat back on and stepped outside. Four inches of snow covered the lane and stray flakes drifted about. Birds flitted from bush to bush, tipping snow off limbs. In the pinewoods, a hawk swooped down, snatched something and sped away. The closer I got to Mary Ann's, the more worried I became. Memories seemed clouded and distant. I searched my mind for the sound of her voice, but it was hidden. *How could I have forgotten?* I felt ashamed.

At the lane to her cabin, a wave of memories washed over me. I recalled the tears streaking her face when we last saw each other and my own tears flowed. *I'm home.* I knocked softly and Mary Ann's mother opened the door. She smiled and motioned me in without fanfare.

"Mary Ann? Someone's here to see ya," Miriam said.

I stood inside the door and waited quietly, playing along with Miriam's ploy.

Mary Ann entered the room, dropped her knitting and hugged me. My blood flowed hot.

"Why didn't ya write?" She stood back and scolded me. "I've been worried sick!"

"We've been on the move for weeks. No mail in. No mail out."

"I need to get somethin' from the barn," Miriam said. "Back in a few minutes." She pulled on her boots and coat and left by the back door.

Alone together, Mary Ann said, "Wonder what she needs from the barn?"

"Nothin' at all, honey." I smiled, pulled her up close and kissed her on the lips. "Your pink's showin'," I pointed to her neck.

"You're showin' too!" she said pushing against me.

When Miriam returned, Mary Ann and I stood side-by-side close to the fire, rocking back and forth. The three of us had coffee and talked. They told me Captain Oldham lived only three weeks after he returned home.

"He was a good officer," I managed to say, but choked over the words. "And careful with his men."

"Think Jesse's feet'll get back to normal?" Miriam asked.

"Sure hope so."

Mary Ann got up and circled the room, looking at me.

"Who's been cuttin' your hair? The Yankees?"

Miriam got the scissors and said, "Let's trim this boy up a bit, shall we?"

Mary Ann's touch thrilled me. After the haircut, I invited both over for supper.

"We'd better get goin' before dark."

"I'm not goin' out in this snow," Miriam said. "You two run along and have fun."

Mary Ann and I walked the lane hand in hand. She kicked at the snow like a child and talked about plans for our future. Her voice was excited and unburdened.

She stopped, faced me, and said, "Are you listenin'?"

"My ears won't quit ringin', honey. The roar's with me all the time. It's like havin' a beehive in my head."

"Well, I'll talk louder," she said and continued.

A couple of minutes later she stopped us again.

"You're not listening! I just asked ya if you'd like to marry Alice and ya said yes!"

"Really?"

"You're not listenin'. You're somewhere else."

She was mad and ran ahead so I caught up.

"I'm sorry. You're right. My mind's troubled. The war … not sure …"

She put her hand on my lips, held up her index finger and looked right in my eyes.

"I'm not lettin' this goldarned war get in the way of our plans!" She was determined, to put it lightly. "You do whatever ya haf to do to get it behind ya." She squeezed my fingers so hard they hurt. "I'll help any way I can."

Her promise and determination sent a surge of energy through my veins. *You have enough courage!* We walked through the pinewoods in silence. The whisper of the wind through the trees usually soothed me, but I couldn't hear it for the ringing in my ears. When Sister's cabin came into sight, I took Mary Ann in my arms and confessed.

"I've done things that are unforgivable." She pulled me tighter. "I wanna love ya like before, but I don't know if I can."

Tears rolled down my cheeks. She stood on her toes, bit my earlobe and whispered, "You'll do fine."

When we reached the door, she pulled my head down and whispered in my ear, "Don't ya worry … I'll make sure."

Supper conversation was lively and filled with laughter. The battle rumbling in my head subsided and the women's voices kindled an ember of hope in my soul.

"How long do ya have?" Sister asked me.

"What da ya mean?" Mary Ann asked.

"How long is your leave?" Sister continued.

"You're not goin' back, are ya?" Mary Ann said indignantly.

"I have to start back day after tomorrow."

Mary Ann jumped up from the table and stomped out of the cabin, leaving the door wide open. Henrietta cried and our peaceful time was over.

"Sorry I asked," Sister said. "Didn't know ya hadn't told her."

"It's alright. It's my fault. I didn't wanna …"

"I'll comfort Henrietta," Sister nodded toward the door. "You'd better go."

I grabbed Mary Ann's coat and went outside. Footprints in the snow led me down the lane to her.

"Mary Ann," I called out. "I'm sorry I didn't tell ya. Please come back."

She turned to face me, tears running down her face. I put her coat around her and wrapped her tightly in my arms. She submitted for a minute and then pushed me away.

"If I'm gonna be your wife," she shouted, "you need to tell me everythin' that's important!"

"I will … I promise …"

After a few minutes we returned to the cabin. Sister and Henrietta sat by the fire, both busy with handiwork.

"Your plans for tomorrow?" Sister asked me.

"I wanna visit Dallas' mother, spend some time with you and Henrietta … and I'm hopin' Mary Ann'll go for a walk with me."

We all looked at Mary Ann.

"Okay," she said with a slight smile. "You talked me into it."

By the time we walked back to Mary Ann's, it had stopped snowing and the breeze blew clumps off the pine needles.

"Stop for a minute," she said. "Listen."

Hoot, hoot, hoot, a whowaa ...

"Our owls," she said.

Her warm forehead touched my chin.

"Wish I didn't have to go back."

"Let's enjoy the time we have."

I slept soundly that night but woke feeling numb and worried. The rigors of soldiering had become so familiar that being safe and warm felt strange and unsettling. My thoughts were with my men and their suffering.

After breakfast the next day, I walked alone to the Townsends'. Birds were moving about and the sunshine warmed my face. *What to say?* It had been five months since Dallas was killed. His mother met me at the door.

"I heard you were back," she said. Her voice sounded tired and sad, and she looked a good deal older than I remembered. "Thank ya for comin'." She took my coat and the bundle of Dallas' things.

"I'm so sorry," I said. "We stuck together like we promised, but it wasn't enough."

"I'm sure ya did your best. You needn't hold on to what might have been. He's with the Lord now."

She got me some coffee, untied the bundle, and picked up the two gray stones.

"I knew these would be here," she said. "I had a dream about this moment." She held them in the sunlight coming through the window. "I want you to have 'em."

"Oh no, Miss Townsend. They belong to you."

She took my hand, slipped them in, and closed my fist tight. "I'm givin' 'em to you!"

She went to the bedroom and returned holding a stack of letters.

"He wrote me often. He was a good son."

It looked like a few dozen letters.

"Is that all you've got?"

"Every single one," she held them to her bosom.

"He wrote many more than that. Three times a week at least, except in prison and when we were on the move."

I handed her the three letters addressed to Emma.

"Dallas wrote these, but never mailed 'em."

She looked at the envelopes and cried.

"Didn't know if I should send 'em or not," I said.

"I'll give 'em to her," she said softly.

She asked about other men in our company and I filled in the details. She nodded, but her heart was somewhere else.

"There's one more thing," I said. "Dallas wanted to give this to Billy." I handed her the bear claw and she turned it over in her hands.

"Thank ya, Andy. He was lucky to have ya as a friend."

"I was the lucky one."

She hugged me.

"I'm headin' back to Tupelo tomorrow," I said.

"Oh, my! Do ya have to? Isn't it futile?"

"It's my duty. I promise to come back and visit ya soon."

She shook her head. "Be careful, Andy. We can't bear any more losses." More tears spilled from her eyes.

I headed down the lane where Dallas and I had walked side-by-side many times, and my tears flowed freely.

Back at Sister's, Henrietta showed me her handiwork, a pile of blue material, cut in pieces.

"I'm makin' a new Sunday dress," she said proudly. "I'm 'bout halfway."

She held it up for me to see.

"That cloth looks familiar!"

It was the same material as the shirt she'd made for me.

"The boys in Company K sure were jealous," I said. "Your shirt kept me warm and lookin' good for a year."

"Don't ya still have it?"

"No. There was a fire."

She looked disappointed.

"You can make him a new one for when he comes home for good," Sister added.

"Wanna help me in the barn, Miss Henrietta?" I said.

"Sure. What are we doin'?"

"Secret." I winked and she followed me out.

In the barn, I split firewood while Henrietta told me about friends, school, and church. We hauled several wheelbarrow loads of split wood and stacked some by the back wall of the cabin and the rest by the kitchen.

"That should be enough for a few weeks," I said.

"Dennis comes over to split wood sometimes."

"Oh, so ya don't need me anymore, is that it?" She laughed. "Before we go in, I've got somethin' for ya. Close your eyes … hold out your hands."

"This isn't a trick, is it?"

"Oh, no. You can trust me."

When she'd closed her eyes, I put one of the polished stones in her cupped hands.

"Okay, open."

"It's beautiful! Where'd ya get it?"

"It's a friendship stone. Good for a lifetime. I've got the other one." I opened my hand and showed her. "They're a pair. Like us!"

Back inside Henrietta showed her stone to her mother and squealed.

"Looky what Uncle Andy gave me!"

Sister looked sad. She knew it once belonged to Dallas.

"Alright ladies," I said. "Off for Mary Ann's now. I'll have supper with them and be back home 'bout eight-thirty."

The second visit was easier than the first. We walked in the woods to be alone.

"What do ya want for your birthday?" I asked.

She looked at me with a puzzled expression. "That's not for seven more months now. You plannin' on shoppin' with the army?"

"No. Just wonderin' what you'd like, just in case."

"Well, I'll do some thinkin' on that and let ya know."

We came to a U-shaped curve on the Big Black, our favorite swimming place. The muddy, brown water was high from melting snow and winter rains. Loose leaves and sticks floated along. We crawled out on a bent tree overhanging the river and sat side-by-side dangling our legs above the water. A log jammed against the bank made the water swirl and gurgle. I dipped my fingers in the cold water and wet one of Mary Ann's cheeks. She put both hands on my chest and pretended to push.

321

"Bet you'd make a real big splash," she said, feigning anger.

"Yeah. Like we did that summer."

She looked deep in my eyes and said, "Playin' in warm water's a lot more fun, don't ya think?"

I was brimming with passion.

"I'll make ya a deal, Mr. Flowers," she said, reaching her arm around my waist. "Get yourself home this summer and we'll get frisky."

We kissed again and when I opened my eyes the sun had come out from behind a cloud. We held each other and watched the river sparkle.

Back at the Hughes's cabin, the three of us had venison, onions, and green beans with corn muffins and elderberry jam. When it was time to leave, Miriam hugged me goodbye and Mary Ann and I stepped outside. The moon lit the night and the wind whispered through the pines.

"I feel happy in the woods with you," she squeezed my hand. "I could stay here forever and not grow tired."

I smiled. "Sweet Mary Ann, I promise I'll be home for your birthday."

"You talkin' about this August or the one after that?" She laughed.

"This one! I promise!"

"I don't know why you'd make a promise like that, silly man."

Hoot, hoot, hoot, a hoowa ...

"There. That's a promise-keeper," I said.

She smiled and we kissed one more time.

I woke early the next day and went out alone. I kicked over old corn stalks and took a turn on the chair swing, renewing peaceable memories. Henrietta came out in her heavy coat.

"Push me!" she demanded.

"How could I say no?"

The swing went higher and higher till Henrietta was nearly even with the limb.

"High enough," she said. "Let the cat die, now."

When she came to a stop we walked down the lane.

"I'll be startin' back to school next week. Miss Rivers says she has some new books this year. I've read most of the ones at school."

"How're ya gettin' along?" I asked her.

"What da ya mean?"

"With your dad away."

"I miss him a lot but made up my mind I wasn't gonna be sad every day till he gets home. I like readin' his letters and writin' back. Momma puts my letters inside hers."

After breakfast, I packed up my things and said goodbye to Sister and Henrietta.

"You going by Mary Ann's?" Sister asked.

"No. We said our goodbyes last night."

"Are y'all gonna get married?" Henrietta asked.

"Yes, we are! 'Less she changes her mind 'fore I come back." Henrietta giggled. "Put in a good word for me, will ya?"

We all hugged.

"I'll be back 'fore Christmas."

"That's what ya said three years ago," Sister yelled as I walked away.

"Yeah, but this time I really mean it!"

We all laughed and that keep me from crying.

At Jesse's place, Martha met me at the door.

"How's the old boy?" I asked.

A voice came from inside. "I can speak for myself. Come on in, baby brother."

Jesse sat by the fire with his feet propped on a stool. He wiggled his toes and flexed his feet.

"They're both workin', but there's not much feelin' in the right."

"Sounds like you'd make the perfect soldier. You could hoof it all day without pain!"

"He wants to go back," Martha said. "But I don't think he can, and I sure don't want him to."

"As a superior officer, I'm orderin' ya to stay home." I saluted. "The war's over for you, Private Flowers."

Jesse smiled and touched his fingertips to his forehead. "Well, I guess that's it, Martha. I'm under orders now."

"I'm gonna tell Colonel Brown ya can't run fast enough to keep up."

"Take this." Martha handed me a quilt and a pair of wool socks. "I don't wanna see any more blue feet!"

We said our goodbyes and I got the mule from the barn. The air was frigid and not a cloud in the sky, and the sunshine warmed my clothes. I didn't see how the Confederacy could hold out much longer.

At the ferry, Sultan was loading a horse and wagon. A row of map turtles slipped off a log jutting out from a sand bar. The ferry crossed, unloaded and I led the mule on board.

"I'll pony up on my way back. Don't have a penny," I told Sultan, turning my pockets inside out. Then I handed him two bits. He grimaced and motioned for me to tug the rope.

When we got to the west side he said, "How's the fight?"

"We're whippin' 'em!" I shouted and that shut him up.

A few miles along, I met two wounded soldiers coming home. In Kosciusko, I returned the mule and spent a cold night on the train station platform. I was glad to be heading back to war and my brothers in arms.

At noon the next day I boarded and took a window seat. *WOOooOOOH, WOOooOOOH,* the whistle sounded, and the train started in motion. The countryside slipped by, empty fields, leafless trees, and swollen creeks. I wished I'd been able to enjoy being home more. I was rude to Sister several times and unwilling to answer her questions. There were some blundering moments with Mary Ann too. *What's wrong with me?*

As the train rolled north, excitement grew within. *Why, why?* The sad truth was that I longed to be with the men more than my dear Sister and Henrietta ... even more than my lovely Mary Ann. The car swayed and the heavy wheels rumbled in my ears. I was ashamed of my love of war, but the devil had me firmly in his grip.

Later a heavy downpour startled me from sleep. Rain peppered the roof and streamed across the windows. I struggled between the burning desire to rejoin Company K and a growing impulse to desert and save my hide. If I deserted I'd have to live with guilt the rest of my life and be called a coward.

The conductor walked down the aisle. He was short and thin with gray hair and sad eyes. I wondered if he had a son in the war.

"Tupelo, next stop. Next stop, Tupelo."

I stepped off the train into the rain. Cold water ran down the back of my neck and under my shirt. The biting air startled my lungs and I felt stunningly alive again. *I'm a soldier!*

Chapter 45

A WHISPER FROM MOMMA
January — April 1865, Mississippi, S. Carolina, N. Carolina

When I got back to winter camp in Tupelo, Eugene had returned. A nasty bruise covered the side of his face, but otherwise he was healthy. His crew had been hit by an exploding shell at Nashville and he was knocked out. When he came to, he followed the retreat route, but it took him a good many days to catch up.

In mid-January, a storm left a foot of snow on the ground. We dug ourselves out, got fires going and cooked. General Loring decided his army was a little rusty, so he divided us into opposing forces to brush up on battlefield tactics. Our side built a wall of snow a hundred paces long across a ridge between two sections of piney woods and made multitudes of snowballs.

Shortly a wave of men carrying sacks of snowballs attacked up an incline toward our center. As soon as they were within range, we shelled them with snowballs. Suddenly, from the woods on our right, another flurry of snowballs bombarded us.

For a half hour we had great fun throwing snowballs and wrestling, and then lay in the snow laughing.

Amos, Woods and I huddled by the fire in our hut the next afternoon, trying to stay warm. The wind blew through every crack it found.

"We need prisoners," Amos announced out of the blue.

"Why's that?" Woods said.

"Looky. Lieutenant needs new boots." Amos pointed at my feet and laughed.

I'd tied ropes around the tips that kept the soles and uppers from coming apart. The Union had newer model shoes with soles stitched to the uppers instead of nailed like ours.

"Now that ya mention it," I looked at Amos, "I could use a better pair. Lemme see if yours fit."

Rations grew short and we had eaten up everything there was around Tupelo. We learned that the Union army under General Sherman was moving toward the Carolinas and there was news of peace negotiations. Enlisted men talked openly about the end and expected it to come soon, and desertions increased as the harsh winter persisted.

On February 1st, we packed up and started east across Alabama traveling by train and on foot till we arrived in Augusta, Georgia on February 22nd. After camping and resting for a few days, we moved on to Kinston, North Carolina in early March.

On the morning of March 8th, the 20th Mississippi and other regiments were ordered to attack Union forces at Wise Forks. We charged the enemy position, running through our own gun smoke. The smoke invigorated me even though it smelled like rotting eggs, my first whiff since returning from home. I was filled with nervous excitement, my mouth was dry, and the devil laughed at me. He knew my craving for war was inferior to nothing else.

The enemy put up light resistance and quite by accident we drove a group of Yanks into a ravine where they dropped their rifles and surrendered. Our attack had come between them and the main Union force. As a result, we won the opening battle and returned to our camp in the woods. The prisoners, about a hundred, were placed in the middle, surrounded by a handful of guards.

After supper, I left my pistol with Amos, picked up some firewood and went among the prisoners. Their conversations stopped immediately. I dropped a log in a campfire and put the rest in their woodpile. A man with a brown handlebar mustache moved over to make a place for me.

"Smoke?" he asked me.

"No thanks. But I'd like some coffee if ya can spare it."

"Randy," the man said. "Get this officer a mug. I'm Sergeant Troyer, Indiana 38th. New Albany's my home."

"Lieutenant Flowers, Mississippi 20th, from Attala County. Your uniforms look mighty new."

"Just drafted. Their first battle. Short one as it turns out."

"We were as surprised as you were, I think."

"You been in from the beginnin'?" Troyer asked.

"Volunteered in July 1861. Our first big battle was in February 1862. Our whole regiment was captured at Fort Donelson … in Tennessee. Ya heard of it?"

"My regiment moved in to occupy the fort after ya left."

"Then I guess we almost met four years ago."

We laughed and the other prisoners resumed their conversations.

"I've been in from the beginnin' too," Troyer said. "First fight was Perryville."

He poked the fire with a stick and stared into the flames. His hands shook, same as mine. He continued.

"Then it was Murfreesboro, Stone's River, Chickamauga, Chattanooga, Lookout Mountain, Missionary Ridge, Buzzard's Roost, Peachtree Creek and twenty-somethin' other places with names I don't remember."

"My best friend was killed at Peachtree," I said.

Troyer looked up from the flames and his eyes were glassy.

"My favorite lieutenant was killed there too," he said. "We'd become friends."

We sat for a few minutes sipping coffee and staring at the flames.

"Is that your Bible?" I asked.

"Yep," Troyer said. "I'm Amish."

"I go to Old Lebanon Church, it's Primitive Baptist. I thought Amish were opposed to all fightin'."

"They are, but God called me to help free the slaves."

"Will your church take ya back?"

"Be surprised if they do. They're stingy on exceptions."

"I b'lieve slavery's immoral."

"Then why are ya fightin'?"

"Protectin' our homeland."

We had more coffee and talked about our plans for after the war. When it was time for me to go we both stood up.

"Brothers in arms," he said and shook my hand.

"I guess you're right about that."

Before sleep I prayed harder than ever that peace would come before anybody else got killed.

The next morning, I had Sergeant Woods take a dozen pairs of boots from our prisoners for our men without shoes. Around noon we were ordered to assault the Union right. At one o'clock, we stepped from the woods and began our charge across a field that sloped down slightly. Enemy cannons commenced after we cleared the woods and their fire was a great deal concentrated. An explosion knocked me over in the muddy field. I struggled to get back on my feet and couldn't find my rifle, so I rejoined the charge with only my pistol. Canister struck the front row of our attack line like a sudden rain blown sideways. Men were mowed down mercilessly. Our force fell back quickly and in ten minutes, we were back in our starting position in the woods. My heart thumped like crazy and mud was caked in one ear.

"They must have known our plans," Amos said. "Do ya think there's a spy among us?"

"I think we're just outnumbered," I said.

Confederate troops north of us captured a dozen Yanks and the prisoners gave information about reinforcements, so General Johnston decided to consolidate his forces and withdraw.

Back among the prisoners at camp, I found Sergeant Troyer sitting by a fire in sock feet.

"We're leavin' now," I said. "Not takin' prisoners."

"Thank you, Lieutenant."

"Hope we don't meet again in battle."

He nodded and handed me a folded piece of paper. "You dropped this when we had coffee together."

I took it and retreated with my men. A half hour after the last gunfire, *cheer, cheer, cheer,* came from the woods. A blue jay flew along our right flank and lit in a stand of trees between the two armies.

"Battle must be over," Amos said.

"How d'ya figure that?" Will asked.

"Blue jays," he pointed. "They only come back when the shootin's over."

The 20th Mississippi was deployed fifty miles west, near the town of Bentonville, North Carolina. The weather remained cold, but we were not hampered by rain or snow. Cavalry scouts reported the Union army following us. Our engineers laid out fortification plans and we traded rifles for shovels and dug in.

That night, I unfolded the paper Troyer gave me:

I can do no more to save my soul
Than awake and love my neighbor,
For it is he whom I can see and hold
Not our Father who is in heaven.

They were my words. Troyer had added a note at the bottom of the page.

Lt. Flowers,
My prayer is that you and I both make it home unharmed. Perhaps we shall meet again someday under peaceful circumstances and shake hands as countrymen and friends. Sgt. Troyer
P.S. Ecclesiastes 3: 1-8 (one of my favorites).

I opened my Bible and turned to the Book of Ecclesiastes: "To every thing there is a season, and a time to every purpose under the heaven: A time to be born, and a time to die; A time to plant, and a time to pluck up that which is planted; A time to kill, and a time to heal; A time to break down, and a time to build up; A time to weep, and a time to laugh; A time to mourn, and a time to dance; A time to cast away stones, and a time to gather stones together; A time to embrace, and a time to refrain from embracing; A time to get, and a time to lose; A time to keep, and a time to cast away; A time to rend, and a time to sew; A time to keep silence, and a time to speak; A time to love, and a time to hate; a time of war, and a time of peace."

On the morning of March 19th, we attacked our enemy. Company K was held in reserve. In mid-afternoon reports of the fighting were hopeful, but at twilight, soldiers from our army began straggling back to our lines. Union reinforcements had stopped our advance. That evening I wrote a letter to Mary Ann.

March 19, 1865

Dearest Mary Ann,

Our army was beaten back again today. All day I've been consumed with a premonition that I'll not be coming home. When that thought is swept out of my head, worrying about John takes over. Of course, that makes me worry for Ellen and Lilly. And sadness about Dallas is always with me. So many losses!

Last week we came upon a row of dead bodies laid in a ditch beside the road. I bet you didn't know that you can actually hear maggots eating flesh when there are enough of them. It sounds like hogs eating corn.

You can't send that, Dallas' words came to me, and I burned the letter.

During the night, a flash rain came, drenching us severely. Our wounded were evacuated across Mill Creek and taken east. The 20th Mississippi was moved from the forward trenches back to guard Mill Creek at the rear. We took position at a bridge on the road to Smithfield and Raleigh. Scattered rifle fire came from the front. Wagons laden with ammunition and food traveled west across the bridge all day, bringing supplies to keep our army in the fight. We spent a cold night at the bridge, our clothes wet from the rain the night before.

The next morning cannons boomed south of us and a light rain began to fall. Rifle fire erupted a half-mile distant.

Colonel Brown rode up. "Union attack comin' our way! We're to hold the bridge. It's our only escape!"

"Do ya think we'll have to retreat?" Woods asked.

"Just keep the bridge open, in case. Any more supply wagons arrive, send 'em back. Got to keep the road clear!"

By noon the rain lessened and by the sound of it, the fighting at the front intensified. It was disappointing that we could do nothing to help sway the fight, yet a strange sense of peace flowed inside me. *Might I make it home alive after all?*

In mid-afternoon, the rain stopped and the fighting slowed. Water dripped off limbs and pattered the leaf-covered ground. Creek water rushed around tree trunks and submerged bushes, carrying leaves and sticks along. Darkness came and we built fires. An hour later the wounded began to arrive in wagons, on mules, and on foot. We stood guard at the bridge as they crossed heading toward Smithfield, then a messenger arrived.

"We're pullin' out now. The whole army." He ran along to tell others.

Mixed among the walking wounded were wagons of dead. Arms, legs, and bloodied heads shown in the flickering torchlights. Columns of soldiers followed, clothes wet and muddy, faces downturned. Many were empty handed.

Colonel Brown returned. "Hold the bridge till everyone's across, then burn it!"

Hour after hour the procession continued under moonlight. I leaned against a willow oak and closed my eyes, but the lines of retreating soldiers continued in my mind. By three o'clock in the morning the procession began to dwindle.

The passing soldiers played tricks with my memory. Twice I thought I saw Dallas among the walking and I hoped for a miracle — to see John. I fell asleep and dreamed I was writing a letter to Dallas' mother. At another point in my dream there was a burning violin. Jack lay on his back in the snow, his face mangled beyond recognition. A voice woke me from the dream.

"Lieutenant!"

It was Sergeant Woods. He shook my shoulder. "You're screamin', sir."

I took a torch and walked along the road against the flow of retreating soldiers, and soon came to a dismounted officer, holding the reins of his horse. He had a short, gray beard and a sword.

"Colonel Mitchell, 24th Arkansas. Rear guard," he said.

"Lieutenant Flowers, 20th Mississippi. Are the Yanks behind?"

"They followed till about midnight, then we lost contact."

"You're almost to the bridge," I said. "We have orders to burn it after your men cross."

"There're 'bout three hundred in our guard. Shouldn't be much longer."

"That's good, sir. I'll leave you now and get back."

Wagon wheels, and the feet of men and mules churned the road into deep mud. *Colonel Mitchell, from Arkansas. Wonder what he'll do after the war?* The first tinges of daylight shot across the southeastern sky as I got back to the bridge.

"Lieutenant," Amos said. "We found dry wood, coal oil and burlap bags in the wagons." My mind was a blur. "To burn the bridge, sir!"

I rounded up our men and gave orders. "Another twenty minutes or so, the last of the rear guard should be across."

We watched as soldiers from Arkansas passed, dressed in all manner of clothing and hats. One whistled the tune "Savior, Like a Shepherd Lead Us," and a few sang along. Colonel Mitchell was the last to cross. *A man of honor.*

Our men spread bundles of wood wrapped in burlap on the bridge and emptied barrels of coal oil on the timbers. Woods handed me a burning torch and I gave it to Amos. He crossed the bridge holding the torch high and set the first row of wood on fire. The flames rose high and black smoke filled the early morning air. He set the last row afire and flung the torch end over end. It landed in the middle and *whoosh*, the bridge burst into flames. We stood twenty paces back on the muddy road and watched it burn as the sun came up behind us. I longed to see the Big Black river back home … without retreating soldiers, wagons of dead bodies, or bridges ablaze.

The next day we marched north to Smithfield. News spread through the ranks that Union forces had occupied Goldsboro and were consolidating forces. The Union army was reported to be over one hundred thousand men. Ours had been reduced to sixteen thousand. Rumors circulated that General Johnston would be seeking peace soon and a curious hopeful feeling sprung up inside me. The idea of defeat was humiliating, but I wanted nothing more than the end.

Over the next two days we marched fifty miles or so and encamped near Durham Station. Our army was in bad shape. The cold, lack of food and warm clothing, and illness far outweighed the hazard of being shot. Morale hit rock bottom and desertions continued. The end was only days or weeks away it seemed. Our generals couldn't fight a war without soldiers.

At the turn into April, the weather grew warmer and rumors of peace swirled. One night in the wee hours I was awakened by the sound of high-flying geese. The sky was awash with rows of long, fast-moving clouds. Moonlight peeked through for brief moments. The steady honking continued for an hour. I pictured the geese in V-formations high above the clouds. Thousands, repeating their ritual of migration … of peaceful life.

I added these words to a letter for Mary Ann.

I promise that I will love you with all my might and with tenderness of heart. And I shall honor and care for you all the days of my life. If God blesses us with children, I pray they will run barefoot in the fields and swim in the Big Black. May we grow old together under the magnolia trees in peace.

On April 9th, the remnant of the 20th Mississippi, one hundred eighty-one men, was combined with other units from Mississippi, Alabama and Louisiana, to form the 15th Infantry Regiment Consolidated. Our new commander was Colonel

Thomas Graham. He set up a schedule of morning and afternoon drills for every day except Sunday. I prayed we would never see action again.

In the night, I awoke to an odd silence and checked my pocket watch. It was one-thirty and no one was stirring. The wind had stopped and soft moonlight filtered through a sheer layer of clouds. *Andy,* a whisper came. It was Momma's voice. *You're goin' home.* Her warm presence surrounded me and I was overcome with gratefulness. Tears came to my eyes. She taught me how to live and love and gave generously of herself. *I'll honor your life through mine,* my words to her slipped through the dark trees. The thin clouds cleared and the soft moonlight made the forest glow. Momma didn't speak again.

On the afternoon of April 12th, Colonel Graham and the other regimental officers were called to General Johnston's headquarters. When he returned he addressed us from atop his horse.

"I have bad news, men. Three days past, General Lee surrendered the Army of Northern Virginia to General Grant at Appomattox Court House."

We stood in shocked silence. A crow flew out of the woods toward the gathering. Three blue jays pursued the crow, calling viciously. Graham turned to look.

"I don't yet know what this means for our army. For now, we'll continue drills and be ready to fight if called upon."

Graham turned his horse to move away, then circled back around to face the men.

"Remember!" he shouted out sternly. "You are still in the service of the Confederate States of America. Deserters will be shot!" He paused and saluted. "Dismissed."

We got fires going for supper. The sky was packed with gray-blue clouds that broke clear a few degrees above the horizon. Suddenly, the sun slid below the cloud cover and brilliant orange light cut across the sky touching us for the first time in days. I pointed it out to the others. We stood and watched the sun swell as it approached the horizon, decrease to a half circle, and then disappear behind the treetops. While the others returned to cook supper, I watched the last rays of sunlight spread underneath the clouds and turn them pink. Then the clouds closed at the horizon and the air cooled quickly. *John, where are ya brother?*

Later, by the fire, Amos offered me whiskey. I took a half mouthful and swallowed straight. It stung, numbed the back of my throat, and my ears burned for a minute.

After supper, the camp was alive with conversations. I walked among the tents and campfires hearing bits of conversation here and there.

"I hope we don't have to fight ..."

"What're ya gonna do when ya get home?"

"I've grown so fond of ya, darling," a man embraced his rifle. "I hope you'll have me as your lawful, wedded husband." The men around him laughed.

"Roasted ham with sweet potatoes … I can taste it now."

I passed another group.
"Gonna lay her back and fuck her long and strong," a tall man gestured with his arms.

Bats skittered over the encampment as I moved along.
"Haven't seen mother in four years. Wonder if she'll rek-a-nize me?"

The wind blew campfire smoke in my eyes.
"She was four when I left; so she's eight now. Lord sakes it's been ages."

Hearing words of pleasure and hope helped soothe my nerves.

On the 18th, Colonel Graham convened an officer's meeting.
"General Johnston's discussing terms of surrender with the Union."
"Is the war over?" Sergeant Woods asked. "Can we tell the men?"
"It's fine to tell 'em, but make sure they understand that this doesn't give 'em permission to leave. We're still a fightin' army. Understood?"
"Yes, sir!"
The following day a rider brought newspapers. I read part of the top story and handed the paper to Woods. President Lincoln had been assassinated. Lincoln, I thought, would not be vindictive to the South, for he seemed a wise and forgiving man. Without Lincoln, I feared, Mississippi would be treated as a conquered state and punishment would be piled on top of our defeat. The enormity of the four years of war hit me like a cannon blast. It had been an out-and-out waste.
A week more passed with no news of peace. Then on April 26th, General Johnston surrendered the armies in North and South Carolina, Georgia and Florida. The war was finally over.

I took off my battered uniform coat, dropped it to the ground and walked alone to a stream. I washed my arms, face and hands, and prayed to God for forgiveness and courage. The prospect of facing peace terrified me. By miracle or luck or both I made it through four years of fighting with only a shortened ear, damaged hearing and a few slight injuries. *Dallas, my dear friend, how'll I live without ya?*

I dunked my head under the water again. *John, you can come home now.*

Chapter 46

EIGHT HUNDRED MILES
*Late April – May 1865, Greensboro, North Carolina to Attala County,
Mississippi*

On April 28th, our regiment was ordered to Greensboro to receive parole papers.
Two days later we arrived at the Guilford County Courthouse, stacked our rifles
and marched east of the town where we camped. Officers were allowed to keep
side arms, but not ammunition, of course. The Yanks also let us keep our purple
and white flag. Other Confederate detachments continued to arrive overnight.

The next morning, the troops were gathered together in a large field. General
Johnston stood on the back of a wagon and gave us parting words. His speech
lasted two or three minutes. The words that stuck with me were about encouraging
us to discharge the obligations of good and peaceful citizens at our homes as well
as we had performed the duties of soldiers in the field.

My insides were all stirred up. I was proud at having done my duty but
questioned what the sacrifice had been for. My best friend was dead and maybe

337

my brother too. I was more than ready to go home, but not sure the devil inside could be tamed. I longed to see Mary Ann and worried that my soul was wounded beyond repair. I wanted to trust God but was not as sure about religion as I was before.

Each officer and enlisted man alike was paid $1.14 (US) in Mexican silver dollars, then we formed lines on the road into Greensboro. The long column shuffled forward a few feet at a time for hours in the hot sun. In mid-afternoon, we were told that the Yanks had run out of parole forms and we would have to come back the next day.

That evening, a merchant came through the camp. He wore a large straw hat and brilliant red shirt, and pulled a cart painted like it belonged in a carnival. It was filled with notions of all kinds including tobacco leaves he called bright leaf. They were vivid yellow. The salesman must have heard we had just been paid or else he had a keen sense of timing. Pipes glowed by the hundreds that night and the men found the bright leaf entirely satisfying.

The next morning, as our place in line got closer to town, I saw Union officers sitting at desks in front of a building filling out forms.

"How we gettin' home?" Amos asked.

"Good question," Woods replied.

Eventually, our group reached the front. A painted sign above the door read: Britton House Hotel. A sergeant named Albright filled out my parole paper and handed it to me.

"Good luck, Lieutenant."

I went to the train station while Amos, Woods and the others got their papers. Six of us from the original Company K decided to travel together.

"How far home?" Amos asked.

"Eight hundred miles!" I said. "I looked at the station masters' map."

"Did ya get us passage?" Amos asked, grinning.

"The railroad's assembling boxcars. There're so many of us, it may be days or weeks 'fore we get goin'."

"Weeks?" Amos exclaimed. "So what do we do in the meantime?"

"Back to camp," Woods said. "Yanks are issuin' rations!"

Soldiering had become our way of life. I had longed for the war's end for years, but when it was over, it left a considerable void. I felt hollow inside and tired to my bones. That evening the fiddles came out and we had quite a frolic. Whiskey flowed without restraint and I joined in. It helped cover the sting of defeat and dull the losses.

On May 5th, our group climbed into a boxcar and headed southwest toward Charlotte. The men were tired and beaten by the years of fighting, disease, injury and hunger. The train slowed to a crawl frequently when we crossed damaged tracks. Conversations became more lighthearted as we rolled along.

"Splendid pistol ya got there, Lieutenant!" Amos eyed my revolver. "Sure wish I had somethin' fine like that to take home."

"Name's Andy now," I said. "My lieutenant days are over."

I held the Colt Navy revolver up in the air and turned it from side to side admiring the polished gray metal. The dark wood handle was scratched, but otherwise it was fully serviceable. I flipped the cylinder open exposing the empty chambers, and spun it around as the men watched.

"No bullets," I said.

"You can buy more bullets," Amos said.

I tossed the gun to Amos, reached in my pocket and pulled out my Mexican silver dollars.

"I got better plans for these dollars when I get home! The dickens if I'm gonna use 'em to buy bullets!"

The men chuckled. Amos turned the revolver over in his hands, pretended to fire it at the roof, and then held it out for me.

"You keep it," I said. "I got no use for a pistol. I got a huntin' rifle and shotgun at home that'll do me jis fine."

Amos grinned from ear to ear.

"It kicks up like the blazes," I said. "Better be standing right by the critter if ya wanna do more'n make noise!"

The men laughed again.

After a few hours in the boxcar most men slept or kept their thoughts to themselves. I read my parole paper.

Greensboro, North Carolina, May 2, 1865. In accordance with the terms of the Military Convention, entered into the twenty-sixth day of April, 1865, between General Joseph E. Johnston, commanding the Confederate army, and Major General W. T. Sherman, commanding the United States Army in North Carolina, *Anderson Flowers* has given his solemn obligation not to take up arms against the Government of the United States until properly released from this obligation, and is permitted to return to his home, not to be disturbed by the United States authorities so long as he observes this obligation and obeys the laws in force where he may reside.

The boxcar lumbered from side to side on the uneven tracks and battles ran through my head. My stomach ached and the rough floorboards scraped my butt. I imagined a summer swim in the Big Black, mud between my toes, and clean clothes. The idea of being home for good was difficult to fathom.

Moonlight flickered through the roof slats. Bodies of men lay about at all angles like fish scattered on ice. The faces of Dallas, Doc Perry, Oldham, Barrett and other dead men rolled through my head. Most of the men I went to war with were not in the boxcar. Some were already home, missing arms and legs. Others were still missing. Some were surely in prisons. I hoped that's where John was. A cloud of sorrow came over me. *Was it noble to fight?* My heart slowed to a crawl as the bitter memories passed one right after another, like the boxcars that were taking us home. I woke with a start, fearing I'd forgotten to breathe, and lit a candle. I read my Bible looking for answers.

The six of us traveled together for a month by train and on foot. We soon ran out of money but met many generous people along the way. In early June, we got off a train at Columbus, Mississippi and stayed overnight in a boarding house. The next day we headed for our homes in Attala County, a hundred miles west. The weather was pleasant for walking, though a ride would have been accepted if offered.

Three days later we reached Kosciusko about two in the afternoon and split up. I struck out alone on the road toward Durant. A few light clouds dotted the sky. Dragonflies were everywhere it seemed, on fence posts, lighting on my shoulders and leading me home. I waved to farmers but didn't stop to talk. About four o'clock I got a drink from a well and took a rest under a shady black oak.

I dreamed I was alone in a killing field after a battle. It was completely silent, and I walked among bodies. Rifles and equipment lay about and pockets of burned grass smoldered. I kicked a loose wagon wheel and it broke into pieces. I spied a saddled horse standing in the field, loose reins touching the ground. I moved closer and saw a man's arm reach up to grab the reins. The gloved hand searched till he found them, and he grabbed and held on. The horse dragged him a few feet before he lost his grip. The horse nosed the man's face, but he lay still in the grass. I ran over to help, but the horse and soldier vanished.

When I woke from the dream, my hands were trembling and the smell of burned hair and gunpowder seemed to be in the air. I fumbled in my haversack, pulled out my Bible and turned to the Book of John.

"In the beginning was the Word, and the Word was with God, and the Word was God. The same was in the beginning with God. All things were made by him; and without him was not any thing made that was made. In him was life; and the life was the light of men. And the light shineth in darkness; and the darkness comprehended it not."

As I stepped out of the shade into the bright sunshine, mosquitoes whined in my ears. My boots and britches were covered with dust from the road and my throat was parched. The Big Black was still a couple of miles away. Black-eyed Susans glowed bright yellow alongside the road. A grove of sweet gum trees loaded with green gumballs waved in the breeze. When Dallas and I were kids, we threw gumballs at each other for fun, and we stopped when one of us got hurt.

"Thou shalt not kill."

I prayed to God with all my might as I put one foot in front of the other. *Will I ever be forgiven?*

Twenty minutes later I heard a bullfrog, *jug-o'-rum, jug-o'-rum, jug-o'-rum, jug-o'-rum,* and knew the river was close.

Sultan's wife sat on her porch doing handiwork. She saw me across the river and waved.

"That you, Andy?" she hollered out.

"It is for sure!"

"You be needin' the ferry?"

"No, thanks, Ma'am. Not today."

She waved back. *A good woman. Deserves a better husband.*

At the riverbank, a blue-gray heron stood on its long, stick legs. Its pointed gray beak and white head with black-striped cap were motionless. A puff of wind ruffled its tail feathers just a bit. We stared at each other for a minute and then the heron cocked its head back and forth, eyeing the shallow, standing water for crawdads and little fish.

The Big Black was low and only fifteen yards across. Brown, sandy mud bars jutted into the river. I held my haversack above my head and waded into the brown water. A row of slate-gray turtles slid off a sunny log a few yards downstream. The water came up to my waist and my boots stuck in the muddy river bottom and pulled off. I ducked under to cool my head and then tossed the boots toward shore. The first came to rest in the roots of an overturned tree. The second came up short, floated downstream a ways then sunk. The mud felt gooey and cool between my toes. A dove flew over, following the river corridor, darting from side to side. It veered off behind me and disappeared.

At the other side my bare feet sunk deep in the warm, white sand. I retrieved the boot and heaved it with all my might. It flew over the river and by a stroke of luck struck the ferry post and rang the bells. *Good riddance, Sultan. You old fart!*

I fell face first in the dry weeds bordering the river, laughing my head off. The yellow straw grass was in my face, a rabbit's eye view. The dusty earth made me sneeze and I laughed again. I rolled over on my back and squinted at the sun. *Home! Home! Thank God, I'm home!*

After lying in the sun a few minutes, I resumed my walk and soon came to a grassy lane, the last turn toward home. At the midpoint of a boggy green meadow a frightening grunt came from the thick bushes, *urr, urrrrrr, urrrrrrr*. A reddish-brown boar stared at me, six feet away. My body froze, muscles tensed, and my heart raced. Its hide was weathered and muddy. My eyes focused on its tusks and a menacing pair of sharp, two-inch cutters. After four years of carrying weapons to kill Yankees, I had nothing to protect myself.

Suddenly there was movement in the bushes behind. Four piglets with light brown fur and circular black bands wandered out of the thick vegetation, grazing the wet soil for roots and acorns. They appeared unbothered till they saw me, then one by one they stopped rooting for food and stood still behind the big boar.

I stood motionless, afraid the boar would rush me. It stood its ground too, muddy sides moving in and out slightly. We were stuck in time together. Abruptly, the boar circled backward and disappeared into the swamp grass and the piglets followed out of sight. My racing heart slowed and muscles relaxed.

I hurried past Dallas' place hoping to outrun my feelings. A sense of despair and guilt came over me and my hands trembled. I sat in the road and opened my Bible again. In Ephesians I found these verses. "Let all bitterness, and wrath, and anger, and clamour, and evil-speaking, be put away from you, with all malice. And be ye kind one to another, tender-hearted, forgiving one another, even as God for Christ's sake hath forgiven you."

Another mile down the lane, I saw Henrietta sitting on the swing reading, her back to me.

"What're ya readin'?"

She jolted and jumped off the swing.

"Uncle Andy!" she squealed, "You scared the bejeebers out of me!"

I spread my arms to give her a hug, but she stopped short and stared at me.

"What happened to you?"

"I went to war."

"No. I mean ... look at you!"

I was wet from head to toe, barefoot, and my clothes were muddy and torn.

"Your forehead's sunburned bad," she said.

It was hot to the touch.

"Don't ya have a hat?" she continued. "You always made sure I had a good hat for a day like this."

Sister came out of the house smiling broadly. "That's not a proper welcome home, Henrietta. Let's help him clean up, then we can hug him."

Eugene came from the barn.

"When did you get home?" I asked.

"'Bout two weeks ago. I'll get ya some clean clothes."

I washed up and the four of us sat in chairs under the swing tree and caught up.

"Did ya walk home alone?" Sister asked.

"Only from Kosciusko. Before that I was with Amos, Woods, Will and a couple others you haven't heard about. We traveled together all the way from Greensboro, North Carolina."

"How long did that take?" Henrietta asked.

"More'n a month."

"Momma. Can I go tell Mary Ann?"

"Sure honey. And invite her and Miriam over for supper. Tell 'em he who was once lost, has been found."

After Henrietta left, I asked Sister. "Any word from John?"

She nodded no and bowed her head.

A half hour later Henrietta returned with Miriam.

"Where's Mary Ann?" I asked.

"She'll be along in a while," Miriam smiled at me. "It'd be a good idea if you went to meet her part way."

I got Henrietta going high in the swing and then left. It felt good to be in clean clothes and not carrying a pistol or anything a soldier carries. I still needed a shave, haircut, finger- and toenails trimmed, and a good, long rest, of course.

Mary Ann walked around a bend with a basket under her arm. She wore a yellow and black checked dress made from the same material as one of the shirts she made for me. She stopped, set the basket down and put her hands on her hips. I was ready to take her right then and there.

"You're late, Mr. Flowers! 'Bout three years late, matter of fact."

"Well ... I kept the other part of my promise."

"What other part?"

"Comin' home in one piece."

She blushed. I turned in a circle and held both fists closed.

"Pick a hand," I said.

She opened my left hand, took the tiny pinecone she gave me before enlistment, and held it to her breast.

"You're one determined fellow, that's for sure."

She smiled, held up her arms and turned around in a circle.

"What do ya plan on doin'?" she said.

"Come here and I'll show ya!"

She took a few steps away.

"Are you ready for me?" she asked.

I picked her up and swung her around. We kissed and pressed our bodies together. She whispered private things in my ear, things she'd never said to me before. I thanked God for sparing me and for so much goodness to look forward to.

We held hands and walked on toward Sister's house.

"Honeysuckle blooms have been done for over a month now," she said. "We'll have to wait till next spring."

"I know a sunny place on the river where they bloom all summer. We're goin' there tomorrow and I'm gonna drip sweet nectar on your lips."

"Promise, Mr. Flowers?"

"I do!"

Back at Sister's we sat with the others, drank apple cider and talked.

"You two gonna get married now?" Henrietta asked.

"I'd sure like to marry her, but I'm not sure she'll have me."

"Why wouldn't she?"

"'Cause I don't have much to offer."

I took off the shoes and put them on the ground next to the hat.

"This all belongs to Eugene."

Everyone but Henrietta laughed, and Sister went to the cabin.

"Ya got your mule," Henrietta said. "And wagon."

"I guess that's a decent start."

"And ya got Mary Ann. I know she's gonna marry ya. She told me herself."

"She did?"

Mary Ann blushed, and Sister emerged from the cabin with both hands behind her back.

"There's one more thing you've got," Sister said.

She spun on her toes and stopped. Father's violin and bow were in her hands.

"Play Lorena for us," Henrietta squealed. "Please Uncle Andy?"

I didn't feel like playing but didn't want to disappoint her.

"Don't know if I remember how. Besides, I had bad luck with violins during the war."

"What kinda bad luck?" Mary Ann asked.

"I'd rather not tell that story right now, but I'll play if you'll sing."

I tuned up and played, and Mary Ann sang ...

> *"A hundred months have pass'd, Lorena*
> *Since last I held that hand in mine,*
> *And felt the pulse beat fast, Lorena*
> *Tho' mine beat faster far than thine.*
> *A hundred months twas flowery May*
> *When up the hilly slope we climbed*
> *To watch the dying of the day*
> *And hear the distant church bells chime."*

After supper, we all sat outside and talked.

"When y'all gettin' married?" Sister asked.

"August," Mary Ann said.

"The 16th," Miriam spoke up. "Mary Ann's birthday."

"I'll make ya a suit, brother," Sister offered.

"I don't have any money."

"I weaved some nice cloth already. Just need to measure ya and get started."

"Sounds like y'all got it all planned."

Sister looked at Mary Ann and Miriam. "We have been doin' a little."

The next day, I got busy helping Eugene and Sister with their crops. It sure was good to be home.

Chapter 47

HOME FOR GOOD
May — August 1865, Attala County, Mississippi

Upon returning home, I believed that having made it through the horrors of war, that my life would be easy, but I was dead wrong. Returning to a peaceful, civil life felt impossible and my good natured self was missing in action.

Mary Ann and I courted that summer. We weren't able to purchase the land near Sallis because all the money we'd saved was in Confederate paper bills and they were good for nothing. Mary Ann was energetic and quite determined that we keep our plans moving, and that encouraged me a great deal, despite the trouble I had adjusting to life after the war.

When I was a child, for instance, I often stood outside and watched the afternoon thunderstorms roll in. Seeing lightning strike and feeling the bone-rattling clap of thunder had been one of my favorite things to do. After the war, though, when I heard thunder in the distance, I went inside and buried my head under a pillow. It reminded me of cannon fire. I stayed away from Sister's kitchen because the smell

347

of wood smoke reminded me of burning hair and my stomach could not stand it. My ears rang constantly, and I had to ask people to repeat themselves often. Sudden movements sometimes startled me, even little birds flitting about.

In mid-July, Eugene and I got the cotton-picking underway. We started on a Monday morning as soon as there was light enough to see. Dozens of grasshoppers flew a couple rows over as we moved. A horsefly took a bite out of my neck before I could slap it off. I picked the cotton fast and stuffed bolls by the handful in the sack tied around my waist. Soon my fingers were pricked and stinging from the sharp hulls. I remembered the promises I made in prison and tried to think of the pain as part of the goodness of peaceful living. *Better the sting of a hundred cuts than the pinch of one bullet.* The bag filled gradually, and we got in several hours picking before the sun and heat took its toll. By eleven o'clock we each had about two hundred pounds and broke off for other tasks.

The work, good food and rest strengthened my body and my feet healed up. Though I was still a young man, I was broken in spirit. I found that I was quite tired sometimes when I'd not been working and I was constantly afraid that mean words would come out of my mouth. Being out in the field with Eugene kept me from exploding at Sister and Mary Ann as much. I tried to talk with Eugene about my rage, but he wouldn't hear it. He just stayed busy with work.

We were both troubled by the war. Before, Eugene had had an easy way about him, and we talked freely. After, he was nervous, didn't seem to be listening when people talked to him, and lost patience easily. Henrietta didn't like to be alone with him. She even asked me if she could come live with Mary Ann and me when we got married. Eugene told me I'd get over the war quicker by piling new living on top. After that I gave up trying to talk with him.

Nightmares plagued me. One night I dreamed that a tall man fell in a heap beside me and lay limp in the snow. He had taken a terrible blast in the face, but I recognized his coat, and a frightful chill surged through my soul. Jack's blood melted the snow and turned it the color of velvet. My body jerked awake and I found that I was lying on the floor and sweating profusely. Jack's shattered face haunted me, and I wished I'd never known him. *Maybe it would have been better if I'd been killed.*

The same nightmare returned the following night. The evening after that I decided to stay awake so I walked up and down the lane till dawn. Some nights Sister got up to check on me when I screamed in my sleep.

Each time I thought of Dallas, I saw his eyes, expressionless, following my lips as I spoke to him during his last hour. The nurse in a black dress with her hair pulled tight in a bun told me, "Your friend asked for you. You'd better talk to him now." Her words came back to me whenever I heard a woman's voice.

Another time I dreamed I came upon the body of a blue-coated man in a stream, his face submerged. One hand bobbed up and down in the current. A cold sadness flooded my soul and I sensed someone was watching me. I would recall this dream every time I washed my hands.

Mary Ann and I went for walks in the woods several times a week. She was alive with energy and hope. I felt flat and exhausted by comparison. *If only she knew. If only she'd seen what I saw.* I didn't really want her to know the horrors of war, of course, but I yearned to be understood and forgiven.

The four years of war seemed like it was my whole life, a living nightmare. I had trouble remembering my childhood, Momma and Father. When you're a soldier you don't know if you're going to live through the fight and when you do, you're afraid about the next one. The next battle could be five minutes later or five weeks later, you don't know for sure. You don't know anything for sure about anything. You could be reading a letter in the woods and a bullet from a sharpshooter's rifle could end your life in a second. A train carrying gunpowder might explode and burn you so horribly your own mother wouldn't know it was you.

My walks with Mary Ann grew increasingly gloomy and I began to doubt if I could ever love her as before. I worried that she'd call off the wedding. She grew testy with me, but somehow stayed steady enough. One afternoon we were a couple of miles out in the woods when a thunderstorm caught us. We huddled together against the trunk of a cottonwood tree and her body was warm against me. She spoke and I felt her voice vibrating in my chest.

"You're gonna have to find a way to forgive yourself, honey. Everyone here loves ya, but ya hate yourself."

I pondered her words and realized she was right. I could not forgive myself. I read my Bible searching for guidance and in the Book of Colossians I found these verses.

"Put on therefore, as the elect of God, holy and beloved, bowels of mercies, kindness, humbleness of mind, meekness, long-suffering; Forbearing one another, and forgiving one another, if any man have a quarrel against any: even as Christ forgave you, so also do ye."

I talked with Pastor Small about the uneasiness I felt in my heart. He tried to console me, but it didn't help. Having not been in the fighting, he didn't understand what soldiers faced. I read my Bible at the start and end of each day and asked for forgiveness.

Before the war, I was able to fall asleep in a minute. After, though, I often lay awake for hours, restless — my ears continually listening. Haunting images came in my sleep like shot from a canister shell. Sometimes at night I felt like I was suffocating, and I woke in panic. One night I dreamed I was crossing a burning

349

field in the dark. My feet touched dead men, horses, and wounded soldiers crawling to get away. I fell and my head came to rest face to face with a dead man and his eyes were open. I crawled over bodies for what felt like hours, without once touching the earth.

It seemed that I was shot through with holes even though the only bullet that hit me with force just nipped my ear. The holes were filled with anger and the anger struck without warning, like the sharpshooter's bullet. I was constantly at odds with others ... especially the people I loved most. Sister listened to me and told me she was praying for me. She assured me that my tender feelings would return even though I wasn't sure at all.

After being home for several weeks, the constant ringing in my ears lessened considerably and I appreciated hearing bird and animal sounds again. Henrietta asked me to play the fiddle and I hated to put her off, but I just couldn't bear to pick it up. I was afraid the sound of the strings would make me so sad I'd slide right down into hell.

One afternoon, in the pinewoods on my way to Mary Ann's, a whisper came, *You're forgiven.* The treetops swayed a bit in the breeze.

I knelt on my knees and prayed out loud.

"I've been obedient to the authority of man. From now on I'll be obedient to your authority. I vow before you, oh God, never to take up arms against any man."

I ran the rest of the way to Mary Ann's. She and her mother were on the porch. Mary Ann brought me a cup of water and I told them about the whisper in the woods and my vow.

The rhythm of farm work and home life slowly tempered the haunts and horrors of war. My nightmares became less frequent and Mary Ann and Sister were remarkably forgiving of my temper when it flared. Sister called it the devil acting up. I tried hard to control my anger and to know when it was going to erupt.

I rented my mule to Larry Rainwater for $2.50 and used $2 to buy our marriage license. The next day, I was playing under the trees with the children after the church service when little Lilly came up to me. Her fourth birthday was just a month away. She grabbed my knee and looked up in my eyes.

"Are you my daddy?" she asked.

Ellen walked up just in time to hear her daughter's question. I looked at Ellen's sad face and then back down at Lilly waiting expectantly for my answer.

"No, I'm not. But I am your daddy's brother."

"Where's my daddy?" Lilly asked.

My throat clogged and my eyes brimmed with tears. I picked her up and took her to the rope swing while Ellen stayed behind. I glanced over my shoulder and saw Ellen crying.

That evening after supper I went for my usual visit to Mary Ann's. All the talk was about the future and saving money for a place of our own. When we were saying our goodbyes on her porch, I asked her for forgiveness. She wrapped her arms around me, and I smelled her hair and felt the moisture of her forehead on my chin. I kissed her and turned to leave.

"Hey, you," she said.

I turned around and she stood with her hands on her hips.

"What ya got planned for August 16th?" she said.

"I'm takin' a wife if she'll have me."

She beamed and said, "You'll do just fine!"

On the way home I paused in the tall trees to listen. A faint breeze passed through the pine needles. A long *chweeeeer* screech of a hawk came in the distance. I lay on the brown straw and watched the dark green needles waving and the shining stars beyond. In a few minutes a whisper came from the wind, *Love one another*. My brother John came to mind.

The dusty smell of fallen pine needles tingled my nose. *WOOooOOH, WOOooOOH, WOOooOOH*. The train whistle blew near the Durant station. Then all was quiet.

Love one another, the whisper came again. The wisdom had been waiting inside me. Waiting till I was ready to hear. The woods were dark, and the air had cooled when I started back down the lane toward home. *Hoot, hoot, a whowaa ... Hoot, hoot, a whowaa*. The call of the owls pierced the silence.

At home I read from the Book of Hebrews. "Let us draw near with a true heart, in full assurance of faith, having our hearts sprinkled from an evil conscience, and our bodies washed in pure water. Let us hold fast the profession of our faith without wavering; for he is faithful that promised: And let us consider one another, to provoke unto love, and to good works."

A few nights later I dreamed I was walking alone in the woods just before dawn. The air was cold and moist, and I heard the rapid *wheo-wheo, wheo-wheo, wheo-*

351

wheo, wheo-wheo of ducks flying fast just above the treetops. A shadowy figure carrying a shotgun emerged from the mist and spoke to me.

"Why don't ya come with us?" It was Dallas.

I was astonished, but before I could answer, a second figure stepped from the woods, my brother John. "You look like you've seen a ghost," he said.

I couldn't speak.

"Why don't ya come with us?" Dallas asked again.

My tongue was silent. The shadow of Dallas passed right through me, and then John passed through me too. I turned to look and both figures disappeared in the fog.

"Wake up Uncle Andy," came a girl's voice.

I opened my eyes and Henrietta stood by the bed shaking my arm.

"Have you been cryin'?" she said. My cheeks were wet. "Why are ya cryin'?"

"'Cause I'm sad."

"About what?"

"I dreamed about ..." I stopped in mid-sentence.

"Today's a happy day!" she said. "It's your weddin' day, remember?"

"Yep, I remember."

"So get up and get movin'!" she insisted. "Mom and I are givin' ya a haircut."

She tugged my arm with both hands, and I followed her out.

AFTERWORD

On the first day of January 1929, twelve days before Anderson Flowers Temple's 88th birthday, he lay fully dressed in his bed, except for his shoes, talking freely with his youngest son, my grandfather, Van Benson Temple. He was not sick, had no pain or suffering, and was in good spirits. Suddenly his head turned to one side and there was a slight, almost inaudible gasp, and he was gone. He died in peace just as he had prayed, "Oh Lord, give us a peaceful hour in which to die."

After returning from the Civil War, Anderson vowed that he would never again take up arms against anyone. He was a peacemaker, and over the years he helped quarreling neighbors talk through their differences and become friends. He was a loyal and patriotic citizen who took courageous stands on public issues. He was an independent person, one who accumulated all the things he needed on his farm, including a blacksmith shop, well-tooled. He loved his family, and he labored hard in its support. When his first child was born, he resolved never to drink whiskey again or have it in his home. He especially loved trees and he planted large pear, peach, and pecan groves.

Anderson was a person who struggled as all do. His name will never be written in the halls of fame, nor find its way to the pages of history, but he was a useful, trustworthy and humble soul whose impression upon the hearts and minds of all who knew him, was laudable and lasting. He was not rich in the goods of this world, but he sought to find a true path and developed character and qualities that would count for most as he moved on into eternity. A host of relatives and friends, including African Americans, gathered at his funeral bearing witness to a life well-lived.

Have you ever wondered if memories of your ancestors inhabit your soul?

ACKNOWLEDGEMENTS

One day in third grade, during reading period in the school library, I became so absorbed in a book that I escaped the pull of gravity and time. I was the lookout in the crow's nest of an 1800s sailing ship riding the rolling waves of the Atlantic. I felt the wind on my face, the sun warming my bare skin, and my heart beating fast as I watched for pirate ships. When the bell rang ending the period, I returned to the present and remembered who I was outside the book. Then a voice inside me said — *To live forever is simple: write stories.* From that day forward I knew I was going to be a storyteller and writer.

Throughout my life I've kept a file of ideas on scrap pieces of paper, napkins, the back side of receipts, whatever was handy at the time. The notes are memory cues, a phrase, a title, a name — just enough to prod my memory later when I have time to write. Over the years I've written dozens of short stories and poems. Sometimes I've shared them with family and friends; other times they've not left my file or computer. In 2016, I self-published *Breakfast At Mema's*, a collection of boyhood adventures and coming of age vignettes from the '60s growing up in a small college town in northern Louisiana.

On a rainy day in 1964 my mother handed me a bronze-colored booklet to read. That was the day I learned about the life and times of Anderson Flowers Temple, my paternal great-grandfather — born 1841, died 1929. I sensed that he was alive and was speaking directly to me. The booklet has a section about family lineage, Anderson's personal qualities, and excerpts from church records at his passing. There are a number of abbreviated stories that Anderson used to tell his children, and nine pages devoted to his Civil War experiences. Each of the stories reveals a slice of wisdom, similar to the way Biblical parables reveal important truths. I came away from this first reading realizing that normal, everyday people struggle with the issues and circumstances of their time and that every person's life is remarkable. Each time I re-read the booklet during my teenage years, I felt Anderson was speaking to me and I wondered if part of him was alive in me. This mystical connection I've felt with my great-grandfather since I was twelve made writing *Whisperwood* truly a once in a lifetime experience.

Whisperwood is my most ambitious writing adventure so far. In the year 2000 I spent a few weeks in libraries in the Philadelphia area where I lived at the time, and was lucky to find a short, firsthand account by a soldier in the same regiment as Anderson, though not the same company. A full regiment is a thousand men and a full company is one-hundred, so Anderson probably didn't know this fellow, but I was struck by the number of similarities in their stories and was then able to correlate Anderson's movements with other bits and pieces of records. The research enabled me to put Anderson's stories in chronological order and fill in gaps. I also researched the specific campaigns that Anderson's regiment was involved in using numerous sources. Two books that were especially helpful were: *The Civil War Day By Day* by E.B. Long, and *The Civil War Archive — The History of the Civil War in Documents*. I collected photos, letters, and military records and then started drafting the story. I got up to about 20,000 words, then my consulting business picked up and I laid the project aside for later.

In 2016 I started taking writing classes at Earlham School of Religion in Richmond, Indiana where my wife Eva was working toward a master's degree. The second class I took centered around writing a substantial piece of work, so *Whisperwood* was a natural choice. Between January 2017 and April 2019, I wrote, researched and wrote more. By this time, the availability of records on the Internet had increased exponentially and that made my research much easier. Internet research taught me about loading and firing a rifle-musket, the foods the soldiers ate, the sounds of war from that era, clothing, diseases, the economy, trains, and sermons given in the North and the South. I even found audio recordings of what it sounds like in the belly of a steam-driven paddle boat. At various points along the way I read passages out loud at writer's group sessions and friends reviewed chapters. This helped test whether or not the narrative was communicating effectively.

By the spring of 2019 the story was finished and the manuscript had grown to a hefty 165,000 words. Today's typical historical fiction books range from 90,000 – 120,000, so I decided *Whisperwood* needed a low-calorie diet and regular exercise. I had heard other writers talk about how much they disliked editing, so I expected that step would be difficult.

After taking a three-month break to add two rooms to our house, I started seriously tightening and trimming the text. Cutting entire scenes and chapters felt like losing fingers at first. The deeper I got into it; however, I saw that some scenes were only making the story longer, not better, and the process became easier and more playful. The leaner manuscript was more fun to read and I could tell that it was becoming a better story. I lost count, but I think I edited the manuscript about fifteen times from start to finish. It was crazy, but I wanted it to be just right. Based on my experience, I'd say that revising, refining and editing is 80% of good writing. By the fall of 2019 I had the manuscript down to a trim 116,000 words and in pretty good shape, so I started the steps towards self-publishing.

Anderson's life story was packed with wisdom and a haunting warning about war. I wrote *Whisperwood* because the story of my great-grandfather's life came alive for me when I was twelve and I wanted to bring it alive for others. *To live forever is simple: write stories.*

I want to thank the Ministry of Writing Program at the Earlham School of Religion, Ben Brazil, our professor, and classmates Janine Saxton, Emily Hollenberg, Evan Underbrink, Staci Williams, and Steven Petersheim for helping me test the dialog of the characters, the vividness of battle scenes, and the balance between action and contemplation. Thanks also to the three writer's groups I belonged to during the crafting of *Whisperwood*: Richmond, Indiana Writer's Group, West Richmond Friends Writers, and the Bayou Writer's Club of Louisiana.

Several individuals were especially helpful for reading and providing valuable input at points along the way. Thanks to Terry Gleeson, Wendy Carpenter, Cindi Goslee, Fritz Rosebrook, Louise Temple-Rosebrook, Sal Giangrosso, Nina Helfert, and Mark Seghers.

Thanks to Anna Zakelj for her black and white sketches that help bring mental pictures alive for readers, especially those who are not familiar with this period of American history. Special thanks also to my long-time friend Karen Todd, for layout and formatting assistance.

Top honors go to my wife Eva Abbott who knows my heart and encouraged me to pursue my dream. A truer partner I could not have.

In many ways the story of Anderson in *Whisperwood* is the story of the universal soldier, a person caught up in a brutal struggle longing to go home. Wars leave scars in everyone who fights and those who stay home. War wrecks societies, destroys the environment, creates poverty, and sooner or later makes things worse. War-making is the ultimate failure of humankind to use our intelligence, creativity, and patience to successfully address issues of wealth, territory, and power. It is my deep conviction that war is not the answer. My dream and my hope is that one day humanity will learn that war-making is never going to solve problems and will insist on finding peaceful ways to address conflict. I believe it is possible.

AUTHOR BIO

Van Temple was born and raised in Ruston, Louisiana, and graduated from Louisiana Tech University. After a forty-three year career in community development, non-profit management, and city government service — a career that spanned Texas, Pennsylvania, Ohio, Delaware, Louisiana, and Indiana — he retired to Abita Springs, Louisiana to focus on his lifelong ambition to be a writer, an ambition originally inspired by his grade-school reading experiences. He has written dozens of stories and poems; his first book, a collection of autobiographical stories entitled *Breakfast at Mema's*, was published in 2016.

Temple's career path in providing services to people in need, as well as his five decades of social and political activism, were shaped by formative experiences in his childhood; his Christian upbringing included family Bible study, regular Sunday School, and involvement in Baptist youth groups. His parents led by example in their own Christian witness for social justice and civil rights. Among these influences was his paternal great-grandfather's experience as a Civil War soldier, which Temple encountered as a boy in the account written by his grandfather, and which was instrumental in Temple's later antiwar activism, conscientious objector status, and lifelong involvement in social justice issues.

CPSIA information can be obtained
at www.ICGtesting.com
Printed in the USA
LVHW090009110721
692197LV00006BA/711